Jack Wolf

Mammoth and Crow

Aurochs Underground Press

Copyright Jack Wolf, 2021

Cover image by Jack Wolf, 2021

The right of Jack Wolf to be identified as author or this work has been asserted by them in accordance with the copyrights, Designs and Patents Act of 1988. All rights reserved.

No part of this book may be used or reproduced in any manner whatsoever without the prior written permission of both the publisher and the copyright owner.

First Edition, 2022

ISBN 978-1-7396972-0-4

Published by Aurochs Underground Press, Bath, UK

Aurochspress.co.uk

Also by Jack Wolf

The Tale of Raw Head and Bloody Bones (Vintage, 2013)

Dog Walking Weather (Aurochs UP / Poetry, 2022)

Mammoth and Crow

For my mother

and for hers

Mammoth & Crow

"Go tell it to the birds"

Traditional

Jack Wolf

Chapter One:

Museum and Train.

Some faery tales, let me tell you, are true.

Some are not. Some are an imaginative rehashing of things that really happened, though not quite as the Storytellers tell them. Others have never held any basis whatsoever in day-to-day reality, but rise instead out of a different kind of truth: an ancient truth, a bloody, breathy, bony truth, a truth of water and earth and fire, that somehow makes sense to the human heart on dark nights, when the fogs are closing in and the mind is able to forget its day to day priorities. And there are some people, let me tell you, who know and understand this truth in the same way that they know the backs of their right hands, without questioning, all day and every day. Some of these people are human. Some are not.

Take, for example, the inhabitants of Bransquite, a tiny Cornish village that lies in a narrow river valley up against the north west shoulder of Bodmin moor. These enlightened folk do not care one way or the other whether the Otherworld of their fabled ghost stories is a place or a state of mind. To them, each is as good as the other, and not that distant from it. Here, truth and myth are known to coexist in a manner in which the normal rules of time and space, left and right, life and death, and so forth, can never properly be applied. The same principle applies to the curious and sinister beings who people both the moor and their grim tales: the misshapen black monsters, the hairy hands, the devil on his horse, the faceless men. Not one of these entities has ever been definitively numbered among the living or the dead, but all are, in some other way, as undeniably real and natural as the wholly this-world tellers of their stories.

Then there are the stories that the moor itself knows to be true: the stories that are carved by wind and rain upon its granite rock faces, woven through the substrate of its thin soil, painted on the shadows of its fogs: the traces of events so long ago in time that, when they were taking place, there was no human mind present to remember them. The moor remembers the coming of the great cold, the sheering winds that blew in over interminable winters from the great northern ice sheet, and froze and thawed its granite surface into strange vertical pillars, and stacked piles of giant flat rocks. It remembers the reindeer, whose warm lips once teased its summer flowers, whose broad feet trod on its mosses and its stones, and whose bones were picked clean white on its surface. It remembers bear and wolverine, red fox and wolf. It remembers the first seedlings of the silver birch, the hazel, and the ash, as those brave young forests of the last epoch spread fast across the open grasslands. It recalls the bubbling of the newborn streams as they flowed fast and bright through its grey gullies and along its conduits. More recently, it has concerned itself with the coming of the men, those long legged, upright pastoralists from the lowland valleys and fertile shores with their stone daggers and bronze sickle blades, their roundhouse fire pits, their singing circles of blue stones, their unbending midwinter gods. At this very moment, let me tell you, it is thinking of the stone cairn that those men constructed in the stony lee of a great craggy tor up on the high north moor. It is remembering the dark-eyed girl they sacrificed and wrapped so tenderly in bearskin, whose body they laid carefully beneath it, to guard both this reality and any other against catastrophe and famine, the slow dying of the world. Utilitarian as this scapegoating clearly was, the moor recalls it was not coldly done, and did not represent, to the eyes of those stone men at least, an unacceptable act of societal violence. Their ethical concerns were exercised much more strongly by war.

Earth time is deep time, long and steady: though to the moor it seems but yesterday those long-ago shepherds came and went, replaced in an eye-blink by another group of hardy souls, it was in fact another thousand years before this second settlement appeared, right on top of the first. These people were tin miners: they brought with them a strange religion, and the understanding of metal to replace that of the dead. They built their long, low, rectangular huts, and made sacred offerings to their gods of Earth and Water. One day, some small distance to the north of their small village, on the sheltered side of the great granite tor, they began to cut a low ceilinged, right angled storage passage into the crevice between two larger rocks. And perhaps because they knew and understood so very little of anything, they were thrown into great anguish when their innocent diggings broke into the buried stone cist containing the already ancient skeleton. They did their best to seal the chamber up, and within a matter of days departed the whole area. All surface traces of their settlement disappeared with them, swept away by rains and fierce winds. But the moor remembers. Two thousand years after their frightened flight, the passage they began lies almost exactly as they built it, three quarters now buried in the soil, a small part of its entrance visible above: a slender triangle of darkness, like a rabbit hole. A Victorian gentleman, hiking on the moor, once stumbled in it, and on inspection identified it, to the best of his limited ability, as a fogou: a low, enclosed passage designed for community defence in case of siege. But then he walked away, and never visited again, so the tunnel's precise location, and that of the grave to which it led, was once again lost.

But the moor remembers. The moor knows. And the moor told the mist, and the mist told the dark night, and the night remembered the fireside stories, and told the faceless men, the sleepers on the far side of the stone; and the faceless men told the Storytellers, weavers of myth and memory.

Let me tell you a story. I'll be your tale weaver, memory spinner, tell-tale-tit. I'll be the whisperer in the twilight who guides you to another world. But I have to warn you that the story I'm about to tell you – which I've learned from the wind, the stones, the rain – will surprise you, upset you, and make you wonder at it, and at me. And make no mistake (because you will): no matter how much the world I'm about to take you to looks like the world you think you understand, beneath its familiar surface lies a faerie tale, and one of the old sort: an eye-socket, thigh-bone, grit-stone history of a world that goes a long, long way beyond the confines of the merely human.

If it's a faerie tale, you ask me, *is it one of the true ones?*

Well that, let me tell you, is something you must work out for yourselves.

Now, this Faerie Tale's real beginning is so long ago that only the Earth and the faceless men remember it; but we'll jump in here: 8:21am on the 2nd December, 1938, in a three storey town house in Chiswick, London. It seems a good moment: entering the story here this allows it to make use of a classic faery tale device. Look: here is a woman in labour, while the universal powers are standing by, aghast. In most faery tales, of course, she'd be the beloved first wife of the King, but in this one she's neither more nor less than Mrs Evelyn Murray, wife of Gerald Murray, Professor of Classics at King's College, London. He's about to take his daughter, whose name is Leto, to the Natural History Museum, to meet the skeletal remains of the Ilford Mammoth.

Ok, stop, you say. *What's the skeleton of a mammoth doing in a faerie tale?*

But of course there is a mammoth. You really must understand that this is not a faerie tale of the sort that you've been used to, pace Grimm's, pace Carroll, pace Lewis. Yes, there'll be a Princess, of a sort, and a wicked Queen, and there is, indisputably, a Wizard: but there will also be a mammoth, because at the root of every faerie story lies the Mammoth: and in the heart of every song vibrates the Spear.

So, back to the tale: and you must promise you won't interrupt again unless you really have to.

Gerald Murray, let me tell you, is not a very engaged father. Since her birth ten years ago, his relationship with his daughter has been limited to being the grudging recipient of bedtime kisses and the stern administrator of paternal discipline. What on earth, he protested this morning, blinking up at Dr Gaskell from his Daily Mail and his soft boiled eggs, was he to do with the wretched child for a whole day? He couldn't take her to Chiswick Common, like the Nanny does. Professor Gerald Murray is a man of standing, not a nursemaid. He was on the point of refusing, when suddenly the fearful thought struck him that if he didn't comply with the doctor's request, some slighted god or other might blast his unborn son. And that was when he remembered Leto's ongoing obsession with the mammoth.

Gerald doesn't know, of course, any more than we do at this moment, that the new baby will be male. Evelyn has insisted that it is, and has done so so often, and so emphatically, that he's come automatically to think of it as such. She's carrying the child, after all, he thinks. And she's confident, so much more confident this time than she's been in several years, of its chances of survival.

At nine o clock, having finished his rudely interrupted breakfast, Gerald folds his newspaper beneath his arm, takes charge of his scrubbed, red coated offspring, and sets off on foot across Chiswick Common to hail a taxi from Turnham Green.

Jack Wolf

Back in the house, shut in the master bedroom, Evelyn Murray is lying on her back, struggling to give birth. The baby's early, as they all have been, but only by six weeks, if her calculations are correct. The labour, like that of the only other child she has successfully carried anywhere near to term, has already taken far too long.

"Please, Mrs Murray," says Dr Gaskell, as Nanny Gould mops Evelyn's wet brow with a folded scrap of white muslin. "You must keep on trying to push."

Evelyn tries. But she's very weak; and the Doctor's words seem, in her exhaustion and her pain, to be coming from far away, like echoes from another time, another place. She's been keeping on trying to push for over thirty hours. She knows this state of affairs is dangerous, for both herself and the baby.

"Very well," says the Doctor, shaking his head, and rubbing his right temple with a frustrated hand. "Stop. Rest for a moment."

Evelyn rests. Her mind begins to wander, and with it, she fears, her sanity.

Leto, she thinks. Why did Dr Gaskell insist on the child leaving the house? Doesn't he know, or care, that Leto's never ridden in a taxi, or on a tube train, or – before today – visited a public institution? Why, the girl has never even attended school. Evelyn has made absolutely sure of that: it would be ridiculous to let a growing girl waste time on team sports and mathematics when her destiny is to become a wife and mother. Leto needs to learn domesticity, not algebra. Besides, sending her to school would place her at risk of picking up dangerous notions from the other girls, and learning to confuse weakness with

11

merit, contra Nietzsche. Better for her to spend her time at home, engaged in pursuits that will entertain her brain and develop her bodily strength while not polluting her mind.

Why on Earth, Evelyn asks herself, is she worrying about Leto now? Now, when she should be concentrating all her energies on the son she's trying to bring into the world: the boy she passionately hopes will be the first of many sons, destined by God or merit or whatever-have-you to become great leaders of men. She tries not to think about her daughter any longer, puts her away inside a box, to be dealt with later.

But instead she only finds herself remembering the American. She met him by chance in a Lyons tea shop at the end of '26. She was seventeen: young, pretty, naive, female, miserably alone; he was much older: sophisticated, blue eyed, silver haired, rich. He called himself a scientist, was a devoted follower of the Harvard eugenicist Charles Davenport, a friendly critic of the interventionist Margaret Sanger, and an avowed admirer of the political fascist Benito Mussolini. He took various measurements of Evelyn's skull, subjected her to an IQ test, and then, to her astonishment, declared her to be of superior genetic stock before seducing and abandoning her with not so much as a by your leave. Psychologically wrecked and broken hearted, Evelyn took solace in the writings to which he'd introduced her, and found therein a purpose that had been sorely lacking in her young, unhappy, life, along with an inflexible ideology that made up for the impossibility of love. Within weeks, she had shrugged the American off and married Gerald – a man old enough to be her father, but a man of great intelligence and status, a writer on Euripides and Aeschylus, whose prizewinning commentary on *Phaedra* had outshone every other publication for the year 1921. Then, just when everything had seemed to be going so well, she gave birth to Leto – *the girl* – whose birth was also too difficult, also too long. The useless, superfluous girl, who on account of her sex could never grow up to command an army, or run a Government, and make the degenerate English great again. The wretched *girl*, whose birth so damaged Evelyn's womb that every son she has since managed to conceive has died at birth, or sometime before it.

She doesn't want Dr Gaskall here, she realises. It isn't only that he's just sent Leto out. It's what he said to Gerald last time, when both men thought she couldn't hear them, muttering their feeble consolations in the hall: there is nothing at all wrong with Evelyn's womb. *What*, Evelyn thinks, furiously, *was that supposed to mean?* That she is carrying some heritable flaw, which tragically inflicts their unborn children with a fatal disorder? Some systemic weakness that causes their embryonic hearts to stop, their fetal cells to cease dividing? It isn't possible. Evelyn is of superior stock. The American told her so, and surely he wasn't lying. And Gerald is too: superior, that is – though he may, she thinks to herself, be something of a liar. He has to be – both – or he'd never have made it to Professor. And if it were the case their very genes were at fault, then how could Leto have survived, while her brothers did not? *There is no flaw,* she thinks. *No weakness. The problem has always been just Leto.*

Please God, Evelyn thinks. *Please God.*

Please save my son. My son must live. Nothing else matters.

Leto Murray is ten years old. She is a solidly built, blonde haired child, not particularly pretty, but quite bright, who – under usual circumstances – talks and jabbers incessantly, as if she's trying to banish silence from existence. Perhaps that is exactly what she's doing, though she doesn't know it. Today, though, intimidated by the rare presence of her father or overwhelmed by the dirty reality of a city to which she's hardly ever been exposed, she is uncharacteristically subdued.

Little Leto is not insensitive: she senses Evelyn's unspoken resentment as loud and clearly as if she were listening to the message being broadcast by the BBC. But if she is hurt, frightened and confused by this rejection, she doesn't show it; not, at least, in any way that would be easily intelligible to her parents. She takes regular comfort in her Children's Encyclopedia, where she reads about mammoths.

Mammuthus Primigenius, Mammuthus Trogontherii: the mighty tusked, woolly coated Kings and Queens of the Pleistocene Epoch, rulers of those thousand mile wide swathes of ice-age grassland that the moor remembers, and which the Encyclopedia calls the steppes: tens of hundreds of thousands of years away from this dirty machine-age London of Nanny Gould and boiled eggs, t-bar leather shoes and diamond patterned pavements, red postboxes, ringing telephones, and a mother who cannot bear the sound of her daughter's voice, or the touch of her little hand.

Standing by her father's side on the far edge of

Jack Wolf

Chiswick Common, Leto is staring at the busy street in front of her, and the bottom falls out of her stomach. For almost ten years, Nanny Gould has been under strict instruction to take her charge no farther than the middle of the green public space where they have picnics and tea parties in the summer, and never to let her wander off, so Leto has never before had proper opportunity to accustom her eyes and ears to the unceasing cavalcade of traffic with which she is now being confronted. There are black cars, red cars, yellow cars, all pumping out clouds of stinking smoke. There are fruiterers' vans and bakers' vans with names like Berry's and Whistler's painted in black script upon their square backsides. There's an old fashioned dairyman, briefly breaking the parade of metal and fume with his huge grey horse and his painted cart, which shoots past in a rattle of chains and hooves; and a gang of builders' labourers in dusty flat caps and shabby grey trousers and waistcoats, pedalling Raleigh bicycles and whistling. At the junction of Chiswick Common Road stands a dark blue uniformed policeman, waving his white clad arm like a flag.

Leto does not like it. She shrinks back, pressing against Gerald's coat. A dark winged butterfly, active out of season, flutters over both their heads before being whipped away on the thin breeze. Leto does not see it.

"The mammoth's name is Huma," whispers Leto to her father; but he, busy hailing a taxi, does not hear her. "She told me so in a dream. And Huma isn't a bull mammoth, no matter what the scientists say." Both male and female mammoths, Leto knows, have tusks. Huma's are for swishing down tall plants and twisting branches from the stubby ice-age trees, not savage weapons of gore and death. She is both wrong and right about these things, as you will see: wrong about the Ilford skull, which did, in fact, belong to a young bull mammoth who died a couple of thousand years before his genus went extinct; and right about Huma, who was not, and is not, the sort of entity who might need weaponry in the first place.

"She's a mother, not a monster. She's Huma, Queen of the Steppes. She's the Matriarch."

Isn't Matriarch a wonderful word? Leto tastes it, like strawberry ice-cream, on her tongue. Matriarch means mother, means strength and protection. It means love. One day, in another time (which is really, I have to tell you, only another place) the Matriarch of a mammoth herd is leading her family carefully toward water and sustenance. She knows where the best pastures are, the sweetest grasses and the tastiest buds; remembers all the signs and subtle changes in the skies and on the earth that give her warning of the coming of the snows, the howling winds of winter. She is careful to pay close attention to the changing songs of birds, the fluttering colours of the ptarmigan. She knows that at the moulting of the hare she'll have to shepherd her beloved family south, out of the path of the freezing northern gales, to keep them safe against the terrible potential of death. She is a guide, a leader, a mother. Everything she does is born of love.

What killed the mighty Mammoth Tribe?

Leto doesn't know, and the Children's Encyclopedia can't help, because the scientists of Leto's day are not at all certain. But she hopes it was the natural end of the ice-age, and not the stone tipped

spears, the savage instruments of Man.
Let's leave her, for the moment, pondering this.

We'll fly now as the crow flies, over the roofs and chimney pots of London, to another, grimier, part of it, and you'll be introduced to somebody else. Because I have to tell you that at this very instant, Miss Jane Fox – almost-but-not-quite native of the moor-side village of Bransquite, Cornwall, which I hope you have not already forgotten – is standing at Liverpool Street Station, waiting for the arrival of a very important train. Miss Fox is forty five years old, a writer, and a spinster of Quaker stock, whose falling out with her family has never been fully understood by any of the parties concerned. She stands five feet eleven inches tall, a great height for a woman of this generation, and her backbone is as straight and stiff as a ramrod. Her hair, which is still dark brown beneath her hat, is tied into a severe bun at the back of her head, and her grey, ankle length skirt and twenty year old lace up boots make her stand out like a sore thumb among the elegantly stockinged calves and smart heeled shoes of the charitable ladies who are also waiting, at the same time, for the same purpose.
The ladies are concerned. They have heard that the train has been delayed, although not – thankfully – intercepted. *Thank God,* they twitter, *oh, thank God.* They press their palms into their breastbones, as if their anxiety should mean nothing until it is telegraphed. Miss Fox keeps her hands clasped resolutely at her midriff.
Miss Fox learned of the existence of the train only yesterday, while visiting her friend and editor, a

very well connected woman who lives in Hackney. This friend, who is active on behalf of several charities, has become involved with the urgent operation to rescue Jewish children from the desperate situation they are facing in Europe, and she told Miss Fox of the urgent plea that just went out over the wireless seeking foster homes for the arriving refugees. Miss Fox at once volunteered her own – though she can't for the life of her imagine what she is to do with a frightened, foreign, orphan child, who mightn't speak a word of English. Now she's standing on the platform of Liverpool Street Station, listening to the nervous mutterings of the ladies and feeling the thudding of her own heartbeat, as its pace increases with every rattle of the oncoming engine. *The engine – yes!* she can hear that, now, too. The train is late, but it is, finally, here. The ladies burst into excited chatter.

Oh, thinks Miss Jane Fox, her hands spasmically gripping her handbag.

The engine slows, and draws up at the platform, its steam brakes screeching. Black smoke billows from its stack, tumbling downwards and swamping the platform in an acrid cloud of dust and dirt. Miss Fox coughs, and waves her gloved hand in front of her face, trying to find a patch of clean air. *Why on earth,* she thinks distractedly, *do I always dress in my smartest clothes to travel on a steam train?* I have to agree with her, by the way: this seems a silly thing to do. I don't know if you've ever ridden in a coal powered locomotive, but if you haven't, let me tell you that the smoke inevitably blows into the open carriage windows, coating everything with grit and grime: clothes, hair, eyelids, nostrils, everything.

Jack Wolf

The children have travelled across two countries and via one rough sea channel from a Jewish orphanage in Berlin which was destroyed during last month's savagery. They have no papers and no parents; only small manila tags with numbers on them hanging round their necks, a proof of identity issued by the British government: *this Document requires no Visa*. The oldest among them are around thirteen or fourteen: wary looking girls and boys with dark, Slavic features and bloodshot, exhausted eyes. The youngest – toddlers, some of them – are staring at the world in uncomprehending shock. Torn from everything they've ever known and loved, they've just fled across half a continent in terror of an unknown tyrant whom they've never seen, but whose name will ring a lifetime in their ears, and the ears of their own children.

One by one at first, then by twos and by threes, finally in an uncontrolled flood, they disembark from the train. For a moment, all is uneasy, frightened chaos, then somebody out of Miss Fox's line of sight blows hard on a policeman's whistle, and the tumult subsides. The children are made to line up one after another in two separate lines, like schoolchildren heading into class; and more quickly than Miss Fox could have expected, each is smartly delivered into the care of his allocated sponsor. Sometimes a home has been found for two siblings together, though never for more. The children weep wholeheartedly at being parted. *But at least,* Miss Fox thinks, clutching at a straw, *they've somewhere safe to go.* Soon, the crowded platform is almost clear. Finally, only herself and one thin, black haired boy of perhaps ten years of age are left.

Miss Fox looks the boy up and down. "Well," she says, awkwardly. "We'd better hurry. We have a long distance to travel today, and another train to catch."

The boy returns her gaze. His expression is far from blank, but behind the inevitable shock, it seems puzzled. *He doesn't understand a word,* thinks Miss Jane Fox. Her heart sinks.

"What – is – your – name?" she asks slowly and clearly, as she knows one must – she is English, after all – when addressing a foreigner. "Your name?" she repeats, pointing at his card. Then she indicates herself. "I am Miss Fox. Who are you?"

The boy narrows his eyes. He's thinking: wondering how, or what, to answer. Then he opens his mouth. "Elijah," he whispers plaintively. "Elijah Rosenstein."

"Oh, my dear," says Miss Fox, without thinking. "That will never do. That will not do at all. We must think of something else." Something less obviously Jewish, and much less German. *Arthur,* she thinks, remembering the book she has been reviewing. No: the name seems wrong, somehow, for such a skinny, fey, half present, little thing. *Merlin,* she thinks, *would be more apt, if it wasn't such an uncommon name outside of Wales.* She remembers the small dark birds that fly every year in and out of the eaves of her little cottage: refugees, too, all of them. "Martin," she says at last. "You'll be Martin. Martin Stone. My nephew."

The Ilford Mammoth, according to the card that somebody has fixed to the presentation case, was discovered in 1824, at a depth of sixteen feet, in a large quarry of diluvian loam and clay that was used for making bricks. Messrs Gibson, Buckland and Cliff, who were called in by the owner of the pit, made every effort to ensure the excavation of the entire skeleton, but unfortunately, despite their best efforts, the bones, being wet, were broken beyond the ability of the museum to restore them. Only the gigantic skull was left intact; but it is perfect in every way, each of the great curved ivories over three times the length of Leto Murray's whole body, thicker and stronger than her father's arm.

And yet, Leto thinks *so very queer to look at.* The whole thing seems peculiarly out of shape: an elephant's head without a face, no trunk, no ears, no eyes, and no hair. She can see the mammoth, in a way, yet *Huma* remains invisible, a memory half superimposed on the now, like a failed trick photograph.

Leto is bitterly disappointed. She had hoped that by seeing the skull up close, she would somehow get a glimpse of Huma in the real, if not quite the flesh; that bone would substitute for warmth, and shape alone bring back before her eyes the living, breathing creature the great Matriarch had been. But here there's nothing but yellowish brown bone in a plain glass case.

Glancing around furtively for the museum guard, Leto creeps below the rope and stands close beside the case, pressing her small, pink, human nose against the glass. Her own eyes, not Huma's, are staring back at her. Grey eyes, tinged with a hint of green in the yellow electric light, startled and watchful, the eyes of a caged thing.

"Huma?" she mouths questioningly, almost

silently. "Huma?"

The mammoth does not answer.

She is not here, thinks Leto.

The disappointment sears like a hot knife in her heart.

Professor Gerald Murray, sitting on one of the long, dark wooden benches, thirty feet away, his head full of concern for Evelyn and his unborn son, does not look up from his newspaper.

Miss Jane Fox takes Martin Stone straight home to Cornwall. They travel by steam train from London to Fowey, where they eat the sandwiches Miss Fox prepared early that morning; and then progress by a series of country buses up onto the moor, finally walking the mile and a half to the remote cottage from the village of Bransquite. There's no traffic, and the night is cold. A light rain began to fall when they reached Bodmin; now the fog has come down over the high moor like a chilling blanket, muffling all noise. Miss Fox is not especially alarmed. She knows the area extremely well in all weathers, and her Bakelite electric torch is powerful enough to show her enough of the road ahead that she won't lose her way, though the silent moor on both sides remains an impenetrable mystery.

The boy hasn't said a word during the long journey, and has sat for much of the time curled up with his head against the rattling window of the train, or bowed forward with his brow resting on the leather back of the bus seat in front of him, his cap tipping over his eye. *Fatigued, poor little chap,* thinks Miss Jane Fox. But she's not sure that, even when his eyes are shut fast, he is sleeping.

What has happened to him? What horrors has he seen in the last few weeks? Is all this – is she – a horror too? Miss Fox hopes not. But who can tell? This is a boy who grew up in a Berlin orphanage – in a city. This soft grey world of clinging fog and shadow spectres of low, twisted trees, of half wild cattle clustering about the roadside water trough, cattle who lift their great shaggy heads in surprise and snort clouds of silvery steam as they are caught in the approaching torchlight, must seem as alien and frightening to him as the far side of the moon. She wonders what he will make of the inhabitants of Bransquite, and whether he will appear as strange to them, and hopes that they'll be able to accept him, despite what she habitually thinks of as their small minded, provincial ignorance.

Although she may have seemed somewhat old fashioned and rustic alongside the charitable ladies with whom she found herself waiting at Liverpool Street station, Miss Fox rightly considers herself several cuts above the poor farmers and semi-literate china clay miners who are her nearest neighbours. She grew up in Fowey, and her family – with whom, as we know, she's fallen out – was a close and loving one, as comfortable as it is possible for a Quaker family to be without appearing immodest. Their values were those of patience, compassion and, above all, education; for, as Miss Fox's father often said, it's only by education that swiftness of mind can be channelled towards an honest love of one's fellows, and an understanding of the true value of mercy.

Until the falling out, which she still doesn't completely understand, though she knows its immediate cause, Miss Jane Fox played the part of the dutiful Quaker daughter her father wanted. She read deeply and widely, attended the Friends' meeting house, sat in contemplative silence meditating on the presence – sometimes, after the outbreak of the Great War, the absence – of God, gave much to charity, and when her brother Thomas was imprisoned for conscientious objection, spoke passionately to a small crowd on Fowey seafront against the unchristian vanity of Kings and Kaisers who would callously inflict such misery on their respective peoples. It did not matter that her words fell on deaf, hostile, ears. As far as Miss Fox was concerned, she was doing what was right, and that was all that mattered.

She came to Bransquite as a visitor in nineteen twenty three, and within a week had spent the last of her mother's inheritance on buying the cottage where she now lives from a farmer who was desperate to sell and move to Plymouth. For the first two years, she barely left the tiny place, repainting its worn doors and tattered window frames, replanting its vegetable garden, and establishing fruit bushes and apple trees. She fed the birds, and left out hazels and peanuts in shells for the small warm blooded creatures that began to populate her woodpile in the winter months. After a while, a rumour began to circulate, as rumours do in places like Bransquite, that she was a witch. It was soon scotched by the Vicar, but it came as a shock to Miss Fox, and she realised it was high time she began to take a little interest in her neighbours. She was a fine maker of preserves, and it occurred to her than this way she might both make acquaintance with and be of aid to those poor village souls who never had enough to eat.

Since then she has become an established figure: *a bit addled,* the neighbours all agree, *but very kind.* She makes a modest living writing literary reviews and articles on jellies and handicrafts for *The Lady* – so when the neighbours knock on her door in the middle of the day selling eggs or hawking clothes' pegs from a wicker basket, they often find her scratching at a sheet of paper with a Parker pen, or sitting with her nose buried in a copy of some recent publication which has come express delivery from London, while sugar syrup bubbles on behind her in the pot.

Now Miss Fox hears, from some distance behind her, a sad, exhausted whimper. She turns, and swings the Bakelite torch. Martin Stone comes back into view at the end of the beam. The boy is beginning to stagger.

A great wave of pity and shame washes over Miss Fox. How could she have forced this cruel march across cold moorland on this poor, unfortunate child, who – *why, surely, I must have seen* – has barely enough energy to stand? What on Earth was she thinking? Was it really of such importance that they should get home tonight, and couldn't have stayed another day with her editor in Hackney, or broken the journey at Fowey for them both to rest?

"Oh, my dear!" cries Miss Fox, running back along the road and taking Martin gently under his shoulders. "I am so, very, very sorry."

With a heave, she lifts him into her arms. He's not at all heavy. *Feather and bone,* she thinks. *Just feather and bone. Poor child. Poor, poor, child.*

The German Jewish boy places his cold, thin arms tightly about her neck, and Miss Fox carries him onward through the darkness, through the mist.

Chapter Two:
The Baby and the Wolf

Gerald Murray is sitting in the corner, watching his wife grieve.

"He was perfect," Evelyn cries hysterically. "Perfect!" Her eyes, while wild and staring wide, are completely tearless.

Perfect, Gerald thinks, *in everything but this: he did not once draw breath.* At what point during his wife's long, difficult labour did her son slip from this world into that of the dead? What bitter travesty: to have gone straight from the comfort of the womb into the jaws of death.

When the Professor returned from the museum, his wife was lying white and silent on the bed, and the baby's too tiny body was wrapped in a white muslin sheet on top of the dressing table. He looked at it just once, closely, then nodded to Dr Gaskell to take it away in his doctor's bag, for burial. He did not want to touch it. The boy had a light fuzz of pale hair covering his head, tiny, oval fingernails, and perfectly formed, rather long, eyelashes – surrounding eyes that would, Gerald imagines, have been a daylight shade of blue, like Evelyn's. He will never know, and thinking about that hurts his heart. But he will never show it.

Nanny Gould, whom I've already briefly mentioned, but with whom you now have cause to become better acquainted, takes Leto upstairs to the nursery as soon as she arrives back at the house, and gives her a cup of hot chocolate and a plate of buttered toast with jam. She tells her nothing of the tragedy that has befallen her family. Professor Murray has been very clear: the incident will be put to one side, the lost baby quietly and secretly mourned, and then, like every other one of Evelyn's lost children, utterly forgotten. There's little point in inviting grief, and even less in indulging it.

But of course Leto has guessed, or half guessed, that something is wrong, and though she daren't ask what, she is desperate to know. So instead of questions, words spill out, words and words and words, one after another in a ceaseless, senseless flood, pushing back the secret, blotting out the mystery until she is no longer troublingly aware of it.

"She was wonderful!" she tells Nanny Gould over and over, bouncing up and down upon her red and blue tapestried stool. "She was magnificent! She was huge, and white as snow. Well, almost white. She was really brown, because of spending all those thousand years in the ground. The acid in the soil discoloured her bones. It says so on the card in the museum. Are you listening? I'm telling you about the Ilford Mammoth. She was the most marvellous thing I have ever, ever seen! She was a hundred thousand times better than riding in the taxi. I didn't like having lunch with Father in the restaurant. It was full of screeching ladies in large hats. Have you seen their hats? Father read his paper the whole time and didn't look at me once. Are you listening? She was wonderful. She was magnificent. And white. She truly, really, was. White, like snow." She says nothing of her disappointment at the skeleton's impenetrable silence; and by the end of the evening has almost convinced herself she never pressed her nose against the empty glass, and whispered: *Huma, Huma.*

Nanny Gould, worrying that her charge is overexcited, and worrying, too, about her own ability to keep hiding the sadness that hangs over her own heart at the family's loss, puts up with the frantic flurry for as long as she can; but finally, when Leto begins to show signs of tetchiness, and her descriptions of the mammoth become tediously repetitive, she sends the child to bed. This sudden firmness on Nanny's part triggers tears and rage. Leto does not want to go.

"I won't!" she shouts. "I won't! You can't make me! You're just a fussy old woman in a silly uniform! A servant!" She will *not* go. Nanny *cannot* make her. Nanny has *no right* to tell Leto Murray what to do. She kicks over her stool, and throws herself, kicking and screaming, on the hearthrug.

But if Nanny Gould has doubts regarding her ability to stop herself from crying, she has no qualms when it comes to dispensing discipline: a hard sharp smack on the haunches for her temper, and a flannel for her dirty face, and Leto is tucked in tight beneath her blankets and yellow crocheted counterpane.

"Can't I *read?*"

"No, you can't, you spoiled little Madam," says Nanny Gould. "You're overtired. Sleep is what you need." She switches off the electric light.

"Can't I say goodnight to Father?" Leto screams, kicking her legs frantically under the covers, stirring them into a maelstrom.

"No," says Nanny Gould. "Not tonight." She shuts the door tight on the child's furious anguish, her unanswerable questioning.

Miss Jane Fox arrives home at midnight, and after lighting the oil lamps on the sideboard, and the bottle powered Belling stove – her cottage, so far beyond the outskirts of Bransquite, has not yet been connected to the National Grid – she wraps Martin Stone in a thick woollen blanket, brings him a plate of bread and jam, some biscuits and a cup of scorched milk, and puts him down to sleep in the guest bedroom. In the morning, she's decided, she'll get out the tin bath from the shed and set it up in front of the kitchen fire, fetch a bar of pears soap, and make the boy scrub himself from the tips of his scrawny ears to the soles of his feet. Then she'll find a fine toothed comb and go through his untidy hair, which she feels certain is infested with lice. Miss Fox's sharp eyes have not failed to notice the red spots that decorate Martin's temples, or the way in which he absent-mindedly raises his hand to scratch the back of his neck. When he's clean and fed, she will launder his clothes, and then she'll take him to the drapers in Camelford and buy some fabric to sew new ones. But right now, all that matters is that the poor child should get a proper rest.

She goes to bed. She's too tired to sleep, and her nerves are too wound up to allow her to think, so instead, after trying for a while to settle underneath a patchwork quilt that feels too heavy, she relights her lamp and takes up her bedside book, and reads until her eyes cannot keep open any longer.

She wakes early, to the sound of crows. Getting out of bed, she pulls back her bedroom curtain, and peers out. Her garden is full of them; great black December birds with sharp beaks and piercing eyes, who stare at her from the bare branches of the apple and pear trees, keeping watch over her soul. "Boy," they caw, triumphantly – or sadly – she can't be certain. "Boy, boy."

"Go away," she says, waving her arms. "Go!"

The crows take flight from the trees. They land in the garden, walking across the frosty soil, staring up at her window, as if trying to ascertain how they might make their way inside the cottage. Miss Fox pulls in her dressing gown, protectively. *There are too many of them*, she thinks. The wild wind is blowing hard off the high moor, scratching like a knife around the window panes. "Boy!" shout the crows, indefatigable, relentless as memory: "Boy! Boy! Boy!"

While combing the lice out of his black hair, Miss Jane Fox begins teaching Martin Stone the serious business of English. English and Englishness: both matters of critical importance if the boy is to last long in Bransquite, or indeed, in England – although, let me tell you, the Cornish, on the whole, don't consider themselves English at all, but the last lingering survivors of the native British race whom the invading Germanic tribes subjugated and displaced. For many, the old grudge still endures. Miss Fox's family, despite living several generations in the county, are not considered Cornish; she knows, to a small extent, how it feels to be a foreigner in a strange and somewhat hostile land. Besides, her early experiences in the village with the local rumour mill and pots of damson jam have impressed upon her how vital it is that one's face should to seem to fit, even if that seeming is an illusion.

She makes a set of cards from the backs of cereal packets, and places them around the house: MISS FOX, says one, and a second MARTIN; another DOOR; another CHAIR, another BED; so the list goes on until there is nothing and no-one in the cottage unaccounted for. Even the huge ginger tomcat, FLUFFY, wears a card on his collar for a few minutes; but then his plaintive growling and scratching moves Miss Fox's pity – or begins to try her patience – and she hastily removes it. Martin Stone, who is wrapped in a bath towel and sitting on the floor before the fire, smiles and quietly holds out his hand to the cat, who rubs himself against it and begins to purr.

"Goodness," says Miss Fox, watching in astonishment her usually standoffish cat becoming firm friends with a stranger. "You certainly have a way with animals, Martin."

"Fluffy," says the boy. "Fluffy, kommen sie bitte heiren."

"Fluffy, yes," says Miss Fox. "But you must say 'come here', in English, my dear, not in German. Try."

"Fluffy, come," says Martin Stone. The ginger cat obligingly does as asked, climbing into his cross legged lap. Martin strokes its head. The cat lifts its chin, closing its eyes. Its purring grows louder, and it rubs its face against the boy's. Martin feels the purr pass through the bath towel into his thin chest. It's comforting. He remembers how his grandmother had a cat, before she died, before he found himself in the Berlin orphanage. When he was very small it used to sleep on his bed, and sometimes, when he woke in the night, its purring was enough to settle him and send him back to sleep. He often wonders what happened to it. Since the attack upon the orphanage, the cat has been the only thing that he has dared to wonder about.

"He likes you," says Miss Fox. "I think he's happy to have found a friend."

"I like him," says Martin, haltingly. He smiles again, at Miss Fox this time. "Good cat," he says. "Good Fluffy."

"Good, Martin," says Miss Fox.

Over the next three weeks, the boy's command of English – if not, alas, Englishness – comes on by leaps and bounds. Miss Fox is impressed and surprised: she hadn't expected much from a child who grew up in such difficult circumstances. Poverty, she has always believed, inevitably has a depressing effect on the intellect. By Christmas, he is speaking regularly, if not confidently, in short sentences, and the number of occasions upon which he relapses into German has fallen almost to zero; although naturally his original tongue is still the language of his thought and heart. The cat, Fluffy, has taken up nightly residence on his bed, and several times Miss Fox has come in after both have fallen asleep to find it lying curled up in the crook of his arm, snoring gently. She wonders if it knows, somehow, that he has no-one else. Miss Fox is disinclined to attribute an emotion like compassion to a cat. Although she is fond of Fluffy, she holds no illusions regarding the animal's predatory nature. She hopes it won't begin bringing in baby mice this Spring, as is its usual habit. Half eaten mice on the pillow are horrible to deal with.

True to her initial plan, she has taken the boy to Camelford, and as an early Christmas present has made him several sets of new clothes – something that has also enabled the quiet disposal of his original ones. Scrubbed clean, with his hair properly brushed, Martin Stone's appearance is not significantly different from that of any other boy of his age, though his hair is very dark. Were it not for his lack of language he would – almost – fit in among the Argyle pullovered, short trousered boys who've been stomping down the lanes at night, singing Christmas carols. Perhaps, thinks Miss Fox, when he's fluent enough in his new language to hold his own, she'll send him to the local school: he might make friends. It isn't healthy, she thinks, for a child to be kept in isolation.

On Christmas Day they sit at the table in the warm kitchen, the Quaker lady and the Jewish boy, eating a cheapish cut of beef and roast potatoes, with Brussels sprouts from the cottage garden, listening to the King on the wireless and Bing Crosby and the Andrews Sisters on the wind-up gramophone. Outside, on the moor, dark shapes move in the mist: cattle and blackface sheep lowing by the wall and huddling underneath the crabbed hawthorns; wild ponies stamping their icy hooves by the field gate. A crow perches on top of the smoky chimney, and caws loud: once, twice, three times to the listening air.

Gerald has insisted that his daughter must share Christmas dinner with her parents – a rare event, but one determined by the need to pretend that everything is normal when it is anything but. So, at six o'clock, Nanny Gould dresses Leto in a sky blue dress that matches her eyes, and curls her hair into Shirley Temple ringlets topped with a blue bow, and sends her off into the dining room to be upon her best behaviour. The child sits silently at the end of the table by her mother's side, her mood caught between awe at being the recipient of such an honour and pout lipped mutiny at being forced to be where she would rather not, kicking her black patent shoes and thinking, though never so much as whispering, about Huma. Since Leto's return from the museum, on some deep level the mammoth has become unspeakable, taboo. *Mammoth, Mama, Monster;* something is wrong, and Leto does not know what, but it pains the very walls of the house, making them tender to the touch.

Evelyn is tipsy. She is never so inferior in her habits as to become drunk – or admit it when she is. But since midday she's been quietly indulging in glass after glass of wine, and port, and latterly gin, and now neither her mind nor tongue remains subject to her usual steely control. She hasn't allowed herself to dwell on the stillbirth, or grieve more than was unavoidable in those traumatic hours after the event itself, but she's still losing blood from it, and a grim horror that she's somehow bleeding through her white cotton underskirt and green taffeta silk dress into the leather dining chair gradually takes hold of her. She doesn't know what to do. She can't stand up, and risk making a disgusting spectacle of herself before her daughter and her husband, but neither can she remain where she is. Fear chafes her thighs. Perhaps, she thinks, if she lifts her haunches and hovers over her chair, she won't bleed; or at least the flux will remain contained within her underwear and not damage her green silk or contaminate the furniture.

"Where is the pudding?" she demands, hoping that this statement will distract her husband, at least, from witnessing her discomfort. "It's awfully late."

"Give the poor chap a chance, Evelyn." Gerald responds, more irritably than he probably intended. "It's Christmas. If the pudding's late by five minutes, it won't kill us."

"Late," Evelyn mutters, shuffling awkwardly. "Always, *always* late. It's no good. And they steal, Gerald. I'm sure Nanny Gould has been pilfering the gin."

She lifts her rear end from her seat, taking her weight on her soles instead. Will Gerald notice, she wonders, if she stands for a little while? Perhaps, even if he does, he will not care. Why should he? Why should anybody care about anything at all?

Gerald clears his throat. "Evie," he says. "I have an idea. My cousin Bertie – you remember him – funny chap, works in the diplomatic service – he sent me a letter last week, quite out of nowhere, don't know where he got the notion from – to tell me he'd recently inherited a cottage in Cornwall. Edge of Bodmin moor. Beautiful place."

"So?" says Evelyn.

"He was asking if I knew anyone who might be able to look after it, just for a little while. Three to six months, maximum, till he can find a stable tenant.

And I'd been thinking, what with you being not quite yourself at the moment, it would be a good idea for you to take a little holiday. To convalesce. And this seems just the ticket. Out of the way. Quiet. Pretty little cottage. Perfect for you and Leto to break the routine. Let in a breath of fresh air. What do you say, Evie?"

Evelyn stares at him. "It's the middle of winter, Gerald," she says, as if she is addressing a madman.

"Well, yes," Gerald admits. "You wouldn't go until the Spring, of course. The Cornish countryside is very pretty in the Spring."

Evelyn grips her wine glass. A sudden urge has seized her to hurl the shimmering liquid in his face, make him splutter and blink and cough; but after a split second, it passes. She hovers uncomfortably over her chair. "I may be expecting by the Spring," she says.

"It would be good for Leto, too. She spends too much time with her head stuck in books. She needs to get some fresh air and exercise. I really want you to consider it, Evie. You have not been well, and I think you would find the place very restorative."

"Didn't you hear me?" snaps Evelyn, standing up completely. "I am not prepared to give up all hope, Gerald, even if you are."

"For goodness' sake, Evelyn," Gerald says. "Sit down!"

"It is all very well for you!" Evelyn cries, suddenly furious. "You have a son already! What do I have? *What?*"

"You have Leto!"

"*Leto?*" Evelyn turns her eyes towards her

startled daughter, who is sitting staring in amazement at this volcanic scene that has erupted, as if out of nowhere, between her usually cold tempered parents. "I had a boy – a *boy*, Gerald, *a son!* And I lost him. *I lost him!*" Her voice rises in pitch and volume, a banshee scream that shakes the holly and ivy decorated window panes.

"I have no son!" Gerald shouts, striking the table top violently with his closed fist. The silverware leaps and falls, like salmon in a stream.

Later, in the darkness, Leto sneaks out of bed. She has been lying awake, listening to the sounds of argument and recrimination that are echoing through the wall from her parents' room – and remembering Nanny Gould's tight-lipped disapproval, which seems to debar all questioning – and a strange, feral consciousness has gradually crept across her.

I am not a human child, she thinks; or rather, knows, in that part of her being Nanny Gould vulgarly calls her water. *I am not a child at all.*

She is a shape-changer, ancient and terrible to behold. She is bat, and bear, and owl, lynx, and wolf, and arctic fox. She is a native of the cold steppes, that long ago, long gone, almost forgotten time. *But not gone! Not forgotten! No!* She, Leto Murray, remembers it. She knows, she feels, and she understands, even if nobody else does. She feels her little heart beating faster and faster, her soul whirling, dancing to the music of the wind between the stones, the rhythm of the ancient place, the lost place, the place belonging to the dead and gone and to the ever living, ever young. A line of poetry whispers in her head: it's from one of her favourites in the Children's

Encyclopedia.

*Come away, O human child,
To the waters and the wild,
With a faery, hand in hand.*

Leto goes over to the bedroom window and looks out. Chiswick lies before her, its bright modern street lights aglow with electricity, its wet pavements shining. The night time air shimmers in the cold.
I am no human child. I am the wild. I am Wolf, thinks Leto.

Leto has been reading about other creatures than mammoths in her Children's Encyclopedia. She's been reading all about wolves: what big eyes they have, what sharp teeth, what loving families – and what less than savoury habits.

Can she defecate on the floor? Of course not. Though she doesn't know it, she is too well trained, too acutely aware of the potential consequences, to make her dirty protest so obvious. But she can pee. That, let me tell you, will be easy.

Leto crouches beside her bedroom door, her nightdress tucked around her waist, exactly as if she were poised over the chamber pot that still lurks like an accusation underneath her bed, and lets out her flow. It feels wrong at first to be piddling on the floor, but once she has got over the residual shame at committing such an act, it feels perfectly right: a wild act, natural and normal. Not since she was a baby has little Leto Murray been able to pee with such satisfying abandon. The musky liquid trickles down between the floorboards. By the morning there'll be little trace of it, not even a stain. But if she continues peeing every night in the same place, eventually the polish will burn from the floor, and the wood will darken. Yes. Then they – Nanny Gould, her parents, the servants, everyone – will know this is not the bedroom of a girl, but the den of a wild thing: a bear, a lynx, a wolf. But they will not know why.

Happy and at peace, Leto goes back to bed; and there we'll leave her sleeping, soundly and dreamlessly, until tomorrow morning.

Chapter Three:
The Birds

It would be wrong to say that Martin Stone knows his birds as well as any expert. He doesn't: at least not in the ways an expert might know them. He can't tell you all their names, or the average number of eggs in a blackbird's nest, or say what colour the eggs were, or explain in detail how the nest has been constructed. What he can do is this: Martin can understand the songs and calls of each and every bird he hears with the same immediacy of comprehension as if he were hearing his native tongue. The harsh screech of the jay and the tic-tic of the robin withhold no secrets from him, but are individual voices speaking out among many; and this speech, queer and avian though it is, sounds within his ear as clear and rational as any man's. This fact, inasmuch as Miss Fox is able to comprehend it, is as astonishing to her as it would be to you or I. She, for one, cannot believe he would have had much opportunity to sit and listen to the trilling of the wren, or the fluting of the blackbird, for long enough to have committed the songs to memory. But if she, or you, or I, were to ask him, he could repeat the alarmed spink of the chaffinch, and tell you why the thrush is singing – or at least, so Miss Fox suspects, for Martin still lacks the command of English such a complicated task demands, and most of his explanations are delivered in a rapid, guttural German that she is unable to follow.

Spring comes later on the high moor than it does in the valleys and coastal reaches of the south west peninsula – though never as late as it did during those cold stone times, those dark ice ages. But bit by bit, it is edging upwards. By mid April, the blackthorn in Miss Fox's garden hedge has come into flower, and the hawthorn by the moor stile at the far end of the bottom field is in tiny leaf. The wild ponies that wander by the roadside and rub their black and white heads on the field walls have given birth, as have the sheep and the shaggy longhorn cattle. Yet despite this passage of time, Miss Fox still hasn't enrolled Martin Stone in the local school. She knows this is something she must do, or risk the wrath of the Board of Education – unless the law doesn't apply to refugee children of unprovable age who have entered the country in a hurry, without papers. Is Martin Stone under, or over, the age of ten? Perhaps his remarkable quickness of mind is because he is not ten at all, but nearer twelve, or even thirteen. If he has been malnourished, she thinks, he won't have grown properly. What were conditions like in a Jewish orphanage in Berlin, between 1935 and 38? You or I might, after a little delving, be able to find out the answer, but Miss Fox feels too uncomfortable to bring the subject up. Better for Martin Stone to forget Germany altogether, she has concluded. They must concentrate on the future, and let the cruel past fade to memory.

Mammoth & Crow

But letting things fade is difficult. Things remember. At the start of the month, Miss Fox read in The Times that Britain has signed a military pact with Poland, and only this morning the BBC radio announcer was saying that Stalin is requesting a similar treaty to be signed by both the British and the French. Miss Fox is worried. Hitler is an abomination, she is sure of it, his ambition unstoppable. She has never believed for one minute in Chamberlain's declaration that he has secured Peace in our Time. Chamberlain is a vain fool, and the wily Chancellor saw through him in seconds. *We are sleepwalking into war,* she thinks, with a shudder. She pushes the idea away and switches off the wireless. Outside the kitchen window, a morning thrush begins to sing, its twin notes like the chorus of a hymn. *War cannot come,* she tells herself. *Not here. Not now.*

She pushes back her chair, walks over to the stove, and places the kettle on the hob. A nice cup of tea will make her feel better. Besides, she has the baking to get on with. She reaches for her apron.

A movement in the garden, outside the kitchen window, catches her eye.

The boy, Martin Stone, is standing in the middle of the vegetable patch, which she sent him to dig after they had finished breakfast. He has driven his spade, upright, into the soil, and he is holding out his arms, like a scarecrow. But he is not scaring the crows. He is feeding them.

Two of them: a pair. Blue-black, shining feathered, unblinking eyed crows. Dead sheep eaters, thieves and vagabonds: avian emissaries of death. One of them is sitting on his outstretched wrist like a trained falcon, pecking and pulling at the crust of toast he is holding in his fingers; the other, perhaps less confident than its mate, is hopping about his feet in the newly turned dirt, staring up at him with one considering eye, head cocked on one side. Wild birds, entirely wild; but to Martin Stone, they are as tame as pets.

Miss Fox's hands fly to her mouth. What is she witnessing? There is something uncanny about the sight, almost sacred; and Miss Fox feels as if she has accidentally stumbled across some oracle that is never intended for mortal, human, eyes.

How long has Martin been feeding them? Surely, this can't be the first time? Surely, such empathy, such affection, can't have sprung from nowhere? She watches in astonishment as the larger crow leaps from Martin's hand to his shoulder, and gently, oh, so gently, nibbles at the corner of his mouth with its savage beak, as if offering him kisses. The boy slowly lifts his hand to his shoulder, strokes the dark violet back of the carrion bird. What can it mean, thinks Miss Jane Fox, when a wild crow will perch graciously upon the living body of a boy and treat him with such gentleness? When it will let him pet it, as if he himself had raised it from its egg, had nourished and provided for it like a mother? How do the crows know not to fear him? How does he know not to be in fear of them?

I should move away from the window, thinks Miss Fox. She isn't superstitious, but the feeling that she is intruding upon some taboo is becoming almost unbearable. If she were a woman of a nervous disposition, which emphatically she is not, she might be fearful of some supernatural consequence. The local clay miners insist the moor is full of spirits: faeries, demons, ghosts. Miss Fox does not believe in such things.

But the crows, she thinks. *The crows.*

The kettle begins to whistle. At once, the crows, perhaps startled by the unfamiliar noise – though it isn't very loud – take flight. For an instant, the small figure of Martin Stone is obscured from view by a thick veil of feathers. Miss Fox ducks out of sight, before he can turn his head and see her standing, watching through the glass, and attends quickly to the kettle.

"Martin," she calls loudly, tying her flowered apron round her waist. "Martin, dear, do you want a cup of tea?"

Miss Fox has lived on the high moor for long enough to have heard most of its ghost stories and goblin tales: the story of the Parson who was accosted by the Devil up at Bronn Wennili; of the wicked Magistrate who made a deal with him and was set the task of emptying Dozmary Pool with a leaking limpet shell in punishment; the Cornish piskies who lead wanderers into the marsh, and tie knots in horses' manes; of the monstrous great black dogs, the red eyed demon hares, the faceless men. But it's one thing to enjoy being frightened by such stories on a cold winter's night, and another to think them possibly true. Such superstitious beliefs, to Miss Jane Fox, are a sign of weak-mindedness or illiteracy, and she suffers from neither. To her, the universe that God has made available to her senses and intellect is enough of a wonder in and of itself to merit her full attention; she has no need or desire to think any Otherworldly power could have an influence upon it. Ghosts are a fiction, faeries a fantasy, and Demon

Parsons a disgrace. *If he ever did meet someone on the moor,* thinks Miss Fox, crossly, *it wasn't the Devil; and if he was robbed, it was as much as he deserved, riding out blind drunk in the middle of the night.*

By the time the kettle has been taken from the hob, and the tea poured in the pot, she has half convinced herself that there is nothing uncanny at all about the sight of the boy and the crows. Perhaps the birds are used to being fed by human hand. Perhaps they were raised in captivity, and have escaped or been set free; and Martin, with his way with creatures, has befriended them. *Yes,* thinks Miss Fox, *that must be it.* They are not wild crows at all, but tame ones. Most probably they have never pecked the eyeballs from a dead sheep in their lives. *Poor, tame, abandoned things*, she thinks. *Some people have no sense, no human kindness at all.*

"Martin, dear," she says, when the boy enters the kitchen, stamping his muddy boots on the mat before bending to unhook their laces. "I was watching you with your friends, the birds. Do you think we should put out some water for them? And some beef scraps from the roast? The poor things must be hungry." She puts the teapot on the table and goes to the cupboard to collect the cups. "Would you fetch the milk jug from the larder?"

Martin Stone looks up, shock etched on his thin features. His dark eyes narrow in suspicion and a small amount of fear, as if he expects the friendliness of Miss Fox's tone to conceal a punishment. She smiles. "It is just, and right, and good to be kind to our fellow creatures," she says. "But I think it's time you had some playmates of your own age – and species.

Mammoth & Crow

It can't be good for you to be stuck here with just a crabby old maid and a few stray crows for company. I'll talk to the Headmaster about finding you a place in school."

The boy eases his boot, slowly, from his foot, and begins unlacing the other. "Please, Miss Fox," he says, slowly, finding his words with care. "I prefer to stay here, with you."

"Nonsense, Martin," says Miss Fox, in surprise. "I'm no company for a growing boy. You need to be in school. Your English is good enough."

Martin Stone shakes his head. "Please!"

Miss Fox is shocked. The boy's expression is so unhappy, his tone so desperate, her kindly meant suggestion suddenly seems unfathomably cruel, and any attempt to persevere in it unthinkable. "Well," she says. "I won't force you. Go and fetch the milk, and I'll pour the tea. There's a tin of biscuits in the larder; you can bring them too, if you'd like."

To her astonishment, Martin Stone leaps from the floor, kicking his foot free of his second boot, and throws himself across the room towards her. She barely has time to steady herself before he cannons into her chest, burying his face into her flowered apron. "My china!" she cries, bewildered. "My dear, be careful!"

Martin makes no reply. Hesitantly, Miss Jane Fox puts her free hand around his shoulders and pats him awkwardly on his bony back. "It's all right," she says stiffly. "It's all right. Don't worry. You shan't go to school. I won't mention it again. Now, be a good boy and fetch the milk and biscuits for our tea."

Evelyn is reading Diodorus upon Carthage.

"There was in their city," she reads aloud, "a bronze image of Cronus, extending its hands, palms up and sloping towards the ground, so that each of the children when placed thereon rolled down and fell into a sort of gaping pit filled with fire."

The pre-classical cultures had many cruel beliefs, Evelyn decides, and many wicked practises, but this was surely the worst of them. Who on Earth – *what* sort of person – would give up a beloved child to placate a bloodthirsty God? Well, yes, of course there is the infamous example of *Iphigenia in Aulis*, but Clytemnestra's daughter was a grown girl by that point, and, anyway, the whole thing's just a myth. This reportage is too real, too horrible. The thought strikes her: would *she – could* she – ever have willingly placed her baby son, if he'd lived, upon that brutal altar? Could she have listened to his agonised screams as he burned to death? *No, no!* The notion is unbearable.

Quickly, she closes the book and shoves it down between the cushions of the sofa. Why, she wonders, did she ever pick it up? What self-injurious impulse made her open it, encouraged her eyes to follow the black text across the page? What prompted Diodorus to write about such an evil practise in the first place? *Surely,* Evelyn thinks, *there are some horrors that really are better forgotten.* She draws a deep drag on her Camel cigarette. The nicotine is potent, even if the taste is mild. It does not help.

Evelyn stands up. The memory of what she has just read is making her feel unclean. She shudders. Children should never be sacrificed, murdered, destroyed. The idea is inhuman, intolerable, vile. There's no excuse for it, no justification. It is a sickness, a wicked delusion of supplication, a savage piety. She can't bear it.

Overcome by a wave of nausea, desperately seeking clean air, she rushes to the window, and throws it open. The delicate glass shakes violently with the sudden force. Her kitten heels are making small dents in the soft Libyan carpet. She can't bear it.

Her baby son is falling, falling through fire.
She can't bear it.

"We're going away for a while," says Nanny Gould to Leto, while she is tucking her into bed. "On a little holiday."

"Where are we going?" Leto asks cheerfully, as if she is used to taking holidays, which, as we all know, she is not.

"To Cornwall," says Nanny Gould. "The countryside. It will make a nice change, won't it?"
The child takes the news on board with remarkable equanimity, given that she has begun to kick up an appalling hoo-ha about everything else. Though, Nanny Gould reflects, she did conveniently forget to mention the fact that Mrs Murray wants Leto to leave her beloved Encyclopedia.

She sniffs. The bedroom has begun to smell. Nanny Gould isn't sure of what, but it's nothing nice. She decides that on their departure she will leave instructions for the maids to scrub the floorboards and check every cranny in case it's a decomposing rat. If necessary, she'll recommend the floorboards be got up: such an unhealthy stench can't be allowed to linger. Leto, thankfully, seems oblivious of it. Nanny Gould kisses the little girl on the head, and puts out the light.

Leto closes her eyes, her head cushioned by her downy pillow. And perhaps she falls asleep: perhaps she's only dreaming that she's wandering though some night time wonderland, in the same way that Carroll's Alice only dreamed of going through the Looking Glass. Perhaps dreams really are nothing but the side effects of thermoregulation in a resting brain, as ephemeral and meaningless as breath. To Leto, though, they are as real as daylight, and so, let me tell you, they will be to us. So as the dreaming child walks through the singing grass and cold, fresh air of the long gone ice-age plain, it's the busy, mechanical world that will be nothing but a side effect: frivolous nonsense dreamed up by the slumbering imagination of the Earth.

She has not been walking very long when she meets Huma, who is drinking from an ice rimed glacial lake, sucking up the silvery water with her long trunk and squirting it into her mouth. The mammoth's kind black eyes peer at her from beneath her shaggy fringe, and she stamps her foot. The ground shakes: an earthquake in microcosm.

Leto reaches out, and pets the end of Huma's trunk. The thick hide feels like lichen covered granite underneath her fingertips. The trunk twists, its finger-like tip rising from the earth to delicately stroke the child's hair, gently exploring the soft lobes of her ears, running over the contours of her face. Leto closes her eyes. The Matriarch is powerful enough to squash her in an instant, if she so chooses, obliterate her like an insect on a screen – but Leto knows, with a deep certainty, she never will. She wraps her arms around the muscular roughness and snuggles against it, turning her face towards the mammoth's warm hide, sucking in the comforting animal smell.

Your Moment will come, Huma says. *Then you will find me, and then you will stay.*

"I want to stay with you here and now. Not there and later."

Then the mammoth winds her trunk right around her, and picks her up, and holds her up close against her own eye, so that she can see her plainly. Leto's reflection peers back at herself from the glistening cornea, her features and her yellow hair oddly contorted by the convex surface, obscuring the depths beneath. Her human eyes flicker in the darkness of Huma's pupil.

Leto reaches out, and spreads her arms about the giant head. It's impossible, of course, for anyone as small as she is in comparison to the mammoth's great bulk to hold Huma; to be anything other than held by her; but still she tries it, tries to cling on, like a baby gripping a parental hand. And like a baby, she knows, without thinking, that the choice of whether she is held or dropped, is loved or is abandoned, lies entirely with Huma, and she has no say in it. But the mammoth is the Matriarch. She'll not let little Leto fall.

Once upon a time, Huma tells her, in another place, another time, this relationship between mother and child, lover and beloved, was that between the world and humankind. The life-giving mammoth steppe cradled humankind in its trunk, just as it cradled elk and wolf and arctic fox – long ago, before the melting of the ice. The Matriarch sustained them all: first the flat browed men of ice, then the long legged summertime invaders who would ultimately outcompete them. They were her children, every bit as much as were the red haired, tusk-less calves that played clumsily about her lichened knees in the spring sunshine, or the young crows that fluttered clumsily between the scattered birch and pine trees and the naked cliffs. They were nothing like the men of steel and gaslight from whom Leto Murray has sprung: those new, forgetful people who will one day dig up a young bull mammoth's brown-yellow skull, so coloured by the rich earth that has cradled it, and place it on show in a cold glass case.

Sleep now, cub, the mammoth tells her. *Sleep, and do not be afraid. Your Moment will come. Everything is good.*

"I love you, Huma," Leto whispers. "I love you."

Chiswick, London.
April 3rd, 1927.

My dear Phillip,

    What on Earth can have possessed you to have left school in such manner? You must go back at once. I have spoken to the Headmaster, and he is prepared to readmit you on condition there is no recurrence of the disappointing behaviour that preceded your running away. I must impress upon you that this generosity on his part represents a favour to me, and I will not tolerate any abuse of it. If your future attitude to your studies and Masters does not live up to what I must expect of my son, I shall remove the large part of your termly allowance by way of punishment. I expect to hear you have returned to school by return post.

    Your loving

    Father

Chapter Four:
The New People

Miss Fox is walking through the village on the way to the bus stop, Martin Stone at her side, her laced boots scraping and clicking on the loose road surface. The springtime air is warm, and the yellow sun is shining weakly through the morning mist. Her mind is on the new shoes she intends to buy in Camelford for Martin and herself, the letter to her Hackney editor that she means to put in the post, and the morning paper, which she quietly slipped, unread, into the waste paper bin before breakfast. Miss Fox knows she ought to read the news, but she's finding it impossible to stomach at the moment.

The walk to the bus stop takes Miss Fox over the clapper bridge and past a large house which has belonged, for most of the time she's lived here, to an eccentric old gentleman by the name of Ignatius Hart. Mr Hart, who has recently died, was not a favourite of Miss Fox's, for reasons including his determined refusal to wash, his violent outbursts of temper, and – though she'd never have admitted it to his face – his loudly voiced belief in the literal truth of those wretched faery tales and ghost stories she considers balderdash. Mr Hart was a folklorist, and also (it was long whispered in the village) a wizard. Miss Fox always dismissed this rumour as springing from the same ignorant prejudice that once branded her a witch, but the common experience never disposed her to view the old gentleman in any friendlier light.

As he had no children, when he died, Mr Hart passed on his property to his nephew, Bertram, who works in some inconsequential role within the Civil Service. Bertram Hart has never come to Bransquite to view the house, much less take possession of it, and by now it's been standing cold and empty for nigh on half a year; so it is with surprise that on turning the corner into the High Street, Miss Fox sees, parked outside it, a large bright green motor car, curving fenders shimmering in the thin sunlight. It looks very out of place: an unwelcome reminder of modernity in a location where time often seems to be standing still.

The driver's door opens, and a man, wearing a crimson chauffeur's uniform and peaked cap, gets out and opens the passenger door. He stands back politely, his nose in the air and his back straight, like a soldier on parade. Miss Fox draws to a halt, intrigued. Martin Stone clutches at her arm, suddenly anxious.

A young woman, maybe in her early thirties, is stepping out of the car, her kitten heeled, black stockinged foot scrabbling for purchase on the slippery cobblestone pavement. Her blonde hair is set in fashionably immobile waves beneath her small blue hat, and her white gloved fingers are clutching with furious anxiety at the small black handbag she is holding closely in front of her. Standing up, she draws her silver wolf fur coat more tightly round her stomach – not as if seeking protection from the cold, but from some other, unseen danger. Her perfect, pink lips twitch once, convulsively, as if suppressing a sudden urge to cry out. *For what,* wonders Miss Fox. *For help?* Hardly surprising – a London lady like her must feel like a fish out of water in a place like this.

The woman steps away from the car, looking up at the stone gateway, the climbing-rose and ivied facade of the house in front of her, her pretty nose wrinkling in distaste. Her complexion is like ivory, notices Miss Fox – and a small, unworthy voice in her head wonders whether it has come courtesy of Max Factor. Then she turns back toward the car, and her expression hardens into something that looks – or so Miss Fox thinks, with a sudden chill – closer to hate.

A sturdily built little girl, perhaps ten or eleven – more or less the same age as Martin, if Martin is as old as Miss Fox believes he is – is clambering awkwardly through the open car door. Her hair – blonde, like her mother's – is tied in two pigtails that swing heavily as she moves. She places her feet squarely on the pavement and stands upright, looking around herself with interest.

"Leto," says the blonde woman, sharply.

The little girl squints at her mother's face; then, hitching up her tartan skirt around her waist, reaches inside her knickers and scratches her right buttock.

The blonde woman gasps. "Stop that!" she hisses. "You are a disgrace! People are watching you."

'People' means herself and Martin, realises Miss Fox. "Come along, dear," she says quickly, unwilling to be drawn into any interaction, even to the point of exchanging pleasantries. Elegant as the woman is, there is some indefinable quality about her that Miss Fox does not trust. And anyway, she thinks, she was never friendly with the uncle – why should matters be any different with any other members of the family? She sets her face away, and begins to hurry down the lane, pulling Martin in her wake.

When Miss Fox and Martin Stone come back from Camelford, the sturdy little blonde girl is sitting underneath the stone archway on the sunny doorstep of Ignatius Hart's old house, inexpertly plaiting a daisy chain. A thickset, older woman in a neat grey jacket and knee length skirt, whom Miss Fox assumes to be the nanny – these well-to-do London families always employ nannies – is seated in a large wicker chair beside her, newspaper spread over her ample thighs and a cup of tea in her pudgy hand. She looks up when she hears the clack of Miss Fox's boot heels on the flags. Miss Fox smiles, and nods her head in greeting.

"Good afternoon," volunteers Miss Fox, a little stiffly. "I hope you are enjoying your tea."

The woman smiles. "Yes, thank you, Madam."

"I trust your journey was a pleasant one – from London, was it?"

"We drove down overnight. It wasn't too uncomfortable."

"Well," says Miss Fox, picking up her long skirt, and beginning to move away. "I do hope you'll enjoy your visit."

"Who are you?" the little girl demands, suddenly.

Miss Fox starts so hard that she almost trips over her own feet.

"Leto Murray, how many times have I told you that it is very rude to ask questions?" exclaims the grey suited woman. "Madam, I apologise. I don't know what's come over Miss recently. She is being very naughty."

"It's quite all right," says Miss Fox, recovering. "She's right; it would have been impolite for me to have come and gone without any introduction. I'm Miss Jane Fox, and this is my nephew, Martin Stone."

"Very pleased to meet you," says the thickset woman. "My name is Mrs Gould, and this is Miss Leto Murray. Her father is the famous Professor of Classics at King's College, London."

"I see," says Miss Fox. "Well – " Miss Fox doesn't often entertain, but now that names have been exchanged, she feels as if she has no choice: it would be offensive to omit the invitation. "If you and Leto would like to come to tea at my cottage," she finishes, with a tight smile, "that would be lovely."

"How kind of you to offer," Nanny Gould says, so warmly that Miss Fox feels guilty. "When would it be convenient for us to call?"

"Tomorrow," says Miss Fox, pulling the date out of thin air, meaning never. "At eleven."

"Tomorrow it is. What would be the address?"

Miss Fox describes the location of her cottage, beyond St Bran's Church, two miles beyond the village, on the very edge of the moor.

"Lovely," says Nanny Gould. "We'll be there, won't we, Leto?"

Mammoth & Crow

Little Leto Murray is staring at Martin Stone. He has dark brown eyes.

Like Huma's, she thinks, unexpectedly. They are strangely ancient eyes: tired eyes, that have witnessed too much and want nothing now except to close and to stop witnessing; but they can't, for the same reason Huma's can't. *He's important,* Leto realises. Seeing him about to walk away, she gets to her feet, and awkwardly, suddenly overcome by a desire she can't explain, thrusts out the daisy chain. "I want you to have this," she says.

Martin Stone looks at her with a bewildered expression on his face. Then he looks at Nanny Gould, and finally at Miss Fox – who, to Leto, is the tall, intimidating woman standing stiff as a pole beside him – as if asking her what he should do. Leto shakes the daisy chain at him in her small fist.

"Here," she repeats. Then, when the boy still doesn't respond, she continues, with increasing impatience: "What *is* wrong with you? Are you deaf, or stupid? Take it. It's yours."

Martin seems taken aback for a moment, but then shrugs his shoulders, and holds out his hand. Leto dashes the daisy chain into it. Then she turns away, suddenly acutely embarrassed by her action, feeling like a toddler who does not know what to do or say next.

"Thank you," says Martin. His accent is unknown, foreign. The thought crosses Leto's mind that her mother would not like him. She likes the thought. She runs quickly up the steps to the old house, and disappears within it, slamming the heavy Georgian door behind her.

"My goodness," says Nanny Gould with a

sigh, as the woodwork rattles. She rolls up her newspaper and tucks it under her arm. "What a pickle she is today. Well, Miss Fox; well, Martin; I shall very much look forward to tomorrow. Good afternoon to you both. It was lovely to meet you."

"Likewise," says Miss Jane Fox, though it wasn't.

She walks home through the flowery lanes with Martin Stone. Although the day has remained sunny, and the descending notes of willow warblers are filling her ears, Miss Fox is unable to shake off the feeling that what was a pleasant day has somehow been irretrievably spoiled. Why did she allow herself to become drawn into conversation with the woman? Why on Earth did she ask her to tea? What does she have to say to any London person, apart from her Hackney editor – even a nanny? And although Mrs Gould comes across as fairly respectable, the family – from the little she has seen of them – seem utterly appalling. A woman who can stare at her own child with such a pointed and un-maternal dislike is unlikely to be kind to anyone else, and as for the daughter... Miss Fox shakes her head. Leto, despite her nanny's efforts to restrain her, has plainly been very badly spoiled. Does the fault lie in the mother's rejection, or the father's overindulgence? Perhaps Professor Murray mollycoddles his daughter.

"What would you like with our steak and kidney for dinner, Martin?" Miss Fox asks. The boy is walking at her elbow, silent as usual, like a small shadow. She puts her arm around him. A singing pipit rises from the far side of the wall. "There are some tinned peas in the larder, or you could see if any winter carrots are ready in the garden."

"I will look for carrots."

"You are a good boy, Martin. I am lucky to have you."

When they reach the cottage, Martin heads into the garden with a trowel, and Miss Fox evicts the reluctant tomcat from her armchair and puts on the kettle for a much needed cup of tea. She deliberately avoids looking out of the window, in case Martin's busy with his crows again. Though she's decided there is nothing supernatural about the sight, no, nothing at all, it still unsettles her. She winds up the gramophone, and takes a record from its sleeve.

> *A tisket, a tasket, a brown and yellow basket.*
> *I sent a letter to my Mommy,*
> *On the way I dropped it.*
> *I dropped it, I dropped it.*
> *Yes, on the way I dropped it.*
> *A little girlie picked it up, and put it in her pocket.*

Miss Fox joins in, singing the version she remembers from school. *I sent a letter to my love.* Why has Ella altered the words? It's always been *love*, and not *Mommy*, as far back as Miss Fox can remember.

Nanny Gould and Leto Murray arrive for tea next morning on the dot of eleven. The little blonde girl has been scrubbed to within an inch of her life, and although it's only Saturday her clothes are fit for Church. Nanny, on the other hand, is dressed very much as she was when Miss Fox met her, although she's changed her crumpled blouse to a starched white cotton one, without a single wrinkle. Miss Fox, for her part, has not dressed up, as such, although she deemed it prudent to rescue her best London clothes, which haven't been worn since Hackney, from the back of the closet. Martin Stone is dressed, like Leto, in what would, in any other household, have been his Sunday best.

    Miss Fox has never asked Martin how he feels about attending – in their case, not attending – Church. The boy is, after all, Jewish, and to expect him to participate in ordinary Christian worship wouldn't be appropriate; but she can't help but wonder sometimes how he feels about the several hours they spend every week in silent contemplation of the divine. Even so, their respective faiths notwithstanding, on their latest visit to Camelford she found herself compelled to buy him a smart set of clothes along with the simply neat and tidy garments with which she has replaced his orphanage rags. She justified the expense by recourse to the rationale that eventually Martin might have to face an immigration tribunal, and he will make a far better impression on those sorts of people if he is well attired. After all, although the Government – as yet – has given no indication of going back on its word, the boy's future security in the country is far from assured. Miss Fox does not trust Chamberlain, and has read some shocking headlines in the *Daily Mail* and the *Express*. Sometimes she wonders whether, in the event of Martin's being required to return to Germany, she would do better to ignore the option of a legal hearing at all, and to hide him rather than offer him up to agents of the Government. The moor is tricksy. It would be easy for a boy to vanish for a while, and hard for those who don't know the land's secrets to find him.

"Good morning," says Miss Fox with a smile, showing her visitors into her little parlour and closing the front door against the suddenly biting Bodmin wind. She calls up the stairs. "Martin, our visitors have arrived."

Nanny Gould and Leto sit on Miss Fox's sofa, while she busies herself in the kitchen making the tea. Martin finds the tin of biscuits from the larder and asks if he should he bring in the Victoria sponge. Miss Fox tells him no, not yet; that's for later, if their guests are still hungry, and then disappears into the parlour with the china teapot, milk jug and flower patterned cups carefully balanced on a black tea tray.

Martin reaches down to stroke the ginger cat, Fluffy, who is purring around his legs. He wishes, as he knows Miss Fox does, that the strangers had not come. They are an unwarranted intrusion into a world within which he has only recently begun to feel safe. Miss Fox isn't at all like his grandmother, but she is kind. More than that, he can tell, she is extremely righteous. If she'd been Jewish, and a man, his grandmother would have decided she was a *tzaddik*, and insisted on her spending *Erev Shabbat* with them, singing out the *birkat ha mazon* in the glowing candlelight. And when she – he – tried to leave, his grandmother would have pressed her with more and more rich food and cheap wine until she collapsed snoring in a corner, like the Rabbi on Purim.

"Who are these people, Fluffy?" he asks the ginger cat. "Why don't they just go away, and leave us alone?"

The cat looks up at him, and gives a long and

guttural miaow. "Oy, glutton," sighs Martin. "All you ever think about is food. One day, you will eat too much, and your belly will pop. Then will you regret. I have nothing for you right now."

The cat wails irritably, and stalks off towards the back door, tail flicking in the air.

"And stay away from the small birds," Martin calls after it. "If you bring in one, dead or alive, I will not share my cream with you tonight. No cream, Fluffy. Hear you?"

The ginger cat jumps onto the window sill, picks its way delicately around Miss Fox's geraniums and auriculas, and disappears through the small window that has been left open for that purpose.

"Martin," says Miss Fox, coming into the kitchen in a rush. "Bring in the biscuits, dear, don't dawdle. Oh, my goodness, Mrs Gould wants three spoonfuls of sugar in her tea, and I forgot to put the bowl on the tray. Whatever must they think of us, Martin?"

Martin can't think of an answer. He shuffles his feet, uncomfortably. What he wants to say to Miss Fox is something like: does it matter what they think of us? We know what we think of each other, and what we think of them. But he does not entirely trust his English, or his nerve.

"Why don't you take Leto into the garden?" Miss Fox suggests. "It will be very boring for you both to have to sit and listen to two middle aged ladies gossiping. And Mrs Gould says that her father is very keen for her to spend as much time as possible in the fresh air. The wind is a little chilly, but you can put on your coats."

Gossiping? thinks Martin in confusion. He

doubts that Miss Fox has a gossipy bone in her body. It's not the sort of thing that she would ever stoop to. Perhaps she imagines that she is doing him a kindness by excusing him from a meeting she herself expects to find tedious. But to be stuck instead with that strange, rude little English girl is not a prospect that he relishes. For a moment, he considers begging Miss Fox to reconsider. But he does not.

"Well, Martin?"

The boy nods. "Yes, Miss Fox."

Martin Stone takes Leto Murray to see the vegetable patch. The little girl looks over the freshly dug rows of peas and carrots, the green growing tops of early cabbages and the faded spikes that were last year's brussels sprouts poking through the soil with an expression that lies somewhere between boredom and confusion. Martin wonders if she has ever seen food growing in the ground, or if it has only ever appeared in front of her, as if by magic, on a plate. He was almost as ignorant once, in the days when vegetables had seemed to spring from market stalls and meat from the window of the kosher butcher. It was a luxury not to have to think too hard about where one's food came from. *But on the other hand,* thinks Martin, *it's a privilege to be able to grow it.* His grandmother, in her tiny Berlin flat, never had the space.

"What is that?" asks Leto at last, curiosity getting the better of her reticence.

"That? Turnip."

"It can't be. They're only for cattle. It says so in the Children's Encyclopedia."

Martin shrugs. "The Encyclopedia is wrong."

"It's never wrong," says Leto.

"Still," says Martin. "That is turnip, all the same. And that is potato, and that cauliflower, and here will be beans, if the birds don't eat the – *jungpflanzen* – seeds – before they have a chance to grow."

"Do birds eat beans?"

"Some do." Martin looks towards the ridge pole of the cottage. The two crows are sitting, like sentinels, one on either side of the chimney pot, cocking their jet black heads as if straining to catch his words. "They do. They do it to tease me. They think it is funny. But it is not."

"Don't be silly," says Leto. "They're just birds. They don't know whether you're angry or not."

"They are my friends," says Martin Stone. "But naughty, sometimes."

"They're scary," says Leto. She shudders. "How they stare."

"They don't scare me," says Martin.

Stepping away from Leto, he holds his right arm straight out in front of him, and gives a raw, unearthly call. It's not a human shout. It's in no human language, contains no discrete units of sound that could be recognisable to a linguist as conveying meaning; but neither is it a formless exclamation, like a man might give in surprise, or when he has stubbed his toe. It's not, in fact, a human sound at all, and all the hairs stand up on the back of Leto's neck when she hears it.

The two crows flap their wings, and rise in unison from the roof of the house, falling like giant black leaves to rest with a low thump on Martin's outstretched arm. Martin laughs. "Oy, you are heavy!

Mammoth & Crow

I didn't want for both of you to come at once. Come, sit on my shoulder, Petra." Obligingly, the large black bird hops up towards his face. Leto Murray stands open mouthed, astonished, horrified, too fascinated by what she is watching to dare scream. The crow's sharp, deadly beak is inches from the boy's unprotected eyes.

"This is Peter," Martin says. "I wanted to name them for the two little dicky birds, like in the rhyme. Two little dicky birds, sitting on the wall, one call Peter, one call Paul. But Peter is really Petra. She is a girl. They have a nest in the rafters."

"How do you know?" Leto breathes. "Did you find it?"

"Not yet, but I know where to look. I am being polite, you see. I am waiting until Petra tells me I will be allowed to see it."

"Tells you?"

"Yes, of course. She is my friend. Would you invade the home of someone who is your friend?"

"No," says Leto, thoughtfully. "I suppose not."

"So you see," says Martin. "Not just birds."

He shakes his arm. The large crow scrabbles to retain her purchase on his sleeve, and then takes to flight. Her mate gives a loud cawing sound, and joins her. For a moment they fly fast in a wide circle round the vegetable patch, like performing clowns in a circus ring. Then Petra gains height, and Paul follows her; and in a sudden draft of wings they are both gone, flying away over the wall and the farmers' fields onto the high moor.

Martin smiles. Leto Murray is staring at him, open mouthed. "How did you do that?" she exclaims.

Martin shrugs his shoulders. "I talk to birds, and they talk back to me," he confesses. "I do not know why, or how I do it, but I do. You will not tell anyone, won't you?"

"Of course not! Nobody would believe me, anyway."

"Miss Fox would. She knows, I think. But she is not frightened. She is too good and sensible."

"It will be our secret," says Leto comfortingly. "Ours and Miss Fox's."

"Thank you," Martin says.

Leto skips across the vegetable patch and bends her face towards Martin's ear, cupping her hands to her mouth. "I have a secret, too," she whispers; perhaps in a spirit of friendship, perhaps out of the wish not to be outdone; or perhaps because a rumbling voice within her head is saying to her: *Leto, speak.*

"Do you?"

"Yes. Her name is Huma. She's a mammoth. She's been dead for fifty thousand years."

Chapter Five:
Horsefeathers

Now, if Leto Murray had made an announcement like this in an ordinary tale, a plain talking, kitchen sink, everyday adult drama grounded in what we think we know of human psychology and the causal mechanics of the modern world, at this point you could assume that you were subtly being invited, or implicitly expected, to decide that she's confusing fantasy with reality as children often do, and interpret everything, both good and ill, that will result from it according to that light. But you and I know that this is no ordinary tale. Yes, it looks like one on the surface, with its mundane talk of cars, and cows, and cups of tea, and Chamberlain, but underneath, it's still a faerie tale: a blood and bone, blue-stone, bearskin, bog-side, blood-river, crow and mammoth tale. It has different rules. And anyway, to let you in on a faerie secret, the real world that you think you know doesn't always work in the ordinary, everyday ways that ordinary people think it does.

Keep it to yourself, his grandmother used to tell Martin Stone, when she caught him standing at the open window in their little Berlin apartment, calling the starlings and the sparrows to his hand. *It is a blessing, but not everyone will understand that. People will be frightened. They will say you are possessed by a dybbuk.*

Leto's is the same species of secret. This is something Martin understands. It belongs, like his talent, to that hidden part of life, whose understanding belongs to the long bearded Rabbis who keep fierce guard over secret tomes, and relate histories of Moses de Leon and the Ari. So instead of disbelieving her, or calling her a silly baby, he says: "How did you meet her?"

Leto hops from one foot to the other. "It was through the Encyclopedia. One night before I went to bed I was reading about mammoths, and then in my sleep I met her in a dream. Only I wasn't dreaming. It felt as real as standing here right now talking to you. I've seen her hundreds and hundreds of times since then, and it's always the same; as if I'm wide awake, and visiting another place. It is a real place, I'm sure of it."

"Is she a – ghost?" Martin asks, uneasily.

Leto scratches her head. "I don't think so. Ghosts live in old castles and go around moaning and rattling chains and trying to frighten people. Huma doesn't do anything like that. She lives on the steppes. Do you know what steppes are? Cold grasslands that are full of flowers in the summer. And she's very kind and warm, and looks after everybody."

"But if she was dead for so many years, then she must be a ghost."

"She can't be a ghost," Leto insists. "She just can't be, because in that other place she's still alive. I can touch her, and everything. It's still a very long time ago there, I think. I'm not sure if any time ever really passes. If it does, it doesn't pass in the same way that it passes here."

"So she is dead here, but not there?" Martin is frowning, trying to understand.

"I suppose so," says Leto, thoughtfully. "I went to look at her skull in the Natural History Museum, once. But it's empty. The spirit's gone. In fact, I'm not sure it *is* her skull, not any more. The scientists say it's a bull's – that's a boy mammoth's – and it seems too small, too *sad*, somehow, to be hers. Perhaps when I think I'm dreaming, I'm really visiting her in heaven. Do you think mammoths go to heaven?"

"I do not know anybody does."

"What do you mean?" exclaims Leto, shocked.

"I do not know what happens when people die. Maybe there is no heaven. Maybe the only thing is life. Or perhaps the dead stay here, watching over everyone, but we cannot see them, and they are unable to speak."

"You're strange," Leto says. She feels that she wants to say something more than this, but she doesn't know what it is.

'No stranger than you."

Leto Murray sticks out her tongue, and pokes him in the ribs with one hard finger. Martin is not entirely sure whether she's being playful or not, and wonders whether he should poke her in return, or whether doing so will get him in trouble with Miss Fox. The blonde girl is solidly built and probably stronger than he is; but he is taller, and older, and a boy to boot. "Do not do that," he tells her.

"Don't," says Leto. "Not do not. Don't. I like

that you're strange. My parents are so boring. All Father ever does is read his Daily Mail, and all Mummy ever thinks about is trying to have a baby boy. She thinks I don't know anything about it, but I do. But Nanny Gould is the worst. She has no imagination. You're the least boring person I have ever met."

A sudden flutter of black wings announces the return of one of the crows, who settles on the garden wall beside the gate, and caws loudly, just once, before cocking its head on one side and staring at Martin with its jewelled eye.

"What does it want?" Leto asks, eagerly.

Martin frowns. "I think he ask us to follow him. Through the gate."

"Onto the moor? Can we go? How thrilling! I've never been on a moor."

"It is too dangerous without compass and a map," says Martin. "Miss Fox says people have lost themselves walking on the moor, and died when the mists closed in."

"I'm sure we wouldn't. You know the pathways, don't you?"

"Not well enough," confesses Martin. "I have not live here very long."

Leto is disappointed. "Where are you from?" she asks, kicking at a clod of earth with her toe. It feels the contact: tumbles, falls, remembers. "You're foreign, aren't you? I can tell by your voice. You don't sound English."

Martin hesitates. Miss Fox has warned him to keep his origins to himself. *People might not understand,* she has told him. It often seems to Martin that people are much better at not understanding than they are at anything else. He looks closely at Leto. Can he really trust this peculiar little English girl, he wonders, whose manners are so odd, and whose curiosity so insatiable? He does not know. On the other hand, he has introduced her to his crows, and she hasn't reacted with the shock and fear he's been conditioned to expect from strangers. He wonders why he let her in on that secret so easily, without a moment's consideration. Perhaps he was trying to scare her, he thinks. He's still not certain if he likes her very much, if at all.

"Miss Fox is my aunt," Martin says.

"I know that, stupid. I heard her tell Nanny Gould. I want to know where you come from."

"Berlin," answers Martin, reluctantly. "Germany."

Leto stares at him. "Germany!" she cries. "Mummy loves your country. She says it's the best country in the world. And she adores Mr Hitler. She has a picture of him by her bed."

Martin stares at her, in mute horror. The urge to take the words back, unravel the moment in which they were said, is as overwhelming as it is futile. He feels sick. He wants to run away, but his legs have begun to shake.

"Please, do not tell anyone," he stammers. "It must stay a secret."

Leto frowns. "Why? That's silly. I wouldn't tell Mummy anyway. I don't tell her anything. She doesn't like me very much." Her expression has clouded.

"Miss Fox says so," Martin says, though already he knows better than to think this answer will be sufficient for Leto. "I'm sorry if your Mother doesn't like you," he ventures awkwardly, attempting to change the subject. "That must make you sad."

"It doesn't." Leto tosses her head. "I don't like her, either. I wish she wasn't my Mummy, but Nanny Gould says we can't choose our family, and have to be grateful for the ones we've got."

Miss Fox chose me, thinks Martin, and something in his heart seems to give a tiny, almost painful, twist. The crow hops from the wall, and lands next to his boot. He bends and strokes its glossy head.

"I have an older brother," Leto says. "Father had a son, years ago, before he married Mummy. I'm not supposed to know about him either. I didn't, until Mummy started talking about him at dinner one evening, when she was drunk. Then they had a nasty argument about it when I was in bed and they thought I couldn't hear them. Father says he's dead to him, but he's not really dead, you know, just lost."

"Did your father and brother have an argument, too?" Martin asks, thinking about Miss Fox and the falling out, which has, of course, never been properly understood.

"I don't know. They might have done. Father doesn't like people who disagree with him."

"Everyone has secrets," says Martin. "People seem simple on the surface, but once you know them, you find out everyone is hide – hiding – something."

The crow looks up slyly, and seeing Martin now distracted, starts pulling up the sprouting beans.

"Your English is terribly good!" says Leto. Martin wonders whether talking about her family is as upsetting to her as it would be to him; wonders whether she even understands what she is feeling. He remembers children like her in the Berlin orphanage:

tough, hard-shelled little boys and girls who'd learned to avoid at all costs acknowledging that anything could hurt. Hurt makes you vulnerable.

"Thank you," Martin says. "Miss Fox taught me to speak it."

"Did you not know any English before you came?"

"A few words."

"You must be very clever."

"I don't think so. I knew I had to learn fast, so I learned. Being clever is doing what you need to do – " to stay alive, he almost finishes; but stops himself in time. There are some things one does not share with a stranger, even a funny little girl whose best friend is a long dead mammoth.

The crow on the vegetable patch gives a sudden squawk, and takes off in a violent clattering of wings. The kitchen door opens, and Miss Fox steps through it. "Martin, dear," she calls. "It's almost time for Leto to go home."

"That horrid old house isn't my home," says Leto loudly. "It's cold and spooky, and I don't want to be there."

"I'm sorry, Leto," says Miss Fox. "But Nanny Gould has finished her tea and says your mother will be wondering where you are. You may have a slice of cake before you go, if you would like."

"I don't like cake," Leto says, although she does. "Can I come to play again?"

Miss Fox looks surprised. "If your family agrees," she says. "Martin, would you like Leto to visit again?"

Martin thinks carefully. He knows the polite answer: he's expected to shrug, and sigh, and say of course he wants to see the little girl again – but he also knows Miss Fox doesn't value the mouthing of empty politenesses any more than he does. She wants the truth.

His answer surprises him. "Yes," he says. "Yes, I would like that very much, Miss Fox."

Evelyn wasn't expecting to like the house, but she hadn't thought she'd hate it as much as she does. It's not, at least, as small and cramped as she had feared – Gerald's description of it as a cottage was misleading – but the building's old, and hasn't been well maintained, despite its owner having had both means and opportunity to have done so. Many of the peeling walls are showing serious signs of damp, and the air in all the downstairs rooms smells musty and stale. Even worse is the condition of the kitchen, which Evelyn feels quite sure hasn't been touched since the middle of the last century. An ancient, blackleaded range squats underneath a broad, brick chimney breast, and a row of rusty bells hangs on the wall: a sorry reminder of the last time the house was occupied by a family. The elderly housekeeper – another relic from the old man's time who's returned to service after six months' retirement – has told her there are five bedrooms, plus a sixth that's been transformed into a library which still contains the late Mr Hart's books and art works. There's also an attic, where the servants once slept, but Evelyn isn't interested in that, and neither need we be. All but one of the bedchambers have been lying under dust sheets for several years. The old gentleman wasn't given to entertaining: the last time some of these beds were occupied was before the outbreak of the Great War.

Yesterday, Evelyn pulled the dusty canvas from her own windows, and insisted that the aged woman washed the curtains and changed the bedding, even though the woman complained that the blankets and quilts were all perfectly clean. Evelyn does not believe that anything that has lain without being properly aired for the best half of a year could still be healthy. She is still worrying about the mattresses, which have not been turned, and the chimneys, which have not been swept; about the foggy chill, and the constant risk of fire; and over and over she has asked herself why in God's name she ever agreed to come here. Worse, why did she consent to bring Leto? The journey here was horrible, the car cramped and the child fractious, her own nerves frayed beyond enduring. This dreadful house is no place for a child, especially a difficult and unpleasant one. What if Leto should catch a chill from the damp? She will be bored, and being bored will become demanding and troublesome, and what is Evelyn to do in order to entertain – or to escape – her? To add insult to injury – though she's trying not to think about it – her period has suddenly begun, which means her body has finally recovered, and she'd have been able to conceive again after the stillbirth. Why, she thinks, was Gerald so ruthless in his determination to send her away? If she was still in London, in her proper place by her husband's side, in her husband's bed, they could try again – and perhaps this time she'd not only carry a son nearly to term, but birth him alive. If she'd been allowed to come to Cornwall pregnant, Evelyn thinks, perhaps she'd have withstood the isolation. She'd have had hope. As it is, all she has is Leto.

Good wife and good mother: *raison d'etre* of a good woman, according to Mussolini, Davenport, and the rest. So how can motherhood mean so little to Evelyn Murray, who wants so badly to be good, when motherhood means Leto? Why can't she love her only daughter, her first born – perhaps her only child, if she never conceives again, if there never *is* another son? In most faerie tales, the wicked Queen isn't the natural parent of the Princess, and the child's own mother – safely dead and buried – is a paragon of gentleness and virtue. Impossible, of course. The truth, let me tell you, is that the simple act of giving birth cannot by itself change a nightmare to an ecstasy, or wake a deluded and unhappy woman from a nightmare that she does not know that she is having. Blood, by and of itself, does not always bond: it is not necessarily thicker than water.

Evelyn shivers. She cannot, just *cannot* feel anything for the wretched brat. If, she thinks, this inability to love makes her a bad mother, a cruel mother, if this unnatural lack of feeling means she is to be punished by the loss of every other child she carries, then she'll have to accept her sentence. Love does not come simply because it is supposed to. But the punishment is brutal. Love's absence should not have such vindictive consequences imposed upon it. Perhaps, for all their wickedness, the ancient Carthaginians held the right idea about God. Perhaps he really is unforgiving, brutal, cruel.

Now, after an uneasy night of very little sleep, Evelyn is standing at the drawing room window with her morning cigarette, watching as her daughter and Nanny Gould walk down the steps and under the stone arch into the lane, turn uphill towards the Post

Office, and disappear from view. A deep sigh of relief escapes her. Although when Nanny first described the woman and her nephew, Evelyn was afraid that they might be an undesirable influence on Leto, it soon struck her as really most unlikely that a middle aged Bransquite spinster would have any interests beyond the baking of scones and the bottling of jam – exactly the domestic skills her daughter ought now to be learning. Perhaps, she thought, it was time for the girl to begin meeting people outside of her own family. As for the boy, if he proved to be a nuisance, Leto could be instructed to avoid him. Gerald said the child needed fresh air.

Well, Evelyn thinks, *now she's getting plenty.* She draws hard on her cigarette. The reflected end glows brilliant red in the grimy glass.

She turns away from the window. There are more matters to attend to in the house.

Evelyn's not particularly interested in the bedrooms, apart from those she's chosen for herself, Leto and Nanny Gould. But she's curious about the library, and demands that the locked room be opened by the housekeeper. She doesn't know what she expects to find there – after all, an old man's reading tastes are most unlikely to reflect her own – but she hopes nonetheless to find something to relieve the tedium of this place, which is already gnawing at her fingers like a rat. A quick conversation with the old woman has already confirmed her suspicion that there's nobody in the village worth knowing except the vicar and postmistress, neither of whom plays tennis. No wonder Cousin Bertie refused to take on the house.

The housekeeper proves surprisingly

reluctant. There's something in that room, perhaps, she does not want Evelyn to see. This naturally piques Evelyn's interest.

"I'm in charge here, now," she sharply reminds her. "I don't care if this is Mr Bertram's house, or what instructions the late Mr Hart may have left. For as long as I'm here, it's my house. If I want to enter any of the rooms, I will. If you won't unlock the door, give me the key."

The old woman mutters under her breath that she'll be handing over any of the house keys over her dead body – but catching Evelyn's expression, fits it into the lock. The key turns with a rusty clunk, and Evelyn seizes the doorknob. The door swings open with a creak, and she marches through it, feeling strangely powerful, like one of the warrior queens of Classical Antiquity storming to victory: like Tomyris, like Artemisia. *How ridiculous!* she thinks. *Is this what I've come to?* Oh, vain, ignorant, foolish Gerald! Is this what you imagine will restore your wife's vitality?

Ignoring the old woman standing behind her, Evelyn strides into the room and drags the dust sheets from the windows, coughing in the dirty rain that falls about her head and shoulders. Daylight rushes in.

As she looks around her, her fading sense of victory diminishes still further toward the Pyrrhic. Mr Hart's supposed library is sparsely furnished, and it stinks, like the remainder of the house, of damp. There are very few books – although a battered Victorian bookcase takes up most of the far wall, and numerous markings in the dust on both its shelves and on the mantle-piece bear wordless testimony to there recently having been books. *Where have they gone?*

Who has taken them? Surely not Gerald's cousin Bertie, who hasn't so much as visited the house, and certainly not the aged housekeeper, who in Evelyn's estimation has the look of never having read beyond her ABC in her entire life.

What remains? Evelyn walks over to the bookcase. The books there now have been placed – or replaced – in a higgledy piggledy fashion, some upside down, some lying flat, some with their spines facing toward the wall, as if whoever last handled them did so in a great hurry, and cared nothing for their condition. Evelyn picks one up, and runs her hand across the shelf. It's dusty, but not as evidently so as the rest of the house. When were the books taken? It can only be a matter of weeks, at most.

Again, the question: who? And why? Were the books valuable enough for somebody to steal them? This, too, strikes Evelyn as unlikely. Unless old Mr Hart took much greater care of the missing part of his library than he did these volumes, they too would have been musty and damp, their pages discoloured, and their leather and board bindings coming loose. *It's a mystery*, Evelyn thinks; and even through her disappointment at finding the room so bare, the word quickens her pulse in a way nothing else has done since the stillbirth.

And it is then, let me tell you, exactly then, whilst her awareness is risen up into this heightened, impressionable state, and the story's settled in a sweet spot, ready, watching, waiting for something significant to happen, that Evelyn notices the red curtain hanging over the mantelpiece, the brass rail, the rope. It is the sort of curtain earlier generations would have used to hide a family portrait that could not, for reasons of propriety, be removed, but whose contemplation remains so odious or painful to its owner that it must be covered up.

Mystery, whispers Evelyn's imagination. She hurries to the curtain pull, and gives it an impatient tug. The velvet slides across in a shower of flies.

There is a painting behind the curtain, but it's not – it can't be – a family portrait. For one thing, it's too amateurishly painted. A figure – a young man – is standing amidst a landscape of grey stones beneath a low, scrubby tree, his back leaning against its twisted trunk, looking out toward the painter, who's chosen to set his composition exactly in the manner, Evelyn thinks, of those country house paintings that were so popular in the eighteenth century. But that's where his attempt at naturalism has, unfortunately, ended. The sky above the figure's dark head is the deep violet of oncoming night, yet the young man's features have been painted in bright whites and brilliant yellows, as if he were standing in full sunlight. And they're queer features, too; slightly stylised, somehow familiar, arrogant and knowing as a King's. But the eyes look wholly real. Too real. The black and sparkling pupils are peering curiously, consciously, out of the painting – and suddenly Evelyn thinks she understands why old Mr Hart, or whoever hung the curtain, felt the urge to cover it up. If she did not know such a thing to be impossible, she thinks, she might come to believe that the figure is watching her. She feels as if it is. She shivers.

"Mr Hart painted that himself," the housekeeper says, in Evelyn's ear. Evelyn jumps. In her fascination with the picture she has not heard the old woman creeping up behind her. "Horsefeathers, we call him."

"*Horsefeathers?* What sort of name is Horsefeathers? Do you know who he is?"

The woman sniffs. "Just a tramp the Master met with some years ago up on the moor. Painted from memory, that was."

"Take it down," Evelyn says, at once. "Take it down, and put it into storage. It is a ridiculous subject, and poorly executed besides. I cannot imagine Cousin Bertie will care to look at it, and I certainly do not."

She looks back at the painting. The dark sky is composed of a seething mass of spiralling forms, in a poor imitation of Van Gogh. She's never liked his work much, either, never understood why so many people make such a silly fuss about it. It's too self-consciously unreal. She peers more closely at the figure under the tree. His face is not the only unnatural element, she realises now: his whole being has been painted in such a way as to make it appear that he's not only leaning against the tree, but emerging from it – or sinking into it, as if it were devouring him, transforming him via some unholy metabolism from man to vegetation. Is that skin upon his face, or bark? Hair beneath his wide brimmed hat, or tendrils of ivy? His hands are wrapped in strangle-weed. Suddenly, as if out of nowhere, she remembers the bronze statues of Carthage, gilded palms outstretched above the pit of sacrifice: the children consumed by the flames.

She shudders violently, as a wave of dizziness washes over her, and fearing suddenly that she's about to vomit, spins about and runs from the room, hand over her mouth. Her kitten heels clatter on the floorboards like hard rain. She'll never go inside that room again, she decides.

She reaches the downstairs sitting room before the fit of nausea has completely passed, and then she realises that she's still holding the book she lifted from the library shelf. She flings it in disgust onto the coffee table and watches without caring as it skitters off the edge and falls open on the dusty hearthrug. Quickly opening her cigarettes, she draws one, applies her Zippo to the tip, and takes a deep, reassuring suck. Her hands are shaking. *What a hideous place this is,* she thinks. Damp, mouldy, full of sick-making so-called art and reeking with the cold scent of abandonment. Why has Gerald banished her? Why has she let him? She should have refused, argued, demanded. She has the right, after all, to remain with her husband. She should not have let him bully her into leaving him, allowed his sorry blandishments and repeated mild suggestions to wiggle their way, like maggots, into her inner ear. What was she thinking? That if she obeyed Gerald in this – as she knew she must in any other thing – some good would come of it? She was foolish. Weak-minded. It's wrong to be weak. Morally degenerate. Professor Davenport would be ashamed.

Evelyn drops onto the sofa, her face buried in her arms. Ash drops from her fingers onto the musty rug. She does not care, or even notice.

But she should pick up the book, she thinks. It's vulgar, common, vile, to let a book fall on the floor as if its contents do not matter. Only the basest people, those who inhabit London's slums, would treat it so. Evelyn has always hated those people, with their low IQs, bow legs, boss eyes, and irregular skulls. They're primarily responsible, she's sure, for the degradation Moseley says has afflicted the country over the past few generations. Stupidity breeds stupidity, and indolence feeds upon it: ignorant, unwashed and lazy, the masses hang about the neck of the nation like a millstone, dragging it down: too stupid to perceive the damage they are doing, too unpatriotic to care; just breeding, like rats, like vermin; breeding, breeding, breeding. *Sterilise them,* Evelyn suddenly thinks. She clenches her fists, suddenly furious, suddenly shaking, suddenly beyond language. She has no idea why this notion that the illiterate poor should continue to produce children, despite their poverty, their inferiority, should suddenly hurt so much, why she is so angry about it; why the dropped book, the dizzying portrait, the vision of Carthage, the instantly suppressed remembrance of loss made her suddenly think of their unreasonable fecundity. Of why, right now, she desperately wants somebody to do something about it: fix things, mend them, put them right. Why it matters so much, so much, so, so, so, so much.

  Evelyn isn't one for weeping. She will not weep. She bends, picks up the book, and puts it on the table. She has no intention of reading it.

Chapter Six:
Water and Stone

Leto is running through the steppe-lands, her brown leather t-bar shoes making soft depressions in the patches of fresh moss that have grown across the cold face of the granite scarp. The wind is warm today, and playful. It lifts Leto's blonde pigtails from her ears, and blows them forward and back, up and down, twisting and writhing like springtime adders in the bright sunlight. The day is dry, its colour beyond blue; bright and cloudless, the ice age sky appears to Leto's delighted eyes to be almost violet, and the sweet air smells of sage, yarrow and tansy. To the western horizon (where, many thousands of years later, will lie the busy little country towns of Camelford and Bodmin, through which she will be driven in the bright green motor car) the many flowered lowland stretches out unbroken beyond the moor: yellow, rose pink, blue and green, its colours punctuated by the distant brown and grey backs of the grazing herds. To her left, a skylark rises up trilling toward the sun.

"Huma!" Leto calls. "Huma!"

There is no sign, yet, of the mammoth, but

Mammoth & Crow

Leto is not unduly concerned. This is her refuge, after all, her place of safety: even should she meet a wolf, a bear, a cave lion, she knows she'll come to no harm. Isn't she one of them? She doesn't belong to any Tribe of Man. Her mother never birthed her. She – Evelyn Murray – does not yet exist.

Leto sits down on a prominent lump of granite, kicks off her shoes, and pulls her white socks from her feet, setting free her toes. She has no need now for shoes, or for socks. The moss and flowers feel cool and delicate against her hot feet, like silken threads, or tissue paper, and the sweet air blows in over them like kisses. She looks up, and around. This time, she feels, she knows – not thinks – that this *here,* this *now* is when the English soil is at its most alive: now, in this ancient world long before Man, when Kings and Queens were living giants instead of great soulless machines, and the air was pure. When you think of the Pleistocene – if you think of it at all – you probably don't think of it like this. Try it, now: chances are you'll find yourself imagining vast, sheer sided glaciers, cliffs of ice as hard as iron, and wind-borne sleet that falls like showers of nails. A world where no-one and nothing can possibly live, because machine Man cannot. How wrong – I'll even say, with Leto, *how silly*. It is true – probably – that the glaciers themselves are largely devoid of life, but let me tell you that every square mile of earth that they cover has been paid for a thousand times over in life on the fertile plains over which they loom. *It's beautiful!* Leto thinks; and its vibrant, and free, and the fact that it no longer exists in our real world is a tragedy. But perhaps that is the nature of time: tragedy. Leto's mother – the one she doesn't have – is always complaining that the world has fallen into in a state of degeneracy and decay. *Though, of course*, Leto thinks, *this isn't what she means.* It would never occur to Evelyn for one second to mourn the loss of wilderness. She cannot bear the notion of a world that is not wholly subject to the Will of Man.

A mountain hare has broken from the sagebrush halfway down the slope, and it is loping toward the clear stream that runs along the bottom of the narrow valley, below the crags. Leto wonders what disturbed it. She can't see any predators. She looks up, scanning the sky for birds of prey. All she can see is a pair of black shapes, switching and diving as if they were writing on the air. *Crows,* she thinks, much too dismissively – but she's only ten, and has not yet learned which things she must see and which she can, quite sensibly, ignore.

Perhaps Huma is in the valley. She's never met the mammoth in uplands like these. It's hard work for a creature of such size and weight to climb from the flat plains onto the high moor, though Leto feels sure Huma would easily be able to pick up any of the large erratic boulders that impede her own, stumbling, progress, and toss it out of her way as easily as a pebble on the beach. She scrambles to her feet. Should she carry her shoes? She's not sure. She leaves them on the granite rock, white socks tucked tidily inside the toes, and wanders down the hill. Flowers bend their necks under her feet, springing smartly back to attention after she has passed. *Just like the flowers in Alice's garden,* Leto thinks; except that this place isn't a garden, as such, and she hasn't passed through any looking glass.

She sees the figure from a few hundred yards

distance, sitting on the edge of the stream. It isn't Huma, of course – any being of the mammoth's size and shape would have been visible over a far greater distance – but neither is it any of the other creatures with whom Leto has become familiar. It has a human shape – or almost human, for as she approaches, it shifts, visibly, into a cataract of clear water, and falls, then continues falling, into the torrent below. Where there once sat a figure there is now a waterfall, shimmering white and cold against the grey-green rocks and purple dryas flowers.

Leto walks over to it, and dropping to her knees, dips her hand in the sparkling water. "Who are you?" she asks.

Who are you? comes the swift retort, as fresh as bubbles.

"Leto Murray."

Who are you?

"I told you. I'm Leto. Who are you?"

Who are you?

"Now stop it," says Leto, becoming annoyed. "I've asked your name three times, and told you mine already. Who are you?"

Somebody else, comes the water's answer. *Every second, someone new.*

"How infuriating you are," says Leto in irritation. She lifts her hand from the water, shakes it, and looks up. The sky is violet, blue, and purple, ribboned colours like the inner bands of a rainbow twirling and spiralling above her head. She'd almost forgotten that this landscape isn't her usual, everyday reality – now suddenly she's reminded, and a sudden fear of waking grips her bones. What if she should wake without having found her Matriarch? What if

Huma isn't here?

You must travel deeper, says the waterfall. *Find the door within the earth, traverse the caves of blood and memory.*

"What?"

Did we say something?

"Yes! You told me something."

The I who told you is already many yards downstream. I told you nothing.

Leto jumps to her feet, and stares along the flowing waters. *Play with us,* says another voice. *Chase us, until no-one has the energy to run.*

"What will happen if I wake?"

You will not wake.

Leto backs away from the stream. There's something now in the way that it is speaking – some sinister implication that makes her think she does not want to play with it, let alone chase it – and it prickles the pit of her stomach. "I think I ought to go home, now," she says, uncertainly.

Stay, says the river. *We want to play with you. Please stay.*

As she retreats further, her eyes upon the waterfall, it rises up, like a fountain; the body of water forming into a column of transparent silvery fluid, which melts and shifts and reshapes itself into the naked likeness of a girl – a girl perhaps Leto's own age, who's now holding out her hands imploringly and smiling, now opening her lips, now begging: *Stay.*

Leto turns, and runs uphill away from the river, faster on her two bare human feet than the hare she has been watching. "Huma!" she shouts. "Huma!"

She runs so fast, and so far, that before much

time has passed – if time has any meaning here – she has reached the top of the crags, and is looking down into the valley from the perspective, she thinks, of the eagles who, according to the Encyclopedia, must surely nest here, though she's never seen any sign of them. Exhausted, she lets herself fall on the soft ground between two large boulders, and lies on her back, catching her breath. *I ought to go home*, she thinks. *I ought to wake up. But I don't think I know how.* She feels suddenly frightened. *Leto, you will not cry,* she tells herself, sternly. *Not here, not there, not in front of anyone, not eagle or human or anyone. You will not cry. You will make yourself wake up.*

One of the two crows who have been circling lands on the larger of the two stones, and stares down at her curiously. Then it gives three loud caws, and takes off, briefly, into the air, before returning to perch once again upon the stone and peer at Leto. It reminds her of the crows who are friends with the German boy, Martin. Perhaps it is friendly, although the Encyclopedia insists that crows are harbingers of death, or scavengers on battlefields. Perhaps sometimes the Encyclopedia really is wrong.

Leto sits up, and the crow caws again. "Shoo," she says, somewhat half-heartedly. "Shoo," Perhaps she means "shoe" – for when she looks down, let me tell you, she sees instead of her bare feet, or the familiar t-bar shoes she left upon the scarp-side, a pair of moccasins: thick soled slippers of white wolf fur and colourful reindeer hide.

"Boy," says the crow. "Boy."

Leto is about to tell the great black bird that she is not a boy; but then the thought strikes her that perhaps it does not mean her, but Martin Stone. Is he here, too?

"Are you going to show me the way back?" she asks the crow.

"Boy," it replies.

Leto gets to her feet. If she can't find Huma, and she can't wake up by herself, there seems little else for it; she can sit here until she dies in her sleep, or follow the crow and hopefully find a way back to reality. "All right, then, crow," she challenges it. "Show me. Where is he?"

"I had a dream," Martin says to Miss Fox over breakfast. It's mid May, and the morning is warm. A gentle breeze is fluttering the red and white gingham curtains on the kitchen window sill, where the large ginger tomcat lies snoozing in the yellow sunshine, his tail draped languidly around the pot of auriculas. "I was walking on the moor behind the house, and I found that girl. Leto Myhrry. I think she was lost. I had to show her the way back home." He dips his bread soldier into his boiled egg.

"Murray," says Miss Fox, carefully, correcting his pronunciation. "Not Myhrr-y. She's a girl, dear, not a present for the baby Jesus. I've been thinking about her too, Martin, as it happens. When I woke up this morning, I wondered whether we should all go up to Rough Tor today, for a picnic, if the weather holds. I think you'd love the high moor, Martin – at least in summer."

Martin nods. "Shall we ask Leto, Miss Fox?"

"I think that would be kind. I expect she's lonely, without company of children her own age. Would you run down to the village after breakfast and ask at the house?"

"Yes, Miss Fox."

"Perhaps they would like some jam. I am sure Mrs Gould would, anyway. She seems to have a very sweet tooth."

Half an hour later, brown paper parcel tucked tight underneath his arm, Martin Stone is hurrying through the lanes towards the Ignatius Hart's old house. Miss Fox's cottage stands two miles beyond the centre of Bransquite, and, like the Church and vicarage, on much higher ground: as the lane drops down towards the village, Martin cannot help but notice the change in temperature. The trees here have some protection from the insistent wind, and have been able to grow much taller than is possible upon the wild moor. Their species are more varied, too. Displacing the blackthorn and the yellow gorse, here grow young sycamores, tall beeches, spreading oaks, ivy and alder already coming into leaf along the verge of the small river that babbles down from the moor top, and the roadside verges are sky bright with bluebells and the half closed greenish spikes of early foxgloves. Blackbirds and robins are fluting loudly in the hedge, and the sheltered air is warm and sweet. *Welcoming*, Martin thinks. He smiles. Hitler and his Nazi *Verbrecheren* can go to hell, if there is one, and vanish up their own backsides, if there is not. He has escaped them. Here, he is safe.

Is he? He remembers what Leto told him – that her mother has a picture of the Chancellor upon her bedside table – and his expression clouds. How many British people, he wonders, would support the Fascists if they came to power here, as they've done in Germany? There's a question to ponder! The thought that any might do so is terrifying: yet it seems such people are not as uncommon as you or I, or Martin Stone, might hope. It hasn't escaped Martin's attention that Miss Fox has developed a habit of switching off the wireless when he comes into the room, and more than once he feels sure she has put the day's paper on the fire before reading it, to stop him from seeing the headline. It could be dangerous being friends with Leto. But on the other hand, she doesn't seem to like her mother.

The village is quiet – most of the younger children are in school, and their fathers gone to work on various local farms and in the local granite and china clay quarries. The only activity Martin can see is inside the Post Office, where two elderly ladies are gossiping in the queue. He crosses the clapper bridge, pausing briefly to watch the sparkling waters cascading down the slope, and wonders how long this river has been running through the valley. How can one tell the age of a river, or a rock? Neither is like a tree, whose age can be determined by counting its rings. Is the answer somewhere in the soil, or in the water? *There's no point in asking the water,* he thinks, *even if I could.* The fluid that is flowing underneath his feet probably fell as rain no more than six months ago on the high moor, and before that was part of the dark grey clouds that sweep across the winter sky on the Atlantic winds. It's river water now, for sure, but that is a temporary state, a brief episode in its ongoing waterly existence. All things are in a constant state of change – both the living and the apparently inanimate.

He pulls a dead twig from one of the large alder trees that grew alongside the bridge, and throws it in the water, intending to count the seconds it will take to pass underneath. The water is flowing so fast, the stick is whisked out of sight before Martin even has the chance to register its tiny splash upon the surface. He runs quickly to the other side. There is no sign of it. Perhaps it got tangled in the roots of the very tree he plucked it from, which are spreading out into the river like a spider's web. *Twig-fly. Spider-tree.* He looks up. A crow is sitting in the upper branches, watching him intently, its head on one side.

"Petra?" he wonders, squinting. "Paul?"

The bird does not answer.

Martin shrugged. *Perhaps it's just a wild crow*, he thinks. From where he's standing, it's too hard to tell. He greets it, anyway, and carries on walking towards the house.

Evelyn has insisted that the housekeeper store the portrait of Johnny Horsefeathers in the attic, in the expectation that this will mean that neither she, nor Leto, nor anybody else will ever have to look at it again. But she hasn't supervised the removal, and as she can't stand to spend any time within old Mr Hart's head spinning library, she remains in ignorance of the fact that the old woman has done nothing of the sort, but merely tugged the curtain closed again and hidden the ugly fellow out of sight.

She has, however, kept hold of the book, and even though she has, still, no intention of reading it, she finds her attention uncomfortably drawn towards it – just as it was once drawn irresistibly to Davenport's *Hereditary*. It's lying on the coffee table where she has dropped it, its embossed title like a banner, a printed command demanding to be read: *The Golden Bough, by James Frazer.* She imagines it must be a novel, with a title like that – probably a retelling of the Judgement of Paris, or Aeneas and the Sybil gaining entrance to Hades. But she's not sure. When she rescued it from the floor its pages fell open, and their contents, which she very briefly scanned, did not strike her as fiction. On the other hand, she's never heard of Mr Frazer. If he is, or was, a Classical scholar, he must be either a very new or a very lowly one for her husband to have had nothing to say upon him; and neither case would seem to recommend his work. The simplest way to find the answer is, of course, to open the book again and look; but that, Evelyn thinks, would mean reading it; and she has no intention of doing that.

She is lying on the sofa, enjoying a mid-morning glass of white wine, when a timid rapping on the front door alerts her to the presence of a visitor. She leaps to her feet. It's unlikely to be anyone worth knowing, she reminds herself, probably only some gibbering village idiot selling hens' eggs, or a dirty gypsy with a tray of clothes-pegs and brightly coloured laces; but nevertheless she can't entirely suppress the ridiculous hope it might be Gerald come to take her home, or at least stay and suffer with her in this absurd, tedious prison. *Find the place restorative*, she thinks scornfully, remembering his words. The only restorative for miles around comes in a green bottle labelled Gordon's. She finds herself wishing that she had given into her impulse to throw her Christmas wine in his face. Perhaps, in that moment, the act would have been enough to derail him, make him give up the silly fantasy before he had grown too attached to it.

She listens to the housekeeper's shuffling

footsteps as the old woman reaches the door and opens it. There's a brief conversation, and then the sound of the door closing. Evelyn sits down heavily, her knees giving way. It wasn't Gerald. Of course, it wasn't. Of course, it never could have been. She knows this, really; but the satisfaction of having her bitter guess proved right is nowhere near enough to fend off her crushing disappointment.

"Mrs Gould," calls the housekeeper's voice. "It's the Quaker boy from up-over-yon, come to see Miss Leto."

Evelyn lifts her head. Perhaps, she considers, looking for a way to rouse herself from her own misery, she really ought to meet this boy, with whom, by all reports, her daughter has become quite friendly. She has no idea, upon her own account, whether he's an appropriate child for Leto to be playing with, or not. But when Nanny Gould returned the other day from the woman's cottage, she brought a positive report. According to Nanny, the family are well mannered, if absurdly provincial, and they seem a decent sort of people; so if the boy is not an ideal companion for Leto, he's definitely to be preferred to the thuggish village brats who are the only other candidates. She supposes that it's good for Leto to learn how to make friends with people her own age. *Certainly,* she thinks acidly, *it's what Gerald would want. Friends, activity and fresh air.* How typical of Professor Murray's affections that he would place his daughter's need for a social life above Evelyn's own.

The spark of anger is enough. She need not meet the boy, she tells herself. Not yet. Perhaps never. Why should she meet him? It's not as if this one brief friendship can have any lasting impact upon Leto's

future, or anything else.
She lifts the wine glass to her lips, wishes it was gin. But it's too early for that.

Martin is waiting for Leto and her Nanny to come downstairs. He didn't want to give up the jam parcel to the housekeeper, whom he feels he can't quite trust, and is still carrying it under his arm. He looks around the hallway. It's a well lit area of about eight feet square, ordinary in appearance, although the light streaming in through the leaded glass panels on the front door is casting a strange multicoloured glow onto the darkly patterned walls. The Victorian paper is peeling away from the plaster in more than one spot, and the air feels damp, as if the walls were rotting. He understands what Leto meant when she described the place as spooky: there's something in the air, above and beyond the whispering smell of mould, that reminds him of a graveyard. He shuffles his feet. The paper parcel is beginning to feel heavy.

"Martin!"

Martin Stone looks up. Leto Murray is standing on the winding staircase just above his head, leaning over the banister, blonde pigtails dangling like ropes.

"Don't just stand there," she calls. "Come up. Nanny is just finishing her cup of tea."

"Miss Fox says to ask if you would like to come on a picnic," Martin says. "And she has sent some jam for Nanny Gould."

"Come up, do! I say, do you want to see the house? It's not nice at all, but it is interesting."

Martin cannot think of a way to refuse this offer that would not seem rude, so he follows the girl up the stairs to the second floor, where one of the bedrooms has been quickly re-designated a nursery. Nanny Gould is sitting by the fireplace, drinking tea. Leto shows Martin in and then shuts the door with a bang. A dark grey pall of coal smoke mushrooms from the fire. Leto laughs.

"You little madam, that was very naughty," says Nanny Gould, coughing. "How many times have you been told to be careful?"

"I don't know."

"Well, I do," says Nanny Gould. "And it's high time you remembered. Hello, Martin. Is that parcel from your auntie?"

"Yes, Mrs Gould. It's jam. Miss Fo – my auntie thought you might like it."

"That's very kind of her, and you make sure you tell her so," answers Nanny Gould.

Martin explains about the fine weather, and Rough Tor, and the offer of the picnic. Nanny Gould sips her tea. "Well," she says. "I don't know, young man. I can't see I fancy the idea of a walk out on the moor myself."

Martin frowns. He isn't sure how to explain that the offer is intended for Leto, alone. It's not that Miss Fox doesn't like Nanny Gould, more the fact that it never crossed her mind to imagine that a girl of Leto's age would need to have a nanny in tow everywhere she went. That isn't, normally, the way that people live. But Leto understands.

"He's asking me, not you," she points out. "And if I want to go, I can, can't I? Father said I need fresh air and exercise, I heard you and Mummy talking about it. That means walks and picnics. I want to go. And if you won't let me, I'll stand here and scream and scream until Mummy comes upstairs to see why, and then she'll say that I can go, and you'll get into trouble with her and Father."

Martin stands by, speechless, and stares at his boots. He's wishing he'd never come – or that he never had the dream that put the notion of a picnic in Miss Fox's head.

Nanny Gould takes a deep breath. Martin freezes, waiting for the eruption; but it never comes.

"Well," says Nanny. "I will ask your mother myself, young lady. And if she says so, you can go with Martin. But you know how your parents feel about you mixing with strangers."

"He isn't a stranger, he's my friend," Leto retorts.

Nanny Gould gets to her feet. "Wait here, then," she says, with a sigh. "I shan't be long."

"Do you want to see something terribly queer?" says Leto, as soon as her guardian is gone from the room.

"What?"

"A painting. Mummy told the housekeeper to hide in the attic, but she hasn't done it. It's still on the wall where she found it."

"Why is it queer?" Martin asks.

Leto heads from the room, peering anxiously this way and that for any sign of Nanny Gould, and leads quickly him along the landing. "Shh," she tells him. "We're not really allowed, but the housekeeper forgot to lock the door."

She stops outside one of the heavy doors, turns the knob, and pushes it open a crack before slipping through. "Come on," she urges Martin. "Be careful, the hinges squeak."

Martin, at a loss for an alternative, follows her.

The room into which they have come was once (as we know, though the children, of course, do not) some sort of library. It's still as dirty and sour as the remainder of the house, but the window curtains are now open, and the floor has been recently swept. Leto ignores the bookshelves and the view from the half open window, and heads straight for the fireplace, over which hangs the dark red velvet curtain on the running pole. Quickly, she tugs at the cord that controls the hanging cloth, and it swishes aside, leaving Mr Ignatius Hart's oil painting in plain sight.

Martin stares at it. "Why is it queer?" he asks. "It's not very good."

"Because I know *where he is*."

"You do? How?"

"I've been there. I *know* I have. I think it's somewhere in Huma's world, the *Otherworld.*"

Martin frowns. "So – " he starts to say. Then he stops. Is Leto really suggesting that the dream-world of her mammoth is as real – and most importantly, as *reachable* – as this world is? *Yes,* he realises, *she is.*

"So where is it?" he asks, reserving judgement.

"On the high moor, somewhere. Only in Huma's time it isn't moor, it's steppe."

"I see."

"So if we go on a picnic, if Mummy lets me, can we look for the place? It must be a special place, you see. It must be a Moment. That's like – " she pauses, trying to decide the best way to explain the idea, which is not a thing she's ever had to do before. "It's like when you're looking in a mirror, and you put your fingers up against your own reflection," she explains at last. "A Moment is the point where this world is touching that one and we can travel through the looking glass, just like Alice. Things become real in a Moment."

"How do you know all this?" Martin can't refrain from asking the question, although he isn't sure, really, that he wants to hear her answer.

"From Huma, stupid." Leto whisks the curtain back across the canvas. "She told me. So can we?" she repeats. "Can we find the spot?"

"It's a very big place," Martin says, doubtfully.

"And when we find it, we can be pirates and mark it on a map with an X, like buried treasure. Then it can be our secret place, and we can come back to it whenever we want. And I can take you to see the plains, and the herds, and the river and everything."

She flashes him a conspiratorial grin, and gives his arm a nudge, before quickly leading him back into her ad hoc nursery. Just in time, he realises, with a jolt. Nanny Gould is in the hallway: he can hear her ponderous footsteps coming up the stairs.

"Well," Nanny says, entering the room with a curiously put out expression on her face. "It seems you are in luck, Leto. Your mother has said you can go."

Leto jumps up from the chair in which she sat down only seconds before, and throws her arms around her nanny's neck. "Thank you, thank you, thank you, lovely, lovely, *lovely* Nanny Gould," she croons, as if the decision were Nanny's, and not

Leto's mother's. Her tone seems false to Martin, and he wonders how Mrs Gould can be taken in by it. But perhaps it is one of those peculiarities of Englishness with which he has still to come to terms: the many ways in which a person might, for reasons of political expediency, hide their true feelings under a display of excessive exuberance. If it is, he doesn't think he likes it.

"Go and get your coat," Nanny Gould says to Leto. "I don't care how warm it seems to be, the wind up on top of that moor is savage. And Martin must bring you back by dinner time, no later. Do you hear that, young man?"

"Yes, Mrs Gould," says Martin, straight away.

"Good boy. And you, Leto, must do as Miss Fox tells you. If you are naughty, I expect to hear about it."

"I shan't be naughty, Nanny," Leto says at once. *Butter would not melt,* Martin thinks. It's what Miss Fox says, every time she catches Fluffy with a mouse. It means extreme guilt with the appearance of wide eyed innocence. He hopes Leto is telling the truth. She would be very silly indeed to run away, and lose herself up on the moor.

Chiswick, London
April 21st, 1927.

Dear Phillip,

Where are you? Today I visited the address to which I have been sending my letters, but was informed you are no longer living there. I have left this note in the hope that you will call some time this week to collect your post, as apparently has been your habit, and will find it then.

You must desist from this rebellious behaviour, and come home at once. I am still hopeful that there is a chance you may return to school, but time and your Headmaster's patience are both running out. I await your reply.

Father

Chapter Seven:
The Fogou

When Martin returns, with Leto in tow, he finds that Miss Fox has packed a wicker picnic basket with various comestibles, and has retrieved a red checked picnic blanket from the bottom of the airing cupboard where it has lain undisturbed for more years than she cares to count. She knows the moor, of course, having lived upon it for so long; but nevertheless she has also tucked her compass into her coat pocket along with an ordnance survey map. It's important to lead by example. It would never do to say one thing to Martin Stone and do another. Besides, she's hopeful that the boy will soon begin to explore by himself, in the way any normal child would do, and so it's vital that he learn how to navigate properly. The last thing she wants is for him to fall into an abandoned mineshaft, or stumble into one of the treacherous bogs that lie in silent wait for the unwary traveller in the most unexpected places.

Miss Fox does not allow the children to linger; she has listened to the weather forecast on the wireless, and the sunshine is reportedly set to stay, but you can never be wholly certain of the high moor, and she's keen to make the most of the time they have.

After handing the blanket to Leto, and the map and compass to Martin, she picks up the basket and leads the way through the busy vegetable garden and over the stile into the enclosed pasture behind the cottage. Leto Murray has never before seen a stile, and Miss Fox, to her own astonishment, has to explain the concept of scrambling over the wooden steps and jumping down into the grass upon the other side.

"That's a cow!" Leto cries, before they have walked more than half a dozen steps. She points.

"Yes, Leto. Of course it is."

"I've never seen a cow. But I like them. The Encyclopedia says 'The Cow Tribe are our sweet natured and generous friends, without whose help we would never have advanced toward civilisation.'"

"Well, dear, I suppose that's true," says Miss Fox. "But do stop waving at it. They can be a little over-curious."

After they have crossed the field, Miss Fox and the children climb over the stone stile into the open country; and then, while Leto stares open mouthed, Miss Fox asks Martin to examine the ordnance survey map and compass.

Martin has had the process explained to him by his foster Aunt many, many times over the preceding winter months, so it's with scarcely a thought that he orients the folded paper according to the northerly direction indicated by the compass, locates the position of Bransquite and Miss Fox's cottage, and ascertains their present position. They are two miles outside the village, facing north east across the grass and gorse and heather covered plateau that stretches, according to the map, as far as Altarnun; from here it's easy to make out the imposing forms of Rough Tor and Bronn Wennilli looming in the distance. The great tors are also less than two miles away, according to the map; but to Martin's eyes they suddenly look much farther, as if they were really part of some other world than this one.

"So, Martin?" says Miss Fox.

"We have to go this way – but there are lots of streams in the way, and I can't see if there's a bridge anywhere."

"So what shall we do?" asks Miss Fox.

"There is a footpath," Martin says, frowning. "A little to the north of here, which heads straight up onto Rough Tor moor. We could follow it and see if it leads to a bridge, or some other place where we can cross."

"Our lives are in your hands," says Miss Fox, which seems overly dramatic to Martin. "Lead on, dear. If we can't get as far as either hill today, we can always find a nice spot on the moor to sit and eat our picnic."

Martin sets his compass and heads north, toward a location where it appears upon the ordnance survey map that their route will intersect with that of the footpath. Miss Fox and Leto follow him.

"It's so huge!" Leto cries after a while. She's stopped walking, and twirls about on the spot like a ballerina, raising her arms above her head. "There's so much sky!" She laughs. "I've never seen so much sky! In London, we only went to the common. This is like being on top of the whole world! Look at those little white clouds! And those birds!"

Martin looks where she is pointing. Black shapes – most probably crows, but not, he thinks, his crows – are circling over a location on the high moor, some hundred yards away. "They've found a dead lamb," he says. He looks at Miss Fox.

"If they have, can we go and see it?" Leto asks, excitedly. "From a distance," she adds, in a more subdued tone of voice, when the others turn to her in some consternation. "I've never seen a lamb except in the Encyclopedia. And I'd rather see a dead lamb than a picture of one."

"Oh, my dear," protests Miss Fox. "It's very out of our way – and I'm sure we'll come across many live lambs on our walk. Wild ponies too, no doubt."

"Wild ponies? Really?"

"Yes. Would you like to see them?"

"Rather!"

"I had never seen them either until I came to live with my auntie," Martin says. "But here they wander all over the moor. You can see them from the cottage in winter."

"I didn't know there were wild ponies here. I thought they were only found on Dartmoor and on Exmoor and in the Welsh Mountains and the New Forest and – "

"Look," Martin interrupts her, pointing. "There's the path."

The footpath is narrow, and constitutes nothing more than a depression in the grass, but it is, in comparison with the surrounding moorland, well trodden. Miss Fox feels proud. As they head towards the two peaks, Leto launches into a long and complicated recital of the many breeds of horse and pony native to the British Isles, all of which she has only read about: their heights, their preferred uses, their great strengths and weaknesses, to which Miss Fox finds herself compelled by politeness and charity to attend. It isn't not long before she realises the astonishing paucity of the child's experience. Although it's not at all uncommon for the children of miners and labourers to live in a restricted universe, it's most unusual for a girl of Leto's class. But it really seems that she's never been exposed to anything, except the inside of her family house and garden; regular, closely supervised, walks to Chiswick Common; and one journey, which she mentions briefly, to a museum.

"Do you play tennis?" Miss Fox asks, remembering that Mrs Gould mentioned the game being a favourite pastime of Leto's mother's.

"Sometimes Nanny and I play on the Common," comes the answer. "But only when it's empty, because Mummy says it is unladylike for me to be seen running about in public."

"Does she? What about cycling? Can you ride a bicycle?"

"I wish I could ride a bicycle! I would adore it! But Mummy says I'm not allowed in case I fall and injure myself so nobody will want to marry me."

"What?"

"I can ride one," puts in Martin. "But I've never had one of my own. My grandmother could not afford to buy me one."

"I'm sure she would have if she could, dear," says Miss Fox reassuringly – though this information, too, is new to her. *So*, she thinks, *Martin was raised by his grandmother before the orphanage took him in. He must have lost his parents very early on. Poor little waif.*

"Father says I have to get fresh air and exercise," Leto says. "Mummy's cross. She wanted to stay in London and try to have another baby, but she had to come to Cornwall because of me."

"Very good, dear," says Miss Fox, quickly. "But things like that are private, Leto. I don't think your Mummy would like to think you'd told me about it."

"I don't care," Leto says. "I hate her. She doesn't like me to have anything I love. She even wanted me to leave the Encyclopedia at home, but I made Nanny pack it and not tell her."

"Ah, look!" Miss Fox exclaims, in relief. "There's the crossing. Well done, Martin."

One by one, the three walkers pick their way over the stepping stones that cross the little river. Miss Fox has already decided not to go too much farther, not because of any fear of the weather, which really is set fair, but because she has grievous doubts regarding Leto's ability to climb a hill as high as Rough Tor or Bronn Wennilli. If the girl has never taken any exercise beyond the occasional half mile walk through Chiswick and rare game of tennis with her nanny, it's unlikely she'll be fit enough to manage such a trek. *Cruel,* Miss Fox thinks, *to keep a child so penned in*. She wonders what on Earth the parents can be thinking. No wonder Leto has such an air of suppressed excitement about her: even sitting down, she seems to buzz and crackle with energy. She is a normal, growing child, and has a normal child's needs for affection, mental stimulation and physical exertion, and from what she has just said it doesn't seem to Miss Fox that her parents are meeting any of them. Miss Fox purses her lips. It's neither her place nor her business to interfere, but she can't help wishing she could give the blonde, fashionable Mrs Murray a piece of her mind. She wonders if the mother is jealous of her daughter. Such perversities are far from unknown, particularly when the mother is as young and modern as Mrs Murray. It must be very hard for somebody like that to watch her daughter grow up, and feel her own youth already gone; stolen from her, perhaps, by that very child. Miss Fox wonders how old the father is. *Older,* she instinctively decides; *considerably older.* Perhaps Mrs Murray married in search of security, and is now regretting it. Miss Fox knows thought like this is idle speculation. She feels a trifle ashamed of herself for indulging in it. It's not at all impossible, after all, that there could be true love between two people of such different ages. Didn't she once fancy herself in love with a man many years her senior? But that love, if love it was, and he are water long gone, and no good ever comes, Miss Fox tells herself, from chasing memories.

They've left the crows behind, but the landscape is far from lifeless. Small, brown, ground nesting birds – skylarks and meadow pipits – are ten a penny here, and every twenty or so yards the sound of their approaching footsteps sends another arcing like a firework from the close-cropped grass. The sky above is bright and dry; from somewhere to the south comes the faint mewing of a buzzard, carried over and over on the thin, restless wind. In the distance, a small free ranging flock of Cornish Longwool sheep is resting placidly upon the soft marshy soil alongside the riverbank. Miss Fox decides to suggest that they should head toward them, in the interest of showing

Leto a living, breathing lamb. She won't go too close, she thinks; they don't like to be disturbed, and it would be a pity to make them run.

The ground between the path and sheep is rough, and pitted with a multitude of small steep sided holes and narrow gorges over which the children are able to leap, but whose navigation poses more of an obstacle to a lady of Miss Fox's years and decorum. Within a minute or two they are several yards ahead of her, while the sheep are beginning to glance in their direction, and one or two are slowly scrambling to their feet.

"Slow down, children," Miss Fox calls. "Be careful not to trip. Stop before you come near to the sheep. You'll upset them."

Leto is much too excited at the longed-for sight of real life farm animals to pay Miss Fox's exhortation any heed. Pretending she hasn't heard, she continues scrambling over the tussocks in eager excitement to get close to the wonderful, woolly things she's read so much about in the Children's Encyclopedia. They're incredible creatures. There were no sheep in the Pleistocene – they came into existence much, much later, bred by stone age farmers from the wild, curly horned creatures that leapt nimbly around the hillsides of Palestine and ancient Greece.

"Stop running," Martin says quietly. "You will frighten them."

His words make an impression upon Leto where Miss Fox's can't. The girl slows, and comes to a ragged halt, balancing unsteadily on the ridge of one of the shallow, bracken filled pits. The sheep have lifted their grazing heads, and those who were lying in the sunshine are now clambering to their feet. They stare at her out of golden eyes, and begin to back away, recognising a natural carnivore.

"It's all right, sheep," says Leto. "We won't hurt you."

"Come away," says Martin. "Slowly, and they will go back to grazing. They want to see what you will do."

"They're so big. So funny looking. Don't you think?"

"They think that you want to eat them," Martin says.

"Silly sheep! I wouldn't eat you. Not unless you were a joint hanging in a butchers' shop, and that's different."

Leto picks her way slowly through the field of pits to where Martin and Miss Fox are standing. The sheep watch her go, intently; then when they're satisfied that she's too far away to pose them any immediate danger, a number of them lower their heads and return to their grazing. A cool breeze rustles the bracken.

"I think they understood what you said about the butchers', Leto," says Miss Fox, with a smile.

"I didn't mean to scare them."

"I'm sure you didn't."

"I think they're super. They won't run away now, will they?"

"Shall we have our picnic here?" Miss Fox suggests, looking up at the great mound which is sheltering the valley in which they are now standing from the rough west wind. "I think it might be a little too windy on top of Rough Tor for us to enjoy it. We can watch the sheep, and listen to the birds while we eat our sandwiches."

This suggestion is met with delight by Leto, and by agreement by Martin, who has no strong feelings one way or the other, so the three of them retreat to a gently sloping area of rocky moorland some fifty yards beyond the pits. Leto lays the chequered picnic blanket on the grass, and Miss Fox puts the wicker basket in the middle of it to prevent it flapping away in the wind. Martin opens the basket lid.

"Don't rush, dears," says Miss Fox, as the children explore the contents. "There are cheese and onion sandwiches for everybody, and some left overs."

"Is that a cake?" exclaims Leto.

"I thought you did not like cake," Martin says.

"I like it now. I like it here."

They sit down on the picnic blanket, and enjoy their sandwiches and Victoria sponge. Then, as the weather's still set fair and no-one wants to go straight home, Miss Fox gives permission for Martin and Leto to explore the local area, providing they don't go too far out of her sight, retrieves a copy of *Rebecca* from her coat pocket, and settles down to read it.

An hour later, Martin returns, breathless with the news that Leto is missing.

"Where did you last see her?" cries Miss Fox in sudden panic, though she knows the question is redundant. Martin will have looked all over for the missing girl before even thinking to sound the alert.

Martin explains that he and Leto were investigating the stream head, which flows through a small rocky area speckled with purple heather some distance to the north, in the lee of the nearby tor. Leto was looking for the spring, and followed the narrow watercourse upwards into the craggy rocks, while he remained downstream in order to keep Miss Fox in his sight. When after five minutes or so she did not return he called her name, several times, and hearing no reply clambered up into the sharp rocks in search of her; but there was no sign.

"Oh, good heavens," cries Miss Fox in horror. "She must have fallen. I should never have let her go."

"I tried to look after her, Miss Fox," Martin says.

"Of course you did, Martin. I'm not blaming you. Leto's a strong willed and lively little girl, who has no idea of how dangerous this moor can be. We must find her." How terrifying to lose a child! How much worse to lose someone else's child, a child whose parents have kept her wrapped in cotton wool, who's been so stultified, so overprotected, that she's never had the chance to hone the natural survival instincts that would have steered her safe away from dangerous crevices and unclimbable scarps, taught her just how far her legs could leap, how strongly her young fingers grip. How absurd of Miss Fox to have imagined climbing Rough Tor beyond Leto's ability. Although, undoubtedly, it *is* – but how's the poor child to know that?

Miss Fox abandons the picnic basket, and follows Martin up into the crags. She can't hurry very fast; fit though she is, her middle-aged joints won't bend and flex as she requires, or with sufficient alacrity. "Leto!" she shouts. "Can you hear me? Are you hurt?"

Her words bring forth no answer, but a mocking caw from a large crow that has perched itself on top of the tallest pile of stones. Miss Fox ignores it.

Martin regards the crow. It's not one of his crows, of that he's certain. It's heavier, and blacker, and it lacks the sleekness of breast and blue-black shine of wing that characterises both Petra and Paul. But it has a knowing look; and as it tucks its head on one side and stares at him out of one calculating eye, the thought strikes him that it knows where Leto Murray is. *Yes,* he thinks, *it knows*; and it can be persuaded to tell – for the right price.

What can he offer it? Crows like shiny things. Trinkets and jewellery, scraps of tin foil and small glittery baubles of ground glass. They also, especially up here on the high moor where food can sometimes be scarce, like cheese and onion sandwiches, and though Martin has eaten most of his, he has tucked the last one into the top pocket of his shirt, for safekeeping, in case he should feel hungry later. Reaching into his pocket, he takes out the sandwich, which he has wrapped in his handkerchief, and unties the cloth.

"Do you want it?" he asks the crow, holding the sandwich up.

The crow eyes it, speculatively.

"Take me to Leto," Martin says. "And I will give it to you. I will leave it right here for you, on this rock."

The crow hops down on to the low grass. It struts about in front of Martin, sticking out one leg

Mammoth & Crow

and then the other, cocking its head and opening and closing its beak. It's weighing up its options, coming to a decision. Martin waits. He can afford to be patient – to a point.

"If you don't want it," he says. "Perhaps the sheep know where she has gone. I can always ask them."

The crow gives a loud, harsh caw, and snaps its beak open and shut. Its tiny black eye stares furiously at Martin.

"Then it is settled." Martin says, putting the sandwich back into his pocket. "You will show me, now; then you will get the sandwich."

The crow appears annoyed. It dances up and down on the spot, its black feathers ruffling up around its head; then it flies up on to the tall standing stone. It caws again, and takes off slowly, into the wind. Martin watches it. It only flies a little way, then drops into the stone thicket, cawing for Martin to follow it.

"Good," Martin says. He looks around. Miss Fox, now some way above him amongst the rocks, is still searching on her own, and has not, apparently, witnessed the interaction. He's glad. It was hard enough for his foster Aunt to come to terms with his befriending the two crows at the cottage, and she's only been able to do that by convincing herself they're not really wild. The possibility he might just have negotiated with an unknown creature of the high moor is one she'll never be able to accept. Making as little noise as he can, he scrambles down from the rocks.

The area of the valley upon which the crow has settled is a rocky, thin soiled and surprisingly steep slope whose marshy grass has been cropped by long horned Cornish cattle. Martin picks his way through the rocks along a narrow sheep path, peering at the soft damp earth for any signs that Leto came this way, and intermittently looking up to make sure that he still has the crow in sight. There's no trace of the girl. The crow caws again, loudly. Martin stops. The bird sounds as if it's laughing. Perhaps it's tricking him. He frowns.

"You do know where she is, don't you?" he says.

In answer, the bird flies a short distance farther, into the lichen draped branches of a single, twisted tree, which is rising inelegantly from between the granite boulders. Martin feels increasingly suspicious. Why would Leto have come so far, or come this way at all? What could she have she been thinking? He narrows his eyes, watching the crow closely; but it betrays no indication that it's lying.

"All right," says Martin. "But if you're leading me astray, Crow, you get nothing. " He presses on into the gorse. "Leto!" he shouts. "Leto, are you here?"

Reaching the base of the hawthorn tree, he stops again, looking up into its branches and down again, peering into the stone thicket. There's no sign of Leto Murray. Martin feels suddenly frightened. What if she's really lost? What if she's hurt, unconscious somewhere in the crags, where nobody will ever find her? "Leto!" he shouts again, through the rising panic in his throat.

A hand grasps his ankle. Martin screams. He looks down. Leto Murray's pink face is grinning up at him from a black, triangular hole in the ground. It's her hand that is gripping his ankle. "Surprise!" she says.

Mammoth & Crow

"Leto!" cries Martin. "Are you hurt? Miss Fox! Miss Fox, I have found her!"

"Of course I'm not hurt," Leto retorts scornfully, releasing his ankle. "You must come down and see this place! It's incredible!"

"Miss Fox is worried to death!" Martin tells her. "She thought you had fallen somewhere and broken your ankle, or worse."

"I was exploring. You remember I told you I wanted to look for the Moment, the special place in the painting? This is it! This is the place! The looking glass! I'm sure of it!"

"How dare you be so selfish?" Martin snaps. "Did not you hear me? My auntie is really worried! Don't you care about that?"

"I'm sorry she is worried," Leto says. "But that isn't my fault, and she isn't my auntie. Come down, Martin, do!"

"I'm not coming down," says Martin angrily. "You must come out, right now, and show Miss Fox that you are not hurt. If you don't, then I will leave you exactly where you are, and you will have to find your own way home."

"I don't care," says Leto. "I could stay here. There's a little room with all sorts of things. If you'll come in and see, I promise to come out and say sorry to your auntie."

Martin stares at her. Her behaviour is outrageous, and her attitude is worse. He wishes he had never agreed to ask her to the picnic, or dreamed about her in the first place.

"All right," he says. "But only for one minute. And how I'm supposed to see very much I don't know, because I left my torch. And then you must come straight out."

Leto scrambles away from the entrance. Without her white face to fill it, the hole appears extremely black, and far deeper than he imagined. Martin hears the sound of falling pebbles somewhere underground. Carefully, he scrambles onto his stomach, and hangs his legs over the sill. "How far is the drop?"

"Only a few feet. It's easy."

Martin shuffles over the edge, and lets his body fall. Leto is telling the truth; the distance to the bottom of the hole is no more than four feet. He looks around. There's very little light, but a faint orange glow is emanating from the far end of what appears to be a low, stone ceilinged passage, no more than five feet in height along its entire length, or three in width. Curiosity overcomes him. "What is this?"

"Come and see what's at the end."

Leto scrambles ahead of him over the surprisingly dry surface, kicking up a number of small stones as she goes. Martin bends and picks one up as it tumbles into the cold remnant of daylight that penetrates the entrance. It's brown and smooth, with one end wider than the other, in the rough shape of a sickle. He puts it in his pocket.

The passage continues for about fifteen or twenty feet before suddenly making a sharp, right angled turn into a larger, square chamber. This chamber is as dry as the passage, despite the fact that the gaps between its ceiling stones have been widened many times by the searching roots of the old thorn tree that is growing directly above it, which now extend through the open space like many pillars into the soil beneath. An amber light, which Martin

Mammoth & Crow

previously assumed to be sunlight streaming through some other entrance, bathes the entire space, but where it's coming from he cannot now tell. Then as his eyes adjust to the light, he sees it: a modern oil lamp, left burning on top of a low, stone table in the far corner of what he now feels the urge to call a room. And then, suddenly, he sees the chair, the camp bed, the sleeping bag, the pile of books, the tins of tobacco and baked beans, the knife and fork.

"We have to leave now," he says at once.

"Why?"

"Somebody lives here. Look."

"It's the man in the painting," Leto nods. "It must be."

"Whoever he is, he won't be gone long. He's left his lamp burning," says Martin. "Come on, quickly."

"I want to meet him."

"Don't be silly. And you promised."

"But – "

Martin ignores her and turns away. He has a debt to pay, now, to the crow. "If you want to stay there till the man comes, then you stay," he says. "But you will be a trespasser as well as a liar. Besides, he might be a criminal. I bet you haven't thought of that. Why else would he hide away up here on the moor?"

"Because he's a wizard," Leto says. "I looked at the books. They are all written in some strange alphabet, and full of pictures of circles and star maps and curious phrases. And there's a human skull with them."

"Maybe he's a murderer, not a wizard. Come on, or you won't know the way home."

"But, Martin!"

Quickly, Martin makes his way back along the low passage to the opening. Leto follows, begging him to stay. He doesn't turn around; he feels too angry, all of a sudden, to look at her. Without another word, he scrambles out of the triangular hole, emerging into the yellow sunshine and looking up, blinking in the brightness, as his eyes seek out the surprisingly honest crow to whom he now owes a cheese and onion sandwich.

Miss Fox is so relieved to see the children approaching across the moor that she almost weeps. As quickly as she can in her long skirt, she makes her way down from the crags and hurries across the close cropped grass towards them.

"Oh, Leto!" she cries, throwing her arms around the little girl. "Thank God, you are safe. I was so worried."

Leto's mouth drops open. Her body is as rigid as a tent pole. Obviously, she isn't used to the sensation of being touched – or perhaps being touched in a manner that is not in some way punitive. Miss Fox puts her hands on her shoulders, and bends down. "It's all right, Leto," she says. "You're not in trouble. But I was very frightened. I thought we had lost you."

Leto stared at her. "I'm sorry, Miss Fox," she says, after a while. "I didn't know."

"The moor is full of dangers, dear. That's why I told you to stay in sight."

"I didn't go far. Only into the stones."

"I found something interesting," Martin says. He glances at the girl. Should he tell Miss Fox everything that Leto found, or will that only make his poor foster Aunt worry more? "This," he says instead, putting his hand into his pocket and pulling out the strange shaped stone. He drops it into Miss Fox's palm.

Miss Fox examines it. "My goodness," she says after a while. "I know what this is. It's a bear claw. Do you see the hole in it? That would have been made by a hand drill. I think it must once have been part of a necklace. It's been in the ground for a very long time. My goodness." She hands the claw back to Martin. "Where did you find it?"

"In a hole in the ground." Leto says.

"You must make sure to look it up in your Encyclopedia, Leto. They are very precious." Miss Fox looks up. The sky, which all day has remained so blue, is now beginning to cloud over, and a cold, damp wind has already begun to curl around the crags.

"We'd better head home," Miss Fox says. "The weather is changing. See how suddenly the fogs can fall. Martin, run ahead and pick up the picnic basket, and get out your compass and map. We may need them on the walk home."

They use the compass to retrace their steps along the pitted river bank as far as the stepping stones, where the path, although already shrouded in patchy white mist, is still visible. Leto is feeling sorry. She's not sure why. It's never in her life occurred to her to consider the feelings of an adult. No adult, in her experience, has ever given the appearance of having any feelings to consider: none, at least, upon which Leto's actions, good or bad, can make an impact. She can't understand why Martin's aunt should have been frightened, or why her anxiety was due to concern over Leto's welfare than the inconvenience of having to look for her. This is not, in Leto Murray's experience, how grown ups behave.

But Martin found a bear claw! As soon as Miss Fox told them what it was, Leto immediately thought of Huma; and now, as she walks, the mammoth's deep rich voice begins to rumble in her imagination, or in her memory, or some other part of her mind: some ancient, blood, bone, fire, stone part, which can communicate without speech, like Martin and his crows.

"Come, wolf cub," says the mammoth. "Come to me."

*Come away, O human child,
To the waters and the wild.*

"How?" Leto whispers.

"Ask Halek-dhwer to reveal the gate. One shall guard, and one be free. Come now."

"I can't," Leto replies. "I don't think Mummy will let me."

"You have no human mother, wolf cub. You have only me."

"I know," whispers Leto. "I know."

Chapter Eight:
The Golden Bough

Evelyn is sitting alone again in the drawing room of Ignatius Hart's old house, blindly staring into the fireplace. Her ashtray is full. Her wineglass, empty now, lies on its side on top of the low coffee table. Wine is dripping from the edge of the table, forming a wet puddle on the carpet. She does not care. Gerald's letter lies half open in her lap.

My son died, Evelyn thinks. *And now I'll never have another.*

The letter arrived mid morning, shortly after Leto and the boy Martin departed for their picnic. Evelyn's very glad Leto is gone. She doesn't like having her daughter in the house at the best of times, and now this cold, lifeless communication, not even written in Gerald's own hand, but typed on his antique Remington with the broken E – when he must have known how deeply she'd be longing for his presence, yearning for some tangible indication, however small, that he still holds her in mind – has made them much, much worse.

He hasn't been unkind – Professor Gerald

Murray almost never is, explicitly – but his message, that he no longer requires or desires Evelyn for a wife, could not be clearer.

My darling Evie, he has written.

> *I trust your journey was not too taxing and that you and Leto are now happily settled in Bransquite. I regret, as you know, the fact that I cannot join you, in the near or even the foreseeable future, but I trust that you will find sufficient entertainment to maintain you both in good spirits. I have, since your departure, heard from Bertie, who has happily agreed to hold off on any possible sale of the property until after your return to London – so you both may remain in Cornwall indefinitely with no fear of being forced to leave. I am sorry if this news does not please you, my dear, quite as much as it does me, but I am convinced that you and Leto will be much happier and healthier away from the capital. I will write again within the fortnight, and hope soon to read of your exploits on the tennis courts of Cornwall and Leto's jolly deeds of derring do.*
>
> *Your affectionate husband.*

Affectionate husband? thinks Evelyn scornfully. Not so. Not so at all. All her worst fears about the meaning of their separation have now been confirmed. She's been thrown away, discarded, like a broken vessel. But a horrible thought is sneaking up on her: perhaps Gerald is right to cast her off. What use is she to any man if she can't bear children? What use to herself? To the future, glorious, Fascist Nation?

She reaches for the empty wine glass, sets it back upon its base, and reaches again for the bottle. She's thankful now that she didn't knock that over, too, when she opened Gerald's letter and was so distressed at its contents that she let the glass slip out of her hand, and the un-drunk liquid spill across the table top. She picks up the bottle, and refills the glass.

Two glasses and three Camel cigarettes later, and now the sunshine slanting through the French windows is illuminating the spine of the old book that she placed previously on the coffee table. Its green binding is dark with spilled wine. Earlier, in her immediate anguish, she neither noticed the risk to the volume nor cared about it; now she suddenly feels a prick of shame at having caused it damage. Good, bad or indifferent, this is still a book, still a work over which the unknown Mr Frazer must have laboured, perhaps for years: on that account alone, it deserves greater respect, and less abuse, than she has given it. And she has to admit that there's still something about it: something in its reassuring, boxy shape, or the embossed letters of its title, which still draws her attention, still whispers of a mystery to be understood. Reaching out, she picks it up. Wine drips from the binding. She wipes it on the plush arm of the sofa. The upholstery's old, worn and dirty: a little wine stain can no longer hurt it. The book, on the other hand, is a vulnerable thing: precious, worth preserving.

Nevertheless, she reminds herself, she still has no intention of reading it. Of that she is certain. But this resolve was made before she heard from Gerald, before he cruelly threw her over; and now the book in her hand is warm and solid, present in a way that he is not: she finds herself wondering why she ever formed it. Was it only out of respect for his academic opinion? *Well, to hell with that! To hell with Gerald! To hell with the bloody Oresteia, and to hell with stuffy, arid intellectualism!* Maybe there is something worth reading in the book. Maybe Mr Frazer has not reached the height of academic acceptability because of something other than the value of his scholarship. Perhaps Gerald, and the established authorities, simply do not like him.

Evelyn lays *The Golden Bough* in her lap, and, at long last, she opens it. *A Study in Magic and Religion,* she reads: *The King of the Wood.*

She drinks, and reads, and reads, and drinks.

Miss Fox and the children reach the cottage just before the mists close in, and Miss Fox at once hastens to stoke the fire and put on the kettle for a cup of tea. She has said nothing more to Leto about the little girl's unfortunate disappearance, and as far as Leto can tell, the subject is now closed. Leto is feeling guilty. She wishes she hadn't made Martin's aunt worry, or been so rude to Martin when he told her they had to leave. He was right, after all. What if the man who lived in that hole really was a murderer, who didn't want his whereabouts known? He might have come back and wrung Leto's neck like a poulterer a pullet's, and then murdered Martin and his auntie too, to stop them blabbing about his crimes. The thought makes her shiver. She wishes Huma had been there to look after them – all of them, including Miss Fox. Huma is so old and good, and so gigantic, she'd have taken care of everybody. She'd never have allowed any man, be he wizard or murderer, to harm them.

Sitting at the kitchen table, closing her eyes, she can still see the mammoth, as plain as if the great beast were standing right in front of her. Huma is beside the stream – perhaps the same stream Leto encountered in her dream, perhaps the very same little river whose channel they traced across the high moor. Her small furry ears are flapping away the biting insects – midges and the like – that congregate wherever there is warmth and blood, and as Leto watches, she draws up a trunk-full of water from the stream and sprays it over and around her face, washing them briefly away. Small pear shaped droplets sparkle like jewels in the sunlight. Where they fall back towards the river, the flowing liquid forms into the shape of a hand, which rises from the surface to catch them in its rippled palm, and the voice of the water giggles like a playful child. Huma lowers her trunk again, and the water's fingers play upon its tip.

"Where is she?" the mammoth says.

Gone, the river laughs. *Gone.*

"She will return."

Everything returns, O Mammoth, Mama, Memory.

Leto opens her eyes. The copper kettle has begun to whistle on the hob. She looks around the kitchen. A large ginger cat is snoozing on the window sill, eyes half open, tail flicking slowly back and forth in front of the whitewashed wall. She feels as if she is flickering back and forth between two worlds, part equally of both; at least for now. Huma has told her *come.* How much longer will it be, she wonders, before she goes into that other realm and does *not* return, cannot find her way, despite the laughing assertion of the river that everything makes its way back, sooner or later, to the place it comes from. But where does Leto come from? And who are they talking about, the mammoth and the water? Are they talking about Leto? If not, then who is *she?*

Martin Stone winds up the gramophone, and Ella Fitzgerald's voice fills the air. Leto closes her eyes again. She can still see the mammoth, and the sloping hillside awash with ice age flowers.

> *Summertime, and the living is easy.*
> *Fish are jumping, and the cotton is high.*

Huma makes a low, rumbling noise that's more than sound but not quite language, and turns away from the river. The water's hand falls back, recedes into the current. Leto watches as Huma twitches her tail, and slowly begins to head up the slope, towards the rocks. She's so tall, she should be able to scratch her shoulders on the largest. Perhaps that's what she's going to do.

> *One of these mornings, you're gonna rise up singing,*
> *And you'll spread your wings and you'll take to the sky.*
> *But till that morning, there ain't nothing can harm you,*
> *With Mammy and Daddy standing by.*

"Leto," breaks in Miss Fox's voice. "I think you had better be getting off home, dear, before the

Mammoth & Crow

rain sets in. Martin, will you walk Leto back to the village?"

Leto opens her eyes. Miss Fox is standing at the kitchen window, cup of tea in hand, looking out anxiously over the high moor. The sky has darkened ominously.

Martin nods, and goes at once to put on his coat and boots.

"Thank you," says Leto awkwardly to Miss Fox, holding out her hand. "I'm sorry if I was a bother. Might I come again?"

"Of course you can," says Miss Fox, kindly, helping the little girl into her red coat. "Martin, don't forget the brolly."

"Brolly?" Martin frowns.

"Umbrella, dear. There, in the stand beside the door. I think you'll need it."

By the time the two children have reached Bransquite, the rain has started. It isn't like the rain in London, Leto thinks, which falls straight downwards: it's a dense cloud of heavy damp that saturates the air like bathwater does a sponge, sometimes seeming to drift and rise, blown upwards into their faces by the faint breeze, soaking through coats and hats and shoes despite Miss Fox's umbrella. She is unusually pleased to get back to the old house, which in comparison with outside for the first time feels warm and homely, a sanctuary rather than a cold and heartless mausoleum. This time, Martin can't – or won't – stay; refusing Nanny Gould's offer of scorched milk, he says goodbye to Leto and heads back into the rain, turning up his coat collar and stamping away underneath the grey stone arch. Leto's sad to see him go. She closes her eyes, looking for

Huma, but the mammoth, too, has departed. The Otherworld has fallen still.

Martin walks through Bransquite, his eyes fixed on the lane in front of him. The sooner he gets home, he thinks, the sooner he will be warm and dry, and can enjoy a cup of hot chocolate with Miss Fox in front of the kitchen stove. He's not as hardy as the crows, whom he's often seen in rough weather, even when no other wild birds dare to fly. He doesn't loiter on the clapper bridge, doesn't look down to see what's happening down by the river, or up over the stone hedges into the fields bordering the lane; and that is why he doesn't see the man until the tall, dark figure wearing a brown Homburg hat hoists itself over the wall barely seven feet in front of him, landing with a faint splash in the puddling gutter. Martin stops abruptly, his heart suddenly beating like terrified wings.

The man shakes the damp from his tatty overcoat, which is tied loosely together at his waist by means of a length of parcel string, and stamps his worn boots on the road surface. Then he lifts his head, and winks at Martin.

He isn't very old, realises Martin – though his face is so filthy it's hard to tell for certain whether the dark creases playing round the corners of his eyes and which run from his nose right to the corners of his lips are wrinkles or ingrained dust. He raises one eyebrow, and the corners of his lip curl up in a smile, revealing a complete set of none too clean teeth. It's not an unpleasant smile, but nevertheless, Martin has no desire to go any closer.

"Felicitations of the moment," the stranger

Mammoth & Crow

says, tipping his Homburg hat.

"I do not know what any of that means," says Martin.

" 'Felicitations': best wishes. Derived from the Latin *'felix'*, meaning happiness; never to be confused with *'felis'*, which means cat. As for 'moment' – well, that's really rather complicated. Never mind the parallaxes of time and space, for now."

"All right," Martin says, slowly.

"So," says the man. "You're the bird boy. I have heard of you."

Martin stares at him. In the dull drizzle, the stranger's eyes look extremely bright. Too bright. Perhaps he's a madman. He's certainly talking like one. Or perhaps he's the man whose cave home Leto invaded up on the high moor. The hairs stand up on the back of Martin's neck. Was he hiding near the tunnel, watching him talk to the crow, listening in on his and Leto's conversation?

"Do you think you could help me?" the man asks.

"I don't know."

"I'm seeking employment here. Do you know anyone who might be in need of my services?"

"No," Martin says, quickly. "I don't."

"That's a pity. I'll have to continue searching, then. Good day to you." The man tips his hat again, and steps past the boy, heading over the bridge into the village. He doesn't seem at all discomforted by the rain. Then he turns, and calls back, half over his shoulder, as if the thought has just occurred to him. "I think we'll meet again, and sooner than you imagine."

Martin watches until he is out of sight, and

then picks up his feet and runs as fast as he can back to Miss Fox's cottage.

The man in the brown Homburg hat (who is, let me tell you, someone we shall spend a considerable length of time in getting to know, as much as anybody can) makes his way through the drizzle to the centre of Bransquite. He comes to Ignatius Hart's old house, and there he stops, and smiles up at the rose covered gateway. *"Aperire,"* he says.

Evelyn ignores the rapping on the front door for as long as she can. But when after a full minute it has still not ceased, and the housekeeper has still not answered, her ragged nerves yank her to her feet. Swaying slightly, she puts the book down on the coffee table, makes her way over to the sitting room door, snatches it open, and shouts for the old woman to see who is knocking or face the consequences. Gerald would think her conduct unbecoming, even degenerate. She thinks that too; but right now, she does not really care.

The useless old woman, who is probably snoring away beside the old fashioned kitchen range with her feet up on the fender, does not come. Evelyn screams in frustration. How she hates this house! How she hates Cornwall. How she hates – but does she really hate Gerald, even though he's imprisoned her here? She doesn't want to think about him like that. Resenting Gerald brings back all manner of unpleasant memories.

The knocking continues. Evelyn staggers toward the front door, and opens it.

"Felicitations, Mrs Murray," says the man in

the brown Homburg hat.

Evelyn screams again, this time in terror, and slams the door.

"Interesting," says the man in the hat, raising his eyebrows. He makes a non-committal sound, and his way around the side of the building to the kitchen door. It opens easily, without complaint, and he passes through it.

The old housekeeper, whom on Evelyn's behalf I have unfairly maligned, is not asleep. She's shovelling coal into the range, and, being rather deaf, simply did not hear the knocking that to Evelyn was so horribly intrusive. She doesn't notice the man in the Homburg hat until he's standing right behind her.

"Hello, Annie," he says.

The old woman jumps violently. Large lumps of coal tumble from the shovel and bounce irregularly on the cracked slate floor.

"Johnny!" she exclaims, putting her hand to her breast. "Creeping up on people like that! You gave me such a horrible fright!"

"I'm sorry, Annie. But it was too good an opportunity to miss."

"What in heaven's name are you doing here?" the housekeeper hisses, hurrying over to the closet to find a dustpan and brush, as the man sits down at the kitchen table. "I was told you'd gone abroad."

"I come and go, Annie, you know that. Like the trade winds and the tides upon the shore, first one place, then another."

"Mr Bertram Hart's let out the house," Annie tells him sternly. "You can't be coming and going any more. There's a lady living here now, with her little daughter."

"I know who she is. Evelyn Murray. Evil-incarnate."

"Don't you be rude about your betters," Annie says. "She's decent enough to me, and anyway, she pays my wages. A bit of a – well, a tartar – but what can you expect? They're London people, Johnny."

"Tartar, or tart? She just answered the front door to me. She's barely dressed, and stinks of alcohol."

"You're not exactly handsome company yourself right now, if you don't mind my saying so."

"I don't mind. It's true. I could very much do with a bath, a toothbrush, and a decent meal, plus a bed to sleep in that has a proper mattress."

"I don't know about that," Annie says. "The bath and meal you're more than welcome to, but you can't stay here. Mrs Murray wouldn't stand it. "

"Mr Hart would be very sad to hear that."

"Mr Hart is dead – and gone to heaven, so I hope."

"I sincerely doubt it. All those Saints and Angels playing harps and reciting psalms? Not his cup of tea at all."

"He doesn't – walk, does he? You haven't seen him?"

"No," says the man called Johnny. "He doesn't walk."

The old woman finishes sweeping up the scattered coals. Casting them into the fire, she carefully closes the iron door and fastens it.

"Damn it, I miss the old sod," the man says, with a sigh.

"He was very kind to you, Johnny."

135

"He was the only human soul to show an ounce of kindness to me in twenty years. Except yourself, of course." The implication hangs like salt spray on the air.

"Oh, very well!" exclaims the old woman at last, in an exasperated tone. "Get the tin tub from the shed, and you can scrub yourself beside the fire. Then I'll fetch down one of Mr Hart's old shirts for you, and some better trousers. But you can't stay here unless Mrs Murray can be talked into agreeing to it. I won't be losing this job over you, Johnny. It only pays a few shillings, but I need every ha'penny."

"Perhaps Mrs Murray's in want of a gardener. I wonder if she could be persuaded to employ one."

"She hasn't engaged anyone. But she'll have to soon, or that kitchen garden'll turn into a jungle right before her eyes. Jeremy Chyneweth was coming in cutting the grass once a week, but Mr Bertram stopped paying him after he let out the house."

"Interesting," says Johnny, sitting back in his chair, and steepling his hands.

The Golden Bough is not a book of Classical mythology, as Evelyn initially supposed. Nor is it a novel. It's a strange book: part anthropological treatise, part imaginative reconstruction of events which, most modern scholars would agree, probably never happened. Evelyn finds it hard to follow beyond the first few pages: there is too much information, and no discernible narrative that can easily direct her somewhat befuddled attention – though her confusion may have quite a lot to do with the amount of alcohol she has consumed. But still, there's some indefinable quality to the text that compels her to keep trying to make sense of it, despite her struggles. Mr Frazer's main contention seems to concern the significance of a barbaric tradition that endured in the name of the Roman goddess Diana Nemorensis in the sacred grove of Arica. The Priest of this grove, of which there was only ever one, had to be chosen by mortal combat, obtaining his position through the bloody murder of his predecessor. The murderer was then proclaimed King of the Wood, whose own eventual human sacrifice would be held to the glory of the goddess in whose service he was now bound, as the living representative of her consort Virbius – or Hippolytus – the only mortal man whose beauty could sway the chaste Diana, just as it swayed the unfortunate Phaedra.

Diana Nemorensis, Mr Frazer says, is a goddess of fertility and childbirth. The connection leaps out at Evelyn, and she instantly remembers the horrors of Carthage. Birth and death, fertility and sacrifice: all over the ancient world, the concepts seem to have been tied closely together in a way she has found too horrific to contemplate. But this telling is nothing like Diodorus'. Mr Frazer's tone is unemotional, unconcerned, scholarly: it does not inspire the revulsion that has always arisen within her before. Perhaps, Evelyn thinks, to him, there is no horror in the thing, no humanity: only bone dry, ancient history. Or perhaps – what a queer thought! – there really *was* nothing terrible in the crowning of a Priest-King whose blood would eventually be shed in honour of the Goddess whom he served. This was not, after all, the murder of a baby, or the deception of an innocent, like Iphigenia. The Priest-King was no more an innocent than any soldier going off to war, even though his was a battle of one against one, and his prize the glory of the Goddess, rather than his Nation.

Evelyn doesn't know. But the reflection that she could even wonder such a thing about such an established horror as human sacrifice – even adult sacrifice, of what must have been a willing victim – unsettles her. Even Caesar condemned it; he who thought nothing of destroying whole armies, whole Tribes, in the mighty name of Rome. Perhaps it's the conflation of death and religion that seems to make the act of sacrifice, in itself, an evil thing, when war seems not. *Dulce et decorum est pro patria mori.*

I should put the book down, Evelyn tells herself, trying to escape her own confusion. *I should put it down and think no more about it.* Obviously, her earlier misgivings were prescient. *The Golden Bough* is neither serious work of Classical scholarship, nor wonderful escapist novel to lift her from her miserable speculations. But when she closes it, and replaces it on the coffee table, it is only to find herself ten seconds later opening it again, perusing its pages with an intent born of some deeply felt internal compulsion that she cannot deny. Something in the book is calling to her, some as yet unread secret truth, which when disclosed, she somehow feels will turn all her confusion into sense.

So she gives in again, and this time reads about the women who left offerings to Diana in the grove: those pregnant, hopeful, fearful Roman matrons whose longing, like Evelyn's own, was for sons who could go on to build a mighty nation. She reads about the concept of incarnate human Gods, and the ancient European belief that deities reside in the bodies of trees. And then she reads about certain Indian peoples of Central America, who believe that intercourse between husband and wife will restore fertility to their fields, and about the Polynesian heathens, who slaughter dogs and pigs in a sacred rite during which the men and women couple in public: and in all these she sees death and life combined to bring about future generation. And she reads of the relationship between the Priest-King and the embodied Goddess: Virbius and Diana – two whose sacred union in the grove was no longer that of mortal man and woman, but a marriage of the Gods. Her hands begin to shake. She lowers the book, and reaches once more for her wine. It's dark red, like the God's blood, like the flowers of Arica. Cornish rain runs down the window. The dying fire smokes in the grate. The greyness of everything around her shocks her senses.

The wine could be a libation, she thinks. She imagines herself pouring it onto the ground, the rich Mediterranean earth drinking it in, while all about her ears she hears the ringing of cicadas. Then the thought hits her, out of nowhere, like a smack to the temple: *Is this why my son died?* Could it be that she, Evelyn Murray, who has always thought herself a modern woman in a very modern world, neglected to perform some long forgotten pagan ritual to Diana or Juno or some other ancient power, which would have secured her son's rightful place among the *ubermensch?* Did the all consuming Goddess of birth and sacrifice seize him instead? Did she snatch him out of Evelyn's own hands, send him tumbling through the fire into the pit of bones?

It was my fault, Evelyn thinks. The thought is

Mammoth & Crow

clear and stark, and dizzying in its immensity. It spikes through her uncertainty like a spear, paralysing her. The wine glass tips as her fingers lose their grip upon the stem: red wine dribbles a small puddle on the carpet. *But it's too late. It's too late, and it will never be enough.*

She's been alone in the sitting room all day now, without really moving, except when she got up to answer the front door. Her daughter has returned from her visit, the coal fire has burned to ash, the scuttle is empty, and, she realises, the blasted wine bottle is finished. She shakes herself, pushing away all thoughts of sacrifice, and trying to suppress the horrible idea that – no, she can't let herself think about that loss again, she won't let herself. She won't sink into self pity.

It would be horribly uncouth to call for more wine. But she still looks for the bell pull to summon the aged housekeeper, and makes her way across the room, knocking over a small bentwood chair on the way. Grabbing the rope, she tugs on it, repeatedly. The old woman appears after a few minutes; Evelyn is certain she has delayed answering on purpose – though you and I know that, being deaf, it's more likely she didn't hear the bell.

"The fire's almost out," Evelyn says, trying to avoid stating the real purpose behind the summons. "It must be time for dinner. Why didn't you answer me straight away?"

"Dinner will be ready at the usual time, Mrs Murray, in an hour," replies the old woman. "But I'll see to the fire, if you like."

"An hour? Perhaps I'll retire to my room for a while."

"So shall I still see to the fire, Madam, or be getting back to see to the roast?"

"The fire, of course! Why is everyone here so slow?"

"I am everyone," retorts the housekeeper. "I'm doing the best I can, but it's hard going on my own. If I had help it'd be easier."

"My servants are all in London, waiting on my husband. Ask Nanny Gould."

"She's busy with Miss Leto right now, Madam. But it isn't only right now I'm thinking of, anyway. If you think I shall be out there in a week's time mowing that lawn you shall be sadly mistaken."

"How dare you talk to me like that!" exclaims Evelyn, swaying back on her heels in her astonishment.

The old woman doesn't seem intimidated. "I'm too old for it, Mrs Murray," she says frankly. "That's God's honest truth. It's a young man's job, that lawn is. If you want, I can ask around the village for anyone who'll be willing to take it on."

"Who used to do it?"

"Jeremy Chyneweth. But he went off to work in a butcher's shop in Callington after Mr Bertram stopped paying him. As I said, I can ask around. There was a young man come to the door earlier today looking for employment."

"Oh, God," cries Evelyn, twisting the bell-rope in her hands as if it was the old woman's neck. "I don't care about the lawn! I really don't! Take on whoever you wish. Just deal with the blasted fire, and hurry up with dinner. If I'm going to have to wait another hour, you may as well bring up another bottle of wine."

"Very well, Mrs Murray," the housekeeper says. "I shall." She turns to leave.

"Wait," Evelyn says, holding up a finger, a horrible possibility occurring to her. "You don't mean that filthy tramp who called here earlier, do you? Because I will not – will not! – have him in the house."

"Oh, no, Mrs Murray," the old woman responds, in a scandalised tone. "He's a very clean and decent young man, and well spoken, too. Would you like to see him tonight, Madam? I can send for him to be here within the hour."

"Good God, no," Evelyn says. "Whatever gives you that crazy idea? Send for him tomorrow morning. I'll see him at eleven, or twelve, or something thereabouts." Without another word to the housekeeper, she stalks unsteadily across the room, throws herself on the sofa, and, having by now completely forgotten her resolve to abandon it, takes up, yet again, *The Golden Bough*. It feels almost like returning to a friend. But the words dance like sparks before her eyes.

Jack Wolf

Chapter Nine:
The Faceless Men

It's June. The cotton grass has grown tall, and upon the marshes of the moor its white feathery tufts wave and flutter in the breeze beneath the blue-grey sky. Meadow pipits are singing all over the crags, and buzzards soar high overhead. The young lambs are growing fast, as are the pony foals born in the early spring. Sometimes Martin Stone stands at his open bedroom window and watches the local herd pass by the moor stile at the far end of the cow field, the piebald stallion standing guard over his harem of brown and dun coloured mares, who plod amiably by with their foals cantering about their hocks, while the many coloured yearlings reach over the wall and nibble the fresh leaves of the hawthorn tree. Petra and Paul have now raised their chicks, and abandoned their nest. The whole family of crows is often to be seen perching in the boughs of the apple trees, or jostling each other cheerfully along the ridge pole of the cottage roof. The young ones will stay around for many weeks, learning what it is to be a crow, before moving on to find mates and territories of their own. The house martins are still busy, dashing in and out of their mud nests, twittering constantly beneath the eaves. Lower down, sparrows chirp ceaselessly in the bushes. The breeze is warm, fresh and clean; utterly unlike the dirty air of Berlin, which stank, Martin now realises, of coal smoke and human poverty, though he was never aware of it at the time. Some of the birds here are the same: sparrows, and starlings. There are pigeons, too, in some of the taller trees down by the river, but they don't have the ragged, dusty look of the feral creatures with whom Martin was friendly in the city, and their calls sound different; happier, somehow; as if pigeons also know and appreciate the differences between concrete and stone.

Martin has not seen Leto Murray since the day of the picnic. He's not deliberately avoiding her, but somehow circumstances, including the unpredictable Cornish weather, have conspired to make it awkward for her to visit again, and he has no desire to spend any time in Ignatius Hart's damp old house under the eye of her nanny – or her mother. Part of him feels guilty about this. He's still not sure whether he likes Leto, but she has befriended him, in her own peculiar fashion, and friendship imposes certain obligations, such as keeping in touch. Another part of him is grateful that she hasn't called again. She was, after all, a nuisance, wandering off and getting into trouble, and she spoke English so quickly that he couldn't always keep up with what she was saying. And he's not sure, in himself, how much he really desires any human company beside Miss Fox. His crows, and the land itself, are beginning to seem enough.

Miss Fox is so pleased with Martin's navigational skills, and was so impressed by his locating Leto among the rocks, that she has given him free use of the compass and ordnance survey map, and has told him that he is allowed to walk up on the moor by himself, providing he uses his common sense, doesn't do anything silly, and tells her beforehand roughly where he's going to be. Martin, however, makes more use of his crows than he does of either compass or map, and though he always tries to give his foster aunt an idea where he is heading, in reality he simply follows where they lead him: flapping ahead to land on twisted tree or stony outcrop and calling him onward with harsh, impatient croaks. So far, the crows have never led him astray, and always managed to ensure he's back in time for tea. They never go as far as Rough Tor or Bronn Wennilli, though they sometimes travel directly across country almost as far as the narrow river before turning back. Martin believes this river demarcates the territory of the crow with whom he struck the bargain, and that Petra and Paul are reluctant to enter it. He sits on the ground beside the river, watching the crags in the distance, but usually sees only the buzzard, soaring unmolested in the afternoon light.

Today being Saturday, and sunny, Miss Fox has let Martin off the gardening, though there are peas to be picked. She's never said so, but Martin imagines that this is a little gesture of respect towards Shabbat, and his heart swells with affection for his foster aunt. He packs up the sandwiches she's made him, and the notebook in which he's begun to record the many bird species he encounters on his wanderings, and climbs over the stile into the bottom field, while Peter and Paul circle round his head like a pair of trained falcons. A cock wheatear gives its scratchy warble from the top of the stone wall. Martin whistles back, but the small grey and yellow bird isn't interested in idle conversation. It's still raising chicks, and there are only twelve weeks left before the great winter migration that will take it south to Africa. It cocks its head, and flutters quickly off.

Martin crosses the field, and makes his way onto the open moor. The sun beats down on the back of his neck, and warms his bare calves. The near silence is comforting. Only the distant whine of an aeroplane engine reminds him that the modern world, with its metal and fume, is there at all. He slips his hand into his coat pocket. The stone age bear-claw, a token from a different world, nestles in the corner, like a key. He's surprised to find it there – he'd fully intended to put it in the shoebox of treasures he keeps in his bedroom. But it doesn't matter. He won't lose it. Martin tightens the straps on his rucksack, and throwing up his arms, allows himself a sudden, loud, laugh. The day is free, the Earth wide open, and the endless sky belongs to him alone.

He follows the crows a long way to the north, towards the distant sea. If he climbs high enough on a day like this, and the weather stays clear, he'll be able to see as far as the coast. But now the ground is dropping away into a low, heather filled valley ringing with the songs of meadow pipits and yellow wagtails. The ground beneath his boots is worryingly soggy. Perhaps, he thinks, he's heading into one of Bodmin's treacherous marshes. Surely, Petra and Paul would never lead him into danger? He sits down on a moss covered stone, opens his rucksack, and for the first time in ages, takes out his notebook, and the ordnance survey map.

It quickly becomes clear that this valley is not easy to locate. He turns the map around, gets out his compass, checks and checks again. Still the map gives him no indication of where he is. It's strange, but Martin's not unduly worried. It's not unlikely the terrain has changed in the twenty years or so since the drawing up of the map; perhaps when the mapmakers explored the moor, the weather had been dry and there was no marsh. Or perhaps they simply neglected to come down into the valley, and failed to notice it. Either way, Martin decides it would be unwise to continue in his journey northward. He has no way of knowing how far the bog extends, or how deep it is likely to be. He doesn't want to end up trapped in it. He stands up, replaces the map in his rucksack, and hoists it back onto his shoulders. He'll return south, he thinks, the way he came.

Peter and Paul have been perched on a low gorse shrub at the side of the marsh while Martin has been reading; now he's on his feet again they both take flight, cawing loudly, insisting he follow them north across the valley.

"I'm sorry," Martin says, shaking his head. "But I can't risk it. I don't have wings like you do. If I get stuck, I'm finished." He turns around; and then, immediately, he freezes.

An unfamiliar movement is taking place at the top of the slope: a low, sinuous, sinister motion. A dark shape, like a gigantic otter, a full twenty feet in length and easily the thickness of a fat man's waist, is weaving slowly, ponderously, down the valley side towards him. Fixed to the spot, Martin stares. *It's not an otter,* he realises, as it comes closer. He doesn't know what it is.

Mammoth & Crow

The creature's fur is dense and dark brown, its fearsomely jawed face bearlike in appearance. But its powerful legs emerge from its body at right angles, like a lizard's or an alligator's, and when it opens its mouth a long, forked tongue, exactly like a snake's, flicks out over black lips. It opens its mouth, panting in the midday heat, and as it does so it reveals a double row of sharp teeth, drooling saliva. Martin begins to back away. He has no idea who or what this is, and his ignorance is as alarming as the thing itself.

The yellow wagtails flutter up in panic. The crows flap round his head, urging him to come away. The Lizard-bear – so Martin decides, for want of a better name, to call it – gives a low growl, and snaps at the air, like a dog after a fly. Then it turns its head toward him, fixing him with an inscrutable, black stare.

Suddenly the marsh does not seem anywhere near as troubling, or the valley half as wide as it did before. Martin reaches a decision, and quickly follows Petra and Paul over the soggy ground. To his great relief, he does not sink.

The north side of the valley, beyond the marsh – whose width doesn't, as it turns out, extend farther than thirty feet along the valley bottom, and isn't particularly deep – is warm, and carpeted with tiny, sweet smelling flowers. At the top of the slope, white tufts of cotton-grass dance against a sky that somehow appears more violet than blue. Yellow tailed bumble bees and dark purple butterflies crowd thickly on the wind. Martin turns, and looks back in bafflement over the moor he has just crossed.

Everywhere he looks, the living land lies breathing underneath a violet sky. The crags and hills to the west loom out of the green earth like the jagged crest of a sleeping dragon, which might one day choose to wake. The air is buzzing with the presence of memory, like static after rain. A little way behind him, along the top of the slope, the air is shimmering as if a giant mirror or thin pane of glass were hanging suspended lengthways in the air. Martin wonders how he didn't notice it before – he must have walked straight through it while he was running from the Lizard-bear. Perhaps the mirage is only visible once one has gone past it.

Martin looks behind him, down the slope. The Lizard-bear has given up chasing him – if that is what it was doing. It's stopped right inside the shimmering oval, and there it's calmly lain down, curled up in the sunshine. The monster's long, reptilian tail is wrapped around its body in a manner that reminds Martin of the ginger tomcat, Fluffy, when he's taken possession of one of the kitchen armchairs. It's still watching him, though, he thinks – watching him intently, as if it's trying to work out who he is, or what it ought to do about him; but it doesn't appear to be considering getting up again. Is it still a threat to him? Does it think him a threat to it? What on earth *is* it? Some kind of giant mustelid, as it first appeared to be, or something else entirely? Perhaps in Martin's panic he imagined the forked tongue, the doubled teeth, the terrifying jaws. Nevertheless, whatever the monster is, he doesn't feel inclined to risk antagonising it by going near it again. He turns, walks across the moor a little way, and, sitting down again, tries to get his bearings. Although he doesn't feel lost, nothing looks familiar. Perhaps, he thinks, if he tries walking south west, he'll eventually reach the crags of Rough Tor where he lost and found Leto, and from there he'll be able to find the path that leads him back to Bransquite and Miss Fox's cottage. He has no intention of returning yet, of course: it's still only midday; but it would be good to know for certain that he is not lost. He turns towards the neck spines of the dragon. This time, his crows follow him.

The day is still warm, and as Martin walks across the moor, the unfamiliar sweetness in the air that he first noticed when climbing up the north slope of the hidden valley persists. The thin soil has come alive with many coloured flowers of species he has never seen before, and the heady air is thick with insects. Above his head a scattered flock of black swifts are shrieking in frantic excitement. Some way off to the north, a buzzard stoops, then rises. Martin smiles. He's still uncertain where he is, or how he'll get home again, but somehow that no longer seems to matter.

He has walked a mile or so from the place where he encountered the Lizard-bear, and the sun has moved a few degrees across the violet sky, when he catches sight of a small group of human figures in the distance, walking slowly along an old, stony track beside what looks to be a rickety ox-cart pulled by a rangy, long-horned bull. It isn't Martin's habit to approach people while he's walking on the moor: this is his special place, and his time alone upon it much too precious to squander upon human company; but this time, he realises, it would be sensible to make an exception. It's likely – or at least hopeful – that these travellers are proper Cornish locals who'll be more familiar with the land than he is, and will be able to direct him back to Bransquite, or at least point out some landmark he might recognise. "Excuse me?" he calls out. "Hallo?"

They show no sign of having heard him. Martin breaks into a run. "Hallo!" he shouts. "Could you help me, please?"

The leader of the group slowly turns his head, and the ox-cart stops. The figures stand silent and still, all of them regarding Martin. There are four of them: two adults, who are on foot, and two smaller figures who must – *surely* – be children, who are riding in the cart. As Martin comes closer still, he realises, to his horror, that the children are sitting on bones: that the ox-cart is piled high with them, in varying states of decomposition. The stink is tremendous. At the very centre of the pile, on a raised bier made from thigh-bones and twisted wood, lies the entire skeleton of a man – at least Martin thinks it is a man, but if it is his bones are unlike any he has ever seen. They have been rubbed all over with some kind of red powder, and the staining has rendered them as dark as blood. He struggles to make sense of what he is looking at. The people are very oddly dressed, but perhaps they're vagrants or circus performers, or rag-and-bone men – which would certainly explain the cart, though it can't quite explain the human skeleton – whose business makes it normal for them to dress in animal skins and furs like Red Indians. The leader is a tall, strongly built man wearing a hooded, tasselled jerkin of pale hide that is fastened and tied about his waist with bright red cord, over breeches of the same material. A section of antler – probably the hilt of a knife – pokes out of what looks like a leather scabbard at his waist.

His feet are clad in calf-high moccasins cut from a darker, thicker leather, which is stuffed, Martin notices in deepening surprise, with what looks like hay. In his right hand, he is carrying a sturdy, dark-wood staff, on top of which – where a walking stick would have its handle – there hangs a bundle of black feathers strapped to the carved, heavy-beaked head of a raven. Behind him stands a woman who is dressed very much the same – but instead of holding a staff, over her arm she's carrying a wicker basket, in which Martin can see a collection of flowers, leaves and what he knows at once to be medicinal roots – though how he knows this is a mystery to him, and I'll not waste time explaining it. Her hair is black, and long, and bound into tight ropes that resemble plaits, but have the look, on the surface, of felt. He cannot see her face.

Martin looks back at the man. He can't make out his features either, though there is nothing obscuring them. Perhaps it's the sunlight hitting Martin's eyes, or some peculiar shadow cast by the leather hood, or some combination of the two; but for all Martin can see of them, the stranger might have had no eyes, or nose, or mouth, or any face at all. But he certainly has a voice, because as Martin stares, it echoes from within the blackness of the hood. It's not unfriendly. "You are not the wizard," it says, in a tone that sounds like surprise, or fascination. "How have you come here, boy?"

"My crows – " Martin begins, and falters. How can he speak a word to these strange people? Who are they? What are they? Are they even people at all? His eyes flicker to the ox-cart with its red skeleton, and he thinks of dybbuks, and his courage dies within him. But then he feels a light thump on first one shoulder, then the other, as first one crow, then the other, lands and caws gentle as a whisper in his ear. *Speak*, they softly tell him. *Speak.*

And with Petra on one shoulder and Paul on the other, Martin feels the warm sun once more upon his back, hears the whistled songs of the birds, smells the flowers on the air. These strange people aren't really so scary, he realises, looking them over again in the summer tinted light. They're just strange – strange in the way that he is strange, and Leto is strange: people who exist outside the norms and expectations of everyday human existence, but are no more unnatural, no less *people* for that. Even the oxcart and the skeleton should really be considered normal, natural things, in a way that makes sense here up on the high moor, underneath a bright sun and a violet sky. And because they are strange, in the way that he is strange, and Bodmin moor is strange, it doesn't feel ridiculous to confess that he has been following the birds; and so he draws a deep breath and explains exactly how he came to find himself lost upon the high plateau, how he fled from the Lizard-bear across the marsh, and how he's hoping that the strangers might be able to direct him towards the correct road to Bransquite.

"You must have a key," the woman says, when Martin has finished. "How did you come by it? Did you steal it?"

"I don't know what you mean," Martin says. "I don't need a key, and of course I wouldn't steal one. Miss Fox always leaves her door unlocked."

"He is the bird boy," says the hooded chief, as if this should provide some sort of explanation. "The

Mammoth & Crow

Gatekeeper has given him permission, as it was given to the wolf cub."

"He is much younger than I expected," the woman says. "And skinnier, too. She turned to Martin. Have you been starved all your life?"

"No," says Martin. The woman's question is extremely rude. His grandmother never starved him, and neither does Miss Fox. As for his time at the orphanage, he has to admit that although there was never a great deal of anything, the managers always made sure that everyone had something to eat and drink, clothes to wear, and shoes on their feet. "I am small for my age," he admits. "But that doesn't mean anybody starved me."

The woman laughs. It's not an unpleasant sound, or an unkind one, but it makes the hairs stand up on the back of Martin's neck.

"We will help you," says the man. "But in return you must do something for us."

"Of course," answers Martin, politely.

"Take a message to Horsefeathers. Tell him the river misses him. Tell him the Gatekeeper is out looking for him, and is angry at his betrayal. Tell him that he must choose swiftly, and choose well. Tell him that the air is turning into glass. The seas are rising. Extinction threatens inside *Pavor Potentia*."

"I don't know who Horsefeathers is," Martin says, wondering if he has understood anything of what the man is asking him.

"You have met him, fledgeling."

Martin doesn't think this can be true, but it seems rude to say so.

"How can I find him?" he asks.

"Follow the music."

"What does the message mean? What is the *Pavor – Pot –* thing?"

The man shakes his head, does not reply. Martin still can't see his face.

"Come," says the woman. "We will take you to the bridge."

The travellers lead Martin along a barely visible, rutted track that snakes westwards across the moor until it meets a small, fast flowing stream, whose channel is narrow enough for him to jump across. There's no sign of a bridge, or of the track's continuation on the other side, only a silvery shimmer in the air, exactly like the one he must have run through previously. His crows, however, who had settled on the bone cart during the walk – to the general annoyance of the little people sitting there, who did not want them pecking at the bones and squabbling over stray bits of flesh and ligament – take off and fly straight across, landing on the heather some thirty feet away, and immediately begin to caw, loudly, for him to follow.

"All right," Martin tells them. "I get that message. Thank you," he says to the man and woman. "I hope I did not take you out of your way."

"You were our way," the man responds.

Curiosity compels him to ask. It's his last chance, he thinks: he's come this far biting his tongue, and if he doesn't ask now he will never get another opportunity. "Where are you going?" he ventures. He points to the skeletal body on the bier. "Please tell me. Who was he?"

The woman turns her hooded face towards him, and for a moment he imagines she is smiling. "He was the man who threw the spear, the man who slew the mammoth," she says, and the hairs stand up and wildly prickle on the back of Martin's neck. "Now we are taking him to the Cave of the Hunters, far beyond the northern river, where his bones will lie untouched in stillness and in silence till the ice has melted into sea, the rivers swollen to a flood. Then he will be discovered, by a man who has no hope of understanding what he has found. Now, leap."

Martin leaps, and the world turns blue.

He lands. The sun is shining brilliantly above his head. Landing awkwardly in the heather, he rolls like a gymnast, and sits up. The whole world seems to have been coated in a coloured wash, like thin paint. His boots have turned a steely grey. His sleeveless pullover is grey, yellow and blue. The green heather and the sheep cropped grass have turned a dull ochre. But most extraordinary of all, the sky is *blue* – the vibrant, vivid blue of near midsummer. Martin stares at it in astonishment. He'd honestly forgotten it could ever be any other colour than violet. He rubs his eyes with his fists, and gradually his leather boots resume their habitual brown hue, and the pattern on his pullover resolves itself again into a trellis of bright red and dark green diamonds.

He peers over the river. The people have completely disappeared. For some reason, Martin doesn't find this at all surprising. It feels, in fact, like the most natural thing in the world. And it doesn't seem at all unnatural, not even remotely strange, that he should have got lost on the high moor underneath a violet sky, and have been guided back to this everyday world by a clan of people without faces, who in return for the favour have given him a cryptic message about a river, a Gatekeeper, and a *Pavor* something for somebody called Horsefeathers.

He looks around. Now he's leapt the stream, he knows exactly where he is. He could have pinpointed his position on the ordnance survey map. Bransquite lies directly to the west, no farther than a mile across the moor; if he sets off in that direction and continues walking, he'll drop down into the valley and arrive at Leto Murray's house within half an hour. But there's no need to turn homewards yet. It's only two o' clock, or thereabouts, and the weather's still set fair. Lying back among the heather, he opens his rucksack and takes out his egg and cress sandwiches. Petra and Paul hop closer.

"Wait a minute!" cries Martin, laughing. "I will give you my crusts. Will that do?"

How is he supposed to get the message to Horsefeathers? *Follow the music*, the man said. *What does that mean?* "Do you know him?" he asks the crows. But Petra and Paul have eyes only for his sandwiches, and refuse to answer. He'll have to ask somebody else.

Martin eats his sandwiches – all apart from the crusts, which he gives, as promised, to his crows – then crumples the brown paper wrapping, and drops it carefully in his rucksack. Miss Fox has impressed upon him the importance of leaving no litter on the moor, not even paper. Then he hoists the bag upon his shoulders, and sets off in the direction of the village. It will take him a little while to get home, if he walks slowly.

Already, the time spent underneath the violet sky seems like a dream. *Did it really happen?* he thinks, or did he simply mistake the direction he was walking in, wander south instead of north, and in his confusion fail to recognise the place where he sat down to examine his map? Perhaps he fell asleep in the hot sun. Such a possibility seems much more likely, here, now, beneath this clear, blue, realist, light, than that he could really have seen a creature that was half lizard, half bear, or met with a group of people who looked as if they belonged to the stone age rather than the present, who had no faces and who disappeared like mist the moment he turned his back on them. Perhaps he has been dreaming, and now he has just woken up. But he's not sure this idea, tempting as it is, makes sense. He remembers leaping over the stream. Perhaps he really did so. Perhaps he was not asleep.

Perhaps, he thinks suddenly, he ought to ask Leto Murray what she makes of it all. She won't automatically assume that the most mundane explanation is the only one. She's the girl who travels to another world in her dreams. He wonders what colour the sky is there.

Miss Fox is listening to the BBC radio service. It's not something she does any more while Martin is in the house, in case there should be more terrible news from the continent, but in his absence she feels safe switching it on. The main story, however, is of the continuing Japanese blockade of Tientsin. There's nothing from Germany. Miss Fox feels relieved – awful as the possibility of war in the far east certainly is, it's nothing compared with the horror of war on Britain's very doorstep. She leaves the wireless playing in the background, and fetches her Parker pen and writing paper.

She received a letter from her Hackney editor

a few days ago, but what with one thing or another has not had time to sit down and compose a reply. Her editor's letter is full of London news, and details of the latest Kinder Transports, as they are now called. She asks kindly after Martin Stone, and expresses her hope that he is well and settling into his new life in Cornwall. It seems some of the children, particularly those who have been forced to leave parents and older siblings behind, are neither well nor settled. They suffer from nightmares, and some of the London ladies have told her that they often wet the beds. Miss Fox is very happy to report that Martin Stone exhibits none of these disturbed behaviours. She doesn't mention the one he does, however: talking to birds is not something that can be put down to homesickness or fear. She tells her friend about his speedy grasp of English, and relates that he's become best friends with a local girl of his own age, who shares his interest in exploring on the moor. None of the latter is, of course, entirely true, but Miss Fox feels compelled to give as positive a report of Martin's progress as possible. Lying isn't a grave sin, if there's love behind it.

She lied to her father, she remembers, when she thought herself in love with the man. She lied to herself, too, of course, but she didn't know she was doing it. She was worried her father would not approve her falling in love with a man so many years her senior, a man who'd been – who still was – a soldier. Then came the discovery, and the falling out, which she still does not entirely understand, and the hidden truths cascaded forth. She wonders how her father is now; whether he's happy her brother married the Portsmouth girl on his release from prison, and settled in Fowey as he'd hoped they might do. It feels strange, not speaking to any of them, even after sixteen years of silence. Strange to be so close in blood, yet so distant in mind. Sometimes Miss Fox has the feeling neither her family, nor her own younger self, ever really existed.

She hopes that if war comes again, as she fears it must, her brother won't be called up to the front as he was before. Whatever anyone thinks of the present German situation, Thomas Fox is still a pacifist, bound by conscience to reject all violence. War, to him, is a form of blasphemy – or rather idolatry – just as it is to her. God simply does not want countless young men to be sacrificed upon the altar of national aggression, any more than he truly wanted Abraham to sacrifice Isaac. But Mr Hitler, she thinks, is a menace, make no bones about it: a megalomaniac of the worst kind. It's evident in the way he speaks, the way he moves – as well as what he says. Can any such man be persuaded out of his nationalistic fervour, or his hatred of the Jews? If he cannot, what is the answer? War will not, cannot work, because war never, really, works. There's always too much loss, too much destruction on both sides, for either to be victorious.

Miss Fox unconsciously stopped writing when she began thinking about her father, and about the man. Now she looks at the clock, and then out of the kitchen window, past the ever present Fluffy, wondering when Martin Stone will return. She's told him that he can stay out until tea time, and the weather here is fine. But there's a grey cloud looming over the high moor, and that might drive him home. Suddenly she wishes that she'd never let him go. The world is not as safe as it appears to be on the surface.

What will happen to the children if there is a war?

What will happen to the world if there is not?

Mammoth & Crow

24th April, 1927.

Father,

I am sorry to have proved such a disappointment to you. I am not sorry, however, that I left school in the way I did. I will not be returning there, no matter what pressure you place on me by way of arguments or harsh financial deprivations. Nor will I be returning home. I made my feelings regarding your marriage to that woman expressly clear when you first made me aware of her existence, and they have not changed. I have no desire to meet her or have anything to do with her. I fail to understand how you could possibly imagine I would be anything other than appalled by your referring to her as my stepmother. I have only one mother, and though she is no longer with us, I cannot but think her horrified by your decision to marry a girl who is closer to my age than yours, and is in all probability nothing but a gold-digger who will give you the run around as soon as your back is turned.

I cannot and will not tell you where I am, but you may continue to contact me via Uncle Ignatius. He does not know where I am either, so do not think that you can find me by bullying him. I have set up various channels by which people can contact me, and my uncle does not speak with me directly, but through a trusted associate.

Your son,

Phillip.

Jack Wolf

Chapter Ten:
Diana and Virbius

Evelyn is sitting in the garden, underneath a parasol. *The Golden Bough* lies unopened in her lap; at her side, on the little wooden table beside the pack of Camels and ashtray, a cold glass of gin and tonic awaits her attention. The hem of her summer dress is fluttering like a yellow butterfly around her stockinged calves. Her shoes are perfect. At the far end of the lawn, the new gardener is mowing the grass.

Evelyn is watching him, closely. He is a tall, loose limbed, almost gangling young man, but despite this failing he seems astonishingly strong, and as he pushes the mowing machine back and forth through the slightly too long grass, his muscles – at least, what Evelyn can make out of them through the narrow gap in his white cotton shirt – bunch and flex like an Olympian's. He's not exactly handsome, she thinks. His hair is just a little bit too unkempt, and his features too dark, almost like a gypsy's; but they are well proportioned, even quite attractive. His nose is too long, but that's not a thing to be held against him: so is Gerald's. How old is he? Twenty five? She hasn't asked him, and something about him makes it difficult to tell. Like many men, she supposes, he's one who on reaching eighteen started looking thirty, and he'll remain so for the next twenty years of his life. It doesn't matter, anyway. He's only the gardener. She just likes to look at him.

Mr Frazer's book has reached an interesting point. He's left off writing about sexual magic and has begun instead upon the topic of royal sacrifice. In many ancient tribes, he states, the old King would have been killed at the end of his reign, to make way for a younger, more vigorous successor. This seems an eminently sensible idea to Evelyn, and one that follows naturally from the notion of a Priest who spills his blood in honour of his Goddess. Surely, it is in keeping with the principle of Survival of the Fittest that any King who's grown too weak to rule his people should no longer be King, but pass on his powers, both official and divine, to him that shall rule after. The strength of the people, after all, is embodied in their ruler. If he should be weak, then so are they. The suggestion echoes Mussolini, and Nietzsche. Surely, Evelyn thinks, the behaviour and attitudes that Frazer is describing would be typical of a race that refuses to be brought low by the mewling of slaves. Her mind wanders to the crisis of the abdication, and she can't help thinking that it ended badly for the country. What on Earth did it matter that the King wanted to marry a divorcee, as long as both he and she were strong, clever, and physically fit – as, indeed, they were? Better the energetic Edward than the mumbling Duke, whose meek demeanour, to Evelyn's eyes, betrays disturbing signs of some congenital weakness. *The weak ought not to rule the strong,* she decides. *Neither ought the old.*

Is Gerald weak? He's certainly – she has to admit it – old.

The gardener has stopped pushing the mowing machine back and forth, and bends to lift off the grass box. It's very full. Evelyn watches him as he carries it casually in one hand over to the compost heap, and tips out the clippings on the very top. She reaches out her hand, and lifts her gin and tonic to her lips. Her lipstick leaves a faint memento on the glass.

Since she left London, Evelyn's barely worn her lipstick, or her kitten heels. There's seemed to be no point. But something about the arrival of the gardener, or her discovery of *The Golden Bough*, has altered matters. Why should she lose her self respect, merely because Gerald does not want her? Damn the man! She'll not let herself go under just because of him, or because of anybody. She didn't go under when her father gave into his own weakness and left her, or when the American went back to his home country, and left her too. She'll show Gerald, and anybody else who may be interested, what Evelyn Murray is made of. She is not a woman to be put lightly aside.

The gardener replaces the grass box on the mowing machine, recommences his strong, fluid, movements.

Evelyn has been sitting outside in the sun for perhaps twenty minutes, and the young man has almost finished with the lawn, when the clatter of t-bar shoes on the paved patio alerts her to the return of Leto and Nanny Gould from their visit to the village Post Office. She turns her head. Nanny Gould is untying Leto's blue hat-ribbon, which is tied in a bow underneath her chin. The sight is unexpectedly offensive. Evelyn doesn't like her daughter, but the child is not a drooling idiot.

"Gould!" calls Evelyn, sharply. "Isn't it time she learned to do that for herself? She's not a baby."

"Yes, Madam, she ought," Gould responds at once. "But this is quicker. And Miss has one of her moods on her today. She has been very naughty."

"I have not!" exclaims Leto, astonished and outraged. "How dare you say that, just to curry favour with my mother!"

"You mind your manners, Miss."

"I haven't done anything!"

"Leto Murray, go to your room!"

"Mummy?" Leto says, hesitantly appealing to Evelyn as arbitrator.

"You heard what Gould said, Leto," Evelyn answers, coldly. She has no way of knowing whether the child has misbehaved or not, but instinctively feels she must have done: Leto is always naughty, always looking for trouble, always finding it.

"But it isn't fair!" cries Leto. "She's blaming me because you just told her off! She's nasty and spiteful."

Evelyn has put down her cigarette, but she still has the gin and tonic in her hand. And now the girl is staring at her, pursing up her lips in an accusing way that reminds her not only of Gerald – *damn him, damn him!* – but her own, much younger, self. Almost before she knows what she is doing – because she can't stop herself, she really cannot stop, not even should she want to – she dashes the alcoholic liquid into her daughter's face.

"You little cockroach," Evelyn says. "Don't speak to me like that. Don't touch those eyes!" she shouts, as Leto puts up her hand to wipe the alcohol away. "If they sting, it's your own fault. Don't you dare show weakness. Don't you dare cry. You see, Gould, this is how you must discipline the child," she continues, speaking to the nanny, but never taking her eyes from her daughter. "You're right about her. She's naughty and disobedient. Take her away. I don't want to see her. Get her out of my sight."

In the long, slow, silent moments after Nanny Gould has escorted Leto away, Evelyn half regrets her outburst. She was quite right, she thinks, to have told the girl off for answering back; but she's far from sure she should have gone so far. Part of her thinks she really ought to have kept a better grip on her temper. Leto is not Gerald, after all; and Gordon's gin is a good deal stronger than Christmas wine. But the real truth is that it feels so *good* to have finally lost it with the wretched brat – such a blessed, blessed relief, after all these years of ruthless self-control, to have let go and allowed her feelings to take over, just for one sharp, expressive instant – that she somehow can't condemn herself for what she's done. *And really,* she thinks, *a glass of gin in the face can hardly be considered an assault, by anybody.* It's not as if she's battering the child; and it's high time the naughty minx discovered that when wicked little girls are cheeky and provocative there will be consequences. She deserved everything she got. Evelyn could, in fact, have been a good deal harder on her. She and Gerald have been much too soft on Leto, and their softness has done the girl no good. They have made the fatal mistake of sparing the rod and spoiling the child.

Well, Evelyn decides, *there'll be no more of*

that.

She reaches for her glass, and it's an odd surprise to find it empty. Then she finds herself fully regretting her momentary loss of control. Regardless of the impact on Leto, good or ill, it was a sorry waste of alcohol, and now she'll have to call the housekeeper for another gin and tonic. But as she opens her hand, a full glass, complete with ice, and sporting a little yellow cocktail umbrella, appears, as if by magic, in it. She looks up in surprise, to see who has put it there. It's the new gardener.

"Thank you – Johnny," Evelyn says. She hesitates before saying his name, trying to convey the impression she can't quite recall it. In fact, it's been lying on the very tip of her tongue all morning. She smiles.

"You're welcome, Madam." The gardener touches his cap, inclines his head, and makes as if to return to his work.

"I now know who to ask for cocktails," Evelyn says, a little stupidly.

The new gardener smiles. There's something wonderfully dangerous in his look. It reminds Evelyn of a predatory bird, or a shark, or any number of fierce creatures that could easily eat one alive, if encountered in the wrong sort of circumstances. Somewhere deep inside, she shivers. It's not at all an unpleasant sensation.

"I make a fine Gin Rickey, and a not so bad Mint Julep."

"What about Be – " Evelyn stops abruptly. "That will be all," she says. "Thank you, Johnny."

"How unspeakably vile that woman is," Johnny says

to Annie later, while the old woman is rolling out the pastry for jam tarts upon the kitchen table. "Do you know what she did to her little girl? Threw gin and tonic in her face. Nanny backed her up, of course – or she was backing Nanny up. I'm not quite certain which way round it went, to tell the truth."

"That child's a handful," Annie says.

"She detests the child," replies Johnny, stealing a strip of pastry and rolling it into a ball. "So that's hardly surprising."

"It's not for us to pass judgement," Annie says, resolutely.

"You're wrong. It is what we do best."

Annie looks up. "Sometimes," she says, shaking her head. "I think you take some of the crazy things Mr Hart used to say a bit too literally, Johnny."

"I am allowed to pass judgement on *her*, at any rate," says Johnny, darkly. "So I will."

The old woman looks at him curiously, but he doesn't elaborate on what he means by this, and I am not about to do so, either. But you may begin to guess.

Leto is furious. She's done nothing wrong. She stayed on her best behaviour the whole time during the long and boring walk to the Post Office and village shops with Nanny Gould, even when Nanny stopped and gossiped for a full half hour with the Postmistress; and now she feels a deep sense of outrage at the old woman's treachery. She doesn't know, of course, that Nanny Gould has privately begun to fear for her position, and is increasingly ready to do or say anything that will keep her on the right side of her employer. But even if she did, it is highly unlikely she would be at all sympathetic. Leto is almost as sick of

Mammoth & Crow

Nanny Gould as she is of her mother.

She is sitting on her bed, in the middle of the afternoon, wrapping her nightdress around her ankles. Evelyn's aim with the gin and tonic was remarkably accurate, and her eyes are sore. *But I will not cry*, she tells herself. No. She's genuinely surprised that her mother should have lashed out at her like that, but she's not upset. Where the upset should be, a dense red cloud of anger and wounded pride has begun roiling slowly over and over. She will not cry, and give her mother – who isn't really her mother at all, just a wicked witch who's dropped into the space where a mother should be, like Snow White's stepmother, or Cinderella's, or the Goose-Girl's – the satisfaction of seeing her tears. *No.* She will never cry again, or argue, or protest aloud. The witch will never even hear her voice. Why should she bother trying to speak to someone who hates her, someone who wants nothing but to cause her injury or pain?

Leto hasn't piddled on the floor since she left London. She has believed that this is because her wolf self hasn't wanted to claim this territory for its own – though, I have to say, it seems far more likely to me that the fresh air and healthy changes in routine following her arrival in Bransquite lie behind it. But now she gets up from her bed, and carefully produces a series of small warm puddles all around the room, paying particular attention to the area right beside the door where Nanny Gould will have to walk. She hopes the pee will make Nanny's shoes smell bad. Then she sits back on her bed and wraps her arms around her knees. The sun is shining outside the window.

Jack Wolf

Evelyn Murray's not her mother, she reminds herself again. Her real mother is Huma, and someday soon Huma will come crashing and stomping out of the Otherworld and laying about her with her stony, lichened trunk, and she'll lift little Leto up and carry her away. Perhaps she'll stamp on Evelyn while she's about it, squash her flat like a cockroach on the sole of her wide, trampling foot. And then Nanny will be sorry – Nanny Gould, who has proved herself her mother's ally in all this, and no friend to the little girl she's raised since infancy. *Nanny can't be trusted, either,* Leto decides. *She's treacherous, and tricksy.*

Come away, O human child.

She does not weep.

At about five o clock she becomes conscious of someone whistling loudly outside her bedroom window. Evelyn doesn't whistle, as she considers it unladylike, Nanny Gould can't, and it seems highly unlikely it could be the old housekeeper, so Leto concludes it must be the new gardener. She gets up off her bed, treads quietly over to the sash, and looks out. The gardener is sweeping the gravel path that runs along the side of the house. As Leto stares, he turns around, as if feeling her gaze upon him, and looks straight up, before smiling and raising his right thumb, to let her know that he is on her side – or at least, she thinks, is not her enemy. After some consideration, she raises her hand and gives him a tiny wave; not enough to be encouraging, but sufficient to show she has seen him and appreciates his gesture of solidarity. The gardener smiles, and mimes to her that she should open the window.

Mammoth & Crow

Leto is not sure. Both her parents have always been very strict about not conversing with servants. But, she reminds herself, her mother's not her mother, and her father's up in London, and if he cares at all, he has no way of knowing anything that Leto does. Very carefully, in order to avoid making any sound that might bring Nanny Gould into the room, Leto undoes the latch, and pushes up the sash. "Hello," she whispers.

"Felicitations, Miss," says the new gardener. "Are you hungry?"

"Why?"

In answer, the gardener reaches into a basket by his feet, and draws out a small, wrapped cheesecloth parcel. "Can you catch?"

"What is it?"

"Jam tarts. Maybe slightly squashed jam tarts. I had to smuggle them out under Annie's nose."

"Nanny says I'm not allowed anything until supper."

"I know. That's why I smuggled them out. Do you do everything that Nanny tells you?"

"No," says Leto, emphatically. "Most certainly not."

"Good," says the new gardener. "So, catch."

Leto half leans out of the window, and the gardener tosses up the parcel. To her own surprise, she catches it, and then runs with it to her bed, where she hides it underneath her pillow. It wouldn't do for anyone to find out she's been given it.

"Thank you," she says, returning to the window. "What's your name?"

"Johnny."

"Johnny what?"

"For now, just Johnny."

"My name is Leto. You may use it."

"I'm honoured, Leto. I'll treat it with care."

"Why are you working as a gardener?" Leto asks. "You don't talk like one."

"That," the new gardener says. "Is a long, complex and not very happy story. Once upon a time, I had a family just like yours. But then my mother died, and my father married again, so I had to run away and fend for myself."

"Was she wicked, your stepmother? My mother is wicked."

"Yes, very. But it was a long time ago. Don't tell anyone. It has to stay a secret."

"I won't, I promise! How did you manage to run away? I wish I could."

"I was a lot older than you, and at boarding school. My father looked for me for a while, but he never found me."

"I suppose it's easier for boys," Leto says thoughtfully. "My parents won't let me go to school," she continues. "They don't want me to mix with inferior children."

"Is that so? That's a great loss on your part, and a shame on theirs. You should always pay attention to your supposed inferiors. They'll have insight into matters you don't know a thing about. And remember, dustmen are human, too, just like you are."

"My mother says dustmen come from very low grade stock. They're practically vermin."

"Does she, indeed?" Johnny says, musingly.

"She says lots of things like that," Leto says.

"And do you listen?"

"Sometimes," Leto confesses. "I think she thinks that I am low grade stock," she adds, in a very small voice.

"Now, you listen to me, Leto Murray," says Johnny, wagging his finger in a stern manner that reminds Leto immediately of her father, *but not,* she thinks, *in a bad way*. "You are not, and nobody else is, either. There's no such thing as human stock, low or high or anywhere in between. Human beings are not cattle or pigs. Your silly old mother is talking applesauce."

"Applesauce?"

"Nonsense. Horsefeathers. Phoney baloney. Whenever you hear her talking complete rot, you must say "applesauce!" to yourself, just like that."

"I will," says Leto, with a giggle. It sounds a nice form of rebellion: like he's given her a spell.

"That's my girl," says Johnny. He winks. "Now, I must finish clearing this path, or Annie'll be after my guts. See you later, old thing."

Evelyn sat outside for so long that the afternoon sun, sloping across the garden into her eyes, eventually began to obscure her view of the new gardener, and her rear end started to feel numb. She's now retired indoors, taking her gin and tonic with her. Over the last few weeks, she has decided strongly in favour of gin over wine; somehow it doesn't seem the same thing to sit and consume a whole bottle of gin by oneself as it does a bottle of white or red, and as the drinks cabinet seems to be routinely kept stocked with at least one bottle – more often two – she's able to avoid drawing attention to herself by calling the housekeeper for a replacement. Not that she cares two

Jack Wolf

hoots what that old woman thinks. This need for circumspection is entirely on her own account: Evelyn doesn't want to admit to herself how much alcohol she's currently consuming.

It's not yet evening, but Evelyn is sleepy. She supposes this perhaps has something to do with the heat, or the outdoor air. She begins thinking idly about the Priest of the Grove, and his role as lover of the divine Diana. Virbius must be something really special, to have tempted that notorious virgin out of her chastity. Then again, no Goddess could mate with a man who was anything less than perfect.

She's not sure at what point she falls asleep, but shortly after settling herself on her sofa (she wishes it was a chaise longue – but there's nothing so comfortable in Ignatius Hart's old house) she finds her mind beginning to drift. She's sitting in the garden again, watching the new gardener clear the beds of the old growth that's strangling the growth of the new season's plants. The muscles ripple in his back as he works, and it doesn't strike Evelyn as at all unusual that he has taken off his shirt. His bronze skin shines with bright sweat in the summer heat.

As she watches him work, a fierce, physical longing begins to burn in Evelyn's belly. Here's a man, indeed! A young, fit, virile, man, whose biceps have grown strong as steel from his labours and whose skin is still as unworn as the wings on a newly emerged butterfly. The gardener turns around – and Evelyn's dream self watches as the tight, layered muscles of his abdomen expand and contract with his every breath. She puts down her gin and tonic. *Come here, Johnny,* she calls. Her voice is candid, bold, commanding. He puts down his hoe, and begins to cross the grass towards her. His face is wearing the predatory expression she saw on it when he brought her the glass, but she thinks she knows how to manage wild things, and she's not afraid of him. Her eyes travel slowly down his body. There's no mistaking the bulge in his trousers. She licks her lips. Now she can hear his footsteps on the patio, as he walks towards her; and she lets him lift her up out of her chair, and thrust her hard against the ivied wall. Now his hand is pulling her hair, and his tongue is in her mouth, and her legs are opening like a flower, and she's wrapping them around his waist as he lifts her up over his hips and –

Nothing. The dream changes. Evelyn is alone. She's standing in Ignatius Hart's old library. Her untouched loins are howling with frustration.

How dare he! thinks Evelyn furiously. She wants to be coarser than this, but even in a dream can't bring herself to swear. She stumbles toward the fireplace. The curtain is still across the painting, which is still just as she left it. Why hasn't the old housekeeper done as she was told to do, and removed it? Evelyn tugs hard on the tasselled cord, and the curtain swishes back. The painting of Johnny Horsefeathers glares garishly from its frame, its colours still outlandishly wrong, its composition still tortured. How she hates this thing. How she hates this disappointment.

The painted figure is reclining – *insolently,* Evelyn thinks, *yes, insolently* – against the tree. His bended knee, his casual insouciance, the jaunty angle of his hat, all suddenly seem to combine to make the very existence of the picture into an insult – and not just to art, as she's previously supposed, but to her.

How dare he! she thinks. She doesn't know which 'he' she means: Mr Hart, the figure in the painting, or the new gardener. She doesn't care. But something has drawn her back to the painting, and although she is disgusted by the filthy thing, she cannot, now, draw herself away from it. She peers closely at the figure. *He has no face*, she thinks suddenly. *Didn't he have a face before?* She can't remember.

Now you see me, now you don't.

The dinner bell rings in the hallway. Evelyn starts roughly awake. She stares muzzily around her. She's in her sitting room, she realises. The late afternoon sun is beating heavily on the blinds, and the stuffy indoor air is dancing with dust motes. Where is the new gardener? She sits up, and adjusts her stockings. Her panties are still in place. Of course they are. What on Earth has she been dreaming about? She straightens the rumpled skirt of her yellow dress, and gets to her feet. She feels unaccountably guilty, and immediately thinks of Gerald. Perhaps she should have dressed for dinner. But on the other hand, with Gerald in London, and no society here, who is to notice, or to care? She shuffles her feet into her kitten heels, and leaves the room.

Chapter Eleven:
Shaydim

At Martin's own request, Miss Fox sends him down to the village with a note asking Leto to tea. Yesterday, when he came in from the moor, he was in an oddly distant and preoccupied frame of mind, and she's relieved that he's now seeking out human companionship. Mrs Murray gives her permission at once, and the two children quickly set out along the flowery lane that leads up the hill past St Bran's Church.

Martin wastes no time in telling Leto what happened to him on the high moor. He's now almost sure that, despite the way that everything he'd just done seemed to slide away from him like water in those few moments after he jumped the stream, making him wonder if he'd just been dreaming, what happened had been no dream; at least, not of any usual sort.

He has remembered how once, among the many curious things he used to overhear during his grandmother's Friday night conversations with the Rabbi and other clever visitors, there was a reference to something called *Shaydim*. These spirits – or so the speaker, somewhat doubtfully, termed them – were not quite belonging to the world of man, but neither were they angels, ghosts, or dybbuks. His tentative hypothesis was that they were a natural part of creation, just like everything else, and no more or less worthy of human concern than a river or a tree. Certainly, there was no reason to fear them, or believe them supernatural in origin. The Rabbi disagreed. *Shaydim*, he argued, in a fervent voice, were manifestations of the *klippoth*: the broken vessels left behind during the initial process of divine creation, and in consequence of this they existed like shadows on the fringes of nature, haunting the darkness into which the mind of a normal man could not quite penetrate. As such, he said, they were unfit for study. And he snapped his fingers, as if that gesture ought to prove the end of the matter. Martin, listening behind the door, had the distinct impression neither the Rabbi nor his debating partner had any real experience of the subject they were talking about. His grandmother had once shown him a picture of an African rhinoceros drawn by a man who'd never seen one, and to Martin, both these learned men sounded exactly like that looked. Everything they said was supposition, based on dubious report. He had returned in confusion to his room, and opened up his window, to listen to the sparrows instead.

But now – after a long night of hard thought – it has become Martin's hypothesis that the faceless people he encountered yesterday on the high moor were, in fact, members of that rarely encountered, not quite supernatural, race; and perhaps that *Otherworld* into which he'd seemed to cross had been their territory: a shadowland, lying on the edge between what is apparent and what is not. He puts this idea to Leto – although, naturally, he omits any mention of the Rabbi, or his own past life.

"Martin," Leto says at once, excitedly. "Do you see what this means? Huma's world is real! I told you it was!"

"And I was able to go there," Martin says, slowly. "Do you think the monster – the Lizard-bear – is part of it?"

"Of course it is!" Leto skips in excitement.

"So what is it?"

"I don't know. I'll ask Huma, next time I see her."

"Have you ever met it?"

"No. I met a Naiad once, though."

"A what?"

"A river."

"How can a person meet a river?"

"The water turned into a girl. She wanted me to stay and play with her, but I was too afraid. I ran away. I wish I hadn't." Leto pulls a face. "I don't like it here. I like you, of course, and now I like Johnny too. But everyone else is horrid."

"My auntie is not horrid," Martin says.

"No, she is very kind. But I don't live with your auntie."

"Who is Johnny?" Martin asks, noticing what Leto has just said.

"The new gardener. Only he's not really a servant. He's very respectable and nice."

"Gardener?" Martin remembers the peculiar tramp who leapt over the wall in front of him; his peculiar question about employment. "What does he look like?" he asks, suspiciously.

"I don't know. Like anybody, I suppose."

"Is he – " Martin stops. He tries to think of a way of putting his question that will not sound ridiculous. "You are sure he's real," he says at last. "I mean, that he's not one of the *Shaydim?*"

"Of course he's not a shade!" Leto says scornfully. "He brought me some jam tarts."

"So what does his face look like?"

"Oh, he definitely *has* a face," Leto says, realising what Martin means. "It's just I didn't really notice what he looked like. After all, he is only the gardener."

"They gave me a message," Martin says, suddenly remembering.

"Who did?"

"The faceless men. Whatever they are. They said to tell someone he must hurry to make a choice, because the river is missing him, and there is danger, or death, or something like that. I can't properly recall."

"Tell who?"

"I can't remember. It wasn't a name that made any sense."

"They must have meant the wizard," Leto says, excitedly. "The one in the tunnel on the moor. You know. Oh, Martin, we must visit again, and see if we can find him!"

"I don't want to go back there," Martin says.

"Why? Are you scared?"

"No. I don't believe he is a wizard. And I don't want to be rude."

They walk on up the sunny lane. Red campion and foxglove flowers filled with white rumped bumble bees wave in the bottoms of the stony hedgerows, and robins twitter in the branches of the scrubby blackthorn trees. The small birds are just gossiping. Everything is as it should be.

As they approach Miss Fox's cottage, a swift rustling in the air and cacophony of raucous cries announces Petra and Paul, who rise from their perches on the ridge pole of the roof and fly straight onto Martin's outstretched arm. He strokes Paul's head, and a few tiny feathers come away in his hand.

"Poor crow," says Leto. "He looks miserable."

"He's begun moulting," Martin explains. "That's why he didn't follow me to the village today. All birds change their feathers at least once a year, when they've finished rearing their chicks."

"I wish I knew as much about birds as you do," Leto says wistfully, although the idea that there should be anything to know about birds beyond the limits of the Encyclopedia is one that has only recently occurred to her. A thought strikes her. "Do you collect eggs?" she asks.

"No," Martin says.

"But you know where to find the nests."

Martin has been telling her about the dunnock's nest he has found in the overgrown wall at the bottom of Miss Fox's garden. There are four eggs in it, which he expects soon to hatch.

"Every egg you take from a nest is a chick who will not live. I would rather have the birds."

"I think you should be a falconer or a gamekeeper when you grow up," says Leto, who has been reading about Country Sports in the Encyclopedia.

"I don't think so," Martin says. "I don't like the thought of hunting with birds. Or shooting them," he adds.

His grandmother was unequivocal upon that score. It is never right, she taught him, to take a life, even that of a small bird, for the sake of entertainment. It's not as if tamed falcons need to hunt. They can be trained to a lure. But it seems somehow equally cruel to Martin to keep the creatures at all, if they're never to be allowed to express their true, wild, predatory natures. But it's too hard to explain all this, in English, to Leto. "What about you?" he says. "What will you do, when you are an adult?"

"Oh, I will just get married," Leto says. She sticks her tongue out in disgust, and giggles.

"All right. So what will your husband be like?" Martin asks.

"Superior, of course. Handsome and rich and clever. Nothing matters except all that, really."

"Nothing matters?" This seems crazy to Martin. "What about being kind, or trying hard, and never giving up?" he asks. His grandmother hugely prized all these qualities in his long dead grandfather. She often spoke of him with great fondness.

"Kindness is all very well. But if you have to try hard at anything it just means you're no good at it. Superior people just find everything really easy, because of hereditary, and they never have to try."

"Who says that?" Martin asks, astonished.

"My mother." She pauses, her brow wrinkling for a moment. "Though actually, I think it might be applesauce."

Martin swings open the wooden gate at the front of the cottage, and walks up the garden path between Miss Fox's flower beds. Petra and Paul fly from his arm and return to the roof, where a squabble of some trivial nature has broken out between the young crows who are snapping at each other in a bored manner, like a gang of boys a month or so too old for school, but who haven't yet started work and have nothing meaningful to do. Petra flies into the heart of the mob like a black torpedo, and they scatter, squawking furiously.

Evelyn has received a second letter from Gerald. She reads it standing in the hall, next to the table where the old housekeeper has left it lying, as if it were nothing but a laundry bill.

> *I am happy to tell you that the University has agreed to grant me a sabbatical leave for a year from September in which I will be able to pursue a new and very promising line of research into the author of the final lines of Seven Against Thebes; and that although this work will necessitate my spending a significant amount of time from June onwards in the libraries of London and Oxford, there is some possibility that I may be able to spare some time in order to join you and Leto for a week's holiday in Cornwall in the late summer. I hope you have happily settled in, and that she is getting all the fresh air and exercise that we had planned, which I am sure will strengthen her constitution no end. I trust you are keeping well, my dear Evie, and are not missing London too much. I expect to hear from you by return.*

Although Evelyn has been longing to read something like this ever since her banishment, the letter does not move her. She does not even mind that the housekeeper neglected to tell her of its being delivered. Gerald talks a fine talk, making his offer of a one week visit, but he's the same as ever: obsessed by his work, and by that unbearable brat. *You and Leto.* What on earth does he see in her? She isn't remotely pretty, she's no budding genius, and her behaviour is so, so bad. *What a waste*, Evelyn thinks, in bitter anguish, that the only one of their children to have survived should have been Leto, and not her brother. If she could, oh, if she thought for one moment it would bring him back, she'd trade one for the other, the daughter for the son, the living child for the dead. Then she suddenly realises what it is that she is thinking, and feels horribly ashamed. She shouldn't be thinking about her own daughter like that. It's un-maternal. Shocking. Wrong. She tries to pretend to herself that she never had the thought; but like thrown gin, it seems that once it is out of the glass, it can never be put back in again. She wishes she could think about something else. *Not Leto. Not Gerald. Not –* But her inner world has shrunk to a cicada.

She returns Gerald's letter to its envelope, and slaps the whole thing down on the hall table. *Hang Gerald and his answer by return!* She'll answer it later, in her own time, and at her own convenience.

The new gardener, Johnny, is trimming the climbing rose at the front of the old house. It's slightly too late for this, but the archway has been neglected for so many months that Evelyn has agreed it doesn't really matter if the plant fails in its second flowering. Anyway, having hired the young man, she feels an obligation to set him to work. She moves quietly to the front door, and peers through the many coloured glass. He, at least, is proving something of a distraction, she has to admit.

Johnny is standing on a set of garden steps, the pruning shears held out in front of him. He's not simply chopping at the thorny stems, but is carefully untangling them, ensuring that the strongest, and most attractively placed, will be left to recover, while the weaker growth is cut right away. The rose arch is being given form and purpose, as well as beauty. Evelyn watches him wipe the sweat from his brow with the back of his hand, and step down from his low ladder to survey his handiwork. Through the coloured glass, his yellow shirt seems to have turned orange, and his skin is as red as an Indian's. She can easily imagine him wearing a feathered headdress, and moccasins, like an Apache chief. The sky beyond the arch glows vivid purple.

Actually, he is extremely handsome, Evelyn thinks, somewhat guiltily – and again the contrast with Gerald strikes her like a blow. For the first time in her life, she is seriously beginning to wonder what on Earth her seventeen year old self was thinking in allying herself to someone so much older than herself, whose vigour was mostly spent. Was Gerald ever really the man she imagined him? Or did she choose him out of inexperience, and, she now has – oh so ruefully! – to admit, want of any better opportunity?

Stop this, she tells herself. *It won't change anything.*

As she stands, still and watchful behind the pane, a figure comes round the corner of the house carrying a tray, upon which rests a tumbler and a jug of clear liquid that sparkles in the sunshine. It's

Nanny Gould, Evelyn realises in displeasure. She watches with increasing unease as Johnny takes the tumbler from the tray, and lifts it to his lips. It must be lemonade. He swallows: even from here, she can see the rise and fall of his Adam's apple, the silver sheen of liquid on his lips. Evelyn feels a stab of pique – or shock, or horror. She doesn't know, in fact, what the feeling is, but it's so sudden, so powerful, so vicious, it punches the breath from her lungs. Gould has no business befriending the gardener. It isn't done for a superior servant to wait on a lesser one. It's shocking conduct, utterly unacceptable. Though on the other hand, a small voice whispers, perhaps it's also inappropriate for a lady to take such an interest in the relationships between members of staff, as long as they continue to do their jobs.

Can she dismiss Gould? Should she? Only if there's nothing for Gould to do, and that, of course, means if there's no child for her to take care of. Can she send Leto to school, then? Of course not. For all that Evelyn dislikes her daughter, consigning her into the custody of others will merely expose her to all the pollutants and degradations from which she's taken such care to preserve her, and make everything that's wrong so, so much worse. Anyway, Gerald will never agree to it. Or will he? Mosley's son is being educated at Eton. *But then again,* Evelyn thinks, *he is a boy.*

Stop obsessing over Leto, she tells herself. *Stop it.*

Perhaps a proper governess would have a better notion of her proper place. A governess would never stoop to bring lemonade to a mere gardener.

Even one as beautiful as Johnny?

Mammoth & Crow

The little girl never stops talking, Miss Fox thinks. Her energy is exhausting. She babbles about the faery stories she has read, and how much she adores Victoria sponge cake, and her favourite poem by W.B Yeats, and Alice's Adventures, and the mating habits of northern European wolves, and the effects of glaciation on the British countryside. There appears to be little rhyme or reason to her monologue, and after an hour or more of constant chatter it strikes Miss Fox that she has no real interest in being listened to, but maintains her constant stream of words to entertain only herself – or keep everyone else at a distance. *It's not really surprising,* thinks Miss Fox. She doubts the child has experienced much meaningful engagement or sympathy in her short life from the adults around her – for even though Mrs Gould seems a decent sort of woman, it became plain from her conversation she regards Leto as something between a duty and a chore: a general nuisance from whom naughty behaviour should always be expected. It seems a sad state of affairs. The little girl doesn't strike Miss Fox as particularly naughty. She simply appears lost.

Right now, Leto doesn't feel lost. She feels, for the first time she can remember, completely at home. Miss Fox's cottage reminds her of every homely place she's ever read about in stories, and in the Encyclopedia. Everything about it is perfect: the auriculas on the window sill, the purring ginger cat curled up in the sun, the battered furniture, the busy garden, bursting with peas and broad beans and all manner of good things, the pretty tiled fireplace – right now empty, apart from a faint trace of ash and the acrid smell of soot. This is Tom Kitten's house, it's Ratty's capital little place upon the Riverbank. It's hardly surprising that a boy lives here who can talk to birds, or that he might have been given an important message for a wizard by an unknown spirit. She wishes she could live here, too. She is sure that Miss Fox, who is so good and kind, and doesn't seem to mind Martin's many oddities, is someone she could talk to about Huma.

Leto hasn't seen the mammoth since her last journey to the Otherworld, though sometimes she still hears her voice, low and rumbling across time and space like a lighthouse bell below water. Sometimes, when she closes her eyes, she can still look into that place, and see it still as clearly as if it were before her open gaze; but though she can watch the Ice Age swifts like flung sickles catching insects in the air, and even sometimes see the shadow of a lynx upon the rocks, or the quick red flash of fox or wolf disappearing out of the corner of her eye, she never sees the Matriarch. It is as if she has travelled somewhere beyond the reach of even Leto's imagination. Sitting at the table, Leto briefly closes her eyes, just to check the steppe-land is still as she last saw it. The image takes a moment to come into focus – like a movie, though of course Leto's never been anywhere near a cinema, and this idea, too, has come from reading about the history of the silver screen in the Encyclopedia. But this movie, unlike most of those whose details Leto has avidly devoured, is a talkie: it has sound. Birds chirrup from the long grass, just as they were doing a few weeks ago from the heather. The river gurgles in the valley as if it – *as if she,* Leto corrects herself – is laughing.

Who can the river girl be laughing at? Is she simply giggling for joy at being alive? There's no sign anywhere of Huma.

Leto opens her eyes. The ginger cat is purring comfortably in the shabby armchair; the tea kettle whistles on the hob.

There's no time to go anywhere after tea, and the weather is on the change, so Leto and Martin head to a quiet corner of the garden out of earshot of Miss Fox, though quite close to the nesting hedge sparrows, and continue their conversation about the *Shaydim*, and the cryptic message they have given Martin. Leto is fascinated by the thought that a wizard might somehow find himself in danger. She presses Martin repeatedly to try to remember everything the faceless man said, but he can't.

"Perhaps," Leto says, at last, "You'll only remember properly when you meet whoever it is you have to tell the message to. That must be it. It's a *spell!*"

Martin feels the lack is due more to the limitations of his memory than any magic, but he does not contradict her. He's never been good at remembering human messages, in any language – and whatever race, supernatural or otherwise, the faceless men belong to, they spoke to him in a clear, unmistakable English.

At seven o' clock, sharp, there is a knock on the door of Miss Fox's cottage. Miss Fox starts. She's not expecting anyone to call, having arranged that Martin will walk Leto home as he has done before, and the surprise puts her into a fluster. She quickly tidies her hair and unties her apron, and opens the door.

Jack Wolf

"Felicitations," says the young man politely, touching his cap. "Is Miss Leto ready to go home? Mrs Gould has asked me to fetch her."

"Oh, my goodness," says Miss Fox. "She is in the garden. I will call her. Do come in."

"Thank you," The young man steps through the doorway, taking care to wipe his feet upon the mat. He takes off his cap. "Mrs Gould said to pass on her thanks, and her hope that Miss has not been a bother."

"No bother at all," Miss Fox replies. "She is charming, and as well behaved as any child her age can be expected to be. Martin!" She hurries through into the kitchen. "There is somebody here to collect Leto. I'm sorry," she adds, turning to the young man. "I don't know your name."

"I apologise. I should have given it. It's Johnny." He holds out his hand, and Miss Fox shakes it.

"It is very nice to meet you, Johnny." Miss Fox wonders why he hasn't introduced himself by his surname, as is proper; but it doesn't seem polite to ask. Perhaps his name is Johnny John, just as some Welshmen are Davy Davy. Serviceable names, but comically repetitious.

The young man looks around the cottage, as if quizzing it. His eye spots the ginger cat, and while Miss Fox calls a second time for Martin he makes his way over to the armchair and holds out his hand for Fluffy to sniff. The cat instantly sits up straight, as if affronted, and hisses.

"I'm sorry, Johnny. He's not fond of strangers," Miss Fox says.

The cat stares measuringly at the young man,

then yawns, stretches, and settles down again, his half closed eyes black slits in his bright orange head.

The back door suddenly opens, and the two children burst through it, laughing after a race across the garden. "Miss Fox!" cries Leto. "I won the race! I won!"

"Well done," says Miss Fox, with a smile. "Leto, this gentleman says he's come to take you home."

"Oh!" exclaims Leto in surprise. "It's the new gardener!"

"Hello, Miss. Have you been enjoying yourself?"

"Oh, yes!" Leto answers. "Martin has been showing me all sorts of things. Did you know dunnocks' eggs are bright blue, like sweets?"

"I haven't collected eggs since I was a boy," the gardener says.

"Oh, he doesn't collect them. That would be cruel. He just watches."

Johnny looks at Martin consideringly. "Good for you," he says, nodding.

"Do I have to go now?" Leto says, pulling a face.

"Afraid so, old girl. I'm sorry. Nanny Gould will have my guts for garters if we tarry."

Leto looks for a moment as if she is about to argue. Then she sighs. "I'll get my coat," she says, in a flattened tone of voice. "Thank you for having me, Miss Fox." She disappears into the hallway.

"It's under the stairs," calls Miss Fox. Then, realising Leto is unlikely to find anything in the dark cupboard, she says "Excuse me," to Johnny, and hurries after her.

Martin Stone stares, suspiciously, at the new gardener. Is this the same man who jumped over the wall? If he is, Martin thinks, then he's dramatically altered his appearance – his hair's been cut and untangled from the straggly mane whose tresses loosely waved from underneath the Homburg hat, and his face seems younger, brighter, and somehow more human, too, unless it's simply that he's taken a long, cleansing bath. He imagines telling him 'Felicitations', and seeing what his reaction might be, but decides against it. Most likely, he thinks, he's not the same man, and Martin will look like a fool. Anyway, if he is, why on Earth would he be willing to admit it? Evelyn Murray isn't the sort of woman to employ a tramp, even if he has taken a bath.

The new gardener smiles at Martin Stone, and says nothing at all.

Chapter Twelve:
River

"What do you think it would be like to be a river?" Leto asks Johnny, as they walk back along the flowery lane to Bransquite.

"That's a philosopher's question," Johnny answers. "Not a little girl's. What set you thinking of it?"

"Something Martin said. Would it be boring, do you think, to be running in the same old channel, all the time, and never see anything else?"

"Nothing's boring about a river," Johnny says. "For one thing, the waters are in constant movement, and constant change. They are never still for long enough to let the river know what boredom is. Or what they are, for that matter. But for another thing, the channel itself is always moving, slowly, over time. Water isn't fixed, not at all. Nor should it ever be. It must be in constant motion to keep the world in balance, running to stand still. These herculean efforts people make to control and contain rivers always backfire in the end. Dredge a river channel in one place and you'll see flooding somewhere downstream. Build a great dam, seven hundred feet high, and you'll kill everything that depends on the continued flow of water, including your own fishermen and farmers downstream along the river channel."

"I've read about the water cycle," Leto volunteers.

"In the Encyclopedia, I know. Nanny Gould told me how much you read. But now you need to learn to see things for yourself, in the real world. Lets stay with your question about what it might be like to be a river. How does the water cycle function?"

"Water evaporates," Leto says. She feels less confident, suddenly, in her knowledge. "Then it condenses in the clouds, and falls as rain."

"So what does it feel like to evaporate?"

"I don't know. I can't imagine."

"Try, and perhaps you'll work out what it is to be a river. What is it like to be a cloud, a raindrop, or a spring? What is it like to flow quickly over cold rocks and to wind slowly through a silted up delta? To be alive with fish, and water boatmen, and dragonfly nymphs with jaws like tiny sharks? When you can imagine these things, old fruit, maybe you'll have some inkling of what that sort of being is."

Leto, for the first time in many hours, falls silent. Johnny has made her think something important. Something that matters, really matters, in a way that hardly anything does. And he has listened to her, taken her seriously, as if she is really a philosopher, and not a little girl at all. Without really thinking about it, she slips her hand into his.

She wishes that he could have been the one to have taken her to see the Ilford Mammoth.

Tonight, she meets the river again. She's been looking for Huma, who must surely be, she feels, close by – though she hasn't heard the mammoth's voice in her dream, or seen her dark shape approaching over the rugged uplands. She asks the waters where Huma is, but the Naiad doesn't know, and giggles like a lunatic when Leto tries to be serious, flowing on over moss and stone, teasing, tempting her to give chase. Leto wonders where the channel will lead her if she follows. She might get lost, or stuck, and – without her daytime self, and most probably, her body, which she suspects is still lying tucked up in bed – either outcome would be very undesirable.

"It's so frustrating," Leto complains, to no-one in particular, "that I can only come here in dreams. I wish I could be here awake. Why did the looking glass let Martin through, not me? It's so unfair!"

It's Midsummer's Day; and the rain has returned. It began to fall, sporadically, on the twenty first, in glistening drifts from the thick grey Atlantic clouds which, let me tell you, are going to remain settled over all of southern England for the remainder of this month. The dampened air has turned distinctly cool. In between the showers, Martin harvests the remainder of the peas and broad beans from Miss Fox's vegetable garden, and plants more. He wonders whether he can ask any of the local population of song thrushes to come down and feast on the many slugs and snails that have suddenly emerged with the wetter weather, but there are none to be found. He decides to keep the request in mind, for later. It's a pity birds can't read, he thinks, or he'd have scratched a message on the garden wall. He has managed to

Jack Wolf

locate some early strawberries, which he and his foster aunt are enjoying with clotted cream and jam on scones, while the white rain splashes on the window sill. Being used to Bodmin moor, and its usually inclement weather, Miss Fox isn't in the least concerned about the sudden disappearance of the sun. The summer hasn't vanished, she knows. Summer rain is warmer, and the winds less chill. It's no less Midsummers' Day for being a washout, though she supposes the inhabitants of those little Cornish towns and villages who still celebrate Midsummers' Eve by lighting bonfires and dancing through the night are less than pleased by this change in the weather.

In Ignatius Hart's old house, the atmosphere is less sanguine. While she was able to sit in the garden, watching the gardener hoe and weed, Evelyn was able to pretend that everything was still somehow normal: that she was not in Cornwall at all, but still in Chiswick, and Gerald was in his study, preparing his lecture on the scholarly text which he would present tomorrow morning. She imagined a lot of other things as well, but this is the only fantasy she's willing to admit to. But now the rain has come, and she's trapped inside a house that smells damp and cold like musty stables; and on top of that, whenever the wind blows in a certain way around the roof, the sitting room chimney smokes, and the only way to stop the room from filling up with soot is to put out the fire. *It's simply horrid*, she thinks. If only she had friends whom she could visit. If only she could play tennis. But there is nobody. Nothing to muffle the shrill of the cicada.

    She has now reached the middle of *The*

Golden Bough. Mr Frazer is arguing that Virbius, who was – as we all surely know by now – the first divine King of the Arican wood, has somehow taken on the character of Hippolytus and been slain by horses; and that the mythic meaning to this gross misfortune is that the horses who killed him were really an embodiment of himself as God of vegetation. Though Mr Frazer has previously taken great care to explain that vegetative spirits are often represented in the form of horses, this association still seems more than a little arbitrary to Evelyn. Why, she wonders, would a divinity of corn or tree choose to appear in the form of a horse, instead of some creature more naturally suited to an arboreal existence, like a squirrel? But she lets it go. Perhaps there are elements of Mr Frazer's argument that are fallacious or extravagant, but they don't really matter – and she has to admit the idea of a hero being mauled to death by squirrels is beyond ridiculous. The central plank of his idea – that the peoples of ancient Latium, like many modern day primitives, cleaved to some sort of divine kingship rite in which the ruler, at the end of his strength, was sacrificed for the good of his people – still seems sound. Moreover, savage rite or not, Evelyn simply can't help but believe the principle a good one. No-one in their right mind should want or tolerate a weak King. It is entirely right he should be disposed of when his time is up: the modern habit of allowing such rulers to continue past their prime seems as ridiculous as the squirrels. She can hardly credit its evolution has been permitted. But now Mr Frazer is suggesting that, later on, the practise evolved – *really,* Evelyn thinks, *degenerated* – to demand the sacrifice of a horse instead of a man;

just as, at Thebes, a sacred ram was offered up once a year to the almighty Ammon. The animal went from being the embodiment of divinity, via the means of bringing death, to the sacrificial victim. Perhaps this is a clue: perhaps the ancients, like the present day British, underwent a process of degeneration, and in all the centuries that followed the civilised world never quite recovered from it. *No wonder Rome fell.* She remembers Diodorus again, and his civilised horror at the Carthaginians; remembers Caesar's horror at the Gauls. Somehow, the thought of all those deaths – which she once found too horrific to contemplate – no longer distresses her in quite the same way that it did. The Sacred Kings had to die, of course, because they were the representatives of their people; but the Carthaginian sacrifices, evil as they seem, were also necessary: vital, even. She is beginning to see that, now. The parents had to give their best beloved children to the flames because they knew the great Goddess would have accepted nothing less than perfection. Surely the question boiled down to this: what price a few screams to secure the vitality, the strength, the continuing survival, of a whole society?

But the Goddess stole my son. I did not offer him.

Evelyn slams shut the book, and on a sudden impulse puts it facing downwards, its spine facing away so that its title can't be seen, next to her empty glass. She takes a deep drag on her Camel cigarette, then leaves the sofa and tugs irritably on the bell pull for the housekeeper – for anyone – to come and attend her. She'll take tea, she has decided, and forget, if she can, about Mr Frazer. It's the respectable

Mammoth & Crow

thing to do at two in the afternoon, even if there's noone to take it with. The rain streams down the window pane, and large drops have begun to find their way down the chimney, making the hot coals hiss. Perhaps she should put on the wireless. The news will, of course, be frightfully dull, but the human voices will at least be company during tea, and there might be some modern music that she might enjoy, that might drown out – She might even get up and dance. Why not? Why shouldn't she dance if she wants to? This imposed solitude is entirely of her own making, after all. And no-one, except you and I, of whose judgement she has no idea, will be watching her.

The sitting room door opens. Evelyn turns, opening her mouth to bark sharply at the aged housekeeper for her tardiness, even though the wait hasn't been a long one by the old woman's standards. But to her great surprise, it's the new gardener. He's carrying a tray.

"I wanted tea – " Evelyn begins. Her voice trails off. Johnny comes into the room with the tea tray balanced in his hands, and shuts the door behind him with his foot. "How did you know?" Evelyn says.

"Annie mentioned that it was your habit to ring for tea at two, so I offered to bring it up to you."

Evelyn doesn't quite know what to say to this. It isn't, and has never been, her habit to take tea at this or any hour; and she has the sneaking feeling she should send the gardener straight away again with a flea in his ear for his presumption. But he's setting the tray down on the coffee table, and she can't help but notice it's a beautifully presented arrangement, on a white crocheted linen cloth, with sugar and milk in a

Jack Wolf

delicate blue flowered china bowl and jug, which perfectly matches the single cup and the small, steaming, teapot. It also contains a small cake on a little silver stand, and a tiny flower vase.

"Oh, Johnny," she finds herself saying. "Thank you."

"Don't mention it, Mrs Murray." The gardener bends his neck – not enough for the movement to constitute a bow, but certainly in a respectful gesture. He makes as if to leave the room.

"Please, Johnny," Evelyn says, unable to stop herself. "Stay a moment."

The new gardener stops in his tracks, and turns. "Of course, Mrs Murray, if you want me."

"I do want you," says Evelyn quickly. "I mean – I want you to stay and talk to me. Where did you come from, Johnny? You're not Cornish, are you? I can tell by your voice."

"No, Mrs Murray. I grew up in Hampshire."

"Oh, please," Evelyn says impulsively. "Call me Evelyn. I can't stand it – being surrounded all the time by servants, with no-one to talk to."

"But I am a servant, Madam," says Johnny.

"But you weren't born to be one, were you? I can tell. I'm sure something very unfortunate must have happened to have brought you to take up the position of a gardener."

"Let's say my circumstances were changed, unexpectedly," Johnny answers. "More than that, Mrs Murray, I'd rather not say."

"Oh! I'm sorry. I didn't mean to pry. But you must admit it's very curious – a man like you, appearing out of nowhere, asking for a job. Where did you go to school?"

"It was a small public school, and quite a new one. You won't have heard of it."

"Take tea with me," Evelyn offers, surprising herself with her own spontaneity. "Go to the kitchen and fetch another cup. No-one need know."

The gardener smiles. "I'd be honoured – Evelyn," he says.

When he has left the room, Evelyn puts out her cigarette, sits down quickly on the sofa, and straightens her stockings before taking out her compact and lipstick. She regards her reflection in the little mirror. There's no time to apply make up properly, she thinks, but a little lipstick won't hurt. It's not done to be seen looking so undressed – why, she is practically scruffy! If Johnny didn't have his own problems to deal with, he'd most probably not have wanted to be seen with her. The realisation gives her a brutal jolt.

Damn and blast this wretched place! How shocked Gerald would be to learn she was reduced to socialising with the gardener – was even worrying that she might not be good enough for him. *Poor Johnny,* she thinks. *I wonder if his family cast him off. I do hope it wasn't because of anything he did himself. He does seem very bohemian. But I suppose one would have to be, to survive such a drop in one's circumstances without losing one's wits.*

The door opens, without any knock, and the new gardener returns, carrying a cup and saucer, and a plate of small mixed biscuits, which he sets down on the tray.

"Shall I pour?" Evelyn offers, at once.

"If you like, Evelyn."

"Sit down, do," Evelyn says, indicating the

armchair in the corner of the room, beside the bay window. "Now, Johnny, you must promise you will not think of yourself as my gardener. In here, we're equal. Tell me about yourself. How long have you lived in Cornwall?"

"A few years. Before that I was in India for a spell, but it didn't work out."

"In India! How wonderful! But you say it did not do?"

"No. I don't have the temperament for office work. I spent too much time playing with the Maharajah's racehorses, and annoyed the Governor. It's a pity, in a way. My life would be much easier if I could just slip on a suit, knuckle down, and fit in, like other people do. But I don't mind. I'm happy as I am, right now."

"I'd love to visit India," Evelyn says. "All those little brown people running about."

"Hmm," says Johnny, thoughtfully, but he volunteers nothing more upon the topic.

Evelyn pours the tea, and plunges the spoon into the sugar.

"No, thank you," says Johnny, quickly.

"No? You can't mean that. Everyone takes sugar. It's practically a patriotic duty."

"Not me. I've taught myself to prefer the taste without."

"Well," Evelyn says. "Then I am in awe of your strength of character, for I never could." She hands him the cup and saucer.

Johnny smiles. "I've had to learn to control my appetites," he says. "Having little means of satisfying them."

For some reason, Evelyn finds herself

Mammoth & Crow

blushing. She hastily changes the subject. "Whatever does one do around here?" she says. "I fear I'm going to go quite mad from boredom. I was told the vicar was bearable enough, but I'm sure I'd find his company tedious. He has no family, as I understand, so his conversation will be all Bible and village gossip."

"And you don't want to become gossip," says Johnny, nodding.

"Oh, most certainly not!" exclaims Evelyn in horror. She pauses. "I suppose I already am."

"Probably. Little minds like to keep themselves busy with little things."

"Oh, yes," cries Evelyn. "Yes, they do! They are such horribly provincial people, here, Johnny! I wish I was in London. Although then I'd never have met you, which would have been a pity."

"Perhaps," Johnny says, slowly and carefully, his eyes fixed upon Evelyn's. "The vicar would probably say Providence was behind your coming here." He lifts his cup to his lips.

"Oh," exclaims Evelyn, softly. *Perhaps it was*, she thinks. Or if not Providence, as such – which she is now inclined to doubt – then perhaps, just perhaps, it was by design of some other ancient Deity, one no longer worshipped by degenerate, over-civilised modern man. Her heart thumps loudly in her chest. "Would you like some music?" she asks, jumping to her feet and rushing over to the wireless. Not waiting for his reply, she switches it on. At once, the strains of Count Basie's jazz orchestra fill the sitting room.

"Do you dance?" says Johnny, getting to his feet.

"To this? Don't be silly," Evelyn says. "I'll find

something else." She begins to fiddle with the radio knob, but can find only the dark grey glare of static.

"Yes, dance to this! I'll show you."

Johnny puts down his tea, and, crossing the room, gently removes Evelyn's half empty cup from her fingers, and places it on the mantelpiece. He takes her hand. She lets him. "This," he says, "is called the Lindy hop. Very popular among young Americans, especially the smart set. Come on."

The Lindy hop, Evelyn soon decides, is crazy, but fun. She's never let herself approve of jazz, for obvious reasons, but here, but now, in the presence of Johnny, who plainly loves it, she can feel something wonderful in the strange, disrupted rhythms and wildly syncopated phrases. Johnny has his hand upon her waist and is twirling and twisting her around the hearthrug, and her heart is thumping with a primitive excitement. *Oh!* she thinks, suddenly. It feels like – it *is* like, *exactly* like – participating in some ancient, tribal rite, for all that the music is as modern as can be. The music, the feral wildness of the jazz, is waking something inside her, transporting her soul back through time to Arica, to the wood: to the dark, secret worship of Dianic mystery.

"Oh!" she exclaims aloud, as the music finishes. "What a shame it's over!"

"Don't you get the opportunity to dance in London?" Johnny asks, surprised.

"Well, I'd like to, of course," Evelyn says. "But my husband isn't young. We don't tend to go out much as a couple. And one can't dance decently without one's husband."

"I'm not your husband, and you're dancing with me," Johnny points out.

"I know, but – " *Jazz isn't decent*, Evelyn almost says. The thought is followed straight away by the habitual reproof: a Good Wife and Mother does not… dance with men she doesn't know. Davenport would be disgusted by her, wouldn't he? *But,* she tells herself, *I do know Johnny;* and besides, out here, in the middle of nowhere, who's to know or care who she dances with, or to what sort of music?

"Aren't you being a little bit old fashioned?" Johnny says teasingly, as if he's been listening to her thoughts.

"Old fashioned?" Evelyn is astonished.

"Come on, old stick," says Johnny, with a wink, as the radio starts up again. "Time for another dance with a strange man?"

Has she been thinking aloud? Evelyn feels herself colouring. She ought to refuse him, of course, she thinks. But she ought never to have got up to dance in the first place, or offered him tea. She certainly ought never to have watched him working in the garden, especially without his shirt on, however enjoyable she found the sight. It's already too late for such silly regrets. And she doesn't want him to think her stiff and boring.

"Oh, yes," she says, brightly. She takes his hand. "Dance with me, then."

"Yes, Madam. Anything to oblige a lady." He bows.

"Oh, stop it, Johnny," Evelyn says, with a laugh. Johnny spins her out around in front of him, and then pulls her in close against his chest. It's a slower dance. She finds herself, to her astonishment, giggling like a schoolgirl.

She hasn't laughed, she realises, since the

stillbirth. That's true: but it isn't the whole truth. The truth is Evelyn Murray hasn't laughed, not properly, since the day she began to realise precisely what it was going to be like being irrevocably bound to Gerald, whose personality was so different from her own, despite his superficially similar politics. Professor Murray's world was well behaved, decent, respectable, quiet: his idea of fun to sit silently in the drawing room with his head buried in his *Daily Mail*, finishing the crossword. For Professor Murray's wife, there would be no parties, no visits to the theatre or the picture house, no trips to the seaside, and certainly, absolutely, no dancing. Ladies' tennis would be acceptable, of course, but only because that's something she could do respectably without him. She wouldn't even to be able to attend Union meetings and political rallies. This, to Evelyn, has always been the biggest outrage.

"But home should be enough for you, Evie," Gerald would say, his small confused eyes blinking uncomfortably as he looked up briefly from his paper. "Why on Earth could you want anything more?"

Gerald has no passion, she knows; neither for her, nor for the Fascist cause he led her to believe he cared about: the cause to which she would gladly have devoted her life. She should have guessed back then that he would be the sort of man who'd one day banish her to the middle of nowhere, with no hope of return. But perhaps, deep down, she did guess it: that day, after all, was the day when she stopped laughing.

And now the music, which has transported her into the past, is carrying her forwards, like a river crashing over rocks. She's helpless in its grasp. She wants to be helpless. It's easy, suddenly, to forget she's married to Gerald – and oh, how she wants to forget him! Him, Leto, all of it! She is rushing towards a different world: one in which she never met him, never threw away her youth on an old man whose time and vital energy was spent, who can not give her the sons she longs for, or anything else. *Dr Gaskell was right*, she realises, with a shock. *The problem really is one of Heredity:* and it does not originate with Evelyn.

But now the song is finishing. Johnny is letting the dance come to an end, and releasing his hold on Evelyn's waist. He steps back, smiling. Then he reaches out, and delicately lifts a strand of hair that has been floating in front of her face, tucking it away behind her ear.

Evelyn stares at him. Her heart is racing. *Why did he do that?* She knows exactly why he did that. *What if he kisses me? Should I let him?*

No, no! Certainly not! She is a married woman: in this world at least. Yet she can still feel the presence of that other Evelyn, that younger self who is still free, still has a chance, hovering just beyond the limits of her senses, encouraging her onward. *What if I leave Gerald?* she asks that other self, wildly. *After all, he's made it very plain he doesn't want me. What if I give him up?*

Impossible! The Good Fascist Woman, according to the creed, is wife and mother come what may. And a good wife, everybody knows, doesn't leave her husband just because of some slight inattentiveness on his part. That's what men are like, after all. A woman should never expect to be the centre of a man's universe. Gerald is a busy man, and an important one.

But he can't give me sons, she answers, in agony. *He is broken. Defective. Degenerate.*

"I should be getting back to work," Johnny says.

"Oh!" Evelyn flushes. "Yes," she says, embarrassed, suddenly brisk. "Yes, Johnny, of course you must. Thank you."

"You mustn't thank me, Mrs Murray," Johnny says quietly.

"No, I suppose that it is not quite done.... oh, but you mustn't see yourself as a servant, Johnny. You're not really of that class. I'm sure your misfortune, whatever it is, will prove to be only temporary."

"I hope so," Johnny says. He inclines his head. "Good afternoon, Madam."

"Good afternoon, Johnny." Evelyn says.

Chiswick, London.
April 25th, 1927

Phillip,

I was extremely displeased by the tone of your reply, and I have to say that it has put me severely out of temper. I did not show it to your future stepmother, who does not deserve to be troubled by such cruel and unfounded allegations as you put forward. I have no doubt at all regarding her affection and loyalty, and I must insist that you make the endeavour to perceive her in a more positive light. I am fully aware of the difference in our ages, but I am also aware, as you, who have never met her, are not, of her unusual maturity and profoundly sensible character: qualities which are not always found in women of twice her years. She is no 'gold-digger', and I resent your use of the phrase. Kindly refer to her with the respect that is her due. Likewise, remember that I am your father, and refrain from addressing me with such contempt. I am disgusted to think that you or your uncle would consider my attempts to discover your whereabouts to be 'bullying'. As your father, it is my right and duty to know where you are living, and to ensure that you conduct yourself in a manner that does not bring shame on this family. I am deeply concerned by your description of your trusted accomplice, as any man who would conspire with another against his father cannot, in my opinion, be trusted. I repeat again that you will give up this nonsensical and destructive behaviour, which I can only conclude is an attempt to punish me for choosing to marry again. The Headmaster has now retracted his offer to allow you back in school, so you have no choice but to come home. Once your last month's allowance is spent, I will be sending no more money.

 Awaiting your reply,

  Your

   Father.

Chapter Thirteen:
Halek-dhwer

Leto has come to a decision. She will cross into the Otherworld, and she will find Huma, or she will die trying. She spends an hour lying on her bed with her eyes closed, willing her body to shift along with her mind into the beautiful place that she can see so clearly in her imagination, but, so far, it has been to no avail. She is moving through the steppe-lands like a ghost, able to see and hear and almost touch, but not truly experience; and what is worse, she's trying so hard that any unexpected noise within the house – a door slamming, Nanny Gould's heavy tread outside the bedroom door, hammering from the garden as Johnny the new gardener sets to work despite the rain on mending the derelict summerhouse – seems to have the power to summon her straight back to the present. Although, she admits, the third time she is jolted rudely out of her daydream, at least this unwanted vigilance on the part of her physical senses will mean there's no risk of her getting stuck accidentally on the other side, and abandoning her body permanently. Perhaps, the trick to getting through for real is to find a Gateway, a door into one of the hollow hills, and walk straight through it. That must be what Martin did, although he didn't know that he was doing it.

But where are the entrances? What do they look like? How can anybody recognise them for what they are, without being told what to look for? Who can she ask for guidance? Not Martin, for all that he's been there already – not only did he not know what he was doing, but he can remember so frustratingly little of the whole experience. He isn't even sure of the message he was told to give to Horsefeathers – and that message, Leto knows, must be really important. The faceless people of the steppe-lands would never have spoken to him at all if it hadn't been. They'd have just left him wandering, lost, until the sun turned cold or he starved to death, whichever was the sooner. *They should have given it to me,* she thinks, resentfully. *I'd never have forgotten it; and I'd have found out who Horsefeathers is and taken it to him by now. I'm sure he must be the wizard.*

It is approaching lunchtime, and Leto suddenly realises she's rather hungry. Perhaps that's the problem. Perhaps, if she wasn't hungry, she might be able to summon up the willpower, or belief, or even magic, to create a Gateway into the Otherworld right here, right now, in this very room. After all, it's already at least halfway out of the human world – she made sure of that when she began piddling it into a wolf den. She calls Nanny Gould to bring her a ham sandwich, and a glass of lemonade. After she's finished both, she lies back on her bed, and resumes her concentration.

So, how, Leto wonders, *can I make a Gateway?* Alice went through the Looking Glass, but Leto doesn't think that will work for her. Anyway, there's no mirror in her little bedroom. She closes her eyes, and instead of heading straight out to the mammoth steppe, pictures the musty little room in which she's lying. Here's the latticed sash window set deep into the whitewashed wall, with the garden and blue sky beyond; here's the fireplace, with its cold ash that no-one, as yet, has carried out, here's the old black iron bedstead, with Leto's body clearly visible on top of the embroidered counterpane. Can creating a Gateway be as simple as picturing the thing into existence? Where should Leto Murray picture it, if so? What would such a Gate look like? The process turns out to be harder than she had hoped. Nothing seems to make sense as a portal to the Otherworld, even those things that are, by their very nature, portal like. The window stubbornly refuses to lead anywhere except the garden, the chimney to the slippery, red tiled roof. In the end, Leto settles for imagining that the head of the iron bedstead has been wrought into the shape of an archway, and that the wall behind the arch does not exist; and finally, her reluctant imagination proves agreeable. The wall turns transparent, and then melts like ice. Beyond it, Leto can see the steppe-lands, bathed in brilliant sunshine underneath a violet sky. Excited, she opens her eyes, and wriggles about on the bed, hoping – no, honestly expecting – to see the wall has vanished here, too. It has not.

It was never a real Gate, Leto realises. It's a crushing disappointment. The Gate existed only in her mind, and there she does not need it. She can imagine her mind into the Otherworld just like that, snap! – by closing her eyes. Suddenly furious at the fact, she sits up, and punches the plaster with her little fist. How dare it be so solid, so real – when, really, really, it is not?

When I do find a Gateway, Leto thinks, *I'll go through it and never come back. I wonder if anybody will miss me? Martin might, I suppose. I don't suppose Johnny will. He hardly knows me, after all. But I think I might miss him.*

But it will be worth it, if I can be with Huma.

She lies on her back, and determinedly closes her eyes. If she can't take her body – oh, inconvenient, too, too solid flesh, that will not melt – she'll have to travel in the usual way, at least for now. She lets herself sink into the Victorian feather bolster. The real world will not matter. She'll make herself forget it.

She lies there, silent, still, counting her breaths. She can see the archway – it's still there, in her imagination – and in her imagination, her dream self takes one final breath, and steps through it.

Her flesh grows cold. Her heartbeat grows fainter.

On the other side of reality, the river awakes, laughing. She has company again.

Leto knows exactly where she is, of course, and it's such a relief to be here. The archway has brought her to the rocky hillside that overlooks the valley, passing between the huge vertical stones where she once met the crow, and has clambered up into the crags to get a better view of the plains that lie beyond the edge of the uplands. She's very fond of this view. It's reassuring to look into the far distance, and see no trace whatsoever of any modern human activity; to know that Bransquite, and Camelford, and London are all many thousands of years away, and cannot touch her. She's safe here, even if she doesn't know where Huma is; even if she can't wholly trust the river. She wonders whether, if she looks hard enough, she might find the faceless men, and ask them to give her the message they previously entrusted to Martin. But there is nothing. Perhaps the shades only permit themselves to be seen when it suits them.

Would it matter, she thinks suddenly, *if I did get stuck?* Would it really, truly matter? She might be only a ghost here, but being a ghost feels better than being alive in a world that doesn't want her. Maybe this is as good as anything is ever going to get.

Pondering this outrageous notion – and she can't help but find it shocking, even though it feels so natural and obvious – Leto slowly clambers down the rocky hillside. This is the spot where she took off her shoes. And suddenly, there they are: twin t-bar leather mementos of a time that hasn't happened yet, a place that does not yet exist. They look lonely; their presence in this world completely alien, unwarranted, an intrusion. She feels sorry for leaving them.

Leto sits down on the hillside, and picks up her abandoned shoes. They're quite dry; either there has been no rain or it has since evaporated, and the socks inside them, though a little stiff and spiky with grass seeds, are fit to wear once she's given them a shake. She draws them over her toes. It's a good thing she began this journey in bare feet. What has happened to the moccasins that appeared before? She hasn't seen them since the moment she woke up. Perhaps the kindly land was loaning them to her, out of its vast store of remembered things.

Fastening her shoes, Leto continues down the hillside, finally plunging waist deep into the long grass that has grown to cover the valley floor. The large grazing herds haven't been here for a while – when they come, this turf will be mown smoother than a carpet. Eventually reaching the river, she dips her fingertips into the icy waters. "Naiad," she calls. "Please come out to play."

The river has been lying low, flooding darkly over the little rocky waterfall on to the gravel bed, quiet and steady as a moment of silence. But immediately on Leto's invitation, the fluid rises in a swirling vertical jet of translucent, bubbling white, which resolves itself rapidly into the familiar shape of the river maiden. *Yes!* the waters answer, clapping their sparkling hands and sending tiny drops of water showering in all directions. *Catch us, if you can!*

Leto thinks she has already made her decision. It's why she has come down the slope, and woken up the river – who knows, after all, only one game. Here, says the Red Queen to Alice, it takes all the running you can do to stay in one place.

"I will!" Leto says.

The river laughs.

The current is fast. Leto finds it hard to keep up. There's no point, she knows, in asking the river to slow down; that's as impossible a thing as slowing time. And it's useless, too, to ask the Naiad – whose shape she can still see, somehow, contained within the larger body of the water – to come closer, or to wait, because the very act of changing course will change her nature, and then she will no longer be the same person, or remember Leto. So she runs, her attention fixed on the shadowy form, and her breath coming in burning pants. Her chest aches, her legs sting from the whipping grasses. It seems she is as unsporty in this world as in the real one, for all she hasn't brought along her physical body. But still, she runs. This is the Naiad's game, and Leto has agreed to play it. Her mother – no, Evelyn Murray, the wicked witch – always insists it's vital never to walk away from a match until it is completely over. Never, ever, concede defeat before you're down. Besides, Leto has a feeling that the river wants to show her something – and unless she follows her to the very end of the channel, she'll never find out what. She hopes – secretly, desperately – that it's Huma.

Eventually, the long grass gives way to scrub, and then gradually to a creeping woodland, unlike anything Leto has ever seen on her wanderings across the mammoth steppe. Here, young birch and alder saplings vie with one another for the light, and brambles are beginning to crowd along the river bank. She has to slow down: she can't run, not here; but the river is now flowing more slowly, too. As the wood grows denser, which it seems to be doing with startling speed, the light is growing greener, and now dimmer, until before long she finds herself in a thickly nettled patch of woodland, shrieking with unfamiliar bird songs, and full of biting midges. Now she's especially glad of her shoes and socks, and grateful to the land for having looked after them for her. The air here feels cold compared with the open plains. Not damp; just cold, in the way of a cave or an abandoned building that is never exposed to the light of the summer sun. She shivers. Where on Earth is she? This is plainly not the Otherworld as she has come to know it. She can't even place this dense wood in her remembered view over the eastern plains. It's as if it has sprung up from the earth in the time it has taken her to reach it. Only the Naiad remains familiar, gliding underneath the surface of the dark green water, smiling up at Leto and waving occasionally, like a Carnival Princess in a parade.

Leto doesn't know how long she has spent walking, either; time, in this wood, seems even less important than it does upon the steppe-lands. Nor can she be certain how far she has walked; all she knows for sure is that the grassy valley now seems very, very far away. But finally the gloom of the understory gives way to brilliant sunlight: a fallen oak, as mighty as a church, has left a space through which the sun can penetrate. Immediately, Leto feels much warmer.

The river is flowing into a beaver pond. Leto takes the opportunity, while the Naiad carefully navigates the dam, to sit down on the wide trunk of the fallen oak, and recollect herself. The sun feels delightful on the top crown of her head. She lies down flat, and lets it warm her body while she looks up at the violet sky. So, this is still her Otherworld, then; she'd almost begun to wonder. She's surprised by the sudden recollection that she's dreaming. *Better not think about that*, she tells herself, sternly: the last thing she wants to do, right now, is wake up.

There is a scrabbling in the clearing. Leto looks up, wondering whether it could be the beaver who built the dam. To her astonishment, a herd of twenty or more wild boar piglets, looking just like a handful of stripy humbugs that have grown legs, is emerging from the edge of the clearing, rooting in between the foxgloves. She props herself up on her elbow, and watches. *Wild boar didn't arrive in Britain till the Mesolithic,* she remembers. *That's what it says in the Encyclopedia. So, is this part of the Otherworld a different time?*

The Naiad is slowly circling the beaver pool, feet first, caught in an eddy. She tries to lift her hand in a wave, but the water is flowing too slowly, and she's unable to summon the energy. Leto feels sorry for her. It's no more pleasant to be trapped than it is to be a ghost.

Go on without me, comes the river's voice. It's little more now than a whisper. *When I next pass through the dam, I will break apart. I may not know you on the other side.* She sounds sad.

"Where should I go?" Leto asks.

Down the stream, down the stream. Find the Gatekeeper.

Something, unseen, silently brushes against the back of Leto's neck. She looks up in surprise. The clearing is slowly filling with huge, black, butterflies. They are pouring down from the canopy, coming faster now: hundreds, no, thousands of insects, insects the size of bats, their soft wings fluttering dark purple in the sunlight. They are settling on the forest floor and on the rotting tree trunk, reaching out with their long spiral tongues with all the eagerness of vultures on a carcass, lapping up the decay as if it were nectar.

If I die here, Leto thinks suddenly, *what will happen to me? Will I die in Bransquite, too? Or will I only die here, and there lie asleep forever and ever, like Sleeping Beauty? Or will I just wake up?* She gets up quickly, and scampers across the clearing. The butterflies part and merge in her wake, like smoke.

Leto is trying to follow the river channel as best she can, but it's growing harder to tell where it leads through the campions and foxgloves that grow thick along the bank, and more difficult to press on now the beaver clearing is behind her. What will she do if the flow should split, as slow moving rivers sometimes do? Which way should she choose? But just as she's beginning to worry, the dense tree cover begins to thin out, and now the river is easy to follow again, as it weaves through a low lying landscape of low walled arable fields full of tall wheat and sweet smelling barley, occasionally punctuated by homesteads of differing shapes and styles – some round, some square, some built in the shapes of ships – from whose thatched roofs woodsmoke rises in soft plumes. *There are people here,* Leto realises, with a shock. *Human people, or, at least, human shaped: shades, faceless men.* She draws to a halt.

Who are you? the river asks her, suddenly.

"I don't know." Right here, right now, it's the truth. Leto walks slowly along the bank, keeping pace with the creature whose face has just appeared in the dark water. It looks like a fish, with large round eyes, no nose, and a hard, scaly mouth.

Why are you here?

"I was playing with you – one of you – a you who isn't here yet. She got trapped in the beaver pond, a long, long time ago, and then she told me to find the Gatekeeper. But I don't know how."

Have you tried summoning it? the fish asks, rolling its eyes.

"Is it as easy as that?"

I didn't say it would be easy.

It would be worth a shot, Leto agrees – though she's not really sure why the river has told her to find this unknown Gatekeeper, when the only person she really wants to find is Huma. It's one of those magical things that makes sense at the time, and in its specific context, but afterwards makes none whatsoever. *Still,* she thinks, perhaps the Gatekeeper, whatever it is, will be able to take her home. She has been walking for years now, after all, and her ghost legs are as heavy as lead. The violet sky seems to be pressing on her head. She wonders if her real body, lying on the bed, is all right. Perhaps it's hungry, or cold, or uncomfortable. She can't tell. Really, she can't tell. Would being cold or hungry in that world make her feel exhausted here? She doesn't know.

She thanks the fish for its advice, and sits down in the barley.

"Gatekeeper?" she says, experimentally. "Are you here?"

There's no reply. Unsurprised by this failure, Leto rests for a second or so, then gets to her feet. Plainly, this will call for a proper, dramatic, stone age style summoning, just like in the picture of the Midsummer's Day Druid calling forth the sun, which she has looked at many times in the Encyclopedia. Breaking off a stem of barley for a staff, and picking up a sharp edged white stone for a knife, she throws her arms wide, and raises her face to the sky. "Gatekeeper!" she shouts. "I call thee hither! Come!" Hopefully, she thinks, it won't matter that she isn't at Stonehenge. "Please?" she adds, in case she's being rude.

Nothing happens. Leto stands still, arms raised, waving the barley stalk. A skylark skitters overhead. She feels a little silly. Then her eye catches sight of a movement in the barley. Something is coming through the field.

It's big, Leto realises, with a sudden apprehension. Very big – perhaps the size of a carthorse, and yet – despite the obvious trace of movement through the field, the flattening of the barley, the deep sunk, long clawed footprints that are now appearing, with horrifying speed, in the soft, chalky earth – she can see nothing of it but a shimmering in the air, a thickening of the light. A musty, animal smell begins to fill her nostrils. *Not mammoth, she thinks, nor crow, nor even wolf.* She should be afraid. She should be terrified. But instead, some ancient, blood, bone, grit-stone instinct tells her to close her eyes and put out her hand towards the looming presence. *Yes,* she thinks, *that's what it is, a presence – a presentness –* and though she cannot see, her fingers graze against dry, scaly skin, and soft, warm fur. *Like Huma,* she thinks, remembering how she once pressed her face against the rough hide of the mammoth's trunk, and how it felt like lichen covered stone.

"Lizard-bear," Leto whispers, softly, realising the truth. "You're Martin's Lizard-bear."

I am the Guardian. I am the Gatekeeper. I am Halek-dhwer.

"I think I'm Wolf," says Leto.

Open your eyes, the Gatekeeper says, and Leto does so.

The creature rearing up before her is immense; bigger and heavier than a modern grizzly on its powerful hind legs, which are attached to its body at right angles, like those of a crocodile. It has thick brown fur on its back, and a soft, wide, greyish muzzle, but its stomach and continually thrashing tail are covered in rough scales, like plate armour, or the belly of a gigantic fish. Its huge, reptilian forepaws are equipped with black bear claws so long and thick that if it so desired it could as easily rip her limb from limb as a cruel schoolboy might pull wings off a fly. Two claws, Leto notices, are missing. The creature's powerful jaws, four feet above her head, sway forwards and back with its every breath. Its fearsome teeth are long, white daggers, and there are two rows of them, like a shark's. They are glistening with spit.

The Lizard-bear looks down at her, measuringly, out of bright, black, crow-like eyes, which are ringed with tiny black feathers. *Not Wolf,* it says. *Not yet. You are just a ghost. You must go back to your own world.*

"It's not my world," says Leto. "I hate it there. And I don't know the way back. I chased the river. I'm lost."

Climb on my back, says the Lizard-bear. *I will take you home.*

Leto immediately thinks of the fox and the gingerbread man. Can she trust the Lizard-bear to keep its word, and not to spin around half way and eat her, whole, in one snap? But bears are trustworthy: at least in stories.

"All right," she says. She remembers not to offer thanks to an Otherworldly being, even in politeness. The Encyclopedia says that to do so would be terribly dangerous. The Encyclopedia, let me tell you, is telling the truth. "What can I give you in exchange?"

The Lizard-bear drops to all fours. In this position it has almost the shape, if not the size, of a giant otter, long and sinuous; but its head is still level with Leto's own. It looks at her. *Its expression is like a rock,* Leto thinks. *Timeless as time itself.*

Freedom, the Gatekeeper answers, gravely. The ground shakes with the power of its voice. *I have been here for a long time, little ghost. Watching. Waiting. Protecting. Now I am tired and broken, and it is time for me to have peace.*

"How can I give you that?"

Do you offer it to me?

"I don't know. Yes, I suppose. If I can. But I don't know how."

Look to your mother, the Gatekeeper says.

"I don't like my mother very much."

The Lizard-bear doesn't answer, but kneels down, lowering its massive head and shoulders to the ground for Leto to climb on. Clutching the thick fur in her fingers, she scrambles on board, burying her face in the soft animal smell. A mix of fur and downy feathers, as soft as those of a duck's breast, tickle her nose.

Then the monster turns, and with the same astonishingly silent speed that characterised its arrival, it begins to run, crashing through the barley. A cloud of dust and milky scented chaff rises in its wake. Leto clings on tightly, her arms round its neck – although the lizard-bear is so huge she can only reach a little way. She suddenly remembers being very, very young, and being carried upstairs by Nanny Gould; or if not Nanny, then somebody who seemed very big and warm and kind. How certain she felt then, how safe. This is not the same sort of feeling, not at all.

It's a long ride, a wild ride. The Lizard-bear runs through arable fields, and round the edges of small villages where faceless men chop wood, and hooded women sit in groups on roundhouse doorsteps, grinding flour in drystone mortars. Eventually, it reaches the uplands, and its wild undulating gallop gradually slows to a walk. Leto lifts her head. She's very glad it hasn't eaten her, like a gingerbread girl. She sits up, and feeling less tired than she did before, looks around. The steep slope rears before her in the west, green and grey and purple with heather, gorse and stone. *This isn't Huma's steppe,* she realises. It is the moor as she and Martin walked upon it. She looks west.

Already below her, in the distance, she can see the river, winding through the fertile farmlands of her own Britain, toward the south coast. She can see country roads, and villages, and towns: there is Bransquite, and there, Camelford. But farther on, a long way downstream, she can see what she can only describe as a strange oily bubble within which lies a location where the river does, indeed, split, as she speculated that it might, but into many channels, not just two: and the land through which these channels flow is constantly flickering and changing, from woodland to farmland, to fume filled city, to flooded wasteland, to blue sea; as if the world doesn't have any idea what it's supposed to be. The confusion, for all that it's a long way in the distance – *somewhere in the future,* she thinks – makes her eyes hurt.

'What is that?" she asks.

The Gatekeeper stops climbing, and looks back. *The men of your world who came here with the eagle legions called it Pavor Potentia. The sea invaders knew it as Ragnarök. The tonsured monks called it Apocalypse. A thousand years ago, it was still smaller than a human eye. I could contain it;*

could protect both our worlds from it. But now, it has grown. And I am not strong, I am not whole, as I was then.

"But what is it?"

It is a Moment – a terrifying Moment, coming into being; an event as yet undecided, undetermined, unfixed; but its potentiality is growing. Someday, the land will show you how it came to be, as it showed me. There is a nightmare threat upon us, little ghost: terrible, colossal, extinctive. If Pavor Potentia should ever touch its reflection in time and in space, it will break through into your reality. Then millions of your kind will die, and millions more of every other living thing, including wolves, and cockroaches, and crows. Your world, and this world, and everything they are, and everything they represent, will be blown away like mist upon the moor. Only the bare land will remember what has happened, for the land remembers everything. Existence, in some lowly, simpler, form, will go on.

"Can't you try to stop it?"

I no longer have the power, little ghost.

"But – " Leto's voice falters.

The Gatekeeper continues to climb.

Finally, they reach the highlands, and Leto recognises the crags. They turns again toward the north, and head into the stone thicket that conceals the triangular entrance to the wizard's den. Here, the Lizard-bear stops, and kneels for Leto to dismount. "Do not forget our agreement," it says. "When your Moment comes, this shall be your Gate, as it was mine. Now pass through it without fear. You will wake."

Leto slips from the great creature's neck. She

turns to thank it – forgetting, for a split second, her manners – but stops herself in time.

The vast bulk of the Lizard-bear blots out the sky. And yet there's something else – a vague flickering, a fuzzy uncertainty to its outline, as if there is a shadow moving underneath the skin, trying to make itself visible. *Is that a human shape?* Leto squints. *A child?* She thinks she can almost make out long, dark, braided hair; clothing cut and sewn from finely tooled leather, worn beneath a thick, fur cloak; a bear-claw necklace. But she can't be sure.

"Are you the wizard?" she asks, in sudden trepidation, as the thought occurs to her.

No, the creature answers, with a low growl. *I am not.*

"Do you not like him?"

He is a grave robber, thunders the Lizard-bear. *An arrogant, flippant, nought-but-human fool who thinks that people are his to play with, and fate his to control. He has no notion of the crimes he has committed, and the harms he will cause, or the punishment he will face. He is a fool, little ghost. A fool. Now, go.*

Leto runs into the tunnel.

Chapter Fourteen:
Names

Martin Stone cannot stop worrying about the *Shaydim*. He must be getting older faster than he knows, because he still can't settle in his mind the question of whether his meeting with them was real or not, and every time he decides it was, a small cold voice of reason in his head tells him it most certainly was not. Talking to Leto, rather than helping him, has paradoxically made him feel more unsure. Something in the way she seized upon the notion and gobbled it up has made him anxious that she's treating the whole thing as a game of make-believe. Yes, Martin knows the world is often strange, and things happen that adults find hard to understand, and difficult to believe – but are those things ever of such a profound magnitude of strangeness as this? Yes, he can talk to birds, but could he really, truly, have crossed into another world? Can reality really be a faerie tale? It seems impossible, in the plain light of the afternoon, with turnips to be weeded, Miss Fox scribbling her magazine piece in the kitchen, and the kettle whistling on the hob. So, he asks himself, did he dream the whole thing, and then let his imagination –

and Leto's – blow it up into something it was not? Of course, he did. But there's still the matter of the new gardener, who, for all he's cleaned himself up and put on fresh clothing, Martin is increasingly sure really is the tramp in the Homburg hat who leapt over the stone hedge. And if he *is*, his presence raises other questions. He remembers how the tramp said, clearly as a bell: "Felicitations of the moment". Not of the afternoon, or the day, but the *moment*: one precise, definitive instant in time and space that is gone almost as soon as it has happened and can never recur again. He remembers how Leto uses the word—with a capital 'M', he's sure – to describe a place and a point in time where the Otherworld and this one are in contact, each mirroring the other, and he can't shake off the feeling that the tramp was using it in the same way. But how could the man have known *that* meaning, when he had, at that point, anyway, never met Leto? *Are Leto's Moments,* Martin wonders, *real?* His common sense screams *No* - but on the other hand, he is the boy who talks to birds.

Just suppose, he argues with himself, *suppose, for the sake of it, they are. Suppose there is an Otherworld, and I crossed into it, and came back again. Couldn't someone else have found his way there, too?*

"Tell Horsefeathers he must choose swiftly, and choose well." The words ring like a crow's yelp in his memory. He still can't recall the remainder of the message.

Could the tramp be Horsefeathers? If he is, then is there anything to lose, Martin asks himself, if he follows his intuition and gives Johnny the *Shaydim's* message? If everything is just a figment of his and Leto's imaginations, nothing will happen beyond the new gardener thinking him a little odd. But his perplexity will be the proof that Martin, right now, thinks he wants: confirmation that the whole thing really *is* nothing but a game. He doesn't want to have wandered into an Otherworld, and met the creatures that dwell there in the shadows and the cracks. The idea it should be possible to do such things, especially without intending to do them, is frightening in a way he can't articulate in any language, which stirs a strange queasiness in the pit of his stomach.

What if the whole thing turns out to be real? "Choose swiftly" doesn't sound very encouraging. And "choose well" could mean any number of things. Choose what? Or whom? For what?

He wishes he could ask Miss Fox for advice – but he knows his foster Aunt has scanty patience with faery tales and moor side stories. They're one of very few things that can make her usually kindly manner grow distinctly brisk. She would tell him in a matter-of-fact tone of voice to stop daydreaming and live in the real world, where there are turnips to be weeded and tea to be made, and eggs to be collected from the farm. His grandmother would have said the same: that it's not healthy or wise to pay too much attention to an overactive imagination, even if one is a boy who can speak to the birds.

But what if –

Martin's right back where he started. Perhaps, he decides, finally, in frustration, if he calls in at Ignatius Hart's old house, not to speak to Leto about it – although he knows he *will* – but to catch a second glimpse of the new gardener, he'll at least be able to confirm whether he's the tramp or not. Then he can decide whether or not to believe that he could also be Horsefeathers, and either give him the message from the *Shaydim* or withhold it. It will at least mean he is doing something, and no longer worrying in silence – because that's getting him nowhere fast.

He puts on his raincoat and galoshes, and picks up an umbrella against the July rain, and then shouts to Miss Fox that he's going to Bransquite to get the eggs. "Is it all right if I call at Leto on the way?" he asks.

"Yes, dear," Miss Fox answers absently, failing to correct his grammar. She is engrossed in the composition of her review of Daphne du Maurier's latest novel, which will be for *The Lady*. She hopes to get at least twelve shillings for it. "But don't be back late."

"I won't," Martin answers. He picks up the wicker egg basket, and sets off. The crows rise briefly from the ridge pole of the roof, then, seeing his intended direction, settle again, shaking their feathers and squawking crossly.

"You could come with me, you know," Martin points out. "There is nothing keeping you out of the village."

The crows do not move. Their martyred disapproval, however, follows him along the lane. Martin shakes his head, in mild exasperation. Birds can be trying creatures while they are moulting their feathers. And when they are not.

Martin chooses to visit the farm first, in case Leto asks him to stay for any length of time. He fills his basket with twelve large, white, oval eggs for Miss Fox, and then, pressured by the pink faced farmer's wife, takes another. "For yourself," the woman says, "for being such a kind boy, and helping her." She looks at him sideways out of sly blue-black eyes, like ripe sloes. "Bad business about that boat, isn't it? Don't know who the ruddy Yanks think they are."

"What boat?" Martin asks.

"The St Louis, of course. Loaded with Jews, it is. They tried docking in Cuba and in Florida, but nobody will have 'em. Last I heard, they were returning to Europe."

Martin does not react.

"I hope they don't try to land it here," the woman continues. "It's not as if we haven't taken more than our fair share in this country already."

"Thank you for the extra egg," Martin says again. "But I must be going now."

"You're more than welcome, my handsome."

No, Martin thinks. *I'm not.* He walks quickly out of the farmyard.

Who is on the St Louis? Martin can't help wondering. *Who are they all, these people whom nobody wants?* Any one of them, under different circumstances, could have been him, or his grandmother, or any one of the Rabbis and Torah scholars who sat round her table on Shabbat. Are any of them the relatives who were unable to take him in when his grandmother died? What will happen to them now? Will they be forced to circle the Atlantic, searching for any port in a storm that has nothing to do with maritime weather?

He wonders why Miss Fox has told him nothing about it. She isn't the sort of person who would not have cared. Is she trying to protect him? It's kind of her to try, but knowledge can't hurt him, not now. After what happened to the Berlin orphanage, Martin Elijah Rosenstein has few illusions left about public attitudes toward Jews, either in Germany or outside it – though plainly things are much, much worse in the old country. *It's safer here,* he thinks, but still, his foster Aunt is right; better to keep his head down and his identity secret, than risk being pelted with eggs instead of given them. Not all Brits are open, caring people. But it's still a shock to think that Florida would turn back refugees so callously. His grandmother admired the USA immensely, and four of her brothers – Martin's great-uncles – emigrated there in the late 1890s. She often spoke longingly of the place as a new and promised land of liberty, truth and justice, to which the children of Israel might openly belong – unlike old, hostile, Europe. This kvetching annoyed the Rabbi, who pointed out that such tolerance was, in fact, already to be found in Berlin. Both she and he would have been heartbroken to learn they'd both been wrong.

We're all searching for an Otherworld, Martin thinks, suddenly. *Not one of us is truly free in this one.* Somehow, although he's thinking of his family, and those generations of Jews who since the rise of Rome have moved and settled and moved on again, an orphan nation forced into a constant motion, the realisation reminds him of Leto. Her people – or at least, her mother's – seem free enough. Free to say and do whatever they like, and care as little as they like for anyone they trample in the process. Modernity is theirs to command, and command it they will – building, mechanising, industrialising towers in the sky. But Leto hates it. She wants to leave it. It's not at all the same thing as his grandmother's yearning for the USA, but perhaps it is fourth cousin to it.

Martin turns the corner, and a white petal lands at his feet. Looking up, he realises he has reached the granite gateway of Ignatius Hart's old house. The now overblown climbing roses are waving sadly in the damp breeze. He stops, suddenly unsure. He isn't certain, now, whether he really wants to spy upon the gardener or not. The notion that he might be Horsefeathers seems childish, even risible in the face of what he has just learned. Of course, Johnny is not a wizard! Of course, Martin hasn't really been into the Otherworld! On the other hand, he is still curious. Johnny might only be an ordinary man, but he is almost certainly still the queer old tramp. How on Earth did he talk his way round Mrs Murray? What does he want? Surely, it could be nothing as simple and honest as a job. *Perhaps,* Martin thinks, *he is a robber.* Or even a spy – though he has to admit that that seems hardly likely. No spy worth his salt would waste his time mowing a Cornish lawn. He'd be in an important place, like London, or Oxford.

He rings the bell, and is shown into the dingy hallway by the old housekeeper, who directs him upstairs, with a peculiar grimace. He keeps his basket of eggs close to his chest, having an odd fear that she has her eye on them, as Miss Fox would say. He wonders what she thinks of the St Louis, and realises he's glad he doesn't know. If she's anything like her employer, she will not be sympathetic.

He arrives at the door of the nursery, and knocks. It opens quickly.

Mammoth & Crow

"My goodness, Martin Stone," says Nanny Gould in surprise. "Leto has a nasty cold. If you've come to ask her to tea, I'm afraid she shan't be allowed."

"Might I visit her?" Martin asks.

Nanny Gould looks at him, with a curiously speculative expression on her face. "Well," she says at last. "I'm not sure. She's been very naughty recently."

Martin frowns. He can easily believe that Leto has been naughty, but it seems a little strange her Nanny should be quite so keen to make him do so. If she wants to tell him to go away, there's no reason she shouldn't be quite plain about it. But perhaps it's just another example of English politeness.

"I'll come back another time," Martin says. "Please tell Leto I was here."

Nanny Gould begins to close the door.

"Is that Martin?" rings Leto's voice from within the nursery. "Let me talk to him! He's my friend!"

Leto fights her way past Nanny Gould, wrenching her shoulder free from the woman's grasping hand, and emerging into the passage. "Hello," she says. She doesn't look as if she's just got out of bed. She's fully dressed, and her yellow hair has been put into thick plaits, which swing as she moves. "I'm not sick."

"Leto Murray, come here this instant!"

"I shan't," says Leto defiantly, spinning round to face her Nanny. "You can't make me. If you try, I'll scream and scream, and Mummy will hear me. And she'll be cross, and you'll get into trouble."

There is a moment's silence. Martin glances

furtively at Nanny Gould. How is she going to respond to this? There's no doubt Leto is being very naughty, right now – *but perhaps,* he thinks, *she might have reason.* And perhaps the threat she's just made carries weight – he feels sure Leto's mother wouldn't shrink from showing Nanny Gould her fury if she were to be disturbed.

"Come on, Martin," says Leto. "Let's go somewhere private." She glares at Nanny Gould. "Somewhere she can't eavesdrop."

"Very well," says Nanny Gould, pursing her lips. "But only down the hall, Leto, not into the garden or downstairs. And be quiet."

"I know," Leto said, rolling her eyes. "Don't upset Mummy. I don't want to."

Grabbing hold of Martin's arm, she propels him quickly along the hallway towards the old library. "Nanny Gould never comes in here," she says, opening the door. "She's frightened of the dust."

"Did you catch a cold?" Martin asks slipping in behind her.

Leto shakes her head. "Well, I've had a mild one," she admits. "So I mustn't go outside and get wet, I suppose. But I don't need to stay shut in my room, and I won't!"

"Oh," says Martin. He doesn't know what else to say. "I was thinking about the *Shaydim*, and Horsefeathers. I was wondering how we might find out who he is."

"But that's obvious," says Leto. "We need to go to the wizard's den, and see what we can find out. He might even be there, and you can tell him face to face. If he has a face. He could be one of the faceless men."

Mammoth & Crow

"I don't think they can cross into this world," Martin says, thoughtfully.

"He might be the man in the painting," Leto says suddenly, in a tone of great excitement, as if the idea has just occurred to her. She hurries across the room, and whisks back the red velvet curtain to reveal the oil painting still hanging behind it. Martin peers over her shoulder, and together the two children stare closely at the portrait of the young man standing lazily beneath the twisted hawthorn tree.

"Oh!" cries Leto, in disappointment. "I can't make out his face at all. Can you?"

Martin frowns. He can't. The painting has been executed in a very modern style that makes the whole scene seem abstract – and if he, himself, hadn't once walked beneath that violet sky (if he really did walk beneath it; but right here, right now, he knows for certain that he did) he'd never have believed it to be anything but a work of pure imagination. But the Surrealist style reaches its zenith in the central figure, who stands half consumed by the very tree upon which he is leaning; or from which, perhaps, he is emerging. It's quite impossible to guess which meaning the artist intended. The figure's face has been obscured behind a tapestry of sharp lobed hawthorn leaves, leaving only a pair of knowing black eyes peering through it; and they are only visible if one looks very hard, for a very long time. *If Horsefeathers looks like this*, Martin thinks, *then he is nowhere I am likely to find him.*

"Did he look like this before?" he asks. It's not a question he'd have voiced in front of anyone but Leto.

Leto puts her head on one side, and pulls a

face. "I don't remember," she says. "I don't think I looked at him properly before. I think my eyes just glided over him, as if he wasn't important."

"Perhaps he doesn't want us to see him," Martin says. "You know," he suggests, somewhat tentatively. "He could be here, in this house, right now. He could have come in here and painted over his face, so we can't see it. He could be pretending to be somebody else."

He watches Leto's expression closely, to see whether she will make the leap: *Johnny could be the wizard.*

"No," says Leto, confidently. "That's not fresh paint. Look at it. It matches the picture perfectly. It's magic! It has to be. Oh, Martin, we have to go back to the den! All the answers will be there, I know it! Blast this rotten, stinking cold! We could go today if only I was better."

She has not made the connection. *Perhaps,* Martin thinks, *that's because she doesn't want to.* He stares at the painting. That hawthorn tree could be the short, scrubby tree he found at the entrance to the underground chamber, and those scattered grey rocks do somewhat resemble the stone thicket, but he can't be sure. "Could you travel there?" he hears himself saying, to his own surprise. "In your dream? Like you told me you can?"

"I suppose I could." Leto seems uncertain. "I mean, I can, obviously – but I don't think I can meet you there, if that's what you mean. You wouldn't be in the Otherworld, so even if we were standing on the same spot, we wouldn't see each other."

"But I walked into the Otherworld," Martin says.

"But you don't know how you did it. It's so frustrating! And I don't suppose you could travel with me, because – " she breaks off. Martin has the uncomfortable feeling she had been about to end her sentence with the words 'that isn't real'. Suddenly he remembers how foolish, earlier, it seemed to him to be so anxious about something that might not be real at all: when the whole idea he rode an ox-cart underneath a violet sky, and Horsefeathers might be the new gardener, had seemed like it must be nothing but an elaborate fairy tale: a game between himself and Leto that was becoming so engrossing it was beginning to extrude into real life.

"I see it, when I close my eyes," Leto says.

"I don't. I don't see anything at all."

The children look at each other. They've reached an impasse. Of course, Martin can't see what Leto can see in her mind's eye. Of course, she can't walk where he has walked. They are separate beings, living, to that extent, in separate worlds. No matter how close their friendship, surely it can never be that close: never close enough for one to pass into the perceptual world of the other, to hear their innermost thoughts, and see through their eyes. Now, that, let me tell you, really would be magic. "What do you see now?" Martin asks.

Leto drops to the floor, legs crossed like an Indian yogi, and closes her eyes. Martin sits down carefully beside her.

"I can see the moor," she says. "It's raining."

"I expect it is," says Martin, glancing out of the window.

'Shh. Don't talk. I need to concentrate."

Martin falls silent. He watches Leto. She's

sitting very still, and it's only by her breathing he can tell she's a living being, not a waxwork. Gradually, that, too, slows and grows shallow. The colour is draining from her face. Martin begins to feel uncomfortable. How long has she been sitting here? Is this how Miss Fox feels whenever she sees him talking to his birds?

"Leto," he says quietly, trying to keep the fear from his voice. "You must come back." When she doesn't respond, he reaches out and touches her hand. Her skin is cold, like death. "Leto!" he shouts. "Leto Murray!"

Leto draws in a deep breath. It's a harsh, shocking sound, like someone reviving from drowning. She opens her eyes, and stares wildly into space. She does not seem to see Martin.

"Are you all right?" Martin asks, urgently. "I was afraid that you were not going to wake up."

After a few seconds, Leto turns her face slowly towards him. The colour is already returning to her cheeks, but she's shivering slightly. "I saw the faceless men," she whispers. "They are on the move."

The air is turning into glass, remembers Martin, suddenly. *Extinction threatens in – something.* It's the message the travellers gave him for Horsefeathers.

"What does extinction mean?" he asks Leto.

"It's what happens to a species when there are none left," Leto says, rubbing her cold knees with the palms of her hands to warm them. "Like mammoths."

Martin feels suddenly sick. "You know," he says. "Perhaps it is too dangerous for you to travel there like that. Perhaps you shouldn't do it."

Leto tosses her head. "Don't worry about me,"

Mammoth & Crow

she tells him, scrambling to her feet. "I do it all the time. I'm only sorry that I can't find Huma. I don't know why, but I haven't seen her for ages."

Extinction, Martin thinks. *Another name for death.*

Having parted company with Leto, Martin leaves the house as quietly as possible, without attracting the attention of the housekeeper or of Nanny Gould. He hasn't forgotten his original intention to spy on the new gardener, especially now he suspects that Johnny has painted – either in pigments or, if Leto's right, in *spells* – over the face of the man in the portrait. There seems to be no logical reason for him to have done such a thing if he is not himself the subject, and trying to hide his own identity. Horsefeathers or not, Johnny is definitely *somebody;* and if he *is* Horsefeathers, Martin has an urgent message to give him.

Choose quickly, and choose well.

As quietly as possible, Martin walks around the side of the house, along the narrow gravel path that separates the wall from the mixed border growing beside it. The air here is very still, the paeony flowers and pink penstemon buds silent; but from somewhere in the house, Martin can hear the unmistakable strains of jazz music playing from a wireless or a gramophone. He can see no sign of the gardener.

At the rear of the house, a set of cracked French windows opens onto a patio, on which sits a dripping wet wrought iron table and chairs. The windows are, of course, currently shut against the drizzle, but Martin can see movement behind the curtains. The music grows suddenly louder.

Jack Wolf

Martin hears laughter. It's not a kind laugh, but it is a spirited one: perhaps the sort of laugh Leto will give, when she's older. On an impulse, despite knowing he will get into serious trouble if he's caught, he creeps towards the window and, hiding to one side, listens intently. It's definitely a woman laughing, not a girl. It must be Mrs Murray. Then to his great surprise, he hears a man's voice, talking in a low, affectionate tone that he can only think of as lover-like. Unable to restrain his curiosity, he peers around the edge of the French window.

Evelyn Murray has her back to him. She is in the arms of the new gardener. From the look of them both, they're dancing – or they have been. But right now they're both standing still, and she's putting her hand around the back of his head, and he's bending his neck and – *Oy gevalt!* Martin thinks in amazement – *kissing* her.

He must have made some small sound – either that, or the new gardener, Johnny, has the power to know when he is being watched. The man lifts his head carefully, as if trying to avoid alarming his companion, and looks straight into Martin's astonished eyes. He gives a little nod, as if in recognition, and smiles. It's not a pleasant look.

Martin runs. He has seen something he knows he ought not: uncovered a secret, a dark, terrible, hidden truth. Mrs Murray is in love with the new gardener. The gardener is in love – no, probably not in love, but he's certainly taking advantage of Mrs Murray. And Mrs Murray is still married to her husband, Leto's father, even though he's many miles away in London. *It is adultery,* Martin thinks. If Leto's father finds out, he'll be furious. Maybe he'll even divorce Leto's mother. Maybe she wants him to. Maybe she's planning to marry the new gardener.

Leto's mother, her fashionable, blonde, hard headed mother, marry a *tramp?* That, Martin thinks, is about as likely as Martin himself marrying the Rabbi's daughter. But perhaps Mrs Murray has never seen Johnny in his tramp's attire. Perhaps she believes the man she sees is who is really there.

Martin has just reached the granite archway when the front door opens. The new gardener appears in the opening. Seeing Martin already running into the lane, he flings himself forward, faster than a rocket, and dashes down the steps. "*Cade!*" he shouts.

Martin glances behind him. The man is very close. He tries to speed up – and that's when he trips, and falls, sprawling, on the cobbled pavement. The wicker basket containing the eggs flies out of his hand, into the roadway.

Now the man is on him. He seizes hold of Martin's shoulders, hauling him to his feet, shoving him roughly against the outside of the garden wall. "You seem to get in everywhere, bird boy," he says.

"Felicitations!" Martin says, furiously. He struggles violently against the man's grip, kicking wildly at his shins; but the man's arms are too strong, and Martin's galoshed feet cannot make contact.

"Perceptive little devil, aren't you?" said the man.

"You're him!" Martin says. "You're not a gardener! You're the tramp I met in the lane!"

"You're right," says the man. "I am. And you're not Miss Fox's nephew. You're a Jewish refugee from Berlin. So we're neither of us quite the people we're supposed to be. But I know to keep my mouth shut about it. The question is, do you?"

"You were kissing Mrs Murray. I saw you."

"What you saw was her kissing me."

"Why? Why would she do that?"

"That's her business. Keep your voice down. We're going to take a little walk along the lane."

"Everyone can see us," Martin says, desperately. "If you hurt me, somebody will call the police."

"I'm not going to hurt you, you idiot. Though I must say I would quite like to give you a hiding. Stop kicking me. It won't do any good and if you keep struggling like this we'll trample on Miss Fox's eggs."

Martin does not know what to do. His instinct is to keep on kicking the man in the shins until he scores a hit, and then run away – but he's always been taught to listen respectfully to adults, and do what he is told. Now the man – Johnny – is telling him he isn't going to hurt him, and something of the impulse to obey anyone in authority is beginning to reassert itself. And – the most alarming thing – Johnny knows who he is, or seems to. He might tell Leto's mother, and tell other people. Miss Fox has been very clear about the importance of keeping his head down and his Jewishness a secret – and after his meeting with the farmer's wife, Martin can fully understand why.

"Let go of me, then," Martin says.

"Very well," says the man. He takes his hands from Martin's shoulders. "Now, you can still run away if you want – but you'll leave your eggs behind if you do."

Martin glares. He rubs his shoulder. It feels sore. "You have hurt me," he says.

"It was accidental. You know what accident

means, I am sure. Ultimately from the Latin *ad cadere:* to fall out, fall upon."

"That's not funny," Martin says.

"It wasn't meant to be."

"Who are you?" Martin says. "Is your name really Johnny?"

The man picks up the basket from the road, and begins replacing those eggs which have, by some miracle, remained unbroken. "Yes," he says. "For all intents and purposes, my name is, really, Johnny. What's yours?"

"Martin Stone."

"Really?" Johnny says. "We shan't get very far if we can't trust each other, bird boy." He begins walking, basket in hand.

Martin sees no alternative but to follow him. "Why should I trust you?" he says. "You don't seem very trustworthy to me. You've lied your way into a job and kissed Leto's mother – or let her kiss you, which is not so different. You know she has a husband already."

"I've no romantic intentions toward Mrs Murray," Johnny says. "Between you and me, the woman is a nightmare. I've started to pity her husband."

"Then why did you let her kiss you?"

"Ah," says Johnny, touching the side of his nose. "That, bird boy, is my business."

"Stop calling me that."

"Tell me your name, then."

"Elijah Rosenstein," Martin says, reluctantly. It's the first time he's spoken his real name since he met Miss Fox on the platform of Liverpool Street station, and the German vowels feels strange and unfamiliar in his mouth.

"Felicitations, Elijah Rosenstein." Johnny stops walking, and holds out his hand, formally. "It is good to finally meet you."

Martin shakes his hand, and takes back his basket of hens' eggs.

"So," says Johnny. "What were you doing, back at the house, peering in at the window?"

"I was looking for Leto."

"No, you weren't. Come, boy, be honest with me, as I have been with you."

"I wanted to see where the music was coming from."

"And you saw more than you expected. I understand."

"I won't tell anybody," Martin says, quickly, lest the man think otherwise.

"I know you won't. And neither will I. We can keep each others secrets, Elijah. Let everyone else think what they will."

"Why is Leto being kept in her room?" Martin asks. "Is she really sick? She doesn't seem it."

Johnny looks at him, with the same thoughtful, measuring look that Martin saw in the eyes of the high moor crow of whom he once asked a similar question. "Nanny says she's getting over a chill," he says. "She was in the garden, and refused to come in. The wind can be tricksy when it blows from the high moor; it can feel warmer than it is. Though, to be entirely honest, she could equally well have caught it from the atmosphere inside the house."

Martin looks up at the man. He seems somehow different from the tramp who came out of the river, or even the frightening figure who not a minute earlier was pinning him against the wall, even though there is no longer any doubt that both times he was, and is, the same man. Is he really also the figure in the painting? It's strange how such superficial things as cleanliness or clothing, or even anger, can seem to alter someone's entire being. He wonders how Johnny would react if he were to give him the message. Perhaps he'd laugh. *I would,* thinks Martin, *if someone asked me if I'd been in the Otherworld – even if I knew for certain that the place was real.* Perhaps there's a way of sounding him out, as sailors do when they are unsure of the depth of the water.

"I met some jolly queer people the last time I was on the moor," Martin says. "They gave me a message for someone in the village. Someone called Horsefeathers." He watches Johnny's reaction carefully.

For an instant, the new gardener seems to hesitate, as if what Martin has said has surprised him; then he recovers, and carries on walking. *So, the name does mean something to him,* Martin thinks. But that still doesn't confirm anything – after all, he might have read it in a faery tale. "They said to tell him to choose swiftly," he says. "And choose well. And something else, about the air turning into glass, and extinction threatening in something, but I can't quite remember what. It was a funny sounding word."

"Well, " says Johnny, slowly. "You seem to have remembered enough."

"Do you know him?" Martin says.

Johnny stops walking. "I think," he says. "We have gone as far as we should, for now."

"Do you know Horsefeathers?"

Johnny looks Martin in the eye. "Yes, I know

him," he says. "As for your message – I'm sure he thanks you for bringing it, but it's too late. His choice is already made."

A cold shiver runs down Martin's spine. He wants to run – but running would mean turning his back on Johnny – who – he's now sure, despite all his earlier doubts and worries, really *is* Horsefeathers, and really *is* a wizard. Was that word he heard him shout an incantation, a charm to bring him down? *Words do have power,* Martin thinks.

"Remember our pact," Johnny Horsefeathers says. "Say nothing of what you saw, and I'll say nothing either. We should be good friends, you and I."

"I will remember," Martin says.

The wizard winks conspiratorially. "Hurry home," he says. "Your crows are waiting."

Chapter Fifteen:
The Savage Gods

Evelyn tells herself she never intended to kiss Johnny. She tells herself it was an aberration, a spur of the moment thing. For a second, he must have looked like Gerald: Gerald as, perhaps, he was some twenty five or thirty years ago, when he, too, would have been young, and strong, and vibrant. And it's not as if she kissed the gardener – not really – for Johnny is, of course, an educated young man from a good family, even if she doesn't know who that family are. Why did he run away from her? *Silly question,* she thinks. Johnny ran away because he recognised the inappropriate nature of what was happening. He ran away because a decent young man doesn't carry on with his employer, especially when she is a married woman. Oh, foolish, impetuous Evelyn! How could she have done it? *But,* she thinks, in rather delicious anguish, *how could I not?* Johnny is everything that she has ever wanted. He's young, and strong, and virile; oh, so virile, in every way that Gerald, poor, feeble, exhausted old King, is not.

For shame! She pushes the idea violently away, and reaches for her gin and tonic. She can't understand where these ideas are coming from, she really can't. She wishes they would stop. But at least they are a distraction from the grieving cicada.

She'll have to regain Johnny's trust, she thinks. She'll have to show him that the kiss meant nothing, and that she has no interest in him beyond platonic friendship. She'll call him back, and she'll be brisk with him, even sharp, as if the kiss was his fault, as if he invited it, as if he forced it on her.

Oh, she thinks suddenly, *if only he had! If only he had not stopped at a kiss!*

Her mind and body are in uproar. How can she call him? How be brisk? It is not possible! As soon as she sees Johnny again, she'll have to kiss him again, and then again, over and over, every part of him; feel his arms around her, pin him down, like Diana and Virbius, like the Goddess and the Priest, perfect beauty and perfect strength. *Oh, yes!* And this, she realises, is why Actaeon was torn apart by hounds, and Hippolytus by horses: this desire, this energy, this lust: this desire that is not safe, is not respectable, that doesn't care two hoots for marriage vows, or conventions, or stultifying, festering decency. This is the master force of life, the divine urge to mate, and to conceive heroes and demigods, whose line will rule eternally. That's a metaphor, of course, Evelyn knows that, *but,* she thinks, *it holds true* – perhaps more true, now, than at any time in human history. This is what the germ-line really wants: perhaps Davenport, with his Victorian, oh-so-American notions of morality, did not, could not, properly understand it. Perhaps she herself has never understood it, until now.

Johnny could give me a healthy son, she

thinks.

She doesn't want to think this way about him. But she can't help it.

Who are his family? She hadn't wanted to pry, but now she'll simply have to force his surname out of him. If she is to leave Gerald and... do what? What is she thinking? How can she, Evelyn Murray, possibly be considering such a thing as to leave her husband, give up her social status, forget everything she's ever believed in – for a young man she barely knows? It is ridiculous.

And what if Johnny has no interest in marrying her? He scarcely seems the type to have any interest in marrying anybody, after all. He's too bohemian, too modern, too exciting, too free.

But surely, Evelyn thinks, pleading with herself – or perhaps with the savage Gods, if they are listening – *if Johnny were to fall in love with me, then none of that would have any appeal for him any more? We could live anywhere. It wouldn't have to be in London. I couldn't stay there, anyway – not after divorcing Gerald. But I could even live here – I could, quite happily, if I had Johnny.* Evelyn has a sneaking feeling, with which we may perhaps agree, that this last assertion is not remotely true – but in the wild romance of her fantasy, she ignores it.

How can I make him mine? How can I make him give me back my son? What do I have to give?

To give to whom?

The striped wallpaper on the chimney breast is shining in the flame-light, like the pillars of a temple. The fire crackles in the grate.

She is beginning to lose her mind, a little. But she doesn't know it.

July continues. The weather remains typically British, and doesn't give up raining until well into the second week. Martin Stone digs the vegetable garden, and discusses with his crows the possibility of going up on the high moor to investigate the antechamber in the fogou, where Leto claims to have discovered the books and human skull, beyond the place where the bear claw found its way into his hand and pocket. Since Johnny – Horsefeathers – is a wizard, Martin tells the crows, then for all his offer of friendship, he's still likely to be extremely dangerous – more so, in fact, than if he was an old robber tramp, or even a crazy murderer, because a wizard's traffic is with things even further outside of normal human understanding than the *Shaydim*: truly heartless, soulless things that dwell in the abyss beyond the farthest edges of creation. So, he says to Petra and Paul, it would be wise to find out as much as he can about who he and Leto (and Leto's mother, nasty as she is) are dealing with. *It's not idle curiosity,* he tells them, as if they were accusing him of that. He has good reason for it. He needs to know if Horsefeathers is as wicked as he fears he could be. And while Horsefeathers is securely installed at Ignatius Hart's old house, running errands for – and stealing kisses from – Mrs Murray, he won't be anywhere near his den out on the moor. This could be the only time Martin can visit it without fear of being caught. He wonders whether he ought to let Leto know what he is planning. After all, she's the one who initially suggested it, and he knows she'll be very cross if he goes on the adventure without her. But Leto, from what he witnessed of her behaviour when Johnny came to collect her from the cottage, and her complete deafness to Martin's hint he may not be all he claims to be, is almost as enamoured of the new gardener as her mother is. She simply does not want to consider he could be the wizard – so even if she finds something in the tunnel to convince her of that, she'll be unwilling to suspect him of malevolence. She might even run straight to him to tell him what they've done. No. *This,* Martin tells the crows, *is something I will have to do on my own. It is better that way.*

Definitely, his crows agree, cocking their heads and strutting eagerly up and down the garden path, like English public schoolboys at a boat race. *Oh, definitely.*

Martin has the feeling they're not fond of Leto. Perhaps they're jealous. It can be hard to tell with birds, even large, black scavengers of sandwiches and carrion.

"Though I could still bring her," he says aloud, experimentally, just to test their reaction. "If there is anything to find in Horsefeathers' tunnel, it would be better for her to see it for herself, rather than for me to tell her all about it afterwards."

His crows aren't happy. *If you are going to spend all your time with that stupid English girl,* they tell him, *go ahead. Don't mind anything we have to say. We don't matter. We are only looking out for your best interests, after all.*

"You sound like my grandmother," Martin says, with a little smile. But for all that it's a blessing, the memory hurts his heart. "All right, I won't bring Leto," he says. "Does that make you feel better? It will just be you and me, like it was before."

Jack Wolf

Before she died. Before the orphanage. Before the screams and shouts and broken glass, the senseless, mindless hate.

Yes, say the crows, nodding enthusiastically. *Before was better, yes.*

As soon as he's finished digging the vegetable patch, Martin asks Miss Fox if he may go for a walk – and she, knowing nothing of how he managed to get himself lost in the Otherworld the last time he went out alone, waves him happily away. She's busy: to her delight *The Lady* accepted her review of *Rebecca* with great enthusiasm, and asked her straight away for another, of a different writer's work, and for more money. Miss Fox is relieved to be writing again. For one thing, it prevents her from listening to the wireless, and worrying herself sick about the fate of those unlucky refugees on whom America – along with the whole civilised world – has turned its back; and about the near inevitability of war.

The high moor is clear, but the threat of mist hangs in the air, and for once, Martin's glad of his compass and ordnance survey map. And he knows where he is going, having been halfway there many times before. He wonders whether his crows will accompany him the whole way – he feels sure now the Rough Tor crags are out of their territory. Really, he decides, watching their black shapes flickering like cyphers through the wispy grey, it was most unreasonable of them to have made such a fuss about the idea of bringing Leto, if they're only going to turn and fly for home before they've even come within half a mile of the fogou. But to his surprise, Petra and Paul don't leave him. He finds the stone thicket

255

remarkably quickly, by following the stream, and both crows settle on the tallest pile of stones, and launch into a shouted cacophony of caws that seem to set the sky vibrating.

"Shut up!" Martin tells them, waving his hands frantically. If they make that amount of noise, they'll attract unwelcome attention. Horsefeathers might not be here, but the strange crow – the one who showed him where Leto was hiding in exchange for a lump of cheese sandwich – might be. Who is to say it's not friends with the wizard, just as Petra and Paul are friends with Martin? It could be a spy. Perhaps that's how Horsefeathers knew who he was when they met, when he leapt over the wall into the lane, and called him bird boy. He wasn't watching the tunnel himself. The crow told him.

Petra and Paul look down at him, their sharp beaks still half open, as if surprised. They're quite put out by his reaction, Martin feels. "Look," he says, reasonably. "I'm very glad you came along – but can you both be quiet? We must not let anybody know that we are here. Do you understand?"

The crows cock their heads, and snap their beaks at him. *Yes,* they answer, they understand the need, if not the reason. But they're not best pleased by it. They want to claim this territory, make it part of their own. They want to shout out their occupation from the tops of the piled stones, which are now their stones, just as the roof of Miss Fox's cottage is their roof. If that means calling down a challenger, so be it.

Crows, Martin thinks, in exasperation. He sighs, and shakes his head.

"Stay here, then," he says. "But please try not to make any noise. If you're not here when I come out, I'll meet you back at the cottage."

After some argument and debate, the crows, at last, agree. They'll be silent as grave robbers, they promise. Martin has the feeling that one, if not both of them, has promised with their fingers – or their feathers – crossed behind their backs; but, for want of any other option, he has to take their word for it.

Leaving the large black birds to their small triumph, Martin scrambles up the damp, grassy slope into the granite thicket. He knows this will be the hardest part. He's probably mad to try it. The wizard's den was hard enough to find in bright sunlight, and now the weather – and visibility with it – is worsening. He stops, and on a moment's inspiration, listens hard. All around him in the quiet air the small birds trill and flutter. Droplets of condensed mist and cold rain from previous nights and days drip from the saucer-like stones into dark brownish puddles at his feet, trickling between the tiny yellow flowers, pooling underneath a miniature, white speckled half eggshell. Somewhere in the distance he can hear the contented bleating of Longwool sheep; farther off, the neighing of a wild pony stallion calling to his mares. He lowers his head. The sentinel – as he's suddenly inclined to think of the other crow – could be keeping watching within the crags. He doesn't want to alert it.

Which way to go? He thinks the scattering of boulders among which he is now standing seems familiar – but wasn't the tunnel opening between the roots of a twisted hawthorn tree, which reared its branches high above the sulking rocks? He peers around him. There *is* a tree, a little way off – though looking up, it's becoming hard to make out its shape properly through the thickening mist. If he weren't sure it was, in fact, a tree, he might have mistaken it for something else, something entirely out of place, here, in rural England, like a bear. There are still black bears in Germany, in the Bavarian forests: Martin saw one, once, when he was much younger, trapped in the bear pit at the Berlin zoo. He hopes Herr Hitler will not try to eradicate the bears, along with everybody else.

Then he remembers the Lizard-bear, and his heart skips a beat. If a tree can be mistaken for a bear, can a *shayd* be mistaken for a hawthorn tree? What if he's not looking at a tree at all, but a queer, hybrid monster: a creature both scaled and furred, with teeth like giant knives and claws like butchers' hooks, standing powerfully erect on clawed reptilian feet, staring at him through the fog? Perhaps the Lizard-bear has eyes that can penetrate any cloud, and it can see Martin now as clearly as he saw it on that day he fled from it, afraid, into the Otherworld.

No, he tells himself, firmly. The looming shape is really nothing but a tree – and if his memory serves him well, it's standing exactly where he needs to go. He turns up the collar of his coat, and picks his way towards it, through the stones.

Finding the entrance to the tunnel, even now he's sure he has a good idea where it is, takes Martin some time. The grass has grown much taller and thicker since his previous visit, and apart from the sheep trails, there's no sign of anyone having intruded into the boulder field for at least that many weeks – which makes sense, if the only other human to ever come here is Johnny Horsefeathers, who is now, as we all know, in Bransquite. The ground is damper than it was, and Martin's hobnailed boots leave clear prints in the mud. He tries to clear them away, stamping in the dirt, but despite his best efforts, the marks persist. *As if the ground is determined to remember,* Martin thinks, in great annoyance. As if the moor itself wants to be the one to tell Horsefeathers all about his visit. There's nothing he can do about it except hope for rain, and for the sharp erasing hooves of sheep. The scrubby hawthorn tree looms over him, its long lichen tendrils waving in the slight breeze.

Oy vey gevalt, Martin thinks in dismay, straightening up. The tunnel must have grown over. How Horsefeathers will find it again he cannot guess. (The wizard, let me tell you, has a better idea than Martin, and will bring a set of secateurs to cut his way through the heather). It seems that this has been a wasted afternoon. Martin thinks longingly of Miss Fox's cottage, with its warm fire and clotted cream. He thinks of the ginger cat purring in the armchair, and how he could have been sitting comfortably with him in his lap and a cup of hot chocolate in his hand. He really should have stayed at home, and listened to the gramophone, or tried to read one of Miss Fox's many English novels. Struggling with a story in a foreign tongue would be preferable to scrambling forward and back between these perilous rocks, for nothing. He puts his hand inside his pocket.

His fingers close on the bear claw. He frowns. He's sure he put it into his shoebox when he came back from the moor, after his experience among the faceless men. He must have imagined it, he thinks, even if he didn't imagine his meeting with them. It's a good thing it hasn't slipped from his pocket. He leaves it where it is, and takes out his compass. He'll make his way back to the cottage.

It's then he sees it: a small triangle of blackness, nestling in the brown earth, appearing exactly where, and exactly how, it is supposed to. He drops to his knees. *Is it – yes, it is!* – the opening to Horsefeathers' tunnel. This is where he found Leto. He's kneeling precisely where he was when she put out her hand, and caught his ankle.

Getting into the hole was not the easiest of scrambles, Martin remembers, and that was on a dry day, when the stones weren't slippery, and the muddy edge of the hole not so terribly treacherous. Very carefully, he sits down and dangles his feet over the rim. One thing, at least, is easier: knowing that the tunnel is as black as pitch, he's brought along Miss Fox's Bakelite torch, and as soon as he's settled himself, he shines the bright beam down, into the darkness.

The drop looks longer than he remembers. The ground beneath the entrance hole is damp, and another muddy puddle has developed in the space directly underneath his feet. He takes a sniff. The air below him smells of soil and root – but there's a freshness to it, too, which he can't explain, as if a breeze is blowing through the sealed stone chamber. He frowns, then, torch in hand, pushes himself through the damp earth into the underground passage.

The tunnel is narrow, and by the light of Miss Fox's torch, Martin can easily make out the method of its construction. Large stone slabs tightly line the walls and ceiling, leaving little room for soil or water to penetrate. The floor is of compacted dirt, covered with a dry, loose soil which must have blown its way in over the centuries – even millennia – since the tunnel was dug. Surprisingly, once he has got away from the entrance, it's not cold or damp, like a cave or an old building. In fine weather, Martin thinks, it's probably a much more pleasant place to be than Ignatius Hart's musty old house. He remembers Horsefeathers' offhand remark about the cause of Leto's chill, and wonders whether the wizard's rueing his decision to move into civilisation.

At the far end of the passage he reaches the sharp, right angled turn into the small antechamber, which he previously saw illuminated by a low oil light. Pausing, he shines his torch carefully into the enclosed space. It seems much larger than he remembers. Perhaps, to it, he seems smaller. Ducking his head to avoid the low cross-stone that forms the lintel, and the many ancient roots that grow across the space, he steps inside. The air in the chamber smells astonishingly fresh, like flowers and dry summer wind. *Could there be another opening?* Martin looks around. All the walls, as far as he can tell, are completely sealed. All apart from one; for there, behind a low, rough table constructed from a plank set on two bricks – on which sits Horsefeathers' tottering pile of books – Martin can just make out a small black hole, where a portion of the wall has, at some time, collapsed, leaving a gap of roughly eighteen inches in diameter across the stonework. Where does it lead? Crouching down, he shines his beam into the darkness.

A human skull grins back at him.

Martin drops his torch in shock. *Of course!* Leto said the wizard's books had a human skull on top of them. Evidently, Horsefeathers has since moved it, or some small creature – a rat, or fox perhaps – has knocked it off, and it has rolled ignominiously into the gap.

He picks up the Bakelite torch, and shines it once again into the hole, this time trying not to look into the unsettling, not-quite-human features of the dead. The opening leads into a small, low, sealed space: a stone coffin, Martin thinks, with a fierce thrill of discovery and shock. A skeleton – the owner of the skull, he supposes – lies curled up like a baby in the centre of it, wrapped in some kind of half decaying pelt. Around its neck is a scattering of small, black, sickle shaped objects.

Bear claws! Martin thinks. Whoever this person was, he – or she – was buried wearing a bear claw necklace. And now Martin has one of the claws in his own pocket.

He reconstructs the scene. Some time ago, Horsefeathers came onto the high moor, discovered the buried chamber, and decided it was a fair place in which to camp out, for a time. Like Martin, he probably had a torch, as well as his oil lamps, and, like Martin, he was led by his inquisitive nature to examine the breach in the chamber wall. But his explorations did not end there. He put in his hand, and dragged out the occupant's skull – breaking whatever cord may still have held the claws in place about the already fragmented spine, and bringing at least one of them out with it: the very claw that Martin later picked up, all unknowing, during his clumsy scramble to join Leto inside the passage.

What a disrespectful way to treat the dead! Martin is appalled. What need has Horsefeathers for this poor skull, except to assuage his callous curiosity? He imagines the new gardener proudly, arrogantly, carrying the skull to a museum, telling the curator how he found it, through his own, wonderful, cleverness, high on the moor. The museum would label it "Iron Age Man" or something similarly inane, and set it up in a glass case for all comers to gawk at, forgetting entirely that these were the remains of a person, not a thing: a real, human, person who was once buried lovingly on the high moor wrapped in a fur cloak, and wearing a necklace of bear claws. *Perhaps the claws were precious,* Martin thinks. Perhaps they had some special meaning, lost to modern understanding. One thing he knows for sure: the burial should never, ever have been disturbed.

Martin sits back on his haunches. He is surprised by how deeply the desecration has affected him. It's not as if he has any idea what such a disturbance might have meant to the inhabitant, after all. Who knows what savage Gods the peoples of the moor worshipped back then, what curious things they believed about death and afterlife? All that is lost to prehistory: only the moor remembers. But he knows how he'd feel if this were a grave belonging to his own people – or if it were his own grave, opened many years in the far distant future. *It's an abominable thing,* he decides, *a despicable blasphemy.*

Can he replace the skull? He suppresses a shudder at the thought of touching death. He has to try. He's sure of it. But can he bring himself to do it?

To distract himself, and give himself time to build up his courage, Martin lifts his torch and peers around the remainder of the chamber. The low table and chair are exactly as he last saw them, but the cot has been shoved roughly to one side, leaving the far wall entirely clear. The giant pile of books casts a long shadow over the rammed earth floor.

Perhaps they really are books of magic, Martin thinks. He walks across to the pile, and opening the volume that lies on top, shines his torch upon its title page. *Cornelius Agrippa,* he reads. *The Philosophy of Natural Magic.* He gives a small giggle. *Well, I suppose that settles that question.*

There's something handwritten underneath the printed title. Martin squints at it. The writing is beautiful—the copperplate of a well educated man – but it's also hurried, as if the writer lacks the patience to form his letters correctly.

To my dear Uncle Ignatius, it reads. *A small gift from me in gratitude for all your affectionate assistance in my time of trouble. Your Johnny.* It's dated July 1, 1929.

That's odd, thinks Martin. The book doesn't appear to have been down here for ten years. 'Johnny,' of course, can only be the new gardener, and Horsefeathers. He wonders who the uncle is. He puts it down beside the tower, and examines the next one.

This proves to be another book of magic – or at least, judging from its title: *The History of Magic* – of magical philosophy. The same untidy copperplate handwriting appears again, underneath.

To my Uncle, on his 70th birthday. With love and affection.

The next three books are marked *ex libris*, but instead of a name, the stamp says simply: *Fireborn.*

Is that a name? Martin wonders. A name in the same way 'Horsefeathers' is a name: a queer, adopted nickname, better fit for use among the *Shaydim* than in human company?

The fourth book is very worn, its spine broken by heavy use, and to his surprise Martin sees it is handwritten, in a painstaking, Victorian script. It seems at first sight to be a private book of recipes, like the one his grandmother used to keep in her kitchen, each dish beginning with a long and complex list of ingredients, followed by a longer page of detailed, comprehensive instructions, and concluding with a number of illustrations and diagrams – some hand-drawn, some printed plates, snipped delicately from some earlier, printed text and glued in place to displaying the intended result. Unlike a recipe book, though, this book has been composed in a mixture of English and a language Martin recognises as Latin, and the pictures are an ugly mix of complex circles, stark geometric designs, and naked human figures festooned with greenery and draped in animal skins, whose style immediately reminds him of the portrait of Horsefeathers in Ignatius Hart's old library. Martin can't bear to look at them. He shudders, closes the grimoire with a thud, and puts it quickly to one side. Underneath it lies a bulging, unsealed, envelope, marked 'sea mail'.

Martin feels compulsion pricking at his thumbs, although he knows he should resist it. These are somebody's – probably Johnny's – private letters, and his grandmother would turn in her grave if she thought he might sink to reading anybody's personal correspondence, whatever his suspicions regarding them. But every instinct he has is urging him to read them. If he really wants to find out who and what Johnny Horsefeathers is, he tells himself, if he really wants to discover if Horsefeathers is as wicked as he fears, he has no choice but to continue his investigations. He reaches down, picks up the envelope, and slides its contents free. There are several letters, exchanged between two people. Old letters, too, dating from before ten years ago. Half of them are written in the same untidy copperplate as the inscriptions, but the other half have been typewritten, and on the same machine: in each one, the capital E is broken. *My dearest Phillip,* the topmost commences.

Martin sits down on the dry floor of the antechamber, and begins to read.

30th April, 1927.

Father,

I wholly repudiate your characterisation of my associate as an accomplice, as if we were criminals. We are nothing of the sort, and I resent your implication and high handed tone. I shall not be coming home, and you will never make me by employing threats and libels.

I do not mean ever to meet that woman whom you call my future stepmother. Not only is she too young to be anything of the kind, she is in utter thrall to an Evil Ideology whose tenets I hold in complete revulsion. You dare to be concerned that I will bring shame on the family, while forging a link to a woman whose beliefs include some of the most vile and abhorrent notions ever dreamed up by man? I cannot belong to a family that would approve of such a despicable concept as Spazio Vitale, and I am appalled to find you, Father, so ready to accept it. I am sure that Mother would have done everything she could to have persuaded you of its abominable and terrifying implications for all people who do not match up to Mussolini's concept of what a man should be, or a woman either: the Slavs and the Jews and the Blacks and the Communists and anybody who dares disagree with him; and I am shocked that instead of doing everything you could, as an older and wiser head, to steer that woman away from it, you have chosen instead to embrace it along with her. There is a saying: 'No fool like an old fool', and I regret to say that you have become the very embodiment of it.

Your disappointed son,

Phillip.

Chapter Sixteen:
The Vicar of Bransquite

The novel that Miss Fox is reading now, in order to review it for *The Lady,* is a sordid tale of a group of desperately lonely nuns living in the Himalayas. Cut off from civilisation, they are slowly going mad – as you or I probably would, if we truly felt ourselves to have been banished to such a distant and barbaric place as British India. Of course, there is a very real sense in which the nuns have banished themselves, but this doesn't make any difference to their feelings of powerlessness.

Miss Fox remembers how she ached when she first arrived in Bransquite. How powerless, how alien, she felt herself to be among the natives of the high moor, who seemed in every way as unlike her as it was possible to be. And how lost, too: how horribly isolated from her own kindred, her own kind. She could easily have gone mad, she thinks. But she did not.

How voluntary was her banishment? Yes, it was her choice, after the falling out, to come up onto the high moor, but was it really a free one? How much pressure was put on her to make it? Why did it matter to her so very much that she remove herself, not merely from Quaker Fowey and her father's circle, but from society entirely? Why did she decide upon exile from life, instead of engagement with it? Did she, really, feel so shunned? If there was pressure, she thinks, then it was never of the open sort, which issues opinions and orders and expects to be obeyed; but it was no less potent for that, and, in its own way, harder to resist. The silencing presentiment of scandal, the frantic, panicking desire to avoid becoming any sort of oddity to be laughed at, or casualty to be mourned over: these were the things that drove her heartbroken younger self to seek compassion in solitude. It didn't matter that her father never told her go, and her brother never said, in so many words, that he considered her conduct a disgrace. She could feel their embarrassment, their voiceless censure; and that was enough.

What had she done? Nothing. Nothing: except fall, briefly, headily and fallaciously, in calf-love with a man whom they considered – and who, to be fair to them, really *was* – unsuitable. A man many years older than herself, who'd spent two years fighting the Boer and was now facing his call up to take part in the great conflict against Germany which the papers cried would be the war to end all wars, the final definitive conflagration of the modern age. And he had known, he had freely admitted that the only thing great about the war was the magnitude of the lie for which it would be fought, and that the papers were foolish, lying lackeys of an equally mendacious and arrogant government. *If you think so,* she begged him, *then don't go. Follow your conscience, please, don't go.*

But I am a soldier, he said, as if he couldn't

understand how she should ask such a thing. *I am a soldier.* It was a matter not of conscience, but of loyalty.

This is not the only reason that he was unsuitable.

Is war ever justifiable? wonders Miss Fox. What would the man think, now, of this new conflict that is presently looming over Europe? What would he say are our alternatives? Are they simply to accept – or watch in horror – the outrages of a tyrant, or should we fight him? Surely not fight. There must be a better way. But unlike the Kaiser before him, what is driving Hitler is more than personal ambition and wounded pride. He is, like Mussolini, even Mosley, a figurehead: an embodiment of a creeping ideology of hate that's seeded itself like a parasitic weed across the whole modern world. In that sense, he is now both more and less than a man: he has become hollowed out by belief, driven by terrible, implacable symbolism. And while it's easy to decide that of course, one should never indulge in war to soothe the ruffled feathers of a slighted King, perhaps this – this fascist menace – is somehow different. Perhaps it can't be dealt with by normal, civilised means. Perhaps aggression is going to be necessary, perhaps justifiable.

Miss Fox shudders. *No.* If matters have already come to that, they've already gone too far – and if the weed's as widespread and plentiful as she fears, the answer can't be to rely on war with one country to uproot it. Such an approach is too simplistic, for all it may seem morally right. Resistance to such evil must involve more than a reflexive return to bloodshed. It has to mean the systematic eradication of the toxic plant in all the places it has taken root, in England as much as in Germany, and America too, and in Italy, and anywhere else where people have begun to think that Might makes Right. This is a battle of minds, not bodies: the combatants, such as they are, are ideas and beliefs, their weapons the human spirit and the steadfast support of a merciful, peace loving, God.

But war's always the first recourse of men, thinks Miss Fox, bitterly. Men will always rush toward the sword instead of the ploughshare. Women will wait, and talk, and pray for peace. And men are praised for it – why, since the very earliest days, male violence has been lauded. The Old Testament is full of war. And the Greek myths – it seems a man can always be found virtuous even when he has committed unspeakable atrocities. Hercules murders his family, and is named a hero. If he'd been a woman, if he'd been Medea, Clytemnestra, Phaedra, he'd have been considered monstrous – as, indeed, he should be.

But, she asks herself, is this belief – her own belief – in the masculine impulse to war not part of the devilish creed that has reached its nadir in the jackboots and salutes of Hitler's Nazis? What assumptions is she perpetuating when she expresses it? That real men go to war, and pacifists are cowards?

She wonders whether this is why the man was so unsuitable. Perhaps, to her father and her brother, both of whom are real men, and real men of peace, her association with him came as a slap in the face, an insult not only to everything they believe, but everything they are.

Well! If that was so, then they – proud,

peevish men – read far much too much into her actions. It was a hopeless, pointless love affair, and in many ways a trivial one. If it had simply been allowed to be forgotten, and life left to carry on as it had done before, then, naturally, Miss Jane Fox would have remained wedded to friendship, not violence. Foolish, irritable, irrational men! The shame, if shame there is, should never have fallen on her. But because she is female, it naturally has.

These unhappy ruminations aren't getting her review written, nor are they in any way soothing to her soul. Miss Fox puts down the novel, and goes to make herself a cup of tea. Activity is the best way to banish melancholy.

Evelyn has gone to see the vicar. She's been forced to walk: the green fendered motor car, which was only borrowed, has long since returned to London with its driver; but fortunately the distance to the vicarage is not above a mile, and though the way's twisty and steep, it doesn't involve any undignified scrambling over stiles, or along little used paths. Even so, her feet, compressed into her kitten heels, are complaining savagely about the roughness of the lane, and chiding her for stepping out of the house in anything less substantial than wellington boots.

She's not really sure why she's going. It was on another impulse: an inchoate motion in search of comfort, springing, I think, from the forgotten depths of habit. Once upon a time, let me tell you, Evelyn Murray was a little girl in a red coat and laced up boots, whose Daddy took her every Sunday to St Martin in the Fields, where she'd sit kicking her legs, and finding an unlooked for comfort in the droning sermons of the Vicar, the heavy music of the organ pipes. Grown up Evelyn is trying to find a way to silence the cicada, trying to find a way to stop thinking about Johnny. Neither Gordon's nor *The Golden Bough* have been much help in this.

The vicarage is situated near St Bran's Church, up on the hill beyond the edge of Bransquite, at the junction of the four narrow country roads that criss-cross this part of the moor. It's an old, dark, granite building, dating to the middle of the seventeenth century, and the half of its face that isn't covered with the waving strands of variegated ivy is cracked and wind worn. From somewhere in the greenery, a late season blackbird is singing. The cries of sheep drift from the open fields; from the nearby forge-and-motor-garage echoes the clang of a hammer on metal. Evelyn totters up the gravelled path, and looks about the shady portico for a doorbell; but there's nothing except a large, rather grandiose, brass knocker. She lifts it, hesitates, then lets it fall.

Receiving no reply, after a while, she tries again. It would be most inconvenient, she decides, for the vicar to be out, when she's made such an effort to come to see him. She sets her jaw, and kicks her heels, and knocks a third time. *Perhaps he's at the Church,* she thinks.

Still receiving no reply, Evelyn steps down from the doorway and casts her eyes over the forbidding visage of the vicarage. A number of the upstairs windows are open, and soft white muslin curtains flutter in the soft breeze, in and out, over the grey stone sills. "Hello!" she calls. "Is anybody home?"

There's a darkly shifting movement behind

one of the windows. Maybe it's nothing but a cat. But then the casement suddenly opens wide, and an elderly head appears in the space.

"Good gracious," says a man's voice. "Good afternoon, young lady. How can I help you?"

"I'm looking for the vicar," Evelyn says.

"In that case, you've found him," says the old man. "Is there anything in particular you require?"

"No," Evelyn says. "I just wanted to introduce myself. And to talk, perhaps."

"Ha! Another troubled soul," the vicar says, in a quizzical tone. "Well, come on in. The front door isn't locked."

"Wherever is your housekeeper?" Evelyn asks.

"Housekeeper? I don't have one – unless you're thinking of Mrs Benetto from the village, who comes and does a bit, you know. What would I want with a housekeeper? I only live in a fraction of the place. The rest is boarded up. Come in, come in. I haven't got all day."

Evelyn pushes at the heavy front door. True to the vicar's word, it swings open. She finds herself looking into a dark hallway, not dissimilar in many ways from Ignatius Hart's old house. A vase of flowers is sitting on the hall table, next to a rather battered Bible, a glass bowl containing a set of keys, and a walking stick. On the floor stands a pair of well worn and rather muddy boots, their laces trailing on the cold grey flags of the old floor. The walls are panelled in some dense wood that's probably oak. Over the centuries the smoke and fume from various fires, oil lamps and cigarettes have turned the plain wood very dark, and the air smells musty. *But it isn't damp, at least,* Evelyn thinks, stepping off the doormat. The problem with this place is lack of use, lack of life, not structural decay.

Leaving the front door open – otherwise it would be too dark to see anything – Evelyn makes her way towards the bottom of the wide staircase that spirals up from the centre of the hall. Perhaps this is a later addition. Evelyn vaguely remembers reading, or perhaps hearing, that buildings of this age would originally have had small stone staircases, sealed like confession boxes behind old doors, in the corners of the rooms. But she's not sure. Still, it's clear for all its age and apparent stasis, the house hasn't remained unchanged throughout the centuries. Modernity has intruded in the form of a patinaed row of bronze bells dangling over what she presumes must be the cellar door, and from somewhere upstairs a wireless is crackling. *A different sort of static,* Evelyn thinks.

"Is it all right if I smoke?" she calls up the stairs.

"As long as you don't set fire to the curtains," comes the dry response. "Don't just stand there, young lady. I'm not coming down. Mounting the Purple Emperor is a delicate business."

Evelyn finds the vicar, finally, in his upstairs study. The light pouring through the leaded casement is falling on his desk, and illuminating the large felted board over which he is bending, as if by some divine presence. He smiles, and straightens up, his spine giving an audible crack, and pushes his thick lensed spectacles onto his forehead. In his hand Evelyn can see some sort of metal object, which she concludes has some use in the preservation of butterflies.

"Good afternoon," he says to Evelyn. "So,

with whom do I have the pleasure of meeting?"

"Mrs Gerald Murray," Evelyn says. "I'm staying in Bertram Hart's house – the one he recently inherited from his uncle. Cousin Bertram is a relative of my husband's."

"Ah, I see!" exclaims the vicar. "Well, it is very nice to meet you, at last." Evelyn feels the censure of that 'at last' hanging in the air, like smoke from the cigarette she hasn't yet dared light. The vicar puts down his instrument, and comes forward to shake her hand. "Forgive me for calling you 'young lady'," he says. "From where you were standing, I could only see your hat. I thought you were much younger. So, how are you enjoying Cornwall?"

I'm not, Evelyn wants to say, but she holds her tongue. She isn't sure what to make of this jovial, peculiar old man, with his spectacles, and quaint, rural hobbies, who lives with all appearance of contentment in a boarded up vicarage, with no housekeeper. How can a man like this be able to comprehend anything of the complex, confusing anguish she is going through?

"It's very quiet," she says. It's one interpretation of the truth.

The vicar eyes her shrewdly. "A little too quiet, perhaps?"

"Oh, no," says Evelyn quickly. "Not at all. I am grateful for the rest." Gerald's words, spilling out of her as if in defence of the man himself.

The vicar gives a chuckle. "Most women of your species – please forgive me if I'm being presumptuous – I mean young, pretty, educated women, as you plainly are – can't wait to get away from the place. Peace and quiet isn't to everybody's taste." He sighs. "Like collecting, Mrs Murray. There are those who see no appeal in pressing insects to a board. They think it an old man's hobby, or a schoolboy's: not worthy of any serious attention. Sometimes, do you know, I quite agree with them. Tell me, do you play tennis?"

"Tennis? Why, yes."

"I used to play, occasionally, when my knees allowed me. Very enjoyable. The to and fro of rally and riposte, the joy of darting to and fro, up and down upon the court. It felt very freeing."

"It does," Evelyn says.

"I wonder," the vicar says. "Whether losing that freedom was what induced me to pin down the butterflies. Perhaps I take out my frustration at no longer being able to play on them."

Evelyn wonders, suddenly, what the vicar already knows about her situation. Has he been talking to the old housekeeper? Or to Nanny Gould? "I assure you," she says, smoothly. "I'm not at all frustrated by Cornwall. I love it here." *What?* Oh, no, that's not the whole truth, nor any twisted version of the truth: it's an out and out lie, and told for no-one's benefit, not even her own.

"So," the vicar says, with a smile. "Should we expect to see you in Church on Sunday? I can't vouch for an exciting sermon, of course, though I do my best."

"I don't know," Evelyn says.

"You should give it a try," the vicar says. "It can be surprisingly rewarding, you know."

"Oh, it's not for want of trying," Evelyn says. "Religion, for me, never seems to take."

The vicar raises his eyebrows. "Well, well,"

he says affably. "Perhaps the ground is not quite right yet. Religion is like seed, you know; it needs the soil to be in the right condition before it can germinate: free of noxious weeds and freshly tilled, those sorts of things. And once it has sprouted, it needs nurturing, too: given regular waterings and pest pickings and the like. It can be quite a task to grow a satisfactory religion."

Evelyn smiles politely. *All Bible and village gossip,* she remembers saying, disparagingly, to Johnny. It seems she was right – the only thing her prophecy failed to include was the butterfly collection. She finds no comfort in the thought. *Please,* she wants somehow to say, *please, help me* – but the admission of need is beyond her, let alone the call for aid. Perhaps, she thinks, her soul is frozen. Perhaps it lost all ability to pray, to keep faith with a higher power, when Gerald threw her away; or when she lost her son. Why should her soil – her soul – be able to grow a religion, when her body cannot grow a child?

The vicar is watching her closely. She wonders what he's thinking. "Please, don't think me a heathen," she says, with a tense little laugh.

The vicar smiles. "Oh, we're all heathens, to some extent, Mrs Murray," he says. "Some of us are simply better at hiding our heathenish tendencies than others. I see religion as being more a moderating force upon our lower impulses than a first class ticket to holiness. It can preserve us from our worst selves, even when it doesn't always make us into our best ones – though it can do that too, of course, if we let it. Now, would you care for a cup of tea? I know how to put on a kettle and stir tea leaves in a pot, though I must admit my culinary abilities end there. Mrs Benetto will be over later with something hot under a cloth, and that will be my salvation, at least from bodily hunger."

"Tea would be very nice," says Evelyn, though she's quite worried that it won't.

"Capital," says the vicar. He rubs his hands together, whether to rid them of stray butterfly scales or in some sort of anticipated triumph, Evelyn cannot tell. "Well, young lady – may I call you that anyway? You still seem terribly young to an old crock like me, you know. My kettle is, of course, in the kitchen, so it looks as if I shall be coming downstairs after all. Follow me, as our Saviour puts it, and I'll show you the way."

The vicar's kitchen, to Evelyn's relief, does not share the damp and stuffy atmosphere that permeates the remainder of the house. The vicar puts the kettle on the range, which, as in most large houses, is always kept hot, and then disappears into the larder in search of fruit cake.

"Mrs Benetto is an excellent cook," he says, emerging with two generous slices of cake on flowered china plates. "I don't know what I'd do without her, to tell the truth. So, you sit there and tell me all about yourself. Your husband is Professor of Classics at one of the London Universities, isn't he?"

"Yes," Evelyn says. Tell me about yourself, the vicar said; yet his immediate question was about Gerald. "He's quite famous for his commentary on *Phaedra.* He is presently working on a new translation of the *Oresteia* for the modern age."

"Ah, Euripides and Aeschylus," the vicar says. "I have to say I find the Greek tragedies quite difficult, although I don't doubt their significance or importance to art. Matricide and patricide, incest and treachery and revenge all over the shop. I sometimes wonder whether we should be encouraging our youth to read them; whether the very artistic merit that makes them worth reading could encourage an impressionable mind to conclude upon a sort of moral greyness, you know."

"I think my husband might not agree with you," Evelyn says. "But I do. I've always considered it of vital importance that we expose developing minds only to positive influences and ideas, especially when it comes to morality and proper behaviour. I do not intend to allow my daughter to read *Phaedra* until she's at least twenty one. Though she may never show any interest in it, anyway. The child is currently obsessed by mammoths."

The vicar chuckles. "All children go through such phases. And some never grow out of them, of course. My mania for collecting – as Mrs Benetto calls it – began when I was a boy."

Evelyn smiles politely. Why on Earth has she come here? she wonders. There's nothing this quiet, pleasant old man can give her: no comfort in his words or in his simple, quaint, oh-so-civilised religion. She was afraid that it would be like this. She should have saved her aching feet, and let her heart bleed on. "Have you always lived in Bransquite?" she says.

"Not at all. I grew up in Oxfordshire. I moved here – oh, it must be forty years ago, when I took charge of the Parish. You wouldn't think it, but it's a very large one, you know – I mean geographically. Some of my parishioners live on the high moor, and see no outsiders except me – and occasionally, the Camelford veterinary surgeon – for months on end. And the Church is the highest one in Cornwall, which is something of an accolade."

"I can easily believe it," says Evelyn, thinking ruefully of how long it took her to walk up the hill. "Who was St Bran? I've never heard of him."

"And why should you? He was a very minor Saint, and a purely local one. The village is named for him, you know. Bransquite – Bran's boundary. Branwalader, to give him his full name, was a tribal ruler during the dark ages – or according to some accounts, a famous storyteller; though I have to say those are very dubious. Lord Crow, his name means, in Cornish. I suppose his people must have considered corvidae to have some special importance. Although it may merely be that he had exceptionally black hair."

Evelyn remembers Mr Frazer's writing on the symbolic significance of horses, and the violent death of Hippolytus. Has the vicar read *The Golden Bough?* She can't help but wonder. But although his comment seems to invite conversation on the topic, she doesn't feel comfortable introducing it. It's too barbaric, too heathen – and she feels sure the chaotic impulses and atavistic feelings the volume has aroused within her will somehow make themselves known to the vicar, and he will be shocked. Or perhaps he *won't* be – which would, in a way, be worse.

"How do you manage, with such a spread out Parish?" Evelyn asks.

"You mean, how do I get people to attend?" The vicar raises an eyebrow. "Well, I haven't yet had to resort to the antics of a colleague of mine, who ended up preaching to cardboard cut-outs. I trust to the consciences of my parishioners, Mrs Murray. And if that fails to work, I get on my pony and pay a conscience-raising pastoral visit. I have a motor car, but I must admit I rarely use it; the roads round here are not really suitable for motors."

"My husband borrowed a car for our journey here, but it's been returned to London," Evelyn says, wistfully. "I miss it terribly. If I had it here, I might go into Camelford, or Plymouth, or somewhere. Anywhere; just somewhere."

"Well," the vicar says. "You might borrow mine, if you had a driver."

"Really?"

"Certainly. As I said, I rarely use it. Perhaps you might repay the favour by attending occasionally on Sundays. You might even use it to drive your family and Annie Tredinnik up the hill, and park outside the Church. But don't worry, I shan't insist."

"I don't know," Evelyn says. "My gardener may drive. I shall find out."

"Lets hope so," the vicar says. "I should be happy to think I've brought a little passing happiness to another human soul, even if it is only of the earthly variety. Who is your gardener? I remember Jeremy Chyneweth used to work for old Mr Hart, before he passed away."

"His name is Johnny," says Evelyn. "I don't know his surname."

"Haven't you made it your business to find out?" asks the vicar, in astonishment.

"Not really." Evelyn pauses. Johnny's troubled circumstances are his own private affair, and no business of the vicar's. "As long as the staff do their jobs properly and keep out of my way, I don't care to know too much about them."

"Hmm," the vicar says. "Perhaps you should. I find it is always advisable to find out everything one can about anybody, especially when one is employing him inside one's house. Take it from an old man with fifty years of bad mistakes behind him. Ignorance is rarely bliss."

"I am sure I've nothing to worry about," Evelyn says airily. "Johnny is a perfectly fine young man."

"I expect he is," the vicar says. "Most people are, when you give them the chance to be. But it would still be wise to make enquiries."

"Well," Evelyn says. "I'll make certain to ask him, when I speak to him about the car. It's so kind of you to offer to lend it."

She swirls her tea-leaves in the bottom of her cup. The pattern into which they're settling resembles the jagged stone tors of the high moor, block upon block. She lifts her gaze from the cup, and stares through the kitchen window. The air is clear enough for her to see the looming forms of Bronn Wennili and Rough Tor silhouetted in the distance against the cloudy sky, like huge, primitive altars. They remind her of the temples of ancient Egypt and Mesopotamia, remnants from the half forgotten dawn of civilisation. She wonders whether she ought to find them, or this archaic resonance, frightening. She feels oddly distanced from the thought.

What would it take for her to tell the vicar what is troubling her? Who would he have to be, this kindly old man who collects butterflies? Not who he is: that much is certain.

If he had been Diana's acolyte, she realises, instead of Christ's, perhaps she could have confessed her confusion. The Priest of the Nemian grove would have given her sound counsel. He would have told her exactly what to do, without blathering on about attendance at a Church in which she no longer has any faith, if she ever did, and the dubious necessity of knowing one's servants. He would have understood the real nature of her conflict, which lies, she suddenly perceives with an epiphanic clarity that hits her like a slap, between a milk-soppish, decadent conservatism that demands she hold fast to her marriage vows and keep her pledge to a failing monarch, and the wild, strong, heathen urge to mate afresh with a young and potent suitor; and he'd have told her, freely, without shame, without fear: go forth, woman, and conceive. The Goddess has summoned her representative and her suitor to the sacred grove, and from their union will spring a young prince fit to rule the coming Age of Man.

It's all deeply metaphorical, of course. Fantastical, even. Even now, Evelyn knows that. Of course she knows her Arica is nothing but a tatty old garden overgrown with honeysuckle, and Johnny isn't really a priest, or a king; but that doesn't make the allegory any less apt: he's not really a gardener, either. *It's the hidden meaning of the myth that is significant*, she thinks, *not its surface composition.* And in this broken, modern world, *this,* not some lily-livered, mealy-mouthed Christian dogma that is centuries out of date, must supply the proper moral code for the coming Aeon. That which was ancient is now modern: that which was for centuries suppressed must now spring free. The wheel has come full circle, the *ouroubos* has seized its own tail. Davenport, though she hates to finally admit it of a thinker by whose teachings she has lived for over a decade, is wrong – and so, too, in his way, is Mussolini. Not in everything, and not because their ideas are particularly radical, or their visions for humanity mistaken; but because they are not radical enough.

"When you have the car," the vicar says. "You might like to pay a visit to Miss Fox, up at Calla. She is an educated lady, you know. She writes for magazines. Of course, she is a Quaker, so I never see her in Church either. Such a pity."

"I've met Miss Fox, briefly," says Evelyn, forcing her distracted attention back to the vicar, and the conversation – though she knows this statement isn't strictly true: Nanny Gould was the person who took tea at the cottage.

"I am not one to gossip, you know, but it's no secret here, and better you learn it from me than Annie Tredinnik. She moved here to escape an unhappy love affair. The man was married, but he conveniently neglected to tell her. A sorry business, and no fault of hers."

"Was he unhappy with his wife?" says Evelyn. She doesn't care, not really. She is thinking of the grove, the Goddess, Johnny.

"I've really no idea. One would suppose so, wouldn't one? Why else embark on an affair?"

"When did all this happen?" Evelyn asks.

"Oh, twenty years ago, or more. She's lived here ever since. One can't help but think it a terrible waste of youth and happiness. Would you like another cup?"

Evelyn shudders. Miss Fox's past seems

uncomfortably like her present. Is twenty years of years of banishment to be her future? *No!* she thinks. *No!* She's no Quaker lady. The similarity is a warning, not a prediction. This is who, and what, you may become, if you don't do something about it.

But she is going to do something about it.

She nods, and smiles at the vicar. "Yes," she says, "I will, thank you." Her words are automatic. She's no longer listening to the old man – if she ever was.

How bright the world is, suddenly. How beautiful. The surface of the tea is sparkling. There's something hypnotic, dreamlike, magical, in the chaotic movement of the fluid, pouring through the teapot spout, swirling down into the china cup. It would be imperceptible to anybody else, she's sure, but Evelyn cannot miss it.

Johnny is going to give me a son, she thinks. *That's why he's here. That's why I had to come to Cornwall.* It's still, admittedly, the obsessive shriek of the cicada, but its key has changed from minor to major: despair to hope, uncertainty to determination.

"I am sure Miss Fox would appreciate the gesture of friendship," the vicar says, and Evelyn is jerked roughly back to the moment. "She has no contact with her family."

"What about her nephew?" she says, frowning.

"Oh, the German boy? He's not her nephew, my dear. He's a refugee from a Jewish orphanage, in Berlin."

"What?" Evelyn says, her hand freezing, her teacup half way to her mouth. The words echo in her head.

"Miss Fox undertakes a number of charitable works," the vicar says. "I must say, she has been lucky with the boy. He seems a very decent sort. Some of them are not."

"Thank you for the tea," Evelyn says quickly, putting down her cup. "I've just noticed the time. This has been a fascinating conversation, but I really must be going."

"Don't mention it, my dear," the vicar says. "You've brightened up an old man's day, which would otherwise have been spent bending over dead butterflies. Do come again, won't you? And at least consider coming to Church. It would be lovely to see you, you know."

Chapter Seventeen:
Honeysuckle

Evelyn walks home. The stone hedges loom over her head, their shadowed oak and holly green intermittently pink with splashes of knapweed and campion, herb robert and valerian. Blood upon the vegetation. Sacrifice on stone. It all makes sense, now, even though the colour is too thin. The flowers watch her, silently.

She is thinking about the politely angry letter she will write to Miss Fox, telling her in no uncertain terms that Martin Stone is no longer welcome in her house. How horrible that the woman tricked her into allowing Leto to associate with such an unsuitable playmate. But she should not have been surprised. Evelyn has never held a very high opinion of the Quakers, with their ridiculous pacifism, and their occult silences.

She won't visit the vicar again either, she realises, though she'll certainly take him up on his offer of the motor car. Johnny can take Annie Tredinnik to Church, if they wish to go; but she, Evelyn Murray, will never again set foot within such a place. Her temple, and her Goddess, are now somewhere else entirely. Perhaps they stand on those high wilderness places of the moor she saw from the vicar's window. What will be her acts of worship? What can she offer that exacting deity? Hymns and prayers, devotion and desire? Will any of those things be enough?

The sticky air feels warm on Evelyn's face, like a lover's breath.

It is four o'clock when she arrives back at Ignatius Hart's old house, and the misty rain is beginning to close in upon the higher slopes. Down in the valley, however, the drizzle is still light, and the glass clear enough for Evelyn to see quite plainly through the French windows to where Johnny is mending the trellis, which has been brought down by the weight of old honeysuckle and young jasmine that scrambled over it. Presumably thinking himself alone, he's removed his shirt, and his damp skin is glistening like pale bronze in the soft light. Every muscle of his strong arms, his powerful chest, his energetic back, ripples smoothly as he moves. Evelyn catches her breath. *Yes*, she thinks, *yes*.

She raises her hand to knock on the window and attract his attention. She has an excuse for summoning him, she thinks: the vicar's car, which she'll shortly send him to collect – at least, assuming he can drive. It doesn't matter if she doesn't send him straight away. She can feel her womb opening inside her, readying itself like freshly tilled soil. *He will give me a son.*

It doesn't matter, either, that she still feels herself in the grip of that peculiar sensation which began to creep across her while she was talking to the vicar: that she is somehow distanced from her surroundings, from her actions, from herself: that nothing, somehow, is entirely real. She doesn't think that she is dreaming; but if this is a dream, then at least it is a comforting one.

But before her fist makes contact with the glass, a figure crosses in front of it: thickset, middle aged, and heavy with femaleness: Nanny Gould. Shocked, embarrassed, furious, Evelyn drops her hand. *Nanny Gould, again.*

The nanny has not seen her. She is crossing the garden, walking boldly, brazenly, towards half clad Hippolytus, wrinkles in her stockings and an enamelled tray in her hands. Evelyn watches in mute, astonished fury as she presents the young man with a glass of lemonade, and stands in front of him, her broad-beamed, grey-clad backside blocking Evelyn's view of him as he drinks it down, standing so she is forced only to imagine the motions of the muscles in his neck, the swelling and sinking of his gullet as he swallows. *Shameless!* Evelyn thinks. *How dare she bring him lemonade!* How dare she stand so close to him, to his beautiful body, close enough to taste his sweat upon the air, close enough to touch him. Touch him? Ha! She'd better not do that, she'd better not touch him; because if she's so shameless, so brazen, such a hussy as to touch him, stroke those greasy fingers across his perfect shoulders, put those fat, dribbling jowls to his sweet lips, then Evelyn really thinks she'll break right through the cracked window pane and rush across the lawn and stab her with the broken glass, yes, stab her, slash her, spit her, spool her bowels on the green green grass. *How dare she!* Oh, how dare she talk to him? How dare she even look at him? Especially now. Especially now. *How dare she, when she's so old, so ugly, the exhausted, heartless, sexless, barren old bitch!* When she is no-one, and nothing. Surely Johnny doesn't want the dirty old whore close to him. Surely, he can't wait for her to leave, take back her disgusting glass and go? Surely, he's only drunk the lemonade because he feels obliged; surely, certainly, he's begun to hate himself before the last drops have been drained, regretting his thirst, wishing Evelyn had been the one who brought him the tray, that Evelyn, and Evelyn alone, had been the one who stood before him, offering herself – oh, vile and wicked Gould!

"Go away," Evelyn hisses, staring at Nanny Gould through the window. "Go." It's a spell, a curse. The nanny can't stay here now, she realises. She can't. Not now. Evelyn will talk to Johnny about the motor car and then, later, she'll make Gould pack her bags and take her ugly backside off the premises, away from him, from everyone. Her era is over.

Johnny hands the glass back to Nanny Gould and wipes his wet mouth on the back of his hand. He smiles, and says something Evelyn cannot hear. Then Nanny Gould turns, and, chuckling – at what? Has Johnny made a joke? Or is the nanny laughing at Evelyn, mocking her supposed innocence, her trusting foolishness? – begins to return to the house. Evelyn steps back quickly from the window, hiding behind the curtain. She doesn't want the vicious old hussy to know she's been seen, and her nasty little game is up. Not yet.

Evelyn takes off her wedding ring, drops it contemptuously into her handbag, and snaps the hasp. *Gerald is nothing,* she tells herself. All that matters now is Johnny.

Mammoth & Crow

The man who calls himself Johnny, but who answers to, as we know, at least one other name, and who is now Evelyn Murray's new gardener, drives the final nail into the trellis and steps back to inspect his handiwork. He's very pleased with it: for a man who left school with no practical skills whatsoever, he has done a decent job. Not only has the trellis been fixed, but the plants that grow upon it have been separated, so each can be retrained to its own, individual support. Now the binding honeysuckle can continue its circuitous twine in confidence that its support will not now suddenly fail, and the delicate winter jasmine can begin to flourish, freed from the overbearing presence of its competitor. Plants can easily be encouraged on a certain course, if they're given the right nudges and allowed the right degree of comfort, just as people can. But they also, Johnny knows, need space to grow, if they are to produce anything of any value.

Choose well, the faceless men have told him.

A sudden, anxious rapping – a hard fist on glass – makes him lift his head. The woman – Evelyn – *Evil-in-carnate,* as he persists in calling her, at least to himself – is standing just inside the French windows, her mouth slack and eyes bulging with a wild, desperate longing, which he thinks he understands. *"Accendate, flammae,"* whispers Johnny. He makes no move to replace his shirt.

Evelyn stands, frozen in the moment, hand pressed against the glass, as Johnny puts down his hammer and nails and strides across the lawn towards her. What is she to say? To do? She wants Johnny. But now she has him – or his attention at least – now he is approaching, crossing, coming (vulgar, filthy, divine, life-gifting word!) over the wet grass, his damp skin shining with drizzle or with sweat – now, she finds herself suddenly overwhelmed by panic. What on Earth has she been thinking? She isn't Nanny Gould, that disgraceful old hag, who can thrust her body at him, making him a present of her sagging breasts, her thick thighs: she's Mrs Evelyn Murray, a woman of style, decorum, and taste. She is Diana's representative on Earth. She can't simply do what every fibre in her body is telling her do, despite the vital force of that need. Johnny hasn't read *The Golden Bough*. He's no follower, as far as she knows, of Davenport. He might not understand. He might assume that her desire is superficial, promiscuous, fleeting, like the girls he's doubtlessly enjoyed in the jazz clubs of London and Berlin, and he might look down on her for it, as he would a common floozy. *No.* She'll have to be more subtle. This isn't about sex, after all, but something more profound than that. Slowly, softly, she allows her hand to slide down the French window pane to the handle of the door. She opens it.

"Johnny," she says. "Oh, Johnny." She tries to sound as if she was simply acknowledging his presence, Mistress to servant: oh, Johnny, there you are, I have a chore for you. But the words creep between her lips as if she's murmuring them to a lover. She flushes. "Johnny," she says, trying – struggling – to be brisk. "The vicar of St Bran's has very kindly offered me the use of his motor car. Do you know how to drive?"

"As a matter of fact," Johnny says, gazing at

her out of those dark eyes, brushing his hands together, as if ridding them of the dust of his prior occupation. "I do."

"Oh, splendid. Can I ask you to do me an immense favour, and go to the vicarage and collect it? If we had a car, we could go for a day out up to the coast, and visit the sea. We could go somewhere pretty. I hear Tintagel's very pretty. That is, if you'd be kind enough to drive."

"I'd be more than delighted to drive you anywhere you want to go," Johnny says. "Will we be including Leto and her nanny on our adventure?"

Evelyn stares at him. "No, Johnny," she answers at last, in a low voice. "No, God forbid. I need – I need to get away from them. From all of it. Quite frankly, I can't stand another moment of this – this dreadful domesticity."

Johnny smiles. "When would you want to go?" he says.

"Tonight. Tomorrow. I don't know. No, tonight. We can sit on the beach and watch the sun set. Unless it's raining."

"It's raining now," Johnny says.

"I know. But it's very light. And perhaps," Evelyn draws a deep breath. "Perhaps it will be clear on the coast."

"Well," Johnny says. "I'll go and change my clothes. It wouldn't do to call upon the vicar in gardening trousers."

"No," says Evelyn.

"No?"

"I meant, yes. Of course you must get out of those clothes. It wouldn't be decent."

"And one must always appear decent in front

of a vicar," Johnny says, softly, half raising one eyebrow. "Even if one is, really, anything but."

"Oh," Evelyn says, flustered. "Yes."

"I'll be back in an hour or two," Johnny says. "I'll try my best to avoid being detained."

"Yes," Evelyn says. "Yes. Thank you, Johnny."

It doesn't take Johnny much more than an hour to walk up the hill to the vicarage and return with the vicar's motor car: a six year old Crossley Golden Saloon with shining wheels and cleanly upholstered dark blue leather seats. Evelyn admires it, delighted. It's not, of course, as smart and fashionable a vehicle as the one which has been returned to London, but it's a car fit to be seen in; although, she realises, she doesn't want anyone to see her in it. Not today. Not with Johnny. Quickly, while he waits in the driving seat, she hurries upstairs to her bedroom to change her clothes. Whatever does one wear for a drive to the Cornish coast? Common sense suggests wellingtons and a raincoat – at least if one's planning to get out of the car – but Evelyn doesn't want anything to do with the restrictive promptings of so-called common sense. She chooses at last to wear a blue-flowered, full skirted summer tea-gown over her new lingerie girdle, which is invisible underneath the tight top bodice of the dress, and gives her body curves where they're required and smooth lines where they are not. This is teamed with a brand new pair of black stockings, satin French panties, and her kitten heels, which despite the fact that she now wears them in the house still add a frisson of sophistication without seeming completely overdressed. Then she sits down in front of her mirror to retouch her make up.

The thought of getting away from Bransquite, if only for a few hours, is wildly, embarrassingly thrilling. What has she become, she asks herself, that the prospect of a mere country drive can elicit such feverish excitement? Evelyn stares at her reflection, and lights up a Camel cigarette. Her empty ring finger chides her from the glass.

It really will be just a drive, she tells her reflection. Whatever her plans are regarding Johnny, it is not as if, right now, she's intending anything more than to spend time in his company, get to know him, throw the line, cast the lure. She takes a long drag on the cigarette, her thirsty blood soaking up the nicotine, lungs revelling in the smoke. A thin stream of grey spirals slowly from between her lips.

We will just talk, she tells her reflection. They'll watch the sunset from the clifftops at Tintagel, or somewhere with an equally good view, and then perhaps they'll find a small and respectable country pub, or similar establishment, in which they'll have dinner. Then Johnny can, for a little while, forget the pressures of necessity which induced him to take employment as a lowly gardener, and be himself again, whoever that self is; and Evelyn will find the appropriate moment to ask him his real name – and he will tell her. After that – well, we'll all have to wait, and see.

"Yes," Evelyn says aloud. "That's what we will do." She takes another long, deep drag on her Camel cigarette, then grinds its tip into the black ashtray. The car is waiting.

Of course, that isn't what they do. It was never going

to be, was it? They set off through the verdant countryside, through Camelford, toward the coast. They don't speak much, exchanging only a few short words, about the vicar, and the poor choice of weather for an outing. They don't look for a place to watch the crashing waves, or view the sunset – not that much of it would be visible if they did, behind the blanket of dark grey cloud – and they certainly don't think for one moment of heading back to civilisation and finding somewhere to have dinner. After a while, Johnny turns the car through rain-washed farmland down a narrow lane that leads towards the high sea-cliffs, and pulls into a murky lay-by overlooking the restless, bottle-green sea. Evelyn doesn't ask why they have stopped.

Johnny turns to Evelyn, and puts his hand upon her stockinged knee. He pauses for a moment, assessing her reaction, then, when she doesn't object, glides it smoothly and determinedly upwards, underneath the neat hem of her summer dress, towards the naked portion of her thigh that lies between her panties and the top of her stocking. Evelyn does not move. She's not sure, for a second, what this is. She wants Johnny, of course she does, but she hasn't really dared imagine it would be quite so easy to get him – after all, didn't he run away from their first kiss? She thought it would take much, much more than this. *And probably,* she thinks, *it should.* She's not some floozy, after all. She remembers herself standing the window, her hand raised, thinking to herself: *I'm Mrs Evelyn Murray.* She doesn't want Johnny to consider her one. But then he moves his fingers higher still, and begins to brush them over the soft fabric of her French panties, caressing her female parts in a manner that would never have occurred to Gerald had she given him a million years. She remembers her meeting with the vicar, and what the Priest of the Grove would certainly have told her do. Perhaps the speed with which events are moving doesn't matter. She no longer needs to adhere, after all, to an outdated, slave morality. As Diana's representative, surely she can do whatever she likes with her Virbius. Then she realises she has already parted her legs, that Johnny is touching her now in a way that would have been impossible if she hadn't spread them as wide as they can go – which isn't really very far within the confined cabin of the motor car. The realisation startles her. Her body, plainly, is some considerable distance ahead of her mind. *I'm not some tart,* she tries to tell him. But it seems the primal forces that are at work are more powerful than this residual shame: her words come out as a low, throaty sigh, and her hips begin to rock against his pressing fingers.

Her hands reach out to clutch his strong shoulders. She gives in, strokes his young face, his strong neck, and pulls him toward her, bringing his lips to hers. He pulls her panties to one side, and slides his fingers inside them, and she realises her womb has already made itself ready, that it is willing, open. *A son*, she thinks. Now the fingers of her left hand are clenching hard around his shoulders, and her right hand is roaming frantically over the top of his shirt, seeking a way in, and she is undoing his tie, and pulling loose his shirt tails, and her fingers are on his trouser buttons.

Johnny gently removes his hand, and, leaning over, engages the lever that will allow Evelyn's seat to recline. Suddenly, she has much more space, and so does he. He carefully clambers over the imposing handbrake and lies on top of her, propping himself up on one elbow.

"Say it," he tells her. "Say it."

Evelyn undoes the buttons, one by one, and now he is free. She spreads her legs again. Now she is on her back, the whole business is much more satisfactory, as she can press her left knee up against the window, and rest her right ankle on the lower rim of the steering wheel. She wishes for a moment they'd been able to lie down together on the grass, or in a bed somewhere – perhaps later they'll go to an inn, and book a room as man and wife – but then she finally stops thinking, because Johnny's pulling her loose panties once more to the side, and taking her hips firmly in his hands, to angle them for his convenience. "Say it," he tells her again.

I can't say it, she thinks. It's so coarse, so vulgar to admit to wanting sex: but if she doesn't, will Johnny pull away, leave her untouched, unsatisfied? That can't happen. He is her Virbius.

"Take me," she whispers. And despite this she's almost surprised when a second later she finds him doing exactly that; and a word she'd never say leaps into her mind, and it's the right word, the perfect word, the only word left that makes any sense. She and Johnny are *fucking,* like primitive heathens, fucking like ancient Gods, fucking like Diana and Virbius in the sacred grove of Arica: fucking in the vicar's borrowed Crossley saloon, on the cliff above Tintagel, in the rain. A wave of deep, profound, primitive pleasure overwhelms her. Quickly, astonishingly, it spreads out, running down the insides of her thighs, making her feet tingle, and upwards into her belly and the hard round nipples of her breasts. Her legs feel weak. Her left knee jerks violently against the window, her right heel slips from the steering wheel, and crashes into the foot well, knocking off her kitten heeled shoe. She doesn't notice. *Virbius, Virbius.*

In the confusion of her orgasm, which is the first she's ever experienced, Evelyn isn't quite sure how long she lies, without moving, on the reclining leather seat, Johnny's weight pressing down on top of her, his hips nestling between her legs. But eventually she realises he's no longer inside her, and puts her hand down to stroke his oh-so-muscular stomach, and – though she isn't yet brazen enough to admit it, even to herself – to see whether there is any chance that his now flaccid manhood can be coaxed back to firmness. The leather seat is slippery; when she lifts her hand, she can just make out the faint shimmer of semen on her fingertips in the dying evening light.

A sudden rage courses through Evelyn's blood, like white-hot venom. She struggles to contain it.

"Did you – " she begins.

"Don't worry. I pulled out, of course. I'm not an idiot, Evelyn."

"Oh..."

"It's my responsibility to look after you, you know," Johnny says.

"You don't have to bother about that," Evelyn says. "I can't have any more children."

"Really?"

"Yes. It's terribly sad, of course." She's lying to him, and she knows it. Lying to a man – the man who's only just become her lover. Conception's never been Evelyn's problem – if anything, she finds that part easier than most. But it has to be done. If Johnny's to give her a son, she needs him to sow his seed within her, not spill it recklessly across the front seat of the vicar's Crossley Golden.

"Let's go to an hotel," Evelyn says. "Now. I want you to make love to me all night, over and over, till I can't stand up."

"Very good, madam," says Johnny. He sits back, and begins to readjust his rumpled clothing, tucking in his shirt and fastening his buttons.

"Promise me you won't ever pull out again."

Johnny clambers back over the handbrake, and regards the rain streaming down the outside of the windows, while Evelyn takes off her stained satin panties and hides them at the bottom of her handbag.

"I don't much want to go out in that weather," Johnny says. "I hope the car will start."

"Promise me," Evelyn says again. "You'll – you know... I want to have all of you, and not be left feeling I've been abandoned halfway through."

"Fair enough," says Johnny. "If that's really what you want."

"Oh, God," says Evelyn. "Let's wait for this wretched rain to ease first. I don't want you to catch your death of cold working the starting handle."

Johnny laughs. "I'm used to cold," he says. "It doesn't bother me."

"But I'm warm," says Evelyn, deciding to push it. She reaches across the handbrake.

They eventually arrive in the village of Tintagel three hours after dusk, and having tidied up each others' dishevelled appearance to some degree of decency, rent a double room under the names of Mr and Mrs Bertie Hart, in the local hotel. In order to avoid suspicion, Evelyn's temporarily replaced her wedding ring upon her finger, though this reminder of Gerald sickens her. They eat a late and hurried dinner in the bar, before heading upstairs to the warm room with its soft, cavernous bed; and there they finally undress, and share a cigarette, and briefly sleep; and then on waking do it all again, until their appetites are satisfied, and a grey dawn is creeping over the horizon in the distant east.

"You don't like your husband very much, do you?" Johnny says, as Evelyn rummages in her handbag for Camel and Zippo.

"No," Evelyn says. "But he doesn't want me, Johnny. He's made that perfectly plain."

"So," Johnny says, leaning back upon the pillows, and putting his hands behind his head. "Have there been many, before me?"

"Many what?"

"Lovers. Men."

"God, no," Evelyn says. She taps a cigarette free from the box, and quickly lights it. "No, you're the first."

"You astonish me, Mrs Murray."

Evelyn drags upon her cigarette. "Don't call me that," she says, sharply. "And it's true. I'm not some cheap tart, whatever you may be thinking."

"I'm not thinking that. But I am wondering."

"Wondering what?"

"What changed? What made you decide I was worth breaking your wedding vows for?"

Evelyn laughs. It has a brittle sound, but she doesn't notice. "Well," she says. "It was your overwhelming virility. Naturally."

"Thank you."

"I married the wrong man," Evelyn says. "I was seventeen, Johnny. How can anyone know what's best for one at seventeen? I should have waited."

"Perhaps," Johnny says, reaching for the cigarette, "you should never have married at all. Women can have careers now, you know. It's the modern way."

"No," Evelyn says, flatly. "I don't approve of career women. It's bad for the race."

"Hmm." Johnny draws on the cigarette, and hands it back to Evelyn. "Well, I do. I think it's a shame how many intelligent and forceful women end up hollowed out and boring on account of getting married. Marriage is a dead end for a smart woman. There are more important things in life than looking after a husband and bearing children."

"Such as?" Evelyn says.

"Art. Music. Literature. Science. Politics. Travel." He flashes her a low, measuring glance. "I've seen places you would not believe. And people who'd make you question everything you think you know."

"Dog headed men?" Evelyn says, a little scornfully.

Johnny laughs. "Maybe."

"All right," Evelyn says, settling down beside him on the pillow. "So tell me: where have you been?"

"A place where nothing is as it appears, and all is in constant flux: where rivers speak, and human beings have no faces. A place where the sky is violet, and the sun never truly rises, or fully sets. And India.

I've also been to India."

Evelyn shoves him, playfully. "I should have known not to expect a sensible answer," she says. "Oh, Johnny, who are you, really? I shan't breathe a word, you know."

"Who am I really? Call me Johnny Nobody, if you're so keen for me to have a name."

"But who are your family, Johnny? Your father?"

"It doesn't matter. I'm dead to him. To all of them."

"Surely not. Surely – "

Johnny reaches over, plucks Evelyn's cigarette from her startled fingers, and stubs it out. "Come here, woman," he says, pulling her towards him. "We're wasting time."

Chapter Eighteen:
Snow

Martin has been reading for some considerable time when he realises the beam of the Bakelite torch is beginning to flicker. The atmosphere within the antechamber has grown cold and still, and somehow the smell of snow hangs in the air. Martin looks up, wriggles his cramped shoulders. He ought to go home, he thinks. It isn't safe to stay – especially if the weather's on the turn. But *snow?* Snow, falling in summer? Perhaps he's mistaken. He looks down at the pile of letters that lies across his lap. It's very wrong of him to be reading them. But curiosity is urging him continue, despite the faltering torch beam and the fact that he is shivering. *There's something very important in these letters,* he thinks; something even more important than the confirmation Johnny is both who and what Martin has thought him, but as yet, he hasn't found it. Can he take them out of the tunnel? But then both he and they will be exposed on the high moor, and the wind might blow the papers out of his hands; or he might attract the attention of the sentinel crow, and the crow fly straight to Horsefeathers with news of his trespass.

Mammoth & Crow

The torch beam is growing fainter, a smear of yellow over the typed letters. But as it fades, the realisation slowly steals in upon Martin that despite this, the chamber is no longer dark. From somewhere beyond the back wall, against which the camp bed stood before being dragged away, there is coming another light: a grey, cold light, like pre-dawn twilight. Puzzled, Martin turns towards it. Somehow, the wall no longer looks as solid as it did before: as if, instead of heavy granite stone, it's suddenly become recognisable as nothing but painted plasterboard, like the set of a play. He folds the letters, scrambles to his feet.

Where is that coming from? Is it reflecting from the surface of the wall? It can't be coming through it, Martin thinks. The world may be full of strange potentialities, but he is confident some things, like the opacity of solid stone, remain fixed. Perhaps the rear of the chamber is larger than he thought. Perhaps it has another opening, no bigger than a slit, somewhere on the high moor – and it's through that tiny gap that the inexplicable scents that were previously of flowers and right now seem to be of snow are finding their way inside.

Perhaps, if he can find it, it will give sufficient light to carry on reading. He can switch off the torch, and save what remains of the battery for his exit – because he doesn't really want to pick his way along the tunnel in the dark.

Martin approaches the back wall. As he closes in on it, it seems to shiver, like the surface of a pond. He remembers the mirror-like silvering of air through which he passed on the day he got lost upon the moor, and instinctively he puts his hand into his pocket, groping for the bear claw like a boy trying to find his door key in the dark.

The claw is warm. Is it from his own body heat, he wonders, or something else? He grips it tightly, and stares at the moving, shimmering surface in front of him. It's no longer a wall. It is a waterfall – a silvery, semi-transparent net of shapes and lines and intersections, dark points of stillness on a moving wave; and through it he can see – or thinks he can see, which may be sufficient, or another thing entirely – snow covered moor, lying silent and hard frozen under a cloud spattered violet sky.

Martin puts his hand up to touch the stone face of the wall. His fingers explore the cold, dry surface: the rough hewn flatness of the stones themselves, the damp, spiderwebby cracks between them. It's still there, right enough: still a solid, stone wall, still impassible, still real; and yet now he can see through it more clearly, as if the land behind it is shifting from one reality to another, transforming to a place in which this tunnel does not exist, and the hillside lies exposed to wintry winds. He lowers his hand. The bear claw in his pocket grows warmer.

What should he do? Should he leave now, run back to the moor that he has left behind, to his crows, and to Miss Fox, before the shimmering veil grows thin enough for him to pass? Will his own world, this world of here and now, continue to exist if he goes through? Will he be able to return, if he dares step forth into the other?

Curiosity killed the cat, Miss Fox sometimes says. It's a very curious expression. Martin's never seen a cat killed by curiosity – though he's all too often encountered the remains of field mice who have met their ends upon the greedy teeth of a curious Fluffy. And cats are usually very adept at extricating themselves from danger. *Anyway*, Martin thinks, *I'm not a cat. I am the boy who talks to birds.*

As if on cue – or in response to this very thought – a shape appears within the shifting, formless image – a definite thing, a black certainty sharply delineated against the infinite whiteness of the moor, flying towards him, coming closer and closer. *A crow.*

Martin stares. The crow lands on the snow in front of him, and opens its beak. "Boy," it says. "Boy."

The glass-like, shimmering surface of the wall expands. It balloons toward Martin, as if inviting him in, like a bubble of liquid enveloping an insect. The bear claw glows red hot against the palm of his hand. He takes his hand away from it. "How will I get back home?" he demands of the crow, guessing if it's come to meet him, it must have done so with some sort of purpose. *Perhaps it is a guide*, he thinks.

The crow cocks its head on one side, and eyes him, thoughtfully. "Claw," it says at last, as if addressing a simpleton.

Martin feels foolish. *Of course,* he thinks. *The claw's a key.* This must be what the faceless people meant when they spoke of his having such a thing. He remembers the man's first words to him: *You are not the wizard.* He's not the only person to possess one, then. Horsefeathers – Johnny – has another. But how did he come by it? Was it a gift, as the woman seemed to think that Martin's is? Or did he steal it?

The crow hops from one foot to another, opens its sharp beak, and flutters its wings, like a fledgeling seeking to be fed.

"I have nothing for you," Martin tells it. He wondered if it's the sentinel. If it is, the last time they met, he gave it a cheese sandwich. "I'm sorry," he says. "I didn't expect to see you." He pauses. "You won't tell Horsefeathers I was here, will you? I promise the next time we meet, you can have all my sandwiches, if you want them."

The crow ceases its fluttering, and stares at him. Martin can't avoid the feeling that it is annoyed. *I hope it's not the sentinel*, he thinks. Though, on the other hand, if it is, it's obviously found its way into the Otherworld – and unless Johnny travels back there, he won't be hearing anything from it for quite a while. This thought makes him feel considerably happier.

The light from the Otherworld is now extremely bright. Perhaps it's midday there, and the sun's reflecting off the snow. Martin wonders how long he'll be able to stand the cold of an Otherworld winter. Perhaps it won't be cold at all, unless he wants it to be. He has no idea.

Curiosity has never killed Fluffy, Martin thinks. *It won't kill me.*

He grips the bear claw tightly in his fist, and steps forward through the shining stones.

On the other side of the Gateway, underneath the violet sky, the snow seems almost pink. Martin stares at it for a moment, remembering how his vision became swamped by blue as soon as he leapt over the stream on the high moor. It's a queer thing, but his memories of that visit seem to be returning. It's exactly like the way that sometimes, when you're dreaming, you will remember an earlier dream, which has completely escaped your conscious mind. *Perhaps dreams are real, too,* Martin thinks. Perhaps, when he's sleeping, he's really visiting some other world, whose physical laws are not at all like those of this one, and whose reality can only be recalled when one is there, actively experiencing it.

But this is real, he decides. The snow, the violet sky, the sentinel crow. Impossible, now, to imagine otherwise. He looks about him. He is standing on a sloping stretch of barren moorland, different only from the one he has left in its season, and the time of day. Here, as he suspected, it is noon, and a stark white sun is shining onto frozen earth. He shivers. The air is very cold, though, thankfully, there is no wind. The low sunlight feels surprisingly warm on the bare skin of his face.

The sentinel crow hops from one foot to the other. It flings itself into the air, black wings beating, and flaps some distance down the snowy valley side, before perching itself upon what looks like a small, branch-less tree, perhaps three and a half feet in height. It caws loudly. *It wants me to follow it,* Martin thinks. He wonders if he should. He was able to trust it before, though then he had had something to offer it. But what danger can the crow be leading him towards that's not already a danger to him? The monsters of the Otherworld can surely find him where he stands. He looks around, thinking nervously of the Lizard-bear, but there's no sign of it. Perhaps today it has better things to do: more dangerous enemies to chase. Martin gives a shrug, and trudges forwards into the white. The icy crust of the compacted snow crunches beneath his boots. He leaves shallow footprints on the slab. The world will remember him, for a time.

As he comes closer, Martin realises that the crow hasn't settled on a tree at all, even a small one. It's sitting on the curved top of a carved and varnished staff, whose end has been driven perhaps a foot deep into a frozen drift. It looks similar to the one that was being carried by the faceless man whom Martin met on the open moor. But there is, of course, no bundle of feathers or bird's skull tied to it: instead, there is a living bird, the crow itself, sharp eyed, alert, and hungry.

Is the staff intended for him? Or does it belong to somebody else, somebody who has plunged it into fresh fallen snow and left it as an anchor, tethering himself to this world even while he walks in another? *Perhaps it belongs to Johnny*, he thinks. What will happen if Martin touches it? Will the wizard know? Or is he now so far away, so focused on his seduction of Evelyn Murray, that he knows nothing else?

Martin puts one hand on the staff, experimentally. The crow squawks, and pecks gently at his fingers. It's not hostile, as such, but it does seem to be giving him a warning. "It's all right," he tells it. "I won't take it. I just want to see if I can move it." He puts his fingers round the black wood, and tries to wriggle the staff out of the snow, but it's frozen solid. How long has it been here? What does time mean, here in the Otherworld?

He removes his hand. The wizard's letters rustle underneath his arm, and begin to slip. Quickly, he readjusts his grip on the escaping papers, and in doing so his eye falls on the letter he was reading before the Gateway presented itself to him. He can read it easily now, without straining his eyes, and he remembers the compulsion he felt to continue reading until he should discover whatever secret is contained within. It seems strange, even to himself, that this should be the first thing he would think of, here, in this new world that must be full of wonders: but Martin Stone is no Jack Trott, climbing the beanstalk purely to learn what is there at the top of it. He's not so easily distracted. There is something in the letters that he needs to know; and perhaps there's something in the nature of this place that will make plain what was indecipherable before, as if it is, in a way, custodian of their meaning, just as it is keeper of the staff.

It won't take long to read them here, he decides. *Not under this brilliant, violet light.*

He looks up, and scans the environment. Everything is still, everywhere empty apart from the crow and himself. The Gateway to the wizard's chamber shivers faintly twenty feet away: it will be easy to return through it, should someone appear.

He lowers his gaze, and begins, again, to read.

Chiswick, London.
May 1st, 1927,

Phillip,

I do not know what on earth you mean by evil ideology, or why you should be worried about Mussolini. Mussolini has only ever expressed respect for the military and economic might of the British Empire, and I can reassure you that his designs are not focused upon us, but upon those countries in Africa and so forth that were previously ruled by Rome, and which have since fallen under the control of barbarians. I am pleased to see that you are keen to take an interest in such matters, but if you are to succeed in politics, you must spend some time educating yourself properly with regard to those theories and ideas that you so naively dismiss. You must agree that it is better for the weak to be ruled by the strong than to fail abjectly in their own governance. That is the principle upon which Britannia is founded and run. Our country requires the strongest government to take her Empire forward to a glorious future, and to defeat those elements within her who would bring her down. Is the acknowledgement of such a principle evil?

I must ask you again, Phillip, to come home. I imagine that your bank account is now empty. I repeat what I said a few weeks ago: there will be no more money until you desist in this ridiculous charade. We will find another school, and you will put this whole shoddy business behind you. We will never speak of it again. Your future stepmother is very keen to meet you, and to put your mind at rest regarding her character, associations, and so forth. The wedding is in six weeks.

Father.

Is Phillip, Martin wonders, yet another of the many names that seem to attach themselves to Johnny Horsefeathers? Perhaps it is, in fact, his real name: he's never been remotely convinced by the man's assertion that 'Johnny' is. He qualified it, after all, by saying 'to all intents and purposes,' which is, as we all know, a phrase that can mean anything between 'for right now' and 'for ever', and have no basis in any self evident truth. To all intents and purposes, Martin is Miss Fox's nephew. Reality can be a fragile thing when it's employed 'to all intents and purposes.' But if Johnny is Phillip, who is *Father?*

A dark, horrible suspicion is beginning to make itself felt in Martin's mind. He pushes it away. *It's impossible,* he thinks. The sentinel crow opens and closes its beak.

Impossible? it says. *Look around you, boy who talks to birds. What, exactly, is impossible?*

Martin stamps his feet in the hard snow. His breath is clouding the still air. He folds the letter and puts it to the bottom of the pile, before unfolding the next.

4th May, 1927

Father,

The fact that you do not see why Mussolini is a monster and his ideas noxious only proves my point. I will not bother to explain, because you are not prepared to listen, and would only dismiss my argument as naive and ignorant.

I have said already that I will not come home and I will not speak to that woman, so I must politely request that you desist in asking me to do so. I have no desire to be at a wedding to which I have the strongest objections, so don't assume that telling me about it will make me change my mind. I don't need any money either.

Phillip

Well. Whatever he is, wizard or liar or anything else, Johnny – Phillip isn't wholly a bad man, Martin thinks, reluctantly. He looks up. The sentinel crow is fluttering on the staff. Tucking its head beneath its wing, it has begun to preen its feathers, its black plumage shimmering dark purple underneath the violet sky. There's still no-one else in sight.

The silence is extraordinary. Martin's never been up on the moor in winter. Miss Fox has always been very clear it's not a wise thing to attempt. He's never imagined that the place could be so quiet, so still. *It is waiting for something to arrive*, he thinks. *Or someone.*

He notices he has begun to shiver. How much more time can he spend here, in this cold, reading these letters? Perhaps he should hurry back to the chamber. He looks behind, to see if the Gateway is still hanging in the air, an oval of distorted light, like a pane of poorly blown glass. To his relief, he sees nothing has changed: the portal remains open. The bear claw, too, is still comfortingly warm in his pocket. Perhaps he doesn't need to worry. But it is uncomfortable standing in the cold. Surely, there must be a sheltered place somewhere nearby where he can sit down, and finish his reading?

Martin turns on the spot like a spinning top, looking around. The great grey bulk of Rough Tor rises to his left, looking like the sleeping dragon he saw – or imagined – on the day he lost his bearings on the moor and met the *Shaydim*. That beautiful, midsummer day, which he had somehow almost forgotten, but remembers now as vividly as if it happened a moment ago. *I can find somewhere to shelter in amongst the crags*, he thinks. There will be north facing places where the snow hasn't settled, or even blown; somewhere he can sit without ending up wet through.

He turns away from the black staff, and begins to trudge uphill. The mirrored Gateway shimmers in his wake. The sentinel crow gives a sharp, sudden caw of alarm, and rises from its perch, flapping around his head. *Don't go wandering off,* it's telling him. *You'll get lost.*

"Not this time, I won't. I know where I am," Martin says, reasonably. "And I won't lose sight of the staff, or of the Gateway."

Remember the little girl. Remember the picnic.

"So that *was* you." Martin feels oddly vindicated. "She was being silly," he says. "I'm sensible. And I have my compass and ordnance survey map."

Neither of which is a lot of use here, the crow remarks.

That's true, Martin remembers. The Otherworld, of course, is uncharted territory. But he continues walking.

Eventually, he reaches a place between two tall rocks, where the ground, though frozen solid, is free from any covering of snow. He sits down, keeping the staff in sight – though it's now a long way downslope, a short, black, vertical line in a flat ocean of white, and he can't see the Gateway to his world at all. He stamps the powdery snow from his boots, and brushes it from his socks. His calves, bare beneath his short trousers, have turned red with cold. He shivers. He will read the last few letters and go home, he thinks.

10th May, 1927

Father,

My uncle Ignatius has sent me word that you ordered someone to his house in search of me. Naturally, I was not there, but my uncle was put severely out of sorts by the business, as the damnable hoods that you employed cracked one of his French windows. As a result, I have decided that it is best for me to cease contact with you altogether, as plainly I am putting innocent people at risk by association. I warned you that you should refrain from this sort of bullying, but you refused to listen to me in this, just as you have in everything else. I hope you intend to make good the financial loss to my uncle. I don't want any more of your money, but you sure as hell owe him a few bob.

Phillip

Martin knows that cracked window – it's the one through which he watched Mrs Murray kissing Johnny. *I think Fireborn must have been Uncle Ignatius*, he thinks. *He was the man who originally owned the books – and Leto's house. He must have been a wizard, too. Perhaps he taught Horsefeathers*

– Johnny – Phillip.

He unfolds the next letter, and continues reading. There are three more, in total, none particularly long, but when Martin has finished the last one, he reads it again over and over in disbelief. When he's recovered from his shock, he rolls it up, and stuffs it, with the others, rather clumsily, into his pocket. He stares across the moor. For all his suspicions, he hadn't really expected to come across the name he has just read. Now, he does not know what on Earth to do. This was the secret, evidently.

"I should tell Leto," he says, aloud, to nobody in particular.

Yes, says the crow. *You should.*

"But I might be wrong. It might be a mistake, or a coincidence."

The low sun is already dropping down the sky. It's long past noon – though what time it was when he entered the wizard's den, Martin can't say. Has any time passed in his own world while he's been lingering in this one? He stands up, and rubs his cold legs in the hope of restoring some circulation. His skin smarts at the touch. *At least I have a coat*, he thinks, grateful for Miss Fox's generosity. If he'd come through the Gateway into this bleak season without one, he'd certainly have frozen.

Looking out over the moor, he scans the horizon. The valley in front of him remains as still and quiet as it was before, but there is movement on the opposite slope. He squints, shading his eyes with his hand, hoping against the sudden gripe of fear it's not the Lizard-bear.

It's not. A group of twenty or so people, human shaped, leather clad, carrying wooden spears in quivers on their backs, is approaching slowly through the snow. *Shaydim*, Martin thinks. *Faceless men*. He remembers Leto warning him that *they are on the move*. But this time, they've no ox-cart with them, being instead accompanied by an uncountable, perhaps ever changing number of red eared, dense furred dogs, who are ploughing their way determinedly though the drifts ahead of them.

Hunters, Martin thinks, *a small party scouting ahead of the rest.* He doesn't know whether he should be afraid. Perhaps these people are the ones who placed the black staff in the snow, and they'll be angry he has touched it. Perhaps they're coming to see what has come through the Gateway. But when he met them before, he remembers, they gave him no cause to fear them – and besides, he has passed on their message to Horsefeathers. It's pointless hiding from them if they are harmless. They might even be friendly. He steps out from between the stones.

The crow flies ahead of him, landing, as it did before, on the staff, and cawing loudly. The hunters see it, and immediately their demeanour changes, and with it their direction. Their progress becomes swift and purposeful, heading towards the noise with a long legged, loping stride that reminds Martin of bears or wolves galloping toward potential prey. The sight is uncanny: not quite human, somehow, like a man who has one brown eye and one blue. *But the faceless men aren't human,* he reminds himself, sharply. *They're both much more and less than that.*

Martin reaches the staff first – he is, after all, much closer to it – and stands calmly waiting by it, with one eye on the faintly glimmering surface of the portal, in case he needs to make a quick getaway. He's not entirely sure the opening will persist for long once the faceless men have arrived. He's pretty sure they can't pass through it, but they seem from his previous experience to have some knowledge of the paths – the *Moments*, perhaps, as Leto Murray would say – that connect the one world with the other. He puts his hand in his pocket, feeling for the claw. It's still quite warm. That's a good sign.

As soon as the leader of the faceless men is close enough, Martin raises his hand. "Felicitations of the Moment," he says.

The faceless men stop moving, as one, and turn their empty hoods towards him. Martin can feel their stares like heat upon his skin, though he can't see their eyes. He stands up straighter, reluctant to reveal any weakness.

"Felicitations, bird boy," says the leader of the men, at last.

He's not the man who gave Martin the message. His voice is younger, thinner, and harsher. But nevertheless, he has recognised Martin; has called him by the name by which the people of the Otherworld – and Horsefeathers – seem to know him. "I found Horsefeathers," he says. "I passed on the message I was given."

The man gives a grunt. *In satisfaction?* Martin wonders. *Or vexation?* Or is it something else entirely? There's no way of telling. How can anyone interpret the reactions of a man who has no face?

"He comes here, doesn't he?" Martin says, suddenly emboldened. "He uses this Gateway. He's a wizard, isn't he? This is his staff."

The man stares at him. Perhaps he's spoken out of turn, Martin thinks. But something drives him on to ask again. "Will you tell me what the message means? What is *Pavor Potentia?* Why are you moving?"

"You will find out in time, bird boy; perhaps sooner than you wish. Then you will never forget."

"Why won't you tell me?" Martin says.

"Because until you have seen it, you will never understand it."

Martin feels insulted by this. *Why won't I understand?* he thinks. He's not, by any measure, a stupid boy: Miss Fox has commented on the quickness of his mind, and so did his grandmother. He shuffles his feet. The looser top grains of piled snow are creeping through the lace holes of his leather boots. "No," he says. "You may be right that I won't understand it *properly* until I see it, but I deserve some idea what it is. It isn't fair you should have asked me to carry such an important message without letting me know anything of what it means."

The leader of the men grunts again. He looks Martin over, silently. *Assessing me*, Martin thinks.

"What do you understand of time, bird boy?" the man asks him, at last.

"Time?" Martin hesitated. Time is supposed to be a line, he knows: an arrow, shooting from the past into the future, pulling everything along with it. But somehow, he doesn't think that, right here, right now, this response is the right one. "I don't think I do really understand it," he says.

"Time," says the man, "is a sea of moments. *Moments.* And these Moments, these events, are constantly in motion: never certain, never fixed, whirling and churning in the waves, like bubbles in beach foam. Your world – which is a reflection of this one, just as this world is a reflection of yours – is constantly coming and going in and out of being as each moment passes. Your people ride like fishermen on small dugouts atop the waves, seeing only the surface, never the chaos underneath. But we who dwell in this world know to look beneath the skin. We watch every event as it develops, spiralling first this way then that, as every variable increases or decreases in probability; until finally potential becomes certainty, and the bubbles burst upon the surface of the sea. So it is that both our worlds are made of nothing more than sea foam, and what comes to pass never lingers long, but vanishes quickly back into the rolling wave. We know this, and we do not fear it. But there are some Moments, bird boy, whose consequences are of far greater significance than most: some poisonous bubbles which if they should be allowed to break would prove so catastrophic they could bring about the extinction of your world and ours with it. Then there would be no-one left to ride the waves, no-one to watch the bubbles burst. There would be only time. One such of these is the *Pavor Potentia*."

The man was right, Martin thinks. He does not understand it. He wonders whether Johnny Horsefeathers does. He stamps his feet, shaking off the creeping snow.

"Where does it come from?" he says. "How did it start?"

"Long ago," the man says, "the people who walked in your world and in ours were as one. Your people knew, as we still know, the blood, bone, fire, stone link between the mammoth and the land. But there came into being a strange, new people, who saw only that they could hunt, and kill, and devour: and they would neither understand nor believe the ways in which the mammoth makes the land, and the land the Tribes of Man. One day, with their sharp spears, they killed a young bull whom they'd found in lowly, woodland scrub. He was not unusual for his kind, nor in any way special amongst them, but his death tipped the scales: when he fell to his knees, then it became inevitable his whole species would follow into extinction. That, bird boy, was his Moment. We had foreseen its coming. Though we grieved, we did not seek to intervene. But what we did not know, to our potential cost and yours, was that at a tiny, pinprick point, somewhere deep in the eye socket of that dying bull, there had popped into existence a second potentiality, of a far more dangerous event: that of the extinction of all things, including these two Worlds of fixity and transformation. It is not yet fixed, not certain, but it exists, none the less; and as your human species progresses through time, it grows. For tens of millennia, it has done so only by increments: tiny, sub-atomic swellings that would be invisible to the eye of mammoth, man, or crow. But now, it is growing."

"Does Horsefeathers understand it?" Martin says. For all the wizard's occult knowledge, he has to doubt it.

"That is a thing I do not know, bird boy."

"I think Horsefeathers is in Bransquite," Martin says. "He's pretending to be Mrs Murray's gardener. I saw him kissing her in the sitting room. I don't think he'll come back."

The sentinel crow gives a loud, shouting caw, and stretches out its wings. *The fool is taking his revenge on those he thinks betrayed him*, it says. *But the air is turning into glass. The seas are rising. Extinction threatens in Pavor Potentia. There's no time to waste upon pursuing petty victories.*

"The river misses him," the man said, nodding his hooded head. "The Gatekeeper is angry."

Martin realises he is shivering. Perhaps it isn't from the cold.

"I should go home," he says. "I've been away a long time, and Miss Fox will be worried. Thank you for explaining to me about *Pavor Potentia*."

The faceless man makes no response.

"I do have a key," Martin says. "But I promise I will put it back, now that I know where it belongs. I'm no thief, even if Horsefeathers is."

"Go," says the young leader of the *Shaydim*. "We shall neither help nor hinder you. But you will come back. You are the boy who talks to birds. Send our felicitations to Horsefeathers – and the little girl."

Something as delicate as a snowflake touches the back of Martin's neck. He looks up. The air is full of dancing, fluttering shapes, like soft, dark flowers. Butterflies.

Impossible, he thinks.

The insects are not only out of season; they're unnaturally huge, and they're swarming so thickly that the violet sky has turned dark over Martin's head. He throws up his hands, trying to brush them away, yet somehow feeling strangely afraid of damaging the delicate scales that cover their wings. He begins to stumble toward the glimmering oval that hangs in the air. He hopes that he will reach it in time, before – but before what?

"What are they?" he shouts.

"Human memories," says the leader of the men. "Ephemera of thought. The final insights of the dying. The fading echoes of Moments long melted in the sea."

Martin throws his hands over his head, and runs as fast as he can back through the Gateway, to the wizard's den.

Chapter Nineteen:
The Lovers

"Can I drive?" Evelyn asks, as they walk out of the hotel to the stable yard where Johnny has left it parked beneath an overhang, which gives the smart paintwork some protection from the rain.

"I don't know," says Johnny. "Have you ever driven a motor car?"

"Lord, no. Gerald wouldn't hear of it. And actually, I've never wanted to. But I would love for you to teach me how to do it."

Johnny laughs. "It isn't hard," he says. "The worst part is starting the motor with the crank shaft. That can be tricky. But then it's just a case of putting the engine in gear and steering where you want to go."

"Can women learn, do you think?"

Johnny raises an eyebrow. "Some women certainly can," he says. "I wouldn't think that it would take you long to get the hang of it."

"Oh," says Evelyn. "Then let me try. I'll sit in the driving seat, and you can sit beside me, and tell me how to work the controls."

"I'll reverse out of the yard first," Johnny says. "We'll hit a straight road pretty soon; I'll let you change seats with me then. Get in, while I start the engine."

The rain, which has continued falling steadily for most of the previous night, has now stopped, and the darkness has given way to a thin, watery sunlight, which Evelyn knows will never last. A faint breeze ruffles the hem of her tea-dress. How crumpled she must look, she thinks, with a sudden flush of shame: just like a woman who has lain in bed all night beside a man who is not her husband. Quickly, she climbs inside the car, and takes her compact out of her handbag. She's not had time to complete her make up before leaving the hotel, and her lips look bare and uninviting, though her hair, which she's barely brushed, hangs about her shoulders in a seductive tangle only vaguely reminiscent of Dietrich.

"Oh, God," says Evelyn. "I look like a hag." She takes out her lipstick and foundation brush, and sets to work improving matters.

Johnny starts the engine, and leaps nimbly into the driver's seat. He puts the car into reverse, looks over his shoulder and releases the handbrake. Soon they are on the open road, heading back towards Camelford and the moor. The landscape here is more open than the river valley with which Evelyn has become familiar, and the road is wider. *It's a relief to be free of the looming Cornish hedges,* Evelyn thinks, *they seal in the narrow lanes so tightly one can barely breathe.* Out here, she can look out of the car window and see verdant agricultural land stretching toward the sea, a scattering of small villages, whose distant churches are poking their sharp spires high above the wheat fields, and several round bellied woods. *This is England,* she thinks. *It's still England, despite...* She sighs, and turning her attention to her reflection, begins to apply her lipstick.

Eventually they reach a stretch of road that runs more or less in a straight line toward Camelford. Johnny pulls into the grassy verge, and opens his door. "Come on, then," he says. "Do you want to drive?"

"Of course!" Evelyn puts her compact away, and scrambles out of the passenger seat, taking care to avoid laddering her stockings on the imposing handbrake.

Johnny walks round the front of the car and slips in beside her. "Now," he says. "In front of you is the steering wheel, and at your feet you have the accelerator, brake and clutch. The clutch is the thing to be careful of. You need to press it down in order to change gear. Right now the car's in neutral, so it's not going anywhere."

"What are all the dials?" Evelyn asks.

"This tells you what speed you're doing," Johnny says, pointing. "We won't worry about the rest. Now, put your foot on the clutch pedal, and press it to the floor."

Evelyn does so.

"Now take hold of the gear stick – and move it – " Johnny puts his hand on top of Evelyn's – "like this – to here. This is first gear. Now lift your foot – slowly – and put your other foot on the accelerator."

"Oh, God, it's complicated," Evelyn says.

"I think you can handle it."

The car begins to move. Evelyn gives a shriek of excitement that's not unmixed with a little terror.

"Easy," says Johnny. "Keep her steady. Good! You're driving, Evelyn! Look! You're driving!"

Evelyn laughs.

"Now, you need to go a little faster," Johnny says. "So put your foot down on the clutch again – right to the floor, yes – and we need to move the gear stick again."

"When do I lift my foot?" Evelyn says.

"When the gears have shifted – there – did you hear that? That tells you it's in second. And – lift."

"You make it sound like a ballet lesson," Evelyn says.

"Put your foot down on the accelerator – not too hard – and take us up to twenty five. Do you see? What speed are we doing now?"

Evelyn looks at the dial. "I don't know."

"What number is it pointing to?"

"Twenty," Evelyn says. "Or thereabouts. It keeps wobbling."

"Good. Lets go faster."

At twenty five Johnny helps her to shift gear again, and now the car is rumbling along at almost thirty miles an hour. Evelyn wriggles in her seat. She feels like a girl again, a light-hearted, red coated little girl who used to ride the cranky horses and shy for coconuts at the steam fair. The girl she was before she was forced to grow up, too soon, too quickly, long before she was in any way ready. In another world, she wonders, would that little girl have grown up to have lived a completely different life? Would she have done as Johnny seems to think that modern women should do, and had a career? Would she have met the American, or read Davenport? She certainly never would have married Gerald, that's a fact; certainly would never have gone through the heartache of losing child after child in a futile effort to have her required *six*. Who would that girl now be, if none of these things had ever happened to her?

"Try steering more towards the centre," Johnny says. "You're drifting too far right."

"I daren't turn the wheel," Evelyn says. "I'm going too fast."

"You don't have to turn the wheel. Don't worry. Just ease slightly to the left." Johnny puts his hand on the steering wheel, and pulls it gently downwards. "That's better."

"This is wonderful!" Evelyn exclaims. "Can you teach me how to turn, and reverse?"

"Not trying to get rid of me, are you?" Johnny says, with a laugh.

"Oh, Johnny!" Evelyn cries. "How could you think that? Who would I have to tend the garden if I got rid of you?"

Johnny laughs again, and then is silent for a while. Then he says, in a serious voice completely different from the one he has been employing: "What are you going to do about your husband?"

"Oh, I don't know," Evelyn says. "Let him divorce me, if it comes to it, I suppose."

"Really? You'd do that? What about Leto?"

"Her father's welcome to her. I can't stand the wretched brat."

"I see," says Johnny.

"He won't find out, anyway, unless I tell him," Evelyn says. When she does get pregnant, she thinks, it will be easy enough to convince Gerald that the baby is his, provided he's still planning to visit within the month – though the idea of sharing any intimacy with Gerald now is not at all appealing. He hasn't written to tell her that his plans have changed. And if for any reason she cannot convince him, and they have to own up to the affair – well, a future with Johnny, rather than with Gerald, could be something to look forward to.

"Oh, look!" exclaims Evelyn. "Rough Tor! Isn't that Rough Tor, Johnny?"

Johnny looks out of the window. The cragged form of the moor top squats a mile or so off in the distance, its shadow side dark grey against the morning sky. "We're coming into Camelford," he says. "Let me have the wheel again."

Evelyn, under supervision, pulls in at the side of the road, and they exchange places.

"I'd love to stop somewhere, for breakfast," Evelyn says. They didn't have time to eat before leaving the hotel.

"We'll find a friendly farm. We won't stop in Camelford."

"Why not? I'm not known."

"No, you're not."

"Are you?"

"Occasionally."

"What does that mean? That someone could tell me who you are? Oh, Johnny, do let's stop in Camelford!" Evelyn laughs. "Please," she says, teasingly, squeezing his free arm.

In answer, Johnny pivots the car sharply to the left, and heads through the centre of the little town at some speed, without showing any sign of doing as Evelyn has requested. *He's annoyed*, she thinks, and for a second she senses something unexpected – an undercurrent of unspoken violence that she felt swirling sometimes around the American, and Daddy – and instinctively she shuts her mouth, and pretends the question was never asked. *It isn't healthy,* she reminds herself, *to provoke the anger of a King.* Climbing the hill, he then takes another sharp right away from the town, along a narrow, winding country lane that rises and falls and lurches with almost sickening regularity.

They follow the road for perhaps a mile, or more, past the entrance to a quarry works and several small cottages, until eventually it runs out. A farm gateway bearing a painted sign saying butter, milk and eggs appears on their left, and the great bouldered scarp of Rough Tor looms before them, just beyond a small river. Johnny pulls into the gateway, and turns off the engine.

"Milk and eggs, so maybe tea and toast," he says, hopefully. "I'll make enquiries."

With Johnny gone to find the farmer's wife, and possibly arrange breakfast, Evelyn stands staring up at the grim, tattered slope of the rough hill directly in front of her. She's been wondering ever since seeing Rough Tor in the distance, from the vicar's study, what it might be like up close; and now that she is here, face to face with the spirit of the high wild, standing at the very gates of Diana's temple, her blood – *heathen blood,* as the vicar almost called it – begins to sing. *It must be fate,* she thinks, that Johnny – her Hippolytus, her Virbius – has brought her here instead of taking her straight home. Whatever impulse prompted him to turn, it must have come from the savage Gods themselves, an irresistible command issuing from his own, inner, darkness, from that terrifying, primitive truth of man that lurks below the thin veneer of civilisation. But why have the ancient deities summoned Johnny to the Tor? Why, more pertinently, have they summoned her? What does the Goddess want Evelyn to do, here in the bare, rock thicketed scarp of her sacred enclosure? What offering does she want Evelyn to make? What divine gift receive? Is it to be the moment of conception, the quickening of Johnny's child? Could it be that? Evelyn clutches her belly. She hopes so, prays so, implores Diana: *Please, let it be that.* The dark, silent Tor does not answer.

They eat breakfast in the farmer's kitchen, while the farmer's grim faced daughter clatters around the scullery, scorching the feathers from a duck. Then Johnny borrows soap and water, and shaves his face, so by the time they go back to the car they're both refreshed and tidy enough to return to Bransquite and explain themselves without incurring too much suspicion. Johnny – who, as we might expect of a man who's lived for several months wild on the moor, knows every road and trackway that crosses this part of it blindfold – doesn't return through Camelford, but takes a side lane that leads onto the open commons before wandering across the featureless landscape. Evelyn does her best to keep Rough Tor in sight as the road snakes east and west, but before long she's become disorientated, and can no longer tell one summit from another. Is that Garrow Tor towards which they are heading, or Bronn Wennili? Where does that faint pathway lead? What are those birds doing in such numbers on that clump of gorse? Is she facing north, or south? From which direction rises the sun? The moor is toying with her. She tosses her head. It doesn't matter. Soon, she'll be nurturing its Priest-King's child within her womb. Then the wind will start to play a very different tune.

It's still only a metaphor, of course.

Of course it is.

When her mother doesn't come home from her drive with Johnny, Leto is, at first, quite pleased. She takes advantage of the opportunity to play for several hours in the garden, and entertains herself with the fantasy that Johnny has driven into a ditch, and though he has – of course – emerged uninjured from the car, her mother's hit her head and is bleeding to death. Johnny, hero that he is, is trying to revive her, but he's failing miserably, and there's no sign of a policeman anywhere. The wicked witch is going to meet her doom, just as all witches inevitably do, in all stories, everywhere. She'll never come home, and Leto will be free of her. But as time passes and the vicar's borrowed car shows no sign of returning, the little girl begins to feel alarmed. She doesn't miss her mother, but her imaginings have become suffused with an oppressive atmosphere of doom, as if the woman's absence should portend some dreadful danger to Leto herself, against which she has no defence. Then the horrible notion strikes her that she, too, is about to die, and that she'll never see Johnny again, or Martin, or traverse the secret pathways into Huma's country. She runs up to her room, shuts the door tight against the world, and slowly, painfully, begins to cry.

Nanny Gould brings her a boiled egg and toast soldiers for tea, and seeing the traces of dried tears on her cheeks, asks her sharply what on earth she thinks she has to cry about. There are children in the world, she reminds her, who have things far worse than she does: orphans starving in the Orient, and little black skinned children running about with no clothes on in Africa. Children who really are cruelly treated, children who are sent down mines and up chimneys, or forced to slave for their gruel in Public Assistance Institutions. So Leto can stop her ridiculous crying, right now. It's undignified and foolish for a girl her age and size to make such a silly, attention seeking, fuss.

If she does not stop crying, Nanny says, she'll give her something to cry about.

Leto has been sobbing silently; she has purposefully not sought to attract any attention or disturb the house, so Nanny Gould's accusation hits her like an arrow in her chest.

"I hate you," she hisses at Nanny Gould. "I hate you, and I hate her!"

"Well," Nanny Gould replies, with a glare and a huff. "I don't think either of us likes you very much." She leaves the room, slamming the door behind her. Her footsteps click mechanically down the stairs.

Leto eats her egg and toast in silence. Then she gets up, prowls around her room, and urinates in several places on the floor. *Like wolves do*, she thinks. *Huma, Huma, where are you?*

Overnight, she dreams again of the river valley, the black butterflies, the violet sky, but sees no sign of the mammoth. At one point, she's almost certain she sees Martin Stone nearby in the company of faceless men, but although she shouts out his name as loudly as she

Mammoth & Crow

can, he doesn't hear her. It's as if he's on the other side of a thick pane of glass: or in a different Moment, a different Otherworldly time – because he seems to be standing on snow, not the rich late summer plains of her own dream time. Is Martin dreaming, too? But then he's gone, and she's alone on the hillside, soft winged insects clustering around her head, their spiralling tongues lapping at the salty corners of her eyes. When she wakes up, she's exhausted and fitful, and she thinks her forehead is burning. Her chill must have returned, and with a vengeance. She whimpers for Nanny Gould.

Nanny comes, but she's distracted. Calling Leto a nuisance and a naughty little Madam, she feels her forehead, and tells her she's not hot, not hot at all; and telling lies in order to worry people is extremely wrong.

"Is Mummy back?" Leto asks. "Is Johnny?"

Nanny Gould refuses to answer her. She has things to do this morning, and does not want to be wasting time on this melodramatic nonsense.

Leto begins to cry again. She really doesn't want to cry, especially not in front of Nanny Gould, but she can't seem to stop herself. A scream is swelling up inside her, like an abscess. She can feel it pressing on her lungs, an unforgiving lump beneath her breastbone, stinging her throat like the cutting tip of a knife, and she knows it is about to explode. How long has it been there? All night? All year? A lifetime?

My mother hates me, Leto thinks. *And Huma is gone. I'm going to die.*

Nanny Gould smacks her hard on the left leg.
The scream bursts.

It's noon before the vicar's car pulls up outside Ignatius Hart's old house. Evelyn looks up with the same sinking feeling of dread that she experiences every time she's forced to contemplate its lacklustre frontage: blank windows staring at a world gone stale. Today, however, the windows are not all empty – in one of them hovers the anxious figure of Nanny Gould, the palm of her right hand pressed flat against the glass – just as Evelyn herself once stood watching Johnny drink down her filthy lemonade. *That woman will go, now*, she thinks.

Evelyn waits for Johnny to open the passenger door, and then steps out onto the pavement. Her kitten heels don't slip, no, not this time. She straightens her skirt, picks up her handbag, and walks proudly into the house. Johnny does not follow her, but disappears around the back of the house. *That will change, too*, Evelyn thinks, *once I've got rid of Nanny.*

"Mrs Murray!" comes Nanny Gould's voice, and Evelyn looks up again, to see her rushing down the stairs. "Are you all right? I was afraid there must been an accident."

"Don't be stupid, Gould," Evelyn says, coldly. "I decided to stay overnight in an hotel. God knows, there's nothing to do here. I hope you didn't upset Leto with your ridiculous fussing."

"No, Madam. I didn't tell her you were gone. I didn't want her to worry."

"I'm going to change my clothes," Evelyn says. "Then I want to see you, Gould, in my sitting room. I'm very unhappy about certain aspects of your recent behaviour."

"My behaviour?" exclaims Nanny Gould.

Mammoth & Crow

"Mine? Why, Madam, whatever have I done?"

"Don't badger me," Evelyn says. "How dare you badger me? I'll talk to you later." She sweeps past Nanny Gould, and mounts the stairs.

Evelyn takes off her dress, her silk stockings, and her new girdle. She washes her face and reapplies her Max Factor, dresses afresh in a clean cotton blouse and tidy skirt, and finally puts on a pair of stockings and new panties to replace the ones she's still carrying in her handbag. She should put them to be washed, but they smell so strongly of sex, she doesn't dare. Once the nanny's gone, she decides, and there's no chance of the jealous old hag reporting her infidelity to Gerald – if infidelity is even what it is, for he abandoned her, didn't he, long before she ever had any notion of betraying him? – then she might surrender them. She lights a cigarette, and smiles. *I wasn't so worried last night*, she remembers, watching the glowing red tip dance in the dressing table mirror. Her reflection, this time, doesn't chide her. But really, they were taking a shocking risk. Making love in a car, of all places! What if they'd been disturbed by a policeman? She giggles, remembering the excitement and the pleasure, and feeling rather embarrassingly girlish. *Pull yourself together, Evelyn! You've a servant to dismiss.* She stubs out the cigarette butt in her ashtray, gets up from her chair, and heads downstairs.

Nanny Gould is waiting for her outside the sitting room. She has tidied her uniform, and put on a clean starched blouse, as if she already knows she's going to stand trial. Evelyn brushes past her, opens the door, and leads her inside. She sits down on the sofa, and – feeling suddenly nervous, though there's no reason why she should – pours herself a measure of gin from the bottle on the low table, and lights a second cigarette, this time for morale support. How should she begin? Slyly, seductively, enticing Gould step by step into an admission of her guilt? Or should she simply confront the wretched woman with the evidence of her crime? She decides on the latter.

"Gould," she begins. "Johnny tells me you've been making unwelcome advances towards him."

"What?" says Nanny Gould, stunned, forgetting her manners in her astonishment. *Because she never expected to be found out,* Evelyn thinks, *not because she's innocent.* "Mrs Murray, I – well, I cannot imagine how he might have gained that impression. A woman of my age – "

"Of your age, Gould, quite," Evelyn interrupts, coldly. "You disgust him. Frankly, you disgust me. I will not have such disgusting conduct in my house."

"But Madam," Nanny Gould says, battling to overcome her shock. "It's not true. I've been friendly to the young man, I'll admit. But it was never more than politeness. I've never had any – what do they call them – *designs* on him."

"You've been chasing Johnny since the moment he set foot inside this house," Evelyn says. "I've seen the way you look at him, Gould. The way you favour him. It's obvious."

"No – I – let me talk to him," Nanny Gould begs. "If he's misunderstood, I'm sure – "

"You will not talk to Johnny!" Evelyn shouts. Nanny Gould starts, takes one small step backwards. "Not now, not ever. You are going to pack your bags and leave. Leto's too old for a nanny, anyway. She needs to learn how to become a young woman. You've been keeping her a baby."

"I've only done what you have asked me, Mrs Murray!"

"Really?" Evelyn snaps. "What about the Encyclopedia? I know you let her smuggle it in her luggage. I told you it was to stay in London, to break her childish obsession with it. You went directly against my wishes. You have become a law unto yourself, Gould. Now it stops."

Nanny Gould stares at her, the colour slowly draining from her face, as the realisation that Evelyn is serious gradually sinks in. "Well," she says finally, in a shaking voice. "I must say, after eleven years of loyal service, Mrs Murray, I expected better treatment than this."

"Loyal service? You can hardly call it that. Pack your bags. I want you out of this house by dinner time." Evelyn sucks hard on her cigarette, and raises her gin to her lips, trying not to let the nanny see her hand is shaking. This interview, as far as she's concerned, is over.

Nanny Gould folds her arms. "I want paying," she says. "If I have to leave, I want the full year's salary you owe me before I move a single muscle from this spot. And some extra, to pay for my fare back to London."

"All of it?" Evelyn says. She looks at Gould, who is standing, chin forward, tremblingly resolute. She could, Evelyn thinks contemptuously, have been drawn from one of those posters so fashionable across Europe, celebrating the Workers of the Nation. The resemblance isn't in any way appropriate. "Very well. Though it will leave me with nothing to pay the grocer until my allowance comes from Gerald."

"That's not my problem, Madam."

Evelyn puts down her glass, fetches her handbag. She rummages within it, making sure to push her incriminating panties to the bottom, where Gould, if she's trying to peer inside, won't see them. All she has is twenty five pounds and six shillings – which would have been enough to have lasted, if she hadn't had this nasty business to deal with, till the end of the month. She takes out a twenty pound note, and hands it to Gould. "There," she says. "That will have to do. If there's any lacking you'll have to apply to my husband for it."

"I want a reference," Nanny Gould says, poking out her lower lip.

"You'll get nothing from me."

"Then I'll ask Professor Murray."

"Do what you wish. Just get out. Get out!" She screams the last – the words welling up inside her like volcanic gas, exploding in a rush. "Out!" she cries again – and if she'd still been holding her gin, she'd have thrown it, glass and all, watched it smash upon the floorboards – better still, on Gould herself.

"Mrs Murray," says Nanny Gould. "I'm going." She leaves the room.

Evelyn flings herself down on her sofa. Her whole body is quivering. She wants Johnny, she realises. She wants him desperately, with a longing so unexpectedly intense it makes her catch her breath; but it's too soon to call him. The pretence that they're still merely Mistress and servant must continue at least until Gould's completely gone. Instead, she reaches for her gin.

Nanny Gould packs her case. The poor woman is in shock. She wants to say goodbye to Leto, but doesn't know how. This dismissal, this parting, is so sudden, so wholly unexpected – except it isn't really unexpected at all, she admits to herself. She's seen it looming on the horizon ever since the move from London. If Mrs Murray's never going to produce another baby, which, quite obviously she's not, there's no real reason for her to retain a woman whose primary expertise is in changing nappies and arranging regular feeds: one who can boil an egg, but can't teach French or German conversation to a young lady. Nevertheless, the suddenness, the uncalled for vehemence of this announcement has caught her completely off balance. How on Earth can she explain what's happening to a child like Leto? Leto won't understand, will cry, will scream and stamp her feet – and to be honest, Nanny Gould, has put up with more than enough of that exhausting rubbish this morning already. Let Leto's mother explain to the little Madam what she's done. While she's about it, she can take the opportunity to explain besides why Leto is now utterly forbidden to spend any more time with Martin Stone, who's the only friend the child has ever had. Let Mrs Murray deal with the heartbreak, the tantrums, the hysterical screaming fits. It's no longer Nanny Gould's responsibility, or even her business. And, she tells herself, if she leaves right now – it's only an hour after noon – there's a chance that she might catch the late night train from Fowey Harbour, and be in London by tomorrow morning. Nanny Gould fastens her suitcase, fastens her coat, and adjusts her hat. Professor Murray will be more than happy to provide a reference, she's sure of that. Then she will find herself a much better position, with a sensible family and a pleasant, happy, well behaved child. She may very well be right in this expectation. Nanny Gould, for all her failings, is a decent enough woman, and though we've tended to see her under strain and struggling to cope with a difficult and disturbed little girl, she is, in truth, a very competent nanny. But we'll never get to know anything about that. She's leaving this story now, and there will be no reason for her to return to it.

Without further ado, Nanny Gould walks heavily down the stairs, through the front door, and out of Leto Murray's life. The door slams shut behind her. The lovers are alone.

Chapter Twenty:

What Martin Knows.

Martin Stone leaves the fogou and runs back to Miss Fox's cottage through the mist, his crows flapping around his ears like anxious thoughts. His heart is beating hard.

He replaced the skull before leaving, so Johnny Horsefeathers won't easily retrieve it again and treat it like a trophy to be stood up on his pile of books, and knocked carelessly to the floor. *It's your duty*, he told himself, *your duty to the dead.* He reached into the dark space and took the smooth cranium in his hand, lifting it from the dry dirt and replacing it into its original location at the top of the spinal column. He felt his fingers brush against the soft surface of an ancient fur, and scraped his knuckles against the end of a hard, twisted cord that could have been made from ligament, or animal intestine. *It's the necklace*, he thought, *or the remains of it*; and he reached inside his pocket for the bear claw he had picked up out of the dirt, intending to put that back in the grave, too.

You may keep it, said a voice inside his head. It wasn't the voice of any crow, or the faceless man with whom he'd just been speaking in the snowy Otherworld. It was a dark voice, an ancient voice: the voice of a bear, or of the granite rocks themselves. A fire voice, stone voice, blood voice, bone voice, eye socket voice. *You have earned the right to use it, bird boy.*

Perhaps the voice was in his imagination. Perhaps, it wasn't. Either way, Martin decided he'd better do exactly as it told him. Now the ancient claw still feels warm and comfortable against his palm; he has replaced it in his pocket.

He reaches the cottage shortly before the mist becomes too thick to see through, and shucking off his coat and soaking boots, replaces Miss Fox's Bakelite torch in the hall table drawer and makes his way into the kitchen. Miss Fox is sitting at the kitchen table next to a newly lit oil lamp, scowling at her literary review and crossing out random words with a determined pencil. She looks up as he enters.

"Martin!" she exclaims, getting quickly to her feet. Her chair scrapes loudly, like a klaxon, on the flags. "Oh, my dear, I am so glad you're back! The weather's closing in again."

"I came back as soon as I saw the mist starting to fall," Martin says, though he knows this isn't entirely true.

"I knew you'd be sensible, dear. But still, I can't help but worry. One hears so many stories of unwary people getting lost upon the moor, and never finding their way off again."

"I knew all the time where I was," Martin says. "I was in the crags below Rough Tor, where we went for the picnic with Leto." He wonders whether he should tell Miss Fox about the letters he has found.

He wants to, but he doesn't know how to start. What if she refuses to listen? What if she tells him off for climbing into the fogou in the first place?

"I'll make us a nice cup of tea," Miss Fox says. "Sit down next to the fire, and dry yourself off. That pullover looks awfully damp."

"It was the mist," Martin says, pulling up a stool. "It seeped inside my coat. I didn't even realise."

"Cornish mists do that," says Miss Fox, putting the kettle on the hob. "It's one of the things that makes them so extremely dangerous."

Martin sits in front of the fire, and slowly relaxes, feeling the dry heat of the coal fire soothe his clammy skin, and warm his bones. His chest aches – though whether from the damp or the exertion of the run, he can't be sure. He stretches out his legs, and puts his feet up on the fender, thinking hard. After some time, the kettle begins to whistle on the hob. Miss Fox gets to her feet, and, somewhat distractedly, as if her mind is on something else, hurries to attend to it. Martin waits until she's finished pouring the hot water and has brought the teapot to the table before speaking.

"Miss Fox," he says. "What is an evil ideology?"

"I beg your pardon?" exclaims Miss Fox. "Wherever did you hear that phrase?"

"I read it. In a – a book."

"Well," says Miss Fox, retreating into the larder, and emerging with the milk. "An ideology is an idea – a big idea, that people find comforting to believe in; an idea which helps them to make sense of how the world works, and decide how they think it ought to work. And if that big idea is unjust, or cruel, or simply too rigid, then the ideology can be a wicked one, and the people who believe it wicked people too."

"Like the Nazis, and Herr Hitler?"

"Yes, my dear," says Miss Fox sadly. "Exactly like Mr Hitler." She reaches absently into her apron pocket, and her fingers began to play with something she has stuffed within it. "Shall we go to Camelford tomorrow?" she says, drawing up a chair and sitting down – changing the subject, Martin notices. "I could do with a new notebook and replacement ribbon for my typewriter. The ink is running low."

"I'd like that," says Martin, slowly. "It's a few weeks since we went into town, and I suppose the weather won't be fit for gardening."

"Camelford it is, then," agrees his foster aunt. "We'll have to catch the bus first thing in the morning." She smiles brightly – *too brightly,* Martin thinks, as she often does when she's worried – and lifts her tea cup to her lips.

Should I tell her? he wonders.

They catch the early country bus from the middle of the village, and reach Camelford by ten. After visiting the stationary shop on Victoria Road, where Miss Fox always buys her professional necessities, they sit for a while on a damp bench in Enfield Park, the site of the old Acetylene Gas Company, and watch the small country town go by. An old man in a grey macintosh is already waiting outside the fish and chip shop, pacing up and down between the puddles left by last night's rain, his rough haired terrier at his feet. A grey heron is silently stalking the river.

Miss Fox is worrying, though she doesn't

want to be, about Germany and Poland. She has heard over the BBC radio service that Mr Chamberlain has once again affirmed Britain's stance regarding the threat of a German invasion into the free City of Danzig. An invasion will now mean military retaliation, and that, of course, will have to mean war. Chamberlain – foolish man! – is being pushed slowly and steadily in the direction that the German Chancellor desires. Hitler actively wants war now: Miss Fox is sure of it. How, other than by martial conquest, can he prove the superiority of Germany over its neighbours? How else impose his twisted notions of order on them?

Miss Fox prays she is wrong; but she has little hope of it. She's been trying to bury her attention in her work, focusing on the isolated nuns of *Black Narcissus* instead of the oncoming crisis, but it hasn't worked. She fears that her review is being coloured by her own looming dread as much as it is a clear reflection on the novel's, and *The Lady* will not want it: that they'll find its tone too dark, its suppressed forebodings too prescient, too alarming. Criticism, according to *The Lady,* is not supposed to be too revealing of the truth. Literature, her editor once reminded her, is not real life.

Well, thinks Miss Fox, bristling slightly at the memory, *that is a lie.* Literature is real life: at least, an important part of it. The word is an immensely powerful thing. What would Fascism be, without the power of words to uphold and empower it? Nothing. But what would our civilisation be, without the constructive power of story? How would we know who we are without narratives to tell us? *The stories that we tell ourselves create us,* thinks Miss Fox.

Martin is watching the road. There's little traffic. Three bicycles, two almost identical piebald horses pulling carts belonging to two different local tradesmen, a milkman's van belonging to the local dairy company; and then, suddenly, a smart, newish looking motor car, which purrs smoothly down the hill with the graceful determination of a hunting tomcat. Martin's attention – along with that of surely every boy who sees it and a fair few of the girls – is immediately captured. It's a beautiful thing, the car, beautiful: its bright green paintwork shining like a neon sign despite the dullness of the day, its four wheels speeding fluidly along the road. It reminds him of the green fendered vehicle that stood outside Ignatius Hart's old house on the day he first saw, then met, Leto Murray. He lifts his hand, shading his eyes, and peers inside as it comes closer.

A woman is sitting in the passenger seat. She has blonde hair, which looks ruffled and untidy, as if she's just left her bed. She's laughing and tossing her head flirtatiously, like the heroine in a movie, and is clutching at the driver's arm, trying to distract his attention from the road in a way that could easily, Martin thinks in alarm, lead to an accident. Then, just as the car speeds by, she throws her head right back onto the leather head rest, and gifts him with a clear, uninterrupted view of the driver's face.

Martin stares. The car whips by him.

It's Johnny, Martin thinks, in shock. *Johnny Horsefeathers – whatever his real name is – with Mrs Murray.* She's borrowed, perhaps even bought, a motor car, and he's driving her somewhere.

But if Mrs Murray's going visiting, why has

she not taken time to brush her hair?

He thinks about the intimate moment he witnessed in the house, and the private letters he found in the antechamber. Johnny swore him to silence, he remembers. But that vow was taken under pressure, before there was any thought that he might stumble on – break in on – the dark secret of Johnny's real identity. *Surely now,* he thinks, *it has to be invalid.* The wizard lied to him, after all, in order to extract it. Lied, threatened, and then lied again, when his threat proved ineffective. How can any promise made upon the basis of a lie be binding? What would his grandmother have told him do? Would she have insisted on his telling Miss Fox both everything he knows and everything he fears, as a matter of truth and honesty? Or would she say that telling Miss Fox anything at all would constitute not only the breaking of his vow, but the spreading of a salacious rumour? Both his grandmother and the Rabbis always proclaimed a morbid horror of loose talk. *Gossip breaks lives*, they told him. *Breaks lives, and destroys families, sets neighbour against neighbour, and friend against friend.* But isn't what Martin now knows something more than rumour? After all, he has seen what he has seen, and read what he has read. He can't – and perhaps he oughtn't – say *nothing*. But precisely how much should he reveal, and how much hold back? He doesn't really know yet what is true, and what is not.

"Miss Fox," he says at last, slipping the question into the conversation as casually as he could. "Is Murray a common name in England?"

"Not really," answers his foster aunt. "It's popular in Scotland, but you hardly ever hear of

Murrays in this part of the world. Why do you ask?"

"I was just wondering," Martin says. He pauses. "When can I go to visit Leto again?"

"Oh, dear," says Miss Fox, looking down, her cheeks reddening. "Martin, I'm not sure you can go at all."

"Why not?"

"Her mother sent me a note," Miss Fox says. "A nasty, petty, angry, vicious little note, to say you are no longer welcome in her house."

"What?" exclaims Martin. "What does she say that I have done?"

"Nothing," says Miss Fox. Her voice is taut. "I don't think you've done anything, Martin. Mrs Murray is a spiteful, small minded woman. I feel very sorry for her poor little daughter."

"It's because I saw them," Martin says, putting two and two together, and making up his mind. "Because I saw her with him. And I just saw them again, one minute ago, in that motor car. I know it was them."

"Saw whom?"

"Mrs Murray. With Johnny, the new gardener. He was kissing her. In the sitting room of the house. There was music playing, and they were alone. I saw them through the French windows. And he chased me away, and made me promise to say nothing to anybody about it."

"Good heavens!" cries Miss Fox. "Are you sure?"

"Yes," says Martin. "I know what I saw, and I remember what he said."

Then he tells her, bit by bit, about the fogou, and how he and Leto found it and realised somebody was living in it. How he guessed this unknown tramp had to be Mrs Murray's new gardener, Johnny. How, yesterday, he went back to the chamber to try out his hunch, and how he found several queer old books there from Ignatius Hart's old house, a number of private letters, and a human skull. He says nothing, of course, about his journey to the Otherworld. But even though the suspicions he has formed regarding *Phillip* and *Father* are beginning to burn like acid in his mouth, he can't quite bring himself to reveal them, either. He doesn't dare. After all, if what he fears is true, then the matter is too shocking to speak of, almost casually, in a public park where anyone might be listening, a place that was once the site of the Acetylene Gas Company. And if it's not, then even to make the accusation, let the cursed words pass his lips, would be a terribly wicked thing. Finally, if Johnny Horsefeathers has any real skill as a wizard, if his muttered incantation really did cause Martin to trip and fall when he tried to run away from him, if he really can come and go between worlds as he pleases, and make friends – and enemies – on both sides of the Gate, he can certainly use whatever black magics might be contained in that old handwritten book of spells to make Martin suffer, should he learn that Martin has betrayed his secrets. And, at least according to the sentinel crow, Johnny – *Phillip* – has something of a taste for finely wrought vengeance.

Perhaps he's already said too much, he thinks, with a sudden twinge of anxiety. "Should we go to the police?" he asks. "They could send a Constable to the tunnel – and – and arrest him."

"Good heavens, no," says Miss Fox. "No, Martin. I don't think this is a matter for the police."

"But if Mrs Murray doesn't know – if he's tricking her – "

Miss Fox makes an embarrassed, throat-clearing sound. "I suspect," she says, gently, "the only person being tricked is Leto's father."

"But he's – he's – he's the gardener!" Martin can't bring himself to say anything more.

"Attraction between two grown up people, Martin," says Miss Fox, in a very quiet voice, "can be an unpredictable thing, I'm afraid. It doesn't always respect the bounds of class, or age, or even, sometimes, decency. Oh, dear. I think it's best if you say nothing of this to anybody. It really is none of our business, and it's – well, it's rather shocking. I have to say perhaps it's a good thing you can't visit Leto any more."

"But Leto doesn't know," Martin protests.

"I'm sure she doesn't. And that is undoubtedly a good thing, too, dear."

"Even if they loved each other, it would be forbidden, wouldn't it?" says Martin, thoughtfully. He doesn't really believe Johnny loves Leto's mother, or she him, but part of him suddenly wants their affair to have some meaning beyond simple lust, or calculated revenge. The world shouldn't always be so bleak, so cold, so ugly.

"Of course it would be forbidden," says Miss Fox, seriously. "Mrs Murray is a married woman. Let's talk about something else, dear. This isn't a nice topic. Not nice at all."

"I'm sorry I spied on them, and I wish I hadn't I broken into Johnny's den," Martin says, with vehemence. "I knew it was prying."

"You felt something wasn't right, and you

were worried about Leto," Miss Fox says. "I think I'd have done the same thing, if I'd been you. But by far the best thing to do, now, dear, is to forget it, and pretend it never happened."

Miss Fox is shocked by Martin's revelation, but she's not, when she sits down and thinks about it, particularly surprised. She's even, in a secret, selfish way, quite glad of it. It's a distraction from her obsession with the terrifying events unfolding in Europe: a local, human sized scandal that her mind can easily comprehend, and it grips her attention in a way that fiction, right now, cannot.

Who is Johnny? she wonders. Is he someone Mrs Murray met in London? He's certainly not a local man, and he is very well spoken, and doesn't conduct himself with the air of a gardener. Perhaps he's one of her husband's students, even his University colleagues. Yes, that really seems quite likely.

They must have planned the assignation carefully, she thinks. He must have travelled to Cornwall ahead of her, if Martin's right in thinking he has spent some time camping on the high moor in a cave while awaiting her arrival, reading Ignatius Hart's ridiculous old faery tales for entertainment. Miss Fox shakes her head. Sleeping in a cave, and then pretending to be a servant! The depths to which some men and women will stoop in order to carry on an illicit affair. She remembers the first time she saw Evelyn Murray, standing in the lane beside the smart green fendered motor car, her Max Factor complexion, silver wolf fur coat and kitten heels marking her beyond all contradiction as a foreigner, an interloper, an *emmet*. She remembers wondering then what on Earth a woman of her type could be doing in Bransquite. Now she knows. Mrs Murray has come to the village to spend time with her lover.

Of course she has! What other reason could there possibly have been? Mrs Evelyn Murray's potential for adultery is, and always has been, as plain as the nose on her exquisitely powdered face, and Miss Fox feels mortified at her naive failure to have recognised it.

Martin's grandmother, let me tell you, would have approved of Miss Fox. She is not given to gossip, considering it a petty act of violence, and believing it generally best to leave people to live their lives as they see fit, providing they do no harm to anybody. But this secret, of course, is not harmless. And the longer she thinks about it, the more it appears to Miss Fox that it could do more damage to keep it hidden than it would to bring it kicking and screaming out into the light. But how is she to expose it? The only person she is sure has any right to know what is going on is Professor Murray, but Miss Fox doesn't have his address. Besides, she considers, it's one thing for her to take Martin at his word, but quite another to expect Professor Murray will. Would it be gossiping to tell somebody else – somebody wholly unconnected – what Martin knows? To ask somebody for advice? But whose advice can she ask? The only person she can think of is the vicar – *and he*, she thinks bitterly, *is not proof against gossip.* Mrs Murray's nasty little note has made that expressly clear.

Perhaps, she thinks, she should write, in confidence, to her Hackney editor. Perhaps her editor, who's so much more a woman of the world than is

Miss Fox, will know what to do. And she isn't local, so the story cannot accidentally worm its way into the open ears of the local labourers and quarrymen, who have no business in being shocked by the scandals of their betters. *Yes,* she thinks, with a sigh of relief. That's what she will do. And perhaps, if her editor is of the opinion that the story should come to the ears of Gerald Murray, then she's much more likely to have the means of ensuring it does so – privately, without having to reveal how she herself came to hear it. Gerald Murray doesn't need the extra mortification of knowing his wife's infidelity with her new gardener has been uncovered – and witnessed – by a young boy who was peering through the sitting room window.

The unlucky man's in for quite enough pain, Miss Fox thinks. *Even if, God help us all, he is a Fascist.*

Jack Wolf

Chiswick,
London
11th May, 1927

Phillip,

    I regret the damage caused to Mr Hart's window, but remind you that the matter is between me and him, and does not concern you. If there is nothing I can do or say from a distance that will make you see sense and return home, then you leave me no recourse but to attempt your removal by proximate force. It is intolerable that you continue to behave in such insolent and blatant disregard of my desires. As for the money, I presume you have found another, presumably illegal, means of supporting yourself. I have informed the Cornish police of your presence and likely criminal activity, and they have agreed to notify me on occasion of their taking you into custody.

    Your

    Father

Chapter Twenty One:
Wild

Nanny Gould's been gone now for two weeks. Leto knows she was given her notice, though she's been offered no explanation why. She misses her. Nanny Gould has been at the centre of Leto's life almost since the day that she was born, wiping her chin, tugging a hairbrush irritably through her hair, tucking in her blankets, fastening her t-bar shoes. Now her annoying, comforting, solid dullness is no longer part of Leto's life, and its sudden absence is shocking, like the unexpected amputation of an arm. What is Leto to do without her? How is she to wash and dress herself? Who is to make her bed and pick her socks up from the floor? Worse, who is to listen when she screams, who to smack her hind quarters when, in her tantrums, she loses the ability to breathe? Clearly, that person is never going to be her mother.

The household routine has changed significantly since Nanny Gould left. Leto doesn't know why this has happened, either, but she doesn't like it. It's not that her mother expects anything more of her, or wants her company. If anything, she sees even less of her. Leto still takes her meals, as she's always done, in her room; but now she sits completely on her own, and they are brought up on their trays by a taciturn Annie Tredinnik rather than Nanny Gould. The wicked witch expects her to keep wholly out of sight, just like Rapunzel. She's no longer allowed to play in the garden, or to visit Martin Stone, and every evening after six her bedroom door is locked, forbidding her even the limited freedom of the old house. Leto hates this particular rule like poison, but though she'd have had no qualms in letting Nanny Gould know how she feels, she doesn't dare to argue with her mother. Like most children's, Leto's survival instinct is strong, and it counsels her against such dangerous provocations. She keeps quiet, too, about the noises she frequently hears issuing from behind the locked door of Evelyn's room, and which resound through the walls at night; terrifying noises: moans and gasps, which unsettle her stomach, and make her brood once more on death. *Show no anger,* she tells herself. *Show no fear.* Fear reveals that one is vulnerable. Vulnerability invites attack. The rule of the wild. The rule of the wolf pack. This must be her life now, under the rule of the witch. The one bright spot is Johnny, who has miraculously continued, in his relaxed, jolly manner, to be her friend, bringing her cucumber sandwiches on china plates and pulling clownish faces; telling her not to be too frightened of her silly mother, who's all bark and no bite. If Leto wants him to put a muzzle on her, he says with a wink, he'll happily give it a go. He mimes struggling with a large, aggressive dog. *Horsefeathers! Applesauce!* Johnny makes Leto laugh; but even his comic turns can't keep the mortal fear at bay for very long, and as soon as he has gone, apologising for the need to lock her bedroom door behind him, it returns. Leto sits on her bed with her legs dangling over the side, and begins to rock her upper body forward and back, forward and back, closing her eyes and wishing herself away to the cold Pleistocene steppes beneath the violet sky: Huma's world, though Huma herself is currently nowhere to be seen. It's a tried and tested method of travelling, and it works, it really works – if only in her imagination.

"Evelyn," says Johnny, seriously, entering the bedroom and putting the key to Leto's room on the dressing table. "This isn't right. You can't go on keeping Leto locked up all the time."

"She'd be in our way if I let her out," Evelyn says. "Surely you don't want that bad tempered little brat poking her nose into all our business?"

"I don't think she is a brat," Johnny says. "She seems very sweet to me."

"You don't know her, darling. She's treacherous, just like her father. Her behaviour is impossible to cope with."

"She's a child," Johnny says. "Children don't behave like adults. You can't expect it. It's what makes them children."

"If she behaved like a child," Evelyn says, lying back upon her pillows and drawing heavily upon her cigarette, "then I'd consider it. But she doesn't. She's like a wild animal, Johnny. Her birth was very difficult, you know. Too long. It nearly killed both of us. I think it left her mentally defective. She should be in an institution, not living in civilised company."

"Send her home, then," Johnny says. "To her father."

Evelyn tosses her head contemptuously. "He won't take her back. He's happy to be rid of us."

"I thought he was fond of her. Didn't you tell me he wanted her to get fresh air and exercise?"

"He doesn't care about her. Not really. He's spent her life having as little to do with her as possible. He's only trying to play the part of concerned father because he thinks he ought. It's nothing more than that."

"What about school, then?" Johnny says.

"What would they teach her at school? Nothing of any value."

"You just said she should be in an institution," Johnny points out.

"Oh, for heaven's sake," Evelyn says irritably, stubbing out her cigarette and holding out her arms. She doesn't want to argue with him, and she doesn't feel like explaining her decisions regarding Leto, either. "Stop fussing about nothing, and come here."

For the first time since their encounter in the vicar's Crossley Golden, Johnny does not immediately respond to her advances. A frown flickers briefly in his eyes, and Evelyn remembers to smile. *He has a temper,* she reminds herself, and she doesn't want to provoke it. He must not begin to feel used – although, she has to admit to herself, that is precisely what is happening. Johnny is being used: both by her, and by her dark Goddess. Her increasing tenderness towards him does not, cannot, challenge this basic fact.

"Come on," she says softly, patting the bed. Her period is a day late: it's likely she's already pregnant, but she knows better than to assume it. She has to keep Johnny happy, keep him interested – at least until she's absolutely sure he has given her exactly what she wants. Of course, there'll be no pressing need to give him up after that; but she doesn't know what will happen after Gerald arrives: if this short time is all that they will have, she has to make the most of it. Anyway, sex with Johnny is hardly a chore. In fact, the very sight of him, across the garden or the breakfast table, open shirted and untidy from their previous night's exertions, is enough to send a tingling through her loins. She has thought of giving up putting on her panties; there seems little point, right now, in wearing any. But despite the savage whispers of the Gods, she is not yet as bohemian as that.

"Tomorrow," Johnny says. "I think you should let her play in the garden."

"Don't be ridiculous."

"Look," says Johnny. "I've some young plants to pot on in the greenhouse tomorrow. I can keep an eye on her if you don't want the trouble."

"No."

"Why not?"

"She'd only be a nuisance."

"Not to me."

"I said no!" snaps Evelyn, her own temper flaring. "I don't want you anywhere near the vicious little bitch! Keep away from her!"

"What?"

"Stay away from her. I'm not going to let her steal you away from me."

"What the bloody hell?" Johnny exclaims, taken aback. "Evelyn, she's eleven years old, for

Jack Wolf

God's sake. And she's your daughter!"

"Gerald's daughter. She's no child of mine."

"You gave birth to her."

"I wanted a boy!"

"What has that to do with anything?"

"Everything," Evelyn says. She glares at Johnny, and folds her arms. "Everything."

"You might not want her," Johnny says, reasonably. "But you can't simply disown her. You're her mother."

"I wish she'd died at birth," Evelyn says.

"That's – " Johnny falters, takes a breath. "That's a terrible thing to say."

"Well," snaps Evelyn. "Perhaps I'm a terrible mother. But if you actually knew Leto, and you don't, you'd agree with me."

"To hell with this," Johnny says, throwing up his hands. "I'm going downstairs to get a drink."

"Don't you dare turn your back on me, Johnny Nobody!"

"Or what? What will you do? Fire me? Go ahead."

Evelyn stares at him. What *is* she to do? she wonders. The fact is that she can't fire Johnny, not right now, and they both know it, though she alone knows entirely why; but the thought of his developing even a cursory affection for Leto is intolerable. Yes, the girl is only eleven; but eleven is a dangerous age. Soon she'll begin to grow, and her childish body will begin to blossom into a young woman's. If Evelyn is still with Johnny – and she has to admit to herself that she does want to be with him, her man, her Priest, her King, her Virbius, even if – astonishing thought! – it ends up costing her marriage to Gerald – what will happen then? Will Johnny begin to prefer the younger version over Evelyn herself? The notion is unbearable, incendiary. *But not*, says a dark, sly voice in Evelyn's head, *impossible*. The potential must be scotched before it can become reality.

She draws a deep breath. She can't argue with Johnny like this. She can't risk pushing him away.

She has to do something about Leto.

"Oh, Johnny," she says, in an appeasing tone of voice. "I'm sorry, darling." She holds out her arms. "I don't want to fight. Come here."

Johnny frowns. He does not move. He reminds Evelyn a little of Gerald when he is irritated. It is a distasteful resemblance, but only a superficial one: the possibility of Johnny's anger is somehow frightening in a way that Gerald's never is. She doesn't want to provoke it.

"If it matters so much," she says. "Then tomorrow I'll let Leto play in the garden."

"Good," Johnny says. He still does not move.

"I think we could both enjoy a drink," Evelyn says lightly, sitting up. "I'll come down with you." They'll make love in the sitting room, she decides. Make up the quarrel, restore some of the excitement of those first moments in the vicar's motor car. There's plenty of room on the old sofa, and sex will be the easiest way to make Johnny feel adored – as well as being useful for practical purposes. She slips from the bed, and walks across the room, taking care to swing her hips in the sultry manner of a dancer at the Follies Bergere. *Show him what's on offer. Reel him in.* Men are easy to manipulate; even when you love them. Especially then, perhaps.

"Hmm," says Johnny. He doesn't appear impressed. Evelyn takes his arm, kisses him on his unshaven cheek. "Darling," she says, in a softly remonstrative tone. "Darling."

For one crazy, panicked instant, she thinks he is going to shake her off. Her heart flips. But then slowly he relaxes, and smiles, and says "of course," and to her great relief, she knows she has him. She should never, she thinks, have been in any doubt.

Leto opens her inner eye, and looks out over the slope towards the golden August grasslands of the Otherworld. The soft, warm air tastes sweet in her mouth, like cotton candy. *I am here*, she thinks. She's made it through; and this time, she'll follow the river girl wherever she might lead. She doesn't care at all about coming back. Better to leave her body behind, and let her spirit fade away quietly in Huma's country than to be conscious of dying, slowly, miserably, imprisoned in the cage the wicked witch has built.

The grasslands are anything but dead. They are humming with the lives of small birds and brown and yellow bees, and in the distance, on the other side of the river, a large herd of aurochs – *Bos Taurus Primigenius*, according to the Encyclopedia – is grazing a broad swathe through the grass, long, curving horns sweeping back and forth across the ground. Leto gazes at them in delight. They're a mixed herd, mostly cows with some of this year's calves and a scattering of dark coated younger bulls. The reddish backs of the giant cattle glow like fire coals in the autumn sunshine, and their dark tails flick away the flies. They're paying no attention to Leto. She's no threat to them, and for all their size and fearsome appearance, they intend no harm to her. But she wonders if they're ever hunted by the faceless men – and whether the faceless men ever hunt the mammoths.

She looks around. She's standing on the side of the valley, in the place where she once left her shoes. She looks for them, to see if they've reappeared again; but they have not. Just as the land remembered their presence, it noticed their subsequent removal. *There is time here, then, of a sort.*

She won't need shoes, anyway. The grass feels soft beneath her bare feet, and she'll tread between the sharp rocks as sure footed as a wolf. She is a wild thing. She belongs. The land can't hurt her. She begins to walk down the valley side, fixing her gaze determinedly on the small, sparkling waterfall. She's going to play with the river, she decides. She's going to follow her through the Mesolithic woods, to the villages, and beyond – she's going to keep on and on, until there is no chance of her ever waking up, until this world is all there is, and she forgets that there has ever been another one.

Ten yards from the riverbank, she pauses. Black butterflies are circling the sedge. The river is singing to herself: a faint, bubbling melody, like a hundred species of birdsong fluting into one: *Oh, where have you gone, my darling Johnny, oh?*

Leto takes a step forward. She knows the answer to that riddle, she thinks. Johnny's at home, drinking gin and tonics with the witch. She wonders if she ought to tell the river. Should she call out to her in greeting? But the river seems older today, somehow: less like a girl of Leto's own age, and more like a grown up. She's not sure now she wants to talk to her, even less try to play with her. And anyway, she doesn't know the river's name – assuming that a thing which doesn't have a stable identity can have one. Perhaps every current answers to a different call. The only names she knows are those of the Matriarch and the Gatekeeper. The creature told her its name, didn't it? And she answered in return: *I am Wolf.*

"*Halek-dhwer.*" She doesn't mean to say it out loud, but no sooner has she heard the word echo within her head than she finds it on her lips. "*Halek-dhwer.*"

And immediately, it is here: the Lizard-bear. Terrifyingly huge, horribly close, looming between Leto and the river: its long, reptilian tail lashing furiously from side to side, flattening the flowers; its great bearlike head, full six feet higher than her own, swaying forward and backward with every rasping breath; saliva dripping from its massive, open, jaws, pike teeth glinting like white knives in the ancient sunlight.

Why have you summoned me, little ghost? comes the deep, growling voice in Leto's head.

"I want to stay here," Leto tells it. She puts out one tentative, pleading hand, burying her fingers in the soft, warm bearskin. "I'm not scared. I don't want to go back there any more. I don't care if I fade."

This is not your Moment, answers the Lizard-bear. *You must go back to your own world, and find it.*

"But I don't want to go." Leto begins to cry. "I want Huma."

Go back, little ghost. Trust your mother.

"The witch is not my mother."

Your mother, the Gatekeeper says again.

Huma, Leto thinks, suddenly. Her tears stop. She lifts her head.

"I don't want to be Leto Murray any more," Leto says to the Gatekeeper. "I want to be Wolf."

Then go, Halek-dhwer tells her. *Be. Become.*

The world turns inside out, swirling and shifting like the colours in a pot of ink and water. Leto puts her hands over her eyes, and clutches her head. When the whirling finally ceases, she opens them again – but this time finds herself looking at the grey evening interior of her bedroom, and realises the Gatekeeper has banished her. *This* is now the Otherworld – this world, that Nanny Gould, and Martin, and Johnny, and everyone else call real. *But it isn't,* Leto thinks. *It isn't real at all.*

Come away, O human child,
To the waters, and the wild.

Be, Halek-dhwer told her. *Be, become.*
But *be* what? *Be Wolf?*

"Let's take the car out for a spin," Evelyn says, pouring a liberal measure of gin for herself and another for Johnny. "We could go to Rough Tor. It's beautiful up there. Leto will be fine on her own for a few hours." They have not made love. Evelyn isn't confident, now, that they will, and this uncertainty on top of the worrisome revelation of the full strength of her feelings toward the wretched man, is making her anxious. She isn't sure, too, whether they're still arguing or if the conflict has somehow been resolved. This is scaring her a little. Perhaps her attempts at appeasement have not worked.

Jack Wolf

"I don't think so," Johnny says.

"Why not? I love the moor. It's so feral."

"You're not built to go feral," Johnny says. "I'd like to see you try to climb Rough Tor in those." He nods towards her kitten heels.

"I'll have you know," Evelyn says playfully, hoping a light tone is the right tone, "that I'm very athletic. I played tennis every day in London."

"Tennis!" Johnny says, with a snort. "The high moor's rather more exacting than a grass court."

"It's a sacred place," Evelyn says. "It makes demands of its visitors." She sips her gin.

"Perhaps," says Johnny, noncommittally.

"You're no fun tonight," Evelyn says. She sits down, less than gracefully, on the sofa, and feeling something hard beneath her, reaches into the cushions and pulls it out. It's *The Golden Bough.*

Evelyn has almost finished the book. Recently, of course, she's had less time for reading, but even so, there have been occasions when Johnny has absented himself for one reason or another, and she's taken refuge in its pages. According to the section she's just finished, the Priest-King was a symbol given form and flesh in the manner of Krishna, or Christ. There's no reason, really, why he shouldn't now manifest in another figure altogether. If Diana can choose her Priestess, then she can call forth her King. There is a space, Evelyn has realised, where metaphor and flesh identify: where what was seemingly abstraction becomes solid, becomes real. Or perhaps this last interpretation is what Evelyn read, rather than what Mr Frazer actually wrote. Either way, it astonishes her now, when she thinks about it, to remember that only a few short days ago she was ready to write the whole idea off as a metaphor, a myth, which could have no application, beyond some kind of ritualised pretence, to modern reality. The message of the Golden Bough of Arica is clear and unequivocal, its truths concrete, its symbols resurgent. She, Evelyn Murray, really is Diana's representative on Earth: the first Priestess of that Goddess to walk in this world since the end of the ancient one; and Johnny, her darling Johnny, is the new Virbius. She's not sure when she began to come to this realisation: perhaps it when she was standing in front of Rough Tor, wondering if her son was kindling in her belly. But there has plainly been a moment when her understanding changed – and not by some great leap of insight, which she couldn't have missed, but slyly, secretly, creeping underneath her reason like a silent snake. Just like her feelings toward Johnny.

"Good grief!" Johnny says, seeing the cover. "Whatever are you doing with that?"

"I found it in Mr Hart's library. It was left behind by whoever stole the rest of his books. I've been very glad of it. It's a wonderful book. Very eye opening."

"Wonderful?" Johnny stares at her, his eyebrows rising. "It's a pile of horsefeathers and applesauce, that's what it is. Frazer's just an old armchair anthropologist, and he makes up too much."

"What do you mean?"

"It's a book of recycled travellers' tales, mixed up with a load of queer romantic notions drawn from an old man's runaway imagination. You do know he puts two and two together and makes twenty two, don't you?"

"Of course he doesn't!" Evelyn exclaims.

"Oh, Evelyn," Johnny says. "I thought you were cleverer than this. You don't mean to tell me you've been taking that fantastic rubbish seriously?" He begin to laugh. It's a feral, unkind sound.

Leto gets up from her bed, and wanders round her room. Halfway round, she drops to all fours, and begins to crawl. It's the most natural thing in the world. She's not human any more. She's Wolf, only Wolf. She's not part of this world. This world isn't real. She belongs to Huma.

Settling in the middle of the floor, she throws back her head and howls. At first, the sound is shrill, hesitant, piping, like a puppy, but then it grows in confidence and volume, and begins to swell, filling the confined space: a billowing balloon of energy, wild and loud, a call that can be heard across miles, across years, across worlds, calling out to Huma, telling the mammoth here is one of her own, a creature of the steppes and violet sky, trapped in an alien land and desperately seeking to escape. *Trust your mother.*

Find me! howls Leto. *Help me! I am here!*

Evelyn is staring at Johnny. Her hands are shaking. If anyone ought to understand, she thinks, it should be him. Surely, it must be him. But he's laughing at her, mocking her, poking fun at the very text which, like *Heredity* before it, made everything clear, calling it the absurdist ramblings of an old man's imagination, saying it's no wonder that the thief, whoever he was, left it behind. Quickly, she lifts her gin to her lips and drains it. *Courage, Evelyn. Strength.* Johnny will understand eventually. He will be made to do so. The birth of his child, if nothing else, will make everything as clear as day.

But perhaps, she thinks suddenly, *he already knows all about it.* Perhaps he knows *The Golden Bough* is, in its dark core, true. Perhaps he's laughing at it to stave off the dread, because he knows what this must also mean: if Evelyn is to give birth to a son, then someday, perhaps soon, his own strength will begin to wane. *Le Roi est mort, vive Le Roi!*

A sudden terrible fear seizes Evelyn then. What if, she thinks, there is a terrible price indeed to be paid for her pregnancy? What if the Goddess will demand a sacrifice? What if she demands Johnny? What if Evelyn's going to lose him, no matter what she wants, no matter what happens with Gerald, just like she lost the American, and lost Daddy – and nothing she can say or do will do anything to change this fate. Her head begins to spin.

"What in hell is that infernal noise?" Johnny says suddenly, looking up in astonishment at the ceiling. "Is that Leto?"

"I told you, there's something wrong with her!" Evelyn says, leaping to her feet. She's grateful, if truth be told, for the interruption, but she doesn't want Johnny to know that. "Oh, she's howling like a demon!" She runs to the door of the living room, and jerks it open. "Stop it!" she screams up the stairs. "Be quiet!"

"Has she hurt herself?" says Johnny, seeming concerned.

"No, she's just seeking attention," Evelyn spits, furiously. "Be quiet!" she shrieks again.

"We ought to go up and make sure," says

Johnny. "I'll do it if you won't. Where are the keys?"

"Damn the girl!" cries Evelyn, her eyes welling up. "Damn her! Damn everything about her, and damn her bloody father! Damn both of them to hell, and hell beyond!"

"Calm down, Evelyn, for God's sake," says Johnny. "I said I'd check on her. You don't have to fuss. You don't even have to move. Sit down and finish your drink."

"Oh, no," says Evelyn darkly, through her tears. "I know her plan. She's trying to come between us."

"Fine, then," says Johnny shortly, his voice suddenly hardening. "Come with me. But she can't be left to bawl like that."

Leto doesn't hear the footsteps on the stairs, though they're anything but quiet. She doesn't notice the key turning in the lock, or, for the first instant at least, the door opening wide. She's marking her territory. She's Wolf, doing what Wolf is meant to do. She's not part of this world. But then she looks up, mid-stream, and sees Evelyn rushing across the room, her arms flailing and her mouth moving, like the villain in a silent movie, the wicked witch come to murder her; and she half scrambles to her feet, raising her arms to protect her head from the savage blows that come raining down. And now she can hear the screaming, the furious, blistering rage, to which she has somehow made herself deaf.

"You, you!" pants her mother. "Filthy! Filthy animal! Filthy!"

Leto topples over and rolls onto her back, curling up into a ball, her hands around her head, her knees protecting her stomach. Evelyn continues to lash out, all pretence of self-control abandoned. She means to kill her, Leto thinks, that is the truth; and as she comes, at last, to this horrible realisation, all her feelings stop, just stop, as if they'd been water flowing through a tap which has now been shut off. She is no longer sad, nor frightened; she just is: a still, grey, heartless Leto who will never laugh or cry or care again for any living thing. Looking at her mother's twisted face, she feels only a faint whiff of contempt, as if the few last droplets of feeling are anger and disdain. *Perhaps I am angry*, she thinks. But she can't feel it. Right now, she has no room for anger; she has to focus on surviving this assault, on staying alive long enough to find her way back to Huma. Evelyn can't really kill her; not like this, not with bare fists and savage screams of temper. It takes more than a few slaps to kill a wolf.

When he thinks about it later – and let me tell you that he will think, long and hard, about it – Johnny Horsefeathers will have to admit that the action he is now about to take is neither as quick as it should be, nor sufficiently determined. He should be more forceful, and less cruel. Yes, he will be right to throw himself into the fray as soon as he realises what Evelyn is up to, and pull her off her daughter before she manages to hurt her; but then he should carry the mad bitch kicking and screaming into her bedroom and lock her in, so that she can do neither Leto nor herself any farther harm. And when he's done that, he should do the one thing he's resolved never to do, and send a telegram to contact Professor Murray, warning him his wife has surrendered what was left of her embattled sanity to an old book and a gin bottle. Perhaps, in some other telling of this tale, where the probabilities work out differently, he manages to do at least one of these things. But he does none of them in this one.

"Evelyn," he says, holding the struggling woman in his arms. "Stop! Please, stop."

"Pissing on the floor!" shrieks Evelyn, hysterically. "Pissing!"

"I saw. But hitting her won't help."

"How would you know!"

"You mustn't beat her like that," Johnny says. "You'll really hurt her."

"How dare you tell me," Evelyn hisses, "how to raise my own daughter! You're nobody – you're nothing but the bloody gardener!"

Johnny Horsefeathers suddenly becomes very still, as if he's been carved from wood. "Really?" he says, his voice dangerously calm. "Is that all I am?"

"Let me go!" Evelyn cries.

Her words fall into a hard, cold silence. Johnny releases his grip, and she falls forward, knees hitting the pissed-on wooden floor. "Certainly," he says. His tone is clipped, precise. "Do whatever the fuck you want, Evelyn."

Evelyn crawls away from him, panting. She makes no move toward Leto.

Johnny stares down at her, and his eyes narrow. "Why should I care about you?" he asks her, softly,

She's never heard him speak to her like this. It's the voice of the undercurrent.

"I don't know – why do you?"

He sniffs. "Truth is, Evelyn, I don't."

"Oh, Johnny," says Evelyn, suddenly realising exactly what, in her uncontrolled rage, she has just let slip to him. "I'm sorry. I didn't mean it. I was angry. Please – " she creeps towards him, on her knees, her hands reaching up towards his face, a supplicating gesture. "Please. You're not just the gardener – you're my Priest-King. My green man. My Virbius."

Johnny flinches away from her approaching fingers. It's a gesture of repulsion, of contempt, not fear. "You're talking like a lunatic," he says. "And a vicious one to boot." He pauses, thinking carefully over what he is about to say next. "Thank God you can't have any more children. You can't even care for the one you've got without abusing her."

"Oh!" Evelyn reels away. She feels as if he's hit her. She wishes he had. She's been readying her body, after all, for violence.

"I feel sorry for her," Johnny continues. "And I feel sorry for your husband, damn his eyes, though I never thought I should. You're not just a bloody Fascist, you're a complete monster."

"I'm not! *Johnny* – "

"To hell with you," Johnny says. He turns away, disgusted by the sight of her, and strides out of the room. Evelyn scrambles to her feet and quickly follows him. The door bangs shut behind her, leaving Leto curled up on the floorboards, like a comma. The key swings from the hole, and falls.

"I'm pregnant," Evelyn blurts out. She hadn't meant to tell him like this, but the words are stronger than her stomach, and she can't keep them down.

Johnny whips about. "You bloody liar," he says.

"Yes, I am a liar. Yes, I am! I am! I was lying

before. But now I'm not, Johnny. I'm going to have your baby."

Johnny Horsefeathers takes a deep breath. Then, slowly, he walks towards her, and grips her shoulders in his hands, bringing his face close to hers, staring into her eyes. For one crazy moment she thinks he must be coming back to her. She doesn't care, she decides, if he hurts her, just as long as he comes back. Violence is only another way of showing love, after all, isn't it? Isn't it?

"If I thought, for one moment, that was true," Johnny tells her, "then I'd do everything in my power to make sure and certain that you lost it. You're a liar, an adulteress and a filthy drunk. You're nothing, and you're nobody. You're not fit to be mother to anybody's child, least of all mine."

"But I – " Evelyn stammers.

Johnny shakes her, like a terrier with a rag doll. Her head snaps back and forwards on her neck. Her teeth snap together on her tongue, and she recognises the taste of blood.

"Everything," he says, grimly. Then he lets her go.

Chapter Twenty Two:
The Tor

Leto Murray does not move. She listens as the argument continues: her mother's voice begging, pleading, crying, screaming, Johnny's quietly resolved, or softly threatening – Leto cannot tell the difference. When things have finally gone quiet, she lifts her head, and looks around the room. The thought strikes her that she has not heard the key turn in the lock. She lifts herself onto her hands and knees, and crawls, as noiselessly as she can, toward the door. Putting up a hand – no, a paw, she slowly, carefully, turns the handle. She's right – the door's not locked. Through the slim gap that appears as she pulls it inwards, she can see the key where it has fallen on the tattered landing rug, easily within her reach. Quickly, she snatches it up, and fits it into the lock on her own side of the door. Should she lock it? She wants to get out, not seal herself inside. Halek-dhwer has made it clear she has to find her way to her Moment if she wants entry into Huma's country, and she's sure the Lizard-bear didn't mean purely in her imagination. A Moment is a place, as well as an instant in time. It's the portal through which she must pass, if she really wants to be Wolf.

But if she doesn't lock the door, Leto thinks, the wicked witch could come bursting in again, and give her another beating. She turns the key, then sits back, staring at the eyeless wood. She doesn't know what to do next, and I'm afraid that neither I, nor the doorway, can tell her.

Johnny Horsefeathers slams the front door behind him and stamps down the front steps, passing underneath the rose covered gateway through which he entered not many weeks previously. He is, to his own amazement, furious with himself. *Evil-incarnate,* he once named her. He's known since the beginning exactly what the woman is, and, in his mind, has kept very clear about the extent and meaning of his intentions towards her – and her little daughter too, concerning whom he's conceived some ridiculous idea of rescue. And yet, even knowing who and what she is, he's somehow allowed Evelyn to catch him off his guard, disarm him and persuade him, against all reason and experience, to run the hideous risk of her impregnation. *Perhaps the bitch is lying*, he thinks. She could be. How long is it since their visit to the coast? But there remains the possibility that she's not, and that he has been carelessly responsible for the quickening of another human soul within a womb – and world – that will only cause it misery.

War is coming. Johnny knows it, and has known it for longer than most. *Pavor Potentia.* It has been, for as long as he's been travelling within the Otherworld, all that the faceless men have whispered about. What else, other than war, could that terrible, dark moment represent? What event, in any world, any time, could be worse? War is coming, and very soon – and the last thing Johnny wants is to beget a child in its teeth, let alone on Evelyn Murray, who to his mind represents everything that war will be against.

You bloody fool, he tells himself. *Now what on Earth or in hell are you going to do?*

He begins to walk slowly up the lane, heading towards that part of the stone hedge from which he originally emerged. "*Transibo per,*" he murmurs.

The air shimmers, like a waterfall. Johnny Horsefeathers vanishes.

Evelyn kneels in the hallway, and watches Johnny leave her. She can't stop him. Her begging, her pleading, even her most savage threats have all proved completely useless when set against his fury. *Not fit to be a mother,* he told her, *not fit to be a wife, not fit even to be my lover. You are nobody and nothing, Evelyn Murray, nothing but a hollowed out, spoilt, pathetic creature not fit even to draw breath. Useless woman! Useless, unwanted, undesired, Evelyn.* But are all those words really Johnny's, or are some of them her father's? Gerald's? The American's? Perhaps, in truth, they're a mix of many men's words, some of which were never spoken to her directly. *Why,* she thinks, *why, why,* do men always choose to leave? Her father was the first, after her mother died and the merry go round stopped turning. Then the American went back to his own country – to his own infinitely superior wife, and flawless children – on the first steamship that would take him, leaving her seduced and confused and utterly alone. And so she married Gerald, and then Gerald abandoned her so that she might fall in love with Johnny, her Hippolytus, her Virbius, her superman; and now Johnny has left her, too.

Could he be right? Evelyn asks herself, in despair. Could it be that she is not, in any sense, the good wife and mother she has tried so hard to be? It's true, she admits, that she's broken her marriage vows – but isn't the continuation and strengthening of the human species of much greater importance than some meaningless words spoken before a God in whom she no longer has any faith? Surely, both Diana and Davenport must agree that it is. But how is she not a good *mother?* It's not her fault if Leto's mentally deficient. Leto is the way she is because of her father's weaknesses, both personal and heritable. It isn't Evelyn's fault. It never was. Leto is a bad child, and a crazy one: a misconceived, useless, makeweight brat, whose wretched existence has stood in the way of so many much more valuable to the race than she can ever be. Boys – who will neither look like Evelyn nor sound like her. Sons – whose strong masculine faces can't remind her, every day, that she, Evelyn, is also nothing but a girl, a useless, worthless, plodding, pathetic girl, clinging to the coattails of some superman, and begging him don't go, please don't go. Sons, boys, whom she can love: sons who will never leave her.

The fight with Johnny wasn't Evelyn's fault, she tells herself. It was the girl's. If the girl hadn't behaved in such a disgusting fashion, pissing on the floor like a beast, the argument would never have happened. She could have soothed Johnny out of whatever black mood had seized control of him, and at this very moment, they'd have just finished making

Mammoth & Crow

love again upon the sofa. He'd be lying here with her, staying here with her, not rushing off angry into the damp half-light of the evening and leaving her with the taste of blood in her mouth and a dull headache between her eyes. Or he would be driving her to Rough Tor, where they would have stood hand in hand in the presence of its ancient divinity, and felt the future growing in her belly, and beneath their feet. She would have made him understand about Diana, and the vital importance of the *Golden Bough*. She would have convinced him of the truth about Virbius, and Hippolytus, and explained to him how the same thing can be both a symbol and be literally true, and how he, Johnny Nobody, can be the Priest-King of the sacred grove while still being Evelyn Murray's gardener, in the little Cornish village of Bransquite.

The girl's fault, all the girl's, if that future never comes to pass.

Evelyn gets slowly to her feet. What is she to do? How can she make Johnny come back to her? *Because he has to,* she thinks. *He just has to.* What if all this upset means that she loses him? She can't lose him. Not her Virbius.

But worse, far, far worse – what if she loses the child?

A horrible thought hits her: what if Johnny meant what he said – that he doesn't want the child, would do everything in his power to bring about its abortion? What power has he to do that? *Only violence*, Evelyn thinks, and he's shown her none. None that really matters, anyway.

Where has he gone? Has he gone to tell Gerald? Ridiculous notion. To the moor, then, that he knows so well? Has Johnny gone to Rough Tor, to speak by himself with the great Goddess, and beg her end the little life that she, Evelyn, petitioned be conceived? What dark and profane magics does he know, that he might use against her?

That's a crazy thought, she tells herself. Johnny laughed at the idea of the Goddess, and called Mr Frazer's great work of science and religion the ravings of a foolish old man. But somehow there is something – a queer niggling in her memory, like a trapped thorn-tip – that makes the thought seem not quite so crazy, after all. She remembers what it is: *the Priest of the Grove,* Mr Frazer says somewhere in his long, meandering tome, *is far from ignorant of sorcery.*

On impulse, Evelyn heads for the stairs. She's not going to Leto – the girl's quiet, now, anyway – but to Ignatius Hart's old library. That's where she first found *The Golden Bough,* and from where she removed it; and where she saw the picture hanging over the mantelpiece.: the ugly violet sky, the twisted tree, the portrait of the man. *Of course,* she thinks, *it will not still be there,* hanging behind the old red velvet curtain – she told Annie Tredinnik to remove it – but still she climbs, compelled by cruel habit to repeat an action she knows will bring no relief. Reaching the library, she puts her hand upon the knob, turns it, and finding it unlocked, cautiously pushes open the door. The smell of dust and the faint green whiff of mould assail her nostrils. Annie isn't cleaning this room. That's unsurprising: no-one ever uses it, and Evelyn vaguely remembers saying something about keeping it permanently shut up. But it's unlocked now. *Has somebody been using it? Who? Johnny?*

She walks into the room. The curtains are open, too; the gloomy evening light is spilling through them, casting a cold glow over the empty bookcases. The pile of unwanted books remains – the thief, whoever he is, has not returned to steal them. And there's something else, too: Ignatius Hart's painting of Horsefeathers, still hidden away behind its curtain. *Well, of course it is,* thinks Evelyn. Annie Tredinnik isn't the sort of woman to put herself out fulfilling what must have seemed a frivolous demand when she has other work to do. She simply closed the door on both the painting and Evelyn's order, and gave no more thought to either.

Evelyn walks across the room, and pulls on the curtain rope. The velvet slides aside, just as it did before, revealing the same scene: the central figure consumed by the entwining branches of the tree; the sickening, surrealist landscape; the black, knowing eyes, peering from that arrogant, beautiful face.

Yes, Virbius, Evelyn thinks, in sudden, though no longer unexpected, recognition. Her breath escapes her, in a low, deep, sigh of mixed relief and dismay. There's no doubt about it: the figure in the portrait is her lover. Ignatius Hart, dreadful painter that he was, knew Johnny. Did he know, too, when he caught the likeness, that he was depicting the high moor's one true Priest? That he was painting its symbolic Spirit-King? Impossible to know for certain; but perhaps he did, for in the background of the painting, beyond the tree and man, Evelyn recognises the broken mound of Rough Tor, ragged against the sky: Diana's Temple. *Johnny knows*, she thinks. *He's known all along.*

Evelyn feels sick. Dizzy. Sick. As if she has

been spinning round and round, faster and faster, without realising she was doing it, and has now, abruptly, stopped. She puts her hand to her head. The room seems to be darkening before her eyes. It's nothing to do with the light. *My baby!* she thinks, clutching at her belly.

Perhaps Johnny didn't really mean what he said about the child. Perhaps his reaction was merely that of a shocked and already angry man unable to deal with receiving such profound news at such a time, and in such a way – and she can hardly blame him for that, she thinks. She'd never have chosen, if she'd been given time and opportunity to choose, to reveal her secret in the middle of a row: the words slipped up, of their own accord, like bile. And even a Priest, especially a King, has the capacity to respond to them with rage and violence. *Yes,* she tells herself. *That must be it.* Johnny wouldn't really harm his child. What man would harm his own child? What Daddy reject his son, even if he should detest his daughter?

Evelyn's ears are buzzing. She puts her hands against her temples. It feels impossible to think. The dizzying, spinning sensation, the sense of distance, dislocation, that she has been feeling to a greater or lesser extent ever since her visit to the vicar, is suddenly getting worse. It's not the gin. She feels as if she is about to faint: sits down, lets her head fall between her hands. She won't let herself faint. She bloody well won't cry, either. Evelyn Murray's not a woman who believes in weeping, especially on account of a betrayal.

I must petition the Goddess again, she thinks. *I must petition Diana, properly, to protect my son from him. From everyone. From everything. From Gerald. From Leto. From this degenerate, terrifying world. I must ask her to help me. Because my son must live. He must live. He must live. This time. This time. Nothing else matters. Nothing.*

Because he was perfect. Perfect.

But what can she offer the dark Goddess in return?

There is one thing, she thinks.

What happened to Iphegina in Aulis was not, let me tell you, Clytemnestra's idea. It was just another version of an old, old story: a sent message gone awry, a journey undertaken in error, resulting in gore and death and, ultimately, war. Blame Troy on the Gods, because if it had been up to Homer it would have been a different story. If those three silly Goddesses hadn't been so appallingly vain, Eris would never have become involved in the first place. And if Zeus had been better able to control his lusts – a curious handicap, in my opinion, for a Sky God to be struggling with – there'd have been no Helen, either. But everything came down, as it inevitably does, to fire and bone; desire and blood.

So despite her understandable horror at her husband's command, Clytemnestra still went along with it; likewise those Carthaginian matrons whom Diodorus found so despicable smothered their own grief and offered up their offspring to appease the roaring god. Such, I have to tell you, has been the case within too many cultures throughout human history. They have all had their own strong motives, clever rationales, and lame excuses for doing so: undoubtedly some were more honourable, if such a word can ever be applied to such a sacrifice, than others.

Evelyn Murray thinks of the child she hopes to carry, the dread doom which seems to threaten him, and the noble future which, she has convinced herself, depends upon his birth: and in the dizzied dream state into which shock has thrown her there seems to be only one solution. A life for a life. Blood for blood. Not the old King's for the new, because that is currently impossible; and anyway, she still can't quite bear to think of Johnny dead – though if she really had to choose between him and her son it would take her less than a heartbeat to make up her mind – but the blood of her other self: *the girl*, who seems now, suddenly, to have been born for this purpose, and this only.

She doesn't belong to me, Evelyn thinks. *She never did. She belongs to Diana; and the Goddess wants me to give her back.*

Miss Fox has unexpectedly run out of eggs, right in the middle of tomorrow's batter pudding. "Run down to the farm," she told Martin Stone, "and fetch a dozen for me, there's a good boy." Martin put on his overcoat and galoshes and hurried down the hill. Now he's returning with his prizes in a basket, and is walking past Ignatius Hart's old house. He's walking quickly: he misses seeing Leto, but it wouldn't be wise to linger, knowing what he knows, and fearing what he fears. And anyway, the church clock has just sounded the three quarter hour; it's nearly eight o'clock, and Miss Fox is waiting in the warm, dry kitchen, listening to the wireless with her pinny covered in plain flour and her glasses perching on the narrow tip of her nose. And his crows – Petra and Paul, and all their half-grown fledglings – are flapping high over his head, urging him to hurry homewards, and not linger upon the encroaching dusk.

The vicar's motor car is parked outside the front door. The driver's door is open, and somebody is clambering inside it, blonde hair bright as a beacon, kitten heels scraping on the damp pavement. She's dressed smartly, in a stylish hat, white gloves and silver wolf fur coat: almost as if she was going to a wedding, he thinks. But no-one, even in England, would hold a wedding in the evening, even during the dog days of high summer.

Where on Earth is Mrs Murray going? He dodges behind the village postbox, and peers across the lane. Mrs Murray scrambles inside the car, and fumbles with the ignition, without success. She gives a sharp shriek of frustration, and tries again. Finally, she gets out of the car again, and begins to hunt around the chassis for the starting handle.

Where's Johnny Horsefeathers? Martin wonders. *Isn't he Mrs Murray's driver, as well as everything else? It should be his job to struggle with the engine.* He squints, and tries to see who else, if anybody, is inside the car. There's no sign of the wizard.

But there is movement on the back seat: a small blonde figure, wearing a red coat, and, bizarrely, a bobble hat, as if it were the middle of winter, or she's being taken somewhere cold: *Leto.* Her expression is curious. She seems to be giggling at something, though as far as Martin can see, there's little to laugh at. As he watches, she lifts a mittened hand, takes off her hat, and slowly starts wiping the car window with it. Then she seems to slump back down into her seat, as if she's been overcome by tiredness, her head lolling against the leather backrest, her mouth dropping open, her eyes closing.

Martin thinks, suddenly: *is Leto drunk?* He's seen people in that state before, usually on Purim. It's typical for drunken bodies to loll about, and people to giggle and laugh uncontrollably at nothing. *But why on Earth would Leto be drunk? Is Mrs Murray drunk, too?* She doesn't seem it – but then she doesn't seem to be quite in her right mind, either – *whatever,* Martin thinks resentfully, *her right mind is. Where are they going?*

There are no suitcases in the car, from what he can see, so his initial thought – that Mrs Murray has decided to drive back to London – can't be right.

Something's wrong, Martin realises. Very wrong, but he can't tell exactly what. Perhaps it's everything put together: Mrs Murray's smart clothing, her increasingly desperate struggles with the starting handle, the mysterious absence of Johnny Horsefeathers, the strange appearance and stranger behaviour of Leto.

Mrs Murray kicks the car. She seems to be upon the point of tears. Martin waits for her to call out for somebody to help her, but she does not.

"Mummy," comes Leto's plaintive voice from within the car. "Mummy, I feel sick."

"Shut up!" Evelyn Murray says.

"I think I'm going to be sick in the car."

Evelyn drops the starting handle in the road, and totters round to the rear passenger door.

"Get out," she says, wrenching it open,

Mammoth & Crow

dragging Leto from the car. "If you're going to be sick, you can be sick in the street."

Leto slumps, retching, into the dirt. *She is drunk,* Martin thinks, in horrified shock. *How did she get into that condition? Did her mother do it?*

Evelyn Murray returns to the starting handle, and determinedly turns it. Finally, the engine catches, and the vicar's Crossley Golden begins to shake and rumble.

Evelyn runs to Leto, and hoists her to her feet.

"Where are we going?" Leto moans.

"For a picnic," Evelyn says, in a peculiar, sing-song voice. "A lovely picnic, on the lovely, lovely moor. We're going to meet someone very special."

A picnic? Martin thinks, in astonishment. *Now?* Who does she imagine they're going to meet up there at this hour? Either Mrs Murray is mad, really mad, or she is lying. A horrible, heavy feeling takes root in his belly. What is he to do? He can't stop Mrs Murray from leaving, or rescue Leto. She is Leto's mother, after all, and entitled to take her anywhere she pleases. He can't run home and tell Miss Fox – not, at least, until the car has gone, because the terrifying thought has just struck him that if Mrs Murray sees him, she might kidnap him, too, or run him over. One of the young crows, irritated at the delay, settles on the postbox. It eyes Martin thoughtfully and opens its beak, as if to scold him.

A sudden inspiration strikes him. Perhaps there *is* something he can do.

"Help her," he whispers to the crow. "Help Leto."

The crow cocks its head on one side, then flies

upwards. For a second, it circles amongst its fellows, disappearing in the whirling coruscation of black feathers; then, like a squadron of dogfighting aeroplanes, or arrows in a mediaeval siege, the crows form themselves into a v-formation and dive upon the car, heart stoppingly fast. Martin gasps as they plunge toward the windscreen. He sees Mrs Murray throw up her arms and shriek in terror, blinded by the attacking mass of birds; sees the car veer sharply off course, almost careering into the front wall of the house opposite; but then the crows, having exhausted their offensive, are forced to rise up and regroup, and somehow Mrs Murray's in control again, steering straight, changing gear – Martin hears the mechanism grind and crunch – and the car leaps forwards like a kangaroo, picking up speed, heading up the hill towards the church, and the high moor.

"Follow her!" Martin shouts to his crows. "Tell me where she goes! Don't let her out of your sight!"

Immediately, the flock divides. Petra and Paul drop from the sky to Martin's side, settling on top of the post box, and stare at him, heads cocked on one side, questioningly. What are *they* to do, they ask him, with their still ragged feathers stopping them from flying fast? The sleek young crows head upwards, splitting up, some venturing ahead, some hanging back, all of them keeping the motor car in sight as it roars up the hill and out of view. Martin is glad that Mrs Murray doesn't, as far as he knows, have a gun.

Still carrying the basket of eggs – though the thought crosses his mind that he could run more swiftly without them – Martin hurries back along the lane towards the cottage. The distance seems farther this time than it's ever done before: by the time he reaches the garden gateway he is out of breath, and a light Cornish drizzle has started falling, coating the road and stone hedges with a glistening sheen. It really is no evening for a picnic.

Petra and Paul head for the ridge pole of the roof, and Martin for the cottage door. "Miss Fox!" he shouts, stumbling through it. "Miss Fox!"

His foster aunt emerges from the kitchen. She's taken off her pinny, and washed the flour from her hands. "Good gracious, Martin," she begins. "What is the matter? Take off your boots and come through to the kitchen, dear. You have a visitor."

"*Frau* Murray *hat* Leto *gemacht.*" The words tumble from him in a torrent. "I think she *hat ihre unter Drogen,* Miss Fox. *Frau* Murray *ist verrückt geworden.*"

"Martin, dear!" Miss Fox exclaims, hurrying forwards and taking the basket of eggs. "Slow down. And in English, please. I can't understand you. Take off your boots."

Martin grinds his teeth. "Mrs Murray has taken Leto up onto the moor," he says. "She was driving the vicar's car – the one I saw Horsefeathers driving – I mean Johnny – in Camelford."

Miss Fox looks acutely embarrassed. "I'd keep quiet about that at the moment, dear," she whispers.

"Why?" Martin asks, loudly. "Who is here? Is *she* here? Mrs Murray?"

"Of course not, Martin, not her – "

"Johnny," Martin says, suddenly realising. "It's *Horsefeathers.*"

Leaving Miss Fox standing in the hall, he

pushes past her, into the kitchen. Johnny Horsefeathers – the new gardener, the tramp in the brown Homburg hat, the wizard – is sitting at the kitchen table in his shirt sleeves, drinking tea from one of Miss Fox's china cups. He looks up as Martin enters. "Felicitations, bird boy," he says.

"No," Martin says. "Not felicitations. Mrs Murray has stolen Leto, and I think she's going to hurt her. And it's your fault. I don't know how, but it is."

"Martin!" exclaims Miss Fox, who has followed him through the door. "Mind your manners, dear! Johnny is our guest."

"It's perfectly all right, Miss Fox," Johnny says. "We're good friends, the boy and I. Isn't that so, Martin Stone?"

"I know your real name, too, now," Martin says, quietly, as Miss Fox disappears into the larder to put away the eggs. "I read your letters to your father. I know who you are. And what. You're a wizard."

Johnny turns his head, eyeing him measuringly. "I prefer the term Occult Magician," he says at last. "And what do you intend to do with this knowledge?"

"That's my business," Martin retorts.

"Touche, I suppose," says Johnny.

"We swore a pact," Martin mutters, angrily. "You broke it. You told Mrs Murray who I was, and that I'd seen you with her."

"I told her nothing. She learned about you from the vicar of St Bran's, not me."

"What are you doing here?" Martin demands. "Did you hear what I said about Leto? Do you even care?"

Mammoth & Crow

"I came to see you," Johnny says.

"Why?"

"Because there are things I can teach you. You're the boy who talks to birds; the boy who had speech with the faceless men, and walked beside the dead cart, and lived to tell of it. And you are also, by your own admission, the boy who had the wit and nerve to break into my camp, and read my private correspondence. If that mattered, by the way, you know I'd have to kill you." He winks. It looks like a friendly wink; but Martin's not convinced. He remembers how afraid he has been of the wizard, despite his efforts to suppress it. "But it doesn't matter; not now. You told me I had to make a choice. So instead of killing you, I have chosen you."

"For what?"

"To be my apprentice, bird boy. And my successor, eventually, just as I was Fireborn's: Ignatius Hart's."

"I don't want to learn anything from you," Martin exclaims, in disgust.

Miss Fox comes out of the pantry. She's wiping the inside of a sugar bowl with a tea towel, and frowning. "Did you say Mrs Murray had taken her daughter up on the moor, Martin?" she said.

"Yes!" Martin cries, relieved that one of the adults, at least, is listening. "She said she was taking her for a picnic, Miss Fox. I think she's drunk. I think Leto is, too."

"Mrs Murray doesn't know the moor," says Johnny. "She won't get very far in the vicar's car, either. She can barely drive, and the tank's low on petrol – though I keep a full can in the back, in case of emergencies. She'll crash into a stone hedge and end up spending the night in a ditch."

"If that's true," says Miss Fox, casting a worried glance in the direction of Johnny, whose voice has not shown any great concern, "hadn't we better go out and look for them? I don't know about Mrs Murray, but the poor little girl will be terribly cold and frightened."

Johnny looks unconvinced.

"You don't care a jot about them, do you?" Martin says.

"Yes," says Johnny, after a long pause, during which the only sounds that can be heard are those of the clock ticking on the wall and the ginger tomcat purring on the windowsill. "I care about Leto. That woman, on the other hand, can break her God damned neck. She's made her bed, and she can bloody well lie in it – "

The mask of politeness slips like melting ice from Miss Fox's face. She gives an audible gasp.

"I apologise," Johnny says. "But if you knew what she was… "

"But I do know," says Miss Fox, drawing herself up to her full height. "And however misguided and distasteful her beliefs, and her recent lapses of judgement – I also know that she is still a human being. She does not deserve to have her death wished on her by a feckless and cruel young man who – I'm sure – has taken full advantage of her deluded foolishness."

Johnny stares at Miss Fox. He tries to reply, but – to Martin's astonishment – both his voice and usual confidence seem to have deserted him.

"Now," says Miss Fox, briskly, hurrying into the hallway to put on her macintosh and wellington boots. "Are you going to help us, or not? How well do you know the moor, Johnny?"

"He knows it very well," Martin says. "He's been camping on the east side of Rough Tor for I don't know how long."

"Rough Tor," says Johnny, as if Martin has said something important. "Evelyn asked me to take her there, this evening."

"Is that where she's likely to have gone?"

"It could well be," Johnny says.

"Then that," says Miss Fox, stuffing her torch firmly in the pocket of her macintosh,"is the first place we will look." She heads toward the door.

"Wait," says Martin Stone. "Miss Fox, you'll be there much faster if you ride your bicycle."

"The boy's right," says Johnny, getting to his feet. "Miss Fox, if you cycle along the lanes, Martin and I will run straight across country to Rough Tor. I swear to God I will not lose him, or myself. I know the moor blindfold in pitch and fog, and – just as importantly – it knows me. "

Martin glares at him. "And I won't lose you, either," he says. "You can be sure of it." *And I'll have my crows,* he thinks. *They'll tell me everything I need to know.*

Jack Wolf

12th August, 1927
Bombay, India

Father,

    As you will tell if you bother to examine the postmark, I am now a long way from Cornwall. I have found employment and have no need of anything from you, including your damned name, which you polluted when you gave it to that woman. Your continued attempts to dig me out will all amount to nothing, so once again I must require you to cease and desist from harassing my friends and acquaintances. None of them knows where I am, and if they did, they would never pass the secret on to you. I never want to see you again or have anything to do with you. As far as I'm concerned you are no longer my father. I never had a father, only a mother; and you bullied and neglected her until she died of loneliness. I'll bet my bottom dollar that you'll treat that woman in exactly the same way as soon as the honeymoon is over. I would feel sorry for her if she wasn't evil. Maybe you deserve each other, and Mussolini can be Master of you both.

Phillip

Chapter Twenty Three:
Petrol and Stone

Trust your mother.

The witch came to the door about half an hour after the argument subsided, and knocked on it. "Leto," she called, not unpleasantly. "Are you hungry? I've got some cake for you, and a glass of lemonade."

It was a simple ruse, which could have been lifted straight from any of the faery tales in the Children's Encyclopedia, but Leto decided to play along with it. She was hungry, and there was a conciliatory tone in her mother's voice, which she'd heard before in Nanny Gould's on the rare occasions Nanny wanted to console her after a tantrum. *Sorry*, it said. And she remembered what the Gatekeeper said, and the thought struck her this was what it must have meant: this choice, this momentary trust. So, despite her doubts, she took the key out of her underwear, and opened the locked door to let the danger in. And she ate the cake, and drank the lemonade although the liquid tasted funny and made her head spin; and she didn't argue when the witch told her put on her outdoor things, because they were going to a special place on the high moor, and it would be cold in the evening wind. The witch was going to take her to her Moment, to *Huma*. For all her power, all her glamour, she was really nothing but a pawn, unknowingly moving into place upon the chessboard landscape of the moor.

Now the witch is driving across the open land, and Leto is sitting on the back seat because there's a picnic basket on the front, and she's feeling sick, and wondering if she should feel frightened, and if the reason she doesn't is because there's really nothing to be frightened of, or because she still can't feel any emotion at all, let alone fear. It's a strange thing, being so emotionally numb: strange and wrong; yet Leto understands that for all this, numbness is the only tool she has left, now, to save herself. Numbness is like being in the still, calm centre of the Naiad's eddy, watching the waters churn around: the only safe place in the river. Nevertheless, being numb doesn't stop her from feeling dizzy and physically sick. She wonders if the witch has poisoned her.

The suspicion should be horrifying, but it doesn't frighten her. She puts it to one side and looks out of the car window. The moorland stretches away on both sides, open and largely flat – on the uplands at least – punctuated by clumps of gorse and the round white backs of sheep. Every time the witch changes gear, the car bucks violently and the engine screams, metal crunching and tyres throwing up vast clouds of dirt and small stones from the rough road surface. Leto can't tell what speed they're going, or in which direction: the lanes twist and coil like hairpins, sometimes doubling back on themselves, travelling up and down steep slopes and through moor gates and over cattle grids with no rhyme or reason whatsoever; and every time one of these things happens the witch curses loudly. More than once she's stopped the car and turned it round, circling up onto the high, gorse covered banks and startling the watching crows – only to turn right back again when she's spotted some landmark or other that she noticed previously. In the distance, the dark ragged peak of Rough Tor stands proudly against the sky – a sky which, Leto thinks, is turning indigo. *It is! It's almost violet.* And again, it doesn't matter what the witch has done, or what she thinks she's doing; all that matters are the distant crags, and waiting Huma.

The car comes to a crossroads, and the witch pulls it, unsteadily, to a halt. She stares round wildly at the darkening moor, and lets out a shriek. Leto covers her ears.

Leaving the engine running, the witch gets out of the car, and begins to run up and down the lane, first along one track, then another, returning each time to the crossroads, and screaming again in frustration, her kitten heels digging deep into the dirt.

She's lost, Leto thinks. *We're lost. But the crags are there, directly in front of us. There's the wizard's den, and the Gatekeeper's Moment. My Moment. Mine.*

"Mummy?" Leto says. "What are you doing?"
"Quiet," snaps the witch. "Let me think."
"Why are we lost?"
"Because of the roads, you stupid girl! Because of the crazy Cornish roads, which don't lead where they're supposed to!"
"But Rough Tor is right there," Leto says, pointing. "And the road's heading toward it."

"It isn't," says the witch, furiously. "It won't. I don't trust it. I don't know where we are."

"Why don't we just go that way and see?"

"These awful roads!" cries the witch. "Why can't the bloody Cornish put up road signs that make sense?"

Talking to Leto's calmed her down a little, it seems. At least, she's no longer screaming, or pacing up and down. After a minute or so, she returns to the car, and settles back into the driver's seat. "We'll try," she says. She puts the car into first gear, and it lurches forwards with a roar, skidding on the wet soil. Leto hugs her knees, and thinks of Huma. Where will the mammoth be waiting? Will she be beside the river, or hiding in the crags? It would be hard for a creature so huge to fit between the stones, but maybe she'll be sheltering below them on the eastern side, where the vast bulk of stone shields the grasslands from the prevailing wind. *She'll be somewhere,* Leto thinks. She's certain of it. Trust your mother.

The car speeds on. Leto's right: Rough Tor is coming closer. At the next junction the witch turns left, and crosses a cattle grid; then after some uncountable distance, she drags the steering wheel violently to the right, and the car swerves sharply, beginning to mount a gentle incline that takes it past a farmhouse. By now, it's almost dark. The witch stops the car, switches on the headlights, and starts up again, despite the protestations of the engine.

A shower of raindrops dashes against the windscreen. The witch lets the car slow down of its own accord, her attention focused upon finding the lever which will operate the wiper. The engine wheezes, coughs, and dies.

Mammoth & Crow

The witch puts her foot on the brake, and swears loudly. She tries to restart the engine, but to no avail. She gets out of the car and kicks the radiator. Then she goes to the rear, and after hunting around for something which Leto, kneeling up on the back seat and peering through the rear window, can't properly see, returns to the front of the car and stares at it helplessly, as if she hasn't the foggiest idea what she should do next, or how to do it. She's holding a fuel can.

Has the car run out of petrol? Leto feels a sudden thrill – not of fear, but of excitement. Perhaps they're going to be trapped here on the high moor all night. Perhaps the witch will leave her alone to get help, and then, while she's alone, Huma will come to find her, or the Lizard-bear will come to carry her to her Moment. And perhaps the witch will fall into a gully and crack open her head, and Leto will finally be free of her, in this world and the real one.

Rain trickles down the car windscreen. Leto watches the witch.

Evelyn Murray, Diana's newest and most devoted Priestess, stands in the Bodmin drizzle with the petrol can in her hand. She is now, by her reckoning, no farther than quarter of a mile from the Tor, and she's sure the road she is now travelling is familiar from the journey she took with Johnny. Somehow, her frantic peregrinations have brought her to the place she needs to be, despite the best efforts of the roads and wretched, wicked crows, to thwart her. She is almost with her Goddess. Perhaps it doesn't matter if there's still a little way to go – she can walk. Perhaps it's better to go this last little way on foot, like a pilgrim.

She puts the can on the ground, and gropes in her handbag for her Camel cigarettes and Zippo lighter. Everything is as it should be. She lights a cigarette, and breathes in deeply. At least, if she's no longer driving, she can smoke. Steering is too difficult with a baton in her fingertips. She can use the fuel, she thinks, to light the bonfire.

Her stomach gives a lurch. *Is it the baby?* she asks the dark Goddess, putting her hand to her abdomen. Is it the new life, already making his presence felt, though he can be no bigger than a tadpole? Or is it something else: awe, even dread? *But he must live,* she thinks. *My son must live. Nothing else matters.* She has to keep repeating the words. Words have power. They are spells.

She does not let herself think about the thing she has here come to do.

Martin and Johnny run pell-mell across the moor. It's not far, as the crow flies, to the craggy outcrop from Miss Fox's cottage, and both of them have travelled that way often enough they know the path without even thinking about it. Petra and Paul are flying overhead.

Martin does not speak to Johnny. He's not afraid of the man, as he was before; wizard or not, he saw how Johnny cowered like a little boy when Miss Fox scolded him, and it's impossible to remain frightened of any man who is afraid of her. Besides, he's confessed – his words had the ring, to Martin, of confession – to a fondness for Leto, and that goes some small way toward mitigating his behaviour toward her mother. And he isn't, after all, a bad man. Not entirely. The writer of those letters never could have been a wicked man. An angry one, certainly, but not wicked. How can anyone who more than ten years ago, when he'd not have been a great deal older than Martin is now, could see through Mussolini, anyone who understood and cared about the danger men like the Italian Duce would always pose to Martin's own people; anyone who was, presumably still is, prepared to stand up and say: 'this is wrong' be wicked? He called the Fascist leader a *monster*.

And Leto's mother, Martin remembers again, *keeps a picture of Hitler by her bed.*

It serves her jolly well right, he thinks suddenly. *Serves her right if she has been deceived. She is a wicked woman. She's cruel to Leto, and her heart is full of hate. She deserves everything she will get.* He remembers the shattering windows of the orphanage, the screams, the panicked flight in darkness to the London train, the weeping, terrified children. Mrs Murray, if Leto is to be believed, thinks that such horrors are entirely fair and just. She is a woman who'd happily watch families be destroyed, livelihoods and lives be torn apart, and think because those lives and families are only those of Jews, it doesn't matter – or worse, that what's happening is right. *She deserves her comeuppance,* Martin thinks.

Then he feels ashamed. It's still wrong, his grandmother would have said, for him to revel in Mrs Murray's humiliation. He's giving in to his *yetzer hara,* which is just as capable of anger and vengeful hate as Mrs Murray's: indulging it will make him little better than she is herself. After all, whatever the woman's vile beliefs, she wasn't part of the Berlin mob who threw the stones, and shattered the orphanage windows.

No, she wasn't, Martin admits, somewhat resentfully. *But she could have been.*

How could any man kiss a woman he does not like? A woman he has, in fact, hated with relentless intensity since long before they even met? How could any man so completely pervert love as to press it into the service of revenge?

Whatever the truth of it, Martin decides, it's impossible that he, Martin Stone, should ever become the wizard's apprentice. He can't imagine anything more ridiculous or less likely. What can he have to learn from a man who deals so roundly in deceit? A man who thinks the way to understand the mysteries of the universe is to learn spells and incantations from a book filled with pictures of naked people. His grandmother would have snorted in derision. The Rabbis would have rolled their eyes, and asked what knowledge Johnny Horsefeathers, of all people, truly has of the esoteric matters he is purporting to teach. If he knew anything of value, they'd have said, he wouldn't now be seeking an apprentice, but another, wiser, Master. A wiser head. Anyway, what use are the so-called mysteries of the *goyim* ever going to be to Martin? Most of them were stolen from the Jews in the first place, and have become garbled and blackened in translation. Trying to learn anything of Johnny Horsefeathers' kind of magic would be as futile as a fish trying to learn to swim from an alley cat.

"Car," says the young crow, insistently. "Car! Car!"

Miss Fox glances in the direction of the sound. The young crow is standing in the road, directly in front of the bicycle, its glossy feathers shimmering deep purple in the pale light from the headlamp. If she hadn't known better, she might have imagined it was speaking.

"Go away," she says, waving her hand at it. She rings her bicycle bell. "Out of the way!"

'Car!" repeats the bird. It doesn't move. Miss Fox is forced to steer around it, veering wildly to the left and almost losing her balance on the rough track. Then she sees the tyre marks, the churned up soil: Mrs Murray has been here. She's going the right way. The crow shakes itself, and flies off, into the dusk.

"Get out, now," says the witch to Leto, dragging the picnic basket from the front seat.

"Here?"

"Yes. We're going to walk to – the special place. Won't that be fun? An adventure. You and me on an adventure, just like in a story book."

She's talking to her now as if she were a baby, Leto notices. "Why are you bringing the petrol can?" she asks.

"In case we need it. To get the fire started."

"What fire?"

The witch laughs. "You can't have a picnic without a fire," she says.

"Miss Fox did."

"I'm not Miss Fox. Stupid, interfering old woman. I wish we'd never met Miss Fox."

"She was very kind to me," says Leto.

The witch's expression hardens. "Get out of the bloody car," she snaps. "And stop asking questions. I'm sick of your questions."

Leto does as she is told. She wants, for a moment, to refuse – to show her mother the same defiance she's shown so often to Nanny Gould – but she thinks better of it. Who knows what the witch might be capable of doing, if provoked? She might never reach her Moment if she annoys her.

Getting awkwardly out of the car, she looks around. Her head is strangely fuzzy, as it was one time when she had influenza, and Nanny Gould brought her hot chocolate in bed, and read to her from the Encyclopedia. It's not the nicest memory, but Leto hugs it to herself like a rag doll.

"Start walking," says the witch, picking up the picnic basket and slamming the car door.

"Mummy, I still feel sick," says Leto.

Her mother glares at her. Leto shivers. The evening air is cold, and the sunless violet sky's begun to deepen into black. She doesn't say anything else.

Evelyn walks along the lane. Her shoes are hurting her feet, but somehow this doesn't matter. Her head is still almost unbearably light; it's not stopped spinning since she found Johnny's portrait; and again she's begun to feel that she is dreaming. The pain is grounding. It will be part of the ritual, the prayer. Her left hand grips the picnic basket; her right, the petrol can. She will build, she thinks, a magnificent bonfire.

She won't let Johnny destroy her son. She'll protect him, preserve him, save him. Yes, save him from everything, even from those weaknesses of her own body that contributed to the deaths of his half-brothers, though they – she – didn't cause them. This last, longed-for son will not die. This boy will be born at the right time, alive and perfect, and he'll thrive and grow. She will make certain of it.

Every gain in life entails a loss: every victory

a sacrifice. And Evelyn is praying now, praying as she walks, her heartfelt plea rising through the damp evening air to the ears of the waiting Goddess. *Let him live. Let my son, my King to be, let him live, let him triumph over his enemies, just as almighty Zeus triumphed over Cronus, as progress subdues time. Let him live, oh proud Diana, mighty mother of us all, who saw our civilisation take its first breaths; let him live, that the human race may prosper and grow into an Empire that will last for a thousand years. Spare him from the fire.*

It seems to take a very long time before the sacred mound finally appears, some short distance to her right, its scattered temple stones a blacker geometry against the darkening sky. Then the lane meets with another. Evelyn turns right, toward the ancient temple, past the farm where she and Johnny once ate ham and eggs. The drizzle is worsening, the ground is already damp. How is she going to build a bonfire? Evelyn has come prepared, but not sufficiently. Why, she thinks, she should have planned properly ahead, should have taken time before today to come up to the Tor and build the pyre, carefully select the gorse, cover it against the rain, make sure every yellow flowered bough will catch alight. She's been a fool. An incompetent, impulsive fool! How can the Goddess accept any sacrifice if it is improperly offered? Why should she?

Again her stomach lurches. What is this sickness? *It is not – it can't be –* the beginning of her period. Because the baby is there, he has to be, buried in the lining of her womb, bathing himself in her blood and life, establishing himself against all and everything who might destroy him. This sickness is something else: some primitive fear, some dread, some terror of the rite, of the savage Goddess herself; and she must not heed it, because if she does, having come so far, everything will be lost. She must go ahead with the ritual, even if she can't do it exactly as she hoped. She has no choice.

Beyond the farm gate, the lane peters out, becoming instead a narrow, rutted track across rough ground. At the bottom of the hill, before the land begins to rise again into the western slope of Rough Tor, the track becomes a low bridge across the little river, then, on reaching the other side, abruptly disappears. Only the sheep trail, leading up toward the summit of the monument, gives Evelyn any hint of where to go; and it's hard to tell, in the fading light, exactly where it leads.

"Come on," says Evelyn to the girl. "We need to climb."

The fogou is strangely easy to find. Martin doesn't know if this is because Johnny is with him, or if some internal compass of his own is guiding him in the right direction; but it seems to him that no sooner have they set foot in the stone thicket than they come across it: a narrow triangle of darkness leading down into the layered earth. Johnny briefly pauses, with the air of a man who has finally come home, and would rather stay than leave, but then presses onwards, up the shattered side of the Tor.

"I can't see any lights," he says to Martin. "Are they here? What do your crows have to tell us?"

"How do you know – " Martin begins, and stops.

"I'm not Miss Fox, Elijah Rosenstein. I know

you sent them to keep watch. Clever. What is happening?"

Martin puts up his arms, and calls his creatures. Within seconds, both Petra and Paul have settled on his shoulders. He strokes their ragged feathers. "Find your children," he tells them. "We need to know what's going on. Where are Mrs Murray and the motor car?"

"Car!" cry Petra and Paul together, rising like dark glyphs against the brooding sky. "Car!"

Martin watches them fly.

"They'll come back," he says to Johnny.

"Of course they will. They are your servants."

"They're my friends," Martin corrects him.

They watch the sky, and wait.

"Bear!" cries the young crow urgently to Miss Fox. "Bear! Bear!"

Miss Fox tries to ignore it. The bird has now been following her on her bicycle all the way from where she found the tyre tracks, flapping round her in a circle never more than twenty yards across, and cawing relentlessly. She's reached the right turn at the bottom of the lane, near the china clay quarry where the tracks tell her the car has veered, wildly, once more onto the turf, and she now begins to cycle up the hill. Johnny's right, it seems, on both accounts: Mrs Murray is heading to Rough Tor, and she can barely drive.

"Bear!" cries the crow again. It flaps in front of the bicycle, a dark spectre in the dusk.

"Shoo!" shouts Miss Fox, finally losing patience. "Shoo!"

The bird flies upwards, its wings booming

round her head. Miss Fox lets out a little scream, and in a sudden, unintelligible, panic, throws up her hand to beat it off. The bicycle swerves, and skids in the dirt, almost toppling over. Luckily, she doesn't fall off.

Miss Fox stops. The wretched crow is over her head, still circling. She shakes her fist at it, and straightens her bicycle. Then, out of the dusk, a movement catches her eye. It's some twenty five yards ahead of her on the lane, heading in the same direction; not the fluttering shock of a bird, but a slow, heavy, earthbound crawling, like the motion of some giant creature. In the fading light she can't tell exactly what it is; only that it is some giant *thing*, some amorphous living mass, made somehow more menacing by its formlessness, as if it isn't fully entered into this world, as if it isn't fully real. Immediately she remembers the moor stories: those tales of hairy hands and devils and black dogs and faceless men at which she's always been so ready to scoff. Is this – this *entity* – one such as those? She shudders. *What is it?* She can't see it, but she feels – knows, somehow, as one does in dreams – that it's twice the length of a crocodile, three times the weight and height of a North American grizzly bear. But is it real? Is it a real creature, or a figment of her stressed imagination?

I will not be intimidated by a phantom, Miss Fox thinks. Whatever it is, however big it is, however devilish, if it's not part of this world, then as far as she's concerned it can have no bearing on it. Let it travel where it will; she has a motor car and a frightened little girl to find, and a foolish, deluded young woman who needs a very stern talking to. She regains her seat, and begins to pedal onwards. When she reaches the place where the creature should have been, the lane is empty.

Evelyn staggers up the slope. The picnic basket is heavy on her right arm, and the petrol can even heavier upon her left. All around her kitten heeled feet, the stone thicket is growing denser, the ground rougher, harder and harder to traverse. What is she doing, coming here in the twilight, which makes it so hard to see? What is she doing? What?

The child is trailing behind her, mewing feebly. *Good,* Evelyn thinks. *The weaker she is, the better.* It's the first time she's acknowledged this thought. Her vision clouds a little. She shakes the dizziness off. "Come on," she calls. "There will be lemonade at the top. Won't that be lovely? Lovely, lovely lemonade. Hurry."

The little girl doesn't answer. Will they even reach the top? Evelyn has to wonder. The ground is growing boggy. Strange, she thinks, that as they head upwards, it should be getting wetter. Perhaps there's a spring somewhere nearby, spilling over the impermeable rock. Or is it only from the rain? Her smart shoes are ruined: wet, filthy, scuffed, and the heel of one of them is coming loose, broken in a stumble over one of the many granite boulders that litter this side of the Tor. Perhaps she should take them off. Go barefoot, like a pagan, like a pilgrim. She remembers how one of them fell into the foot well of the vicar's car during her first, wonderful, encounter with Johnny; how she found it afterwards and replaced it: Cinderella's slipper.

Onwards and upwards. Is the Goddess

watching? Has she heard her prayer?

At the top of the mound, the ground begins to level out. Evelyn isn't sure, but she thinks she can see a narrow path leading to the right, up into the crags themselves. Perhaps its only there in her imagination. Perhaps that doesn't matter: she still feels as if she's dreaming, despite her aching feet, despite the pain, the exertion of the climb; and if the Tor is functioning like a dreamscape, it will do what she needs of it. The closer she can get to the temple, she thinks, the closer she will be, symbolically and really, to the Arican grove, to Diana: and the greater will be the chance of her sacrifice being accepted. She begins to pick her way, slowly, through the stones.

Leto follows her mother. She doesn't know what else to do. The witch told her, "come", and now, like an enchanted heroine, she's doing exactly that, even though it's increasingly plain that nothing good can come of it. *Where is Huma?* she thinks. *Where's my Moment?* Perhaps she's wrong to have listened to the Gatekeeper, foolish to have trusted the witch. She's glad she's put on her coat and mittens. The night wind is blowing in fast and cold from the distant strait, and the drizzle in her eyes is making it harder and harder to see.

Can she escape? Can she run away? But where can she go? She has no idea where she is. Are those her own crags up ahead? Or just the twilight playing tricks upon her eyes?

Lights are twinkling in the valley. A farmhouse? Leto vaguely remembers passing one during their walk along the lane, although she barely noticed it: she was thinking of Huma, and wondering when and where the Matriarch would reveal herself. She was so, so sure Huma would be here, watching, waiting. But now she's standing on top of a remote, rocky hill in a cold rain, and Huma has never felt so far away, never so much only part of her imagination. *She will not come,* Leto thinks. Will not, because she cannot. Huma isn't part of the world – this world, this real world, this boring, terrifying, everyday machine-run world of t-bar shoes and boiled eggs, and Nanny Gould, and Mummy: not some wicked, faerie-tale witch, just Mummy – staggering through the darkness with a petrol can, and a basket of poisoned lemonade.

"I want to go home," says Leto. "I want to go home!"

Evelyn's ankle twists. The kitten heel finally snaps: she casts it off and puts her stockinged foot down, gingerly, onto the wet ground. The cotton-grass feels soft against her toes – almost pleasant, for an instant, till the chill seeps through her skin. She gasps in shock. Her silver wolf fur is so warm, she hadn't realised how cold it is up here on the high moor, how greedily the earth sucks heat from naked flesh.

"Only a little further," she says, breathlessly. "Then we can sit down and have our picnic."

"I want to go home," the child repeats. "Please, Mummy, let's go home."

Evelyn turns around. The path is bathed in darkness. *What on Earth am I doing?* she asks herself, suddenly. An instant of clarity. She stares out into the black. She is standing on top of a rainy hill, in the middle of Cornwall, in the dark. This is madness. But then the picture of Johnny swims before her eyes, and she remembers her cruel

Goddess, and *The Golden Bough*, and Davenport – and *oh, my son, my son*. "Come here," she says, holding out her hand. "We can walk together."

Can she do it? Can she really offer up the child: sacrifice the girl to give her brother life? But what other offering will satisfy? What else will have the power to bring forth the Brave New World? Johnny's son, *her* son will be a child of the future: a modern man for a modern age, for an Age of Progress, an era of petrol and stone. *Leto was born for this purpose,* Evelyn tells herself. It is the reason she has thrived, despite her deficiencies, when so many have died: the dark Goddess has singled her out, and claimed her; now, at last, she is to take her.

Isn't that right? Isn't it? Isn't it?

Perhaps the girl is not enough. She's very far from being her mother's best beloved, after all. She's not even really Evelyn's child, after all, only Gerald's, in the infuriating ways that she takes after him, that pathetic, treacherous worm of a man. But she is all, right now, that Evelyn has. The thought almost makes her want to weep. But tears are not a luxury Evelyn Murray will allow herself. Not now. Not here. Not anywhere.

But how, she thinks, is she to do it? She has been seeing the vision in her head, over and over, a terrifying vision, inescapable as knife and fire – but there's no pyre, due to her own lack of preparation, and can she really bring herself to cut her daughter's throat? Now she thinks about it, did she even bring a knife? The girl is looking up at her, her face an innocent white oval underneath her bobble hat. Evelyn's stomach twists. *The ancient Carthaginians gave their babies to the Priests,* she thinks. *They didn't have to do the deed themselves.*

How does one kill a child? One's own child? How?

But she's not mine, Evelyn reminds herself. *Not really.*

They'll call it murder. They won't understand.

The whole purpose of the weak is to exist in the service of the strong.

She is only a girl. What worth is that of Woman, when compared to Man? What is it Apollo says, in that line from the Oresteia?

> *The mother of what's called her offspring's no parent,*
> *But only the nurse to the seed that's implanted.*
> *She harbours the blood-shoot, unless some god blasts it.*

Vain, cruel, ignorant, lying god! But it's true enough of the girl, isn't it? True enough of Leto.

Nothing and nobody. Only a girl. Soil.

Only soil.

Her whole body begins to shake. Thoughts tumble brokenly through her mind, like little bodies falling into fire.

Chapter Twenty Four:
Fire Gate

Martin Stone holds out his arms, and the crows descend. One, two, three: all the fledglings except one, fluttering black shapes like the floating embers from a burning building, carried upon superheated air.

"Where are Mrs Murray and Leto?" Martin asks them. "Where is the motor car?"

"Car-thage!" cried the young birds, in a chorus. "Car-thage."

"What does that mean?" Martin exclaims.

The young crows open their beaks, and cock their heads onto one side, eyeing Martin with a disappointed air. *Why don't you understand?* they ask him. *Are you stupid?*

"Tor," says one of the young crows. "Tor."

"Have they climbed it?"

The crow stares at him, silently, almost disdainfully. It has answered once, it seems to be saying. It shouldn't need to answer twice. Then it flies upwards, circles once, and disappears in the direction of the stone thicket. *Yes. They have climbed Rough Tor. Yes.*

"I can't see any sign of them," Johnny says, peering up into the crags. "There are no lights."

"I don't suppose Mrs Murray thought to bring a torch," Martin says. "And Leto won't have one."

"Evelyn!" shouts Johnny, suddenly. "Evelyn Murray! Leto! Leto!"

"The wind's too strong," Martin says. "And it's blowing in the wrong direction. They can't hear us."

"I know a way up," Johnny says. "Come quickly, bird boy. Bring your crows."

Evelyn sits down in the lee of an overhang, out of the wind, and catches her breath. Her stomach is sore. She has no idea why. She won't let herself think about it. She has taken off her second kitten heeled shoe and thrown it away, as trying to walk with one shoe proved nigh impossible; and though to some extent this has made matters easier, now she misses it. The soft skin of her feet is unused to walking even on friendly ground, and now they are cold, grazed and bruised, and probably as blue as two blocks of ice. Now the damp is spreading up her calves, into her knees, running along her inner thigh, chilling the place where Johnny ran his hand, moving upwards, upwards, towards her griping womb. She puts the picnic basket down, beside the petrol can, and rummages in her handbag for her Zippo and a cigarette.

I have to perform the sacrifice, she tells herself. She has to perform it here, and now, before she loses her nerve or the wretched girl begins to cry, or runs away into the dark. But she can't do it while Leto is awake. That would be too cruel. Another hearty dose of gin, and the little brat will be completely senseless. Then – she doesn't know what, then. She takes a long, deep drag upon her cigarette. The tip glows scarlet in the dark.

It will be like killing herself.

"Come and have some lemonade," she says. "And let's build a little fire, to warm us up."

"What with?" Leto says. The hillside is bare, except for some small tussocks of wet grass, and a few small piles of dung left by the moorland ponies.

"There must be some twigs. Look around."

"I can't see," Leto says, in a mutinous tone of voice. "It's too dark."

"For God's sake," snaps Evelyn. "Search!"

Leto stands quite still, staring at her mother. Then slowly, deliberately, she takes off her mittens, and throws them on the ground. The bobble hat follows. Then the belt of her red coat.

"What are you doing?" Evelyn says. There's a panicked tone, suddenly, to her voice.

'Burn them," says Leto. "There's nothing else." She begins to unbutton her coat.

"Stop that nonsense this minute," snaps Evelyn. "You'll catch your death of cold."

Leto takes off her coat, and throws it on the ground along with the rest of her things. "There's nothing else to burn," she repeats.

Is this defiance? Evelyn can't tell. Is this simple, barefaced *cheek* – the wretched brat testing her, yet again, to see what she will do, where the line is drawn? Or is it something else: something more profound and yet more horrible – has the girl somehow guessed the real purpose of the picnic, and is she now offering herself up to her fate, like

Iphigenia, divesting herself of those articles of which she will have no need in death?

It will be like killing herself.

What in the Great Goddess' name do you think that you're doing, Evelyn Murray? Are you really going to kill your own child? Really?

Of course not, Evelyn realises, reason snapping back to her with sudden, shocking, terrifying clarity. She reels back from the blow. She cannot love Leto, but of course she isn't going to kill her. That would be *madness*, not devotion but *madness,* and of course she isn't –

It would be like –

Thus with the death of Iphigenia begins the war.

"Stop it!" Evelyn screams. "Stop it!"

Leto sits down on a rock, and begins to unbuckle her shoes. There's a calmness to her actions that drives Evelyn wild with rage and grief arising in a violent torrent: and there's fear there, too. Fear of the child, as well as for her. Fear of her own terrible, unfathomable self.

"Stop it, Leto!" shrieks Evelyn, leaping to her feet. "I can't bear it! Stop it! Stop it! Stop it! Stop it!"

Leto does not stop.

Losing control, Evelyn springs forward. She isn't sure if she's trying to embrace the child, or beat her; whether she's more angry at Leto's defiance or more terrified by her own behaviour, by the insane belief that, only moments ago, held her enthralled within its grasp. Perhaps she's trying to save her daughter, throw her arms protectively around her, rescue her from the now too horrifying fate for which, minutes ago, the girl seemed destined. *Crazy thought!*

It would be like killing herself. But it is dark, and despite this last minute revival of her sanity, Evelyn is still rather drunk. The alcohol coursing through her blood has made her clumsy. Her frenzied hand deals Leto a heavy blow to the side of her head, which knocks her flying. Leto tumbles backwards, over the far side of the rock, and disappears into the darkness.

"Fine!" screams Evelyn, panicking, torn halfway between shock and rage: giving in to rage. Rage is safer. Rage doesn't risk half as much as any admission of tenderness: blaming the child seems to obviate the chance of any tragedy befalling her. "Fine! If that's what you want, then they can burn! Come back here this instant, and we'll stand and watch the damned things burn!"

She picks up the petrol can, her cigarette still in her hand, and runs back to the pile of clothing. "Burn!" she says again, unscrewing the lid of the can, and violently upending it.

The explosion is so bright that the sky above her head turns, for one brief moment in time, from black to violet.

From his position halfway up the slope, Martin watches the conflagration, as if it were the final scene in an old Hollywood movie. *It can't be happening,* he thinks, stunned. It's too surreal a sight – even for him, the boy who talks to birds, who followed the dead cart with the faceless men. Mrs Murray is at the top of the Tor, amongst the rocks, and she is on fire; her wolf-fur coat burning, blazing, like a giant silver candle, and her hands are flapping frantically at the flames, but nothing is happening, and now the fire is in her hair and at her feet and in the grass, why, it's even flowing out over the stones themselves, as if it were some demonic fluid that can burn by itself, with no substance to feed upon. But perhaps it is real, because now Johnny Horsefeathers is running up the hill, scrambling across the scattered boulders faster than Martin has ever seen any man run, screaming at the top of his voice: "*Extinguere! Extinguere!*" Perhaps it is real, because now he's leapt inside the tower of flames, and is throwing Mrs Murray to the damp ground, beating out the savage fire with fists and boots, dragging the burning pelt right off her body, kicking it away. But the flames are still spreading, and suddenly here is Leto – a shadowy flickering across the face of the inferno, scrambling down the side of the Tor towards him, and he shouts: "Leto!" but she doesn't seem to hear him. She looks up towards the top of the hill, and her face glows brilliantly golden in the light of the flames. She's wearing neither hat nor coat, and her blonde hair is shining with what looks like blood. Martin clambers towards her, waving his Bakelite torch in an effort to attract her attention. "Leto!" he shouts again. "You're hurt!"

Leto slows down, and looks around, confusion on her features. She puts her hand to her head, and seems astonished when it comes away wet.

"You're hurt," Martin says.

"Martin?"

"Yes. We came to look for you. What's happened?"

"It's Mummy," Leto answers. She looks back up the slope.

The flames are dying down now. The conflagration has lasted for a matter of seconds, but to Martin it has felt like an eternity.

Jack Wolf

"I'm scared of her," Leto says. "I'm not going back. I'm never going back. I think she wanted to kill me." She begins to shake. "She wanted me dead."

"We'll tell Miss Fox," says Martin. "She'll know what to do."

Leto begins to stagger down the side of the Tor, weaving cautiously through the rocks.

"Where are you going?" Martin shouts.

"Home. I'm going home. You can come with me if you like."

"You just said you were never going back." Martin scrabbles along a gully.

"I'm cold," says Leto.

"Horsefeathers!" shouts Martin. "Johnny Horsefeathers! Help!" There's no response. *Of course*, he remembers, *Johnny is probably injured too: he threw himself on top of Mrs Murray to beat out the flames.* "We need to get to shelter," he says, making a decision. "We'll wait for help in the wizard's den. It's not far."

Leto doesn't seem to hear him. "Wait for me!" cries Martin. "I'm coming!" *Go*, he tells Petra and Paul. *Tell Johnny I've found Leto. Tell Miss Fox what has happened. She must find a telephone box, and ring for an ambulance.* He doesn't stop to wonder how an ambulance will reach them, up on the high moor. Such considerations are the responsibility of adults. Martin is happy, for once, that they should be so.

Shadows are moving in the darkness; a blacker black against the unlit moor. Martin swings the beam of his torch towards them, and immediately they vanish. *What are they? Are they the faceless men?*

Mammoth & Crow

Petra and Paul, sitting on his shoulders, let out a sudden, unified squawk. They don't like this dark, they tell him. *It's full of monsters.* They don't want to leave him, but they're afraid to stay. He remembers how he was afraid of the sentinel crow, and the Lizard-bear, and the hairs prickle on the back of his neck. Is that monster here? What could it be doing, out there in the darkness and the cold, relentless rain?

Leto keeps on walking, as if in a dream, or in response to some summons that she alone can hear. Martin finally catches up to her, and snatches at her arm.

"You're freezing!" he exclaims.

Leto stops, and turns to stare at him. Blood is running down her face. "You've hit your head," Martin says. "Did you fall over?"

"I don't remember," Leto says.

"Come with me," Martin says. "We will be safer out of the wind. And we don't need to be frightened of the wizard. I know who he is."

When the explosion lights up Rough Tor like a beacon fire, Miss Fox is at the farmhouse. She passed the abandoned Crossley Golden some while before, and since then has been cycling more slowly, calling out for Mrs Murray and Leto at regular intervals, in case they're just a little way ahead of her: stopping to scan the moor and nearby fields for any sign of torchlight or Mrs Murray's blonde hair. But there's been nothing, and Miss Fox has decided that perhaps even a woman as determinedly foolish as Evelyn wouldn't try to climb Rough Tor in the darkness and the rain, so she's turned into the farm gateway overlooking the mound, and knocked on the kitchen door, as confident as she can be that Mrs Murray and Leto will be sheltering within. A few explanations later, however, she knows this is not the case. The farmer scratches his head, pulls on his boots, and comes stomping out into the yard; and they both look over toward the Tor, wondering aloud how a London lady and a little girl who do not know the land could possibly manage its ascent in the dark.

Then the fireball blazes on top of the crags, and Miss Fox screams, knowing without questioning that some very terrible thing has happened out there in the rainy darkness. And the crows descend, black letters tumbling out of a blacker sky. Martin's crows, Martin's messengers, Martin's written words.

"Oh, my goodness," Miss Fox says, her hands flying to her mouth. "I think somebody has been badly hurt."

The farmer shouts for his son to fetch the motorbike quick out of the tool shed, and ride to Camelford to fetch the police. He won't be long, he says. And in the meantime, he himself will find a torch, and he and Miss Fox will go up Rough Tor together, to see if there is anything that they can do. "Tourists," he says, shaking his head in sorry exasperation.

The shadows are coming closer. Martin can hear them – if it's possible to hear something that is no more substantial than darkness – whispering. For the first time ever up on the high moor, he feels afraid. The great creature is circling around them, teeth and claws bared, ready to lunge, and it is lashing its terrible tail, and breathing heavily, every breath the latent buzz of electricity. Petra and Paul have taken flight, cawing loudly. He hopes they won't lose themselves in the dark.

"Come on!" he says to Leto, pulling her arm. "We have to run. Something's following us."

He was right to choose to shelter in the fogou, he thinks, as they crawl inside. The air below ground is dry and still, and considerably warmer than above the surface. Hopefully the Lizard-bear, or whatever the monster is, won't find them. Even if it does, it must surely be too big to fit through the triangular gap. He flashes the torchlight along the low passage. It's empty. And yet as his nostrils accustom themselves to the earthy, musty scent, he realises he can smell something else: the scents of summer flowers growing on an open plain, of sweet, drying, grass, and clean, crisp, air. *Is the chamber open?*

Leto sways against him, and puts her hand to her forehead. "I feel sick," she says.

Martin helps her along the passage, and into the antechamber. He's worried. What if Leto's badly hurt? What if help doesn't arrive? What's happened to Johnny Horsefeathers, and Leto's mother? He makes Leto sit down on the camp bed, and scrabbles round in the darkness for something to light the oil lamp. He doesn't think Johnny would have left matches, but it's still worth looking for them, just in case. He didn't think of searching when he visited before; but then he was on his own, and the world wasn't so frightening. Eventually, his hunt turns up a small yellow box of Swan Vestas, nestled in the space between two magical books. The box is nearly empty, but it's dry enough to make it worth trying to strike a light. He turns his torch upon the lamp, and begins to investigate it.

"Halek-dhwer," Leto whispers, suddenly.

"What?"

"Halek-dhwer," says Leto, more loudly. It sounds to Martin as if she is speaking someone's name.

"Who is Halek-dhwer?" he asks.

"The Guardian of the Gate," Leto says.

The prehistoric grave, Martin thinks. A shiver runs down his back. The bear claw, the rotted cloak, the ancient skull: *Halek-dhwer.*

"It's the Lizard-bear," Leto says.

"Don't call it," Martin says, urgently. "Don't!"

Leto looks at him through the long fringe of her bloodied hair, and smiles. "But I want to," she answers simply. "I want to." And she says the name again, softly; and as she does so it seemed to Martin Stone that the chamber has suddenly grown extremely warm, and the still air is now stinking with the ripe, carnivorous smell of some huge animal, half mammal, half reptile, with potential to be either or both: a creature frozen forever in a moment of transformation, all the more terrible to human eyes on account of that queer, unnatural unfixity. He closes his eyes, trembling. It is less frightening to be unable to see the monster because of something he has done, than because it is choosing to remain invisible. But now, with his eyes shut, he can picture it looking in every detail exactly as it looked on the day it chased him over water into the land beneath the violet sky, the land of the *Shaydim,* the faceless men. Is the monster in his head? Is it physical? Leto seems to think so. Perhaps it doesn't matter.

Something large and warm, like a muzzle, snuffles round his head. His hair moves in the stale wind of its breath.

What is the Lizard-bear? he thinks, wildly. Was it fashioned by the hands of God, to be part of his creation – or is it something else, a creature of the cracks, the shadows, existing on the edges of reality – an echo of what was, of what is never to be? *What are the Shaydim?* Why do they exist? Where, and to what reality, do they belong?

You are the bird boy, says a dark voice, in his head. *You treated me with kindness, with respect. You replaced my skull.*

"Yes," stammers Martin.

I am so, so sorry for your loss.

"What do you mean?" Martin says.

The voice does not answer.

Leto understands what she must do. She was wrong to doubt Huma. The Matriarch is here, waiting on the other side of the thin veil that separates this narrow world of machine-men from that of her mighty kindred. All Leto has to do is to find the gate, and walk through it. But Halek-dhwer is the Gatekeeper, and it is only Halek-dhwer who can open it for her, in exchange for the peace that she has promised it.

So she closes her eyes, and calls the name. Again. Again. Again.

So, Halek-dhwer says. *So, little ghost. You have come.*

"Is this my Moment?"

Yes, Halek-dhwer says.

"Will you open the gate for me? Can I go through now?"

You will not come back if you do.

"I don't want to come back," Leto says,

fiercely. "Why does everybody think I should? I don't want to!"

"Leto, don't go!" cries Martin Stone. "Please don't."

"Why not?"

"You'll become one of the faceless men. They'll make you ride the bone cart. And I'll never see you again."

"I won't be one of them. I will be Wolf," says Leto. "And I will be with Huma."

"Is that all you care about? A long dead mammoth?"

"She's not just any old mammoth," Leto says. "She's the *Matriarch*."

"If you go, I'm going with you," Martin says. "I've done it before. I crossed the river. I travelled the road. I stood under the violet sky. I have a key." He puts his hand in his pocket. The bear claw is there, of course, as it always is: he's never remembered to put it among his treasures. It grows warm to his touch. *It's reacting to the presence of the Otherworld,* he thinks. *It's getting ready to take me through.*

"Come then," says the Gatekeeper. "Come away, o human child, to the waters, and the wild."

The animal smell grows stronger, hotter, as if the Lizard-bear is crouching over them, predator or protector; then it's gone, transformed or blown away by the warm breeze that is now entering the chamber; a breeze sweet with the untainted scents of a late Pleistocene summer: the small steppe flowers, the ripening grass, the berrying trees, the roaming herds.

"Can you smell it?" Leto says.

"Yes. What is it?"

Leto opens her eyes. "The world," she says.

"It is the world."

Miss Fox finds Johnny on top of Rough Tor, with Mrs Murray lying across his lap, rocking her back and forth like a baby, and muttering softly in what might be Latin. He's wrapped her in what looks to be a picnic blanket. She's not moving. The remains of her silver wolf fur coat lie some yards away, smouldering; beside it lie the open basket, and the empty petrol can.

"Johnny!" cries Miss Fox, hurrying over. "What happened? Where is the little girl?"

Johnny lifts his face, and stares at her blankly, as if he can't understand what she is saying. "Johnny!" she repeats urgently, seizing his shoulders and shaking him. "What happened?"

"Evelyn's hurt," Johnny says, seeming to come somewhat to his senses. "I can't heal her. I don't know where Leto and Martin are. I think she must have tried to light a fire."

Miss Fox looks down in horror. "With *petrol!* How could anybody be so silly? Oh, the poor, *foolish* young woman!"

"This is my fault," cries Johnny. "I made her believe I loved her, when I didn't. I don't."

Miss Fox flashes him a scathing look.

"It's true," he continues, pitifully. "It's my fault."

Miss Fox draws herself to her full height. "Even if it is," she says. "Now is not the time for self recrimination and self pity. Indulge in them later, if you must. Leave Mrs Murray with me, and find Leto and my nephew, before there is another tragedy."

"It's all my fault," Johnny repeats.

"Leave her with me," says Miss Fox, firmly. "The police have been called, and I'll go with her to the hospital if need be. You know this moor better than I do, by all accounts, and I've no doubt I'm better at taking care of the injured than you are. Find the children."

The plains stretch in front of Leto, miles upon miles of golden grass beneath a violet sky. Swallows rattle high above her head, and warblers chatter in the marshy sedge that grows at the bottom of the river's valley, where the icy waters run as clear and fresh as light. Yet, this is still a picture, she realises: a movie projected on the far wall of the chamber, as if upon a silver screen. The lines of rough hewn neolithic stone are interrupting the surface of the image, making it seem somehow less present, less real, and to belong to another time than just its own, as if both the long gone Age of Farming and the current Age of Steel were also contained within it. It is three times within one. Three Moments, all somehow connected, each one dependent on the others.

This is my Moment, Leto thinks, excitedly. *This is what my Moment looks like.* "Where is Huma?" she says. "Where is my Mammoth?"

Johnny Horsefeathers scrambles down the south side of the Tor. He doesn't know where Martin's gone, but it doesn't seem unreasonable or unlikely that a boy seeking shelter from wind and terrifying flame would have made his way to the fogou – assuming he remembers where it is. If he isn't there, Johnny reasons, then he doesn't know where or how to find him – not, at least, without employing magic. But once he's underground and has his grimoire to hand, then if he has to do this then he can, and if he has any skill at all, he should be able to locate both children before anything else goes wrong.

His hands are shaking, and his skin's beginning to sting. He was very lucky to have escaped serious injury when he threw himself on top of Evelyn. Very lucky, yes – unless the spells he kept on chanting had some effect on him even if they did not heal her. Perhaps the truth is he was not lucky at all, and it's only now that the immediate terror is over, and his adrenaline levels are beginning to drop, that he's becoming aware of the damage that the fire has done to him. It's too dark to tell, and he left the Bakelite torch with Martin. How badly has Johnny Horsefeathers burned himself, beating back the inferno?

His usual confidence has deserted him. All this time, he's been imagining himself in full control: of Evelyn, of Leto, of everything. He's successfully escaped his enemies in one world and revenged himself upon them in another, planning his exit strategy with more than military precision. He's chosen a successor. Now his mission is unravelling in a way entirely beyond his expectation, and he doesn't know how to mend it; or if, indeed, such thing is even possible. Perhaps it's not. Perhaps Evelyn Murray really is going to die, and Leto really vanish into the darkness of the moor, Martin Stone with her. The story has edged ahead of him, and he can't predict it. This sudden reversal is shocking, disorienting – even, though Johnny Horsefeathers rarely admits to such a feeling, frightening. Where did he go wrong? Whom, or what, did he misjudge?

Everyone, apparently.

"Martin!" he shouts. "Leto!"

The entrance to the fogou is at his feet: he plunges through it.

Trust your mother. Trust Huma, the ancient Matriarch of the plains, the wise old grandmother who always knows where to find the clearest water and the sweetest grass, who guides the young ones, teaching them how to live, how to thrive in this changing world of sun and ice. Huma, whose mighty kind are so essential, so utterly key to the well being of this long forgotten community of soils and plants and creatures that, when finally, they die, the steppe-lands will die too: unfertilised, unmaintained, becoming frozen wasteland, tundra, lifeless rock and snow. Huma is the greatest of them all: the great Queen, most revered, the first Goddess: she whom the moor holds, in one shape or other, forever in its memory. *Trust your mother.*

"I trust you," says Leto. "I do."

Halek-dhwer opens the gate.

Chapter Twenty Five:
Choose Swiftly and
Choose Well.

Leto takes Martin's hand, and together the two children walk into the Otherworld.

The late afternoon sunlight is dazzling; after the darkness of the fogou and the dimming evening light of the moor, it seems to Martin Stone that every star has come out at once and begun to blaze with the intensity of the sun. The brightness hurts: he lifts his arm, hiding his eyes and crying out in pain. *Is this how Mrs Murray felt,* he thinks, *when she was caught in the explosion?*

"It's beautiful!" Leto cries out. "Oh, Martin, it's so beautiful!"

"I can't see," Martin says. "It hurts."

"It's much realer than I imagined it," Leto says. "But it's the same, somehow. There's the river, and there are the crags, and there's the sea in the distance, and *Pavor Potentia,* and everything."

The pain is gradually beginning to recede. Martin drops his arm and opens his eyes again, squinting in the light. In front of him the high plains stretch away to the east like a vast, panoramic portrait, the long black shadow of the Tor lying across the late summer grass like a smudge of charcoal. *This is the moor when it was young*, he thinks. The land is still untouched, unaltered by human hand: an ancient world of Mammoth and of Crow, of peoples long forgotten by everything except the deep earth and the ever watching sky. And yet, when Martin looks very closely, he realises it cannot be composed wholly from memory, because in addition to the grazing herds, the summer bees and the sweet scented flowers, here too, are creatures which never existed in any past epoch. Here, yes, almost at his feet, crouches a creature he'd have thought a hare if not for the budding antlers on its head – antlers which are growing bigger even as he watches – and for way the long back legs are becoming proportionally shorter as the forelegs lengthen, clawed toes vanishing, paws turning into tiny cloven hooves: if not for the manner in which the roebuck stands up, shakes its white tail, and bounds away towards the babbling river. Above his head, wispy cirrus clouds form and disperse, appearing and disappearing into the violet sky.

Everything in this place is in flux, Martin thinks. The Otherworld is just energy, raw energy, with no settled form: changing and shifting and growing, pausing and shrinking, questioning and answering, but never falling still.

"Did you see – " he begins to ask Leto, but then the words stop dead in his throat. The Lizard-bear has followed them through the gate. The gigantic mustelidine monster begins to circle closely round them, its forked tongue flicking in and out, its scaled tail lashing ceaselessly from side to side. What does it mean, that constant irritable movement? Is the

Gatekeeper an enemy or a friend?

Martin clutches Leto's hand, tightly. *She's not afraid of it,* he thinks. *She summoned it, she named it, she asked it to open the gate.* Perhaps her relationship to the Lizard-bear is like his friendship with Petra and Paul. Perhaps, even if the monster is a wild thing, a Spirit-creature much too proud and far too powerful in its own right to ever serve another, it's happy enough to befriend on equal terms a little girl who treats it with respect. He hopes so, anyway.

Suddenly, the giant *shayd* rears up on its hind legs, and towers over both the children, blotting out the sun. It gives a dark brown, rumbling, roar – then suddenly it's charging, leaping over both their heads, flinging itself towards something – or someone – they cannot see; something – or someone – who is climbing through the still half-open gate, calling, shouting out a word, a name, his unexpected human voice jarring the still air. The ground shakes under Martin's feet.

He turns about. There is a body in the grass – a man. The Lizard-bear, in its furious leap, has knocked him off his feet, and sent him flying, Martin guesses, at least a dozen feet beyond the Gateway. But it hasn't knocked him back through it; instead, the opening hangs in the air, a shimmering, transparent oval almost like a window, but one through which one can see two worlds simultaneously, one superimposed on the other; and the Gatekeeper and intruder are behind it, wrestling upon the stony earth of the Otherworld: *Man against Nature – or Super-Nature,* Martin thinks. Man's putting up a good fight. He's plainly very brave, and very strong, too, punching at the terrifying muzzle like a hero; or perhaps in his desperation to survive the Lizard-bear's frenetic attack he has discovered a strength he'd never ordinarily have had. Martin watches the struggle with a curious detachment: it doesn't seem to matter, in this moment, whether Man lives or dies: whether the Lizard-bear succeeds in biting off his head, or he succeeds in strangling the Lizard-bear. All possibilities are open, and none more desirable than any other. *All things change,* he thinks. Then Leto screams: "Johnny!" and suddenly his whole perspective shifts. Before him struggles not Man, but a man: Johnny Horsefeathers; and whatever wicked things Johnny has done, he's Martin's link back to the real world – back to Miss Fox, to Petra, to Paul.

"Stop!" Martin shouts, running forwards, dragging Leto with him. "Stop! Don't kill him!"

How can he have failed to recognise Johnny Horsefeathers? Who else would have found his way to the Gate? Who else have had the courage, the arrogance, the brazen nerve, to have thrust himself uninvited into a place he knew not where?

Is there something in this place that feeds on memory? Martin thinks. *Perhaps that's why the Shaydim have no faces. They have no faces because they have no individual selves. They've lost their names, forgotten their personal histories, if they ever had them: now they're just part of the ever changing flux, part of the world, like the grasses or the sky. Perhaps sometimes they even are the rocks, or the trees. But I still have a name, and so does Leto; and so does Johnny, even though he calls himself something else. And so does –*

"Halek-dhwer!" shouts Martin. "Stop! Please,

stop!"

The Lizard-bear has pinned Johnny Horsefeathers by the shoulder with one, long, vicious claw. It lifts its massive, savage head at the sound of Martin's voice, and turns its beady, black crow eyes upon him. Johnny thumps it in the throat. It does not appear to notice.

What do you want of me, bird boy? The voice vibrates the rocks, like an earth tremor.

"Why do you want to kill this man?" Martin asks, hoping that his intuition is correct. "What has he done to you?"

He is a grave robber, comes the immediate answer. *He has no honour, no respect. The old magician taught him of the existence of this world in good faith, that he might continue the great work he had begun, and humankind come at last to understand the true nature of all manifest things. I opened the gate for him. The land accepted him. The faceless men looked to him as a prophet, one who would carry into your world the warning of what shall come to pass if Pavor Potentia be allowed to burst. But he has proved himself nothing but a base liar and a thief, and he has used this world only for a robber's den, a secret highway by which to pass undetected through your world, to engage upon his mischief without trace. He has neglected his sacred duty; broken the Covenant of trust. He believes that both mankind and myth are his to control, and Earth and Sky and Time do not remember him. He is wrong.*

"Johnny Horsefeathers!" shouts Martin. "Do you hear it? You must give back what you stole. I know you have it. So does the Gatekeeper."

"What did I steal?" cries Johnny. "I've taken

nothing from it! Nothing! It's the robber, if anyone is! It has stolen you!"

"I came here with Leto, by my own choice!" Martin shouts. "And she came because she wanted to come! Because you and her mother have made her life so unhappy she would rather join the faceless men than stay with you!"

The Lizard-bear gives a low growl.

"It's the claw!' shouts Martin. The wizard is so stupid. "The bear claw you took from the necklace, in the grave. You didn't steal it in this world! You stole it in ours! You took it when you found the skeleton. The claw belongs to it!"

It is a key, the Gatekeeper says. *A key to which you have no right. You did not find it by honest accident, as the boy did; neither did you offer to return it. You purposefully stole it, because you guessed what power it contained and hoped to wield it for yourself.* It lowers its open jaws towards the wizard's head. *You are no longer welcome in this world, grave robber.*

Johnny struggles desperately against the creature's crushing weight. "Let me give it back to you, then!" he pleads. "I can't move! The claw's in my pocket! Let me find it!"

"Please!" Martin shouts. "Give him a chance, Halek-dhwer! He'll promise never to come here again, if you do. Won't you?" he demands, switching his attention to Johnny. "Won't you?"

"Yes. Yes. I'll promise. Get off me, monster! You'll have your trinket back. I swear."

Trinket? roars the Gatekeeper. *Trinket, say you? How many times have you conjured a false gateway by means of that trinket? How many secrets stolen? Coward and thief, you lie to yourself if you think the mysteries of this Universe are yours to command. Death is coming. The air is turning into glass. The seas are rising. Will you sink beneath the flood?*

"Don't call me coward!"

What are you then, if you are not that?

"Let me go," Johnny says, suddenly furious. "I'll give you back your bloody key. I'm no coward! I know death is coming. There's going to be another war! But I've stolen no damned secrets from this wretched world, because this world holds nothing that could be of any use to me!"

Is he still lying, even now? Martin can't tell, one way or the other. Perhaps, for the first time since we have met him, Johnny Horsefeathers is, in fact, telling the unadulterated truth. "Please let him go," he says. "He's obviously learned nothing of value. You can let him go."

The Gatekeeper hesitates. *It's considering,* Martin thinks: weighing up what he has said, wondering whether a mere boy can really judge the marrow of a man; whether his word, as much as the wizard's own, can be trusted. He stands still and waits.

"If you will promise that this man will never walk again beneath the violet sky," the Gatekeeper says, "then, yes, I will give you his life."

"I promise," Martin says. It's what his grandmother would have done. Even a promise to a *shayd* has to be permissible if it's given to save a life. He hopes Johnny will honour it. What will happen if he doesn't? Will the wizard drop down dead upon the spot?

Jack Wolf

The Lizard-bear rears up onto its hind legs, towering over the man lying in the grass. *Massive as a mountain,* thinks Martin. *Massive as the moor.* From this angle, the monster looks just like the high crags of Rough Tor, whose young form, unweathered in this ancient world, rises up behind him. Johnny Horsefeathers sits up, and fumbles frantically in his coat pocket, finally bringing forth a small, dark object. He holds it out in front of him, his hand shaking. The Gatekeeper holds out one great, scaled paw – a paw which, Martin realises, is missing one claw – and paw and object seem at once to fuse. And as they do so, the creature's body, which until now has seemed so solid, so heavy, so horribly immense, grows transparent, shifts and breaks, like a reflection on the surface of disturbed water. The dark shape shivers, its edges blurring; and suddenly it begins to shrink, becoming more human-like with every instant; until standing over Johnny is a child, a girl maybe of Leto's age, perhaps a year or two older, dressed in finely tooled leathers and a soft, capacious, bearskin cloak. A child who was once carefully buried, curled up in furs like a foetus in the nurturing soil, her precious bear claw necklace safely round her neck. Halek-dhwer – the terrifying Guardian of the Gate – is the child who was buried in the fogou.

She's a girl. Martin wasn't expecting that – though you, I, and the moor itself, surely remember.

"You saw what you expected you would see," Halek-dhwer says. "What do you see now, wizard?"

But Johnny, staring stupidly into space, does not seem capable of any answer.

Halek-dhwer turns to Leto. "Now, you must help me," she says. Her voice is now the voice of a

Mammoth & Crow

child, no longer strong enough to shake the rocks or agitate the sea. "Give me the freedom that you promised. Trust your mother."

These words seem to shock Johnny out of his reverie. "Wait!" he shouts. "What promise has she made you?"

"Freedom," says Halek-dhwer. "She promised me peace."

"You promised to bring me to Huma," Leto says, speaking for the first time since Johnny Horsefeathers' unexpected tumble through the gate. "Where is she?"

The girl lifts her hand. "There," she says, pointing towards the eastern horizon. "There." The children's eyes follow her finger.

Martin's mouth drops open. There is not one mammoth: there are at least twenty. A glorious, triumphant herd of mammoths, approaching in slow, deliberate formation over the whispering grass. Mammoths as tall as trees, mammoths as huge as buses, towering over the low boulders of the granite forest. Mammoths in the prime of life, ripe with the knowledge of their own potency. Gentle, fearsome giants, with ivory tusks longer than telegraph poles, and legs as thick as towers of masonry. *Mammuthus Primigenius, Mammuthus Trogontherii,* architects and rulers of the ancient mammoth steppes.

"Huma?" whispers Leto. She steps forwards, hopefully, hesitantly – *awed,* thinks Martin, by the sheer enormity, the overwhelming presence of the creatures. *But at least she's able to speak,* he thinks. His tongue can't form a single word. Language has deserted him.

Leto takes another, tentative step. "Is it you?"

she whispers.

The leader of the herd raises its trunk, as if in salute. Is it, too, a female? *A mother?* Martin doesn't know how to tell. Is it Leto's beloved Huma, come at last in answer to the little girl's relentless calling? He remembers, suddenly, the children in the Berlin orphanage, and how similar to them Leto once appeared. How hard, how lost, how desperately in need of love. *Mammoth, Mama. Mama.*

Who is Huma? he wonders. If nothing here is really as it seems, if the Lizard-bear can shape shift and become an adolescent girl, then who, then *what* is Huma? She is not – can't be – one of the faceless men. She has a name; unless that, too, is a thing in flux, and sometimes her identity answers to other names, other calls. *What is she? Is she a memory?* A grandmother, perhaps, or some other beloved old woman, half remembered, half imagined, her substance drawing form from the only authority for which the older Leto has any respect: her Children's Encyclopedia. Is she a toddler's fantasy given power and sculpted by the girl's potent imagination and frustrated need? Or is she wholly, objectively real? If Leto has not defined her, then from where, from what mind does she ultimately derive her shape, her self? Is she shaped by the memory of the Earth? Or by the memory of God? Both?

Leto makes a decision. She slips her hand out of Martin's, and begins to scramble down the near side of the valley, half stumbling, half falling, toward the mammoths. "Huma!" she calls. "I'm here! I'm coming!"

The lead mammoth raises her trunk again. *It*

really is Huma, Leto thinks, excitedly. *She's here at last, and that means I can stay, and never have to go back to the Otherworld.* She breaks into a run, her t-bar shoes crushing the grass. How hard it was to walk up Rough Tor earlier, in the fear that Huma had deserted her, and the witch meant only to murder her! How faithlessly she doubted the mammoth, how shamefully forgot to believe. *'Mummy'*, she called the witch. 'Mummy'! It seems so silly now her mother is here – her real mother: *Huma*, the *Matriarch*, the wise old Queen who never leaves her children to starve, or suffers them to weep. *Huma,* whose trunk is warm and strong, guiding the infant calves to take their first steps and comforting the old, the dying and the sick. Now she is running, swift as the wind across the valley floor, and her feet – her paws – are flying over its surface, claws digging into the rough dirt. Now she has come to the river. She knows she can leap it, cross that silver thread in one flying bound, stretching her body like a rubber band, delighting in the unexpected power of muscles she's never known she has: muscles in her shoulders, in her neck, her back, her forearms, in her strong hind legs – and landing, landing forepaws first, the silvery ruff of fur about her neck swinging forwards with the force of impact and settling back into place about her head; and now she is pricking her ears, and lifting her paws, and plunging onwards through the tall sea of sedge, her thick, silver fur coat keeping her from cutting herself on its razored leaves; and her tongue is hanging out between her long, sharp teeth, and her nose is suddenly alive with a million different smells: the water, the sedge, a small family of plovers hiding in the grass. A broken, torn up tree, its exposed roots freezing in the clean cold winds and icy soil of the Pleistocene steppe. And the mammoths: stone and mud, sweat, hair and ivory, blood and bone. And Huma, Huma. Mammoth, Mama, Memory.

Martin sees Leto beginning to run, and snatches for her arm, but he's not quick enough to catch her. "Leto!" he shouts. "Stop!" He starts to follow, scrambling awkwardly down the slope. But she's already several yards ahead of him, and the gap is widening – as if the very land itself is propelling her onwards, and holding Martin back. He's some thirty or forty feet behind her when she reaches the river, and he watches her leap and land; watches astonished, almost disbelieving his own eyes, as the transformation takes effect, and what left the ground as human falls to it again as wolf: red eared, red eyed, long legged and rangy, like a puppy just approaching adulthood; a silver coated she wolf, with strong, white fanged jaws and a long, waving tail like a silky banner. *She's beautiful,* he thinks, in the same instant that the terror seizes him. Leto is gone, Leto is lost: she has, in leaping the river, thrown herself across some Rubicon, some invisible line only passable by those who belong, by nature or compulsion, to this world, and this world only. *She's never coming back.*

Johnny appears, panting, at his shoulder. The wizard is exhausted, as if he's been fighting his way for several hours through sticky mud. He puts one hand on Martin's shoulder to steady himself, and bends double at the waist, wheezing and holding his stomach.

"We've lost her," Martin says. "She's gone."
"No," Johnny says. "That can't be."

Mammoth & Crow

"Didn't you see what happened? She's become a wolf – just like the prehistoric girl became the Lizard-bear."

"The Gatekeeper," Johnny says. "She's going to be the Gatekeeper. That's what it meant by asking her to set it – her – free." He stares wildly across the stream, toward the approaching behemoths. "Leto's going to die," he says. "In our world, anyway. In this one she'll be trapped for eternity."

"Can we rescue her?"

"I don't know. But that won't stop me from trying. I'm not giving up on my little sister without a God damned fight."

My little sister. Martin catches his breath. It's the first time he's ever heard Johnny admit the fact.

"So I was right," he says. "You are Phillip Murray."

Johnny is searching for a way across the waters. "I no longer use that name, Elijah Rosenstein."

"There's no comparison between us," Martin says, scornfully. "My name was taken from me. You hid yours from everyone in order to get revenge on your father."

"You really did read my letters," Johnny says, without looking up.

"Yes. And I'm glad I did, even if it was prying, because if I hadn't, I wouldn't have understood what kind of man you are."

"And what kind of man is that, bird boy?"

"A foolish man," Martin says. "But not really a wicked one. Whereas Mrs Murray is both foolish and wicked, and your uncle Ignatius Fireborn was neither."

"I chose better than I knew, when I chose you," Johnny says. He takes a tentative step forwards into the flowing stream. Immediately, the river rears in front of him, spiralling upwards in a fountain of shimmering white, forming into the shape of a woman, beautiful and treacherous as a whirlpool under winter ice.

"Get out!" Martin shouts, in sudden panic. He does not want to lose Johnny now, having only just redeemed him from the Lizard-bear. Besides, if Leto is lost, if she's truly lost, the wizard is his only link back to the human world, and without him he might never find his way back to the Gateway. Is the Gate still open? Has Halek-dhwer closed it? Where is she, the Guardian of the grave? Who is the Guardian, now? Is it Leto? Will his bear claw key still give him passage, if the Guardian has changed?

We miss you, Johnny, ripple the many voices of the water. *Come and play.*

The river misses him, the faceless men warned. "Get out!" shouts Martin, again. "She's going to drown you! Get out!" He scrambles onto the river bank, holding out his hand. "Take my hand! Here!"

Johnny stares mutely at the woman for a second or so, as if he's hypnotised by her swaying torso, her spinning skin; then some survival mechanism in his brain seems to kick into gear, and he begins to skitter backwards through the water like a rat retreating from a flood, and struggles back up Martin's side of the bank.

Come back to us, wizard, the river whispers, softly. *Seductively,* Martin thinks.

"No," Johnny says. "The boy is right. Your so-called play would mean the death of me."

But what about your sister? Your darling little sister? Won't you play the hero to save her?

"Oh," Johnny says, darkly, staring across the open plain. "I will. But I won't play it your way. Damn this place! Damn it, and damn you!"

The woman smiles. *She looks like Mrs Murray,* Martin thinks suddenly, with a shock. And another part of him answers: *but of course she does.*

Martin shades his eyes, staring across the river toward the plains, across which the mammoth and her kin are still walking slowly towards him. Where is Leto? Where's the silver wolf? What should he do?

Look, says the river woman, laughing. *Look.* She raises her hand and points. Following her gesture, Martin sees no sign of Leto.

Extinction beckons in Pavor Potentia, the river says. *The choice is yours. Choose swiftly, and choose well.*

The view directly beyond the stream is shifting, changing, Martin realises suddenly. The world is growing uncertain, darkening with the terror of possibility. There lie the open steppes, but there too, flickering in the same space like a poorly wired electric light bulb, sits a vast, sprawling industrial complex, a wicked metropolis of smoke and metal that seems to dwarf any city he's ever encountered. It's bigger than London, crueller than Berlin: a brutal empire that will bring subjugation and terror to every being of every kind who lives beneath its crushing heel. And there's sound, too: the metallic, grinding, crunching, all consuming noise of factories and foundries and hammers clanging endlessly on iron; the mad hum of incessant production, of frantic, malignant growth. A machine world, a machine: humankind reduced to moving parts, the earth itself to dust. And Martin somehow knows, though he'll never be able to explain how, that what he sees is not happening only in the Otherworld, but also his own: neither in the present, nor the future, as yet – *but it is a future that could be*, Martin thinks. *It could be.*

Choose swiftly, and choose well. The very words he himself passed on to Johnny Horsefeathers, and which Johnny, for reasons of his own, chose to believe referred to his choosing an apprentice. They mean nothing of the sort. The choice is much more elemental. *Resist or surrender. Choose life, or die.*

"Do you see it?" he shouts. "Do you understand it?"

"I see it," Johnny says.

"What do we do now?" Martin says.

"Run," Johnny says, seizing Martin by the arm. "We run."

Chapter Twenty Six:
Promises

Martin and Johnny Horsefeathers pelt up the slope towards the Gateway. Behind them, the hellish sounds emanating from *Pavor Potentia* are swelling to a cacophony, a deafening pounding of machinery and flesh, a wailing of misery. Martin tries to put his hands over his ears, but it's too hard to make his way at speed over the rocky ground without free movement of his arms; he stumbles, tripped and almost falls. Johnny hauls him up, pulling him onwards.

"Come on, boy, run! That thing will soon spread across the river."

Martin looks back; he can't help it. The vision – or the breach, whatever it is – has reached the far side of the river bank. *It's trapped,* he thinks, *trapped like a giant soap bubble in a blower.* He can see its skin ballooning out over the surface of the icy water, trying to break the physical bonds that hold it in the hoop, but thankfully failing to do so. But in the short time it has taken for himself and Johnny to have made it to the crest of the ridge, it's already swelled to ten, perhaps twenty times its initial size. The evil thing is spreading, swelling, eating up the plains, darkening the sky, turning the sun blood red.

"What is it?"

"War," answers Johnny, shortly. He is severely out of breath; the sprint has cost him far more than it cost Martin.

"It is the future, isn't it?"

"One potential future. The likeliest, right now, by the look of it. A Brave New World of soulless suffering and state appointed death. Unless – "

"Unless we change it," Martin says.

The volume of noise undergoes a sudden, sharp increase. The greasy bubble of possibility has found a path across the water. Now it's crawling steadily up the slope towards the crags: towards them. Johnny swears loudly, crudely, and seizes hold again of Martin's arm. "Where's the Gatekeeper?" he shouts. "Halek-dhwer?"

The girl in the bear fur cloak has vanished. Martin didn't see the moment of her disappearance: his attention was all focused upon Leto, and then the river woman, but he's been expecting it. The Gateway shimmers faintly in the air, its substance almost evaporated.

"She's gone," Martin says. "She's not bound to it any more."

Johnny curses again. "No!" he spits. "Leto's only a child, for God's sake! A little girl!"

"Leto!" shouts Martin. "Leto Murray!"

She is Wolf, and she is running.

Running with Mammoth, with reindeer, with hare. New formed, new forged, in eye socket and thigh-bone, in sinew and hair, in muzzle and fang, in pad and claw. Leto is Wolf, and now Wolf is free.

The sweet air is a tonic in her lungs. How wonderful to run across the cotton-grass and leap the young rocks, to taste on her tongue the fresh spores of fungi and damp skins of worms, the cast off feathers of birds rotting on the earth. How sweet to scent the distant ice, the first molecules of coming winter on the autumn air. Everything is apparent, tangible: the world withholds no mysteries, holds no loneliness. There is only running. There is only Wolf.

The mammoths don't seem to mind her presence, as she tags along behind them, panting, tail waving, red tongue lolling out over her teeth. They know she poses no danger to them. What possible harm can one half grown cub offer creatures large enough to crush her with one foot, send her flying with one casual sweep of the trunk? She makes her way gradually to the front of the herd, weaving between gigantic bodies, seeking out the one mammoth, the *Matriarch*, who raised her trunk in salute. *Huma. Huma. Mother. I am here.*

Out of nowhere, a name: *Leto. Leto Murray.*

And she is still running, running; but she feels the compulsion, the connective inevitability of cause and effect, potential and realisation, drawing her back, back across the river, back, back to the place from which she began. She can't refuse it, because the possibility of her resistance is not part of the structure of this world. *They call your true name, Gatekeeper, and you come.*

She doesn't need to turn about. She can keep on running, while the world around her reorients itself, sending her gliding across the swelling surface of *Pavor Potentia* like a skater on an ice rink, or a droplet of water diverted through an oily channel. There is no friction, no time, no space; only speed, only her own momentum, carrying her onwards and back towards the fulfilment of her promise.

"Leto!" Martin shouts again.

A ripple crosses the surface of the bubble, like the V shape left in water by a swimming snake, or in the wake of a ferry boat. Giant forms appear in front of it, walking slowly, inexorably up the hill toward him. They are mammoths, and yet Martin can see that, at the same time, they are not. Beneath the surfaces of their skins flicker the shapes of men and women dressed in ornately tooled leather, faces obscured by their own braided hair or hidden under cloaks: the faceless men, the people of the moor, conveyors of the Dead, preservers of memory, bringing their ox-cart of bones along with them.

And then the wolf appears right at his side, just as if he were a shepherd summoning a collie dog: a silver wolf, red eared, bright eyed, looking exactly as it did in its wild leap over the stream; and a voice that's not quite Leto's, not quite the land's own, says to him, in his head: *Do you want to go home, Martin?*

"Yes," Martin answers.

Are you afraid of Pavor Potentia? It's going to be more frightening out there, you know. There's going to be great evil, and war, and battles, and death. An awful lot of death.

"But," Martin says. "Miss Fox is out there too, and so are my crows. I promised them I'd come back safely."

Huma is here.

"I know," says Martin. "But she isn't *my*

mammoth. I don't love her as you do."

Won't you stay?

"No. I can't. This isn't my world."

Your world, Leto answers, *is too full of weeping.*

"It's your world, too," Martin pleads. "Despite everything your mother's done to you, it's still where you belong. You should come back with me, before it's too late."

The silver wolf looks at him, its head – *her head,* Martin thinks – cocked on one side like a puzzled dog's. It's an unsettling sight. *It's too late, already,* he thinks. He'd feared as much, but somehow in all the confusion of running away from *Pavor Potentia,* and calling out her name, and hearing her voice, he had almost forgotten.

I'll open the Gate for you, says Leto's voice. *But I'm not coming back. Not ever. Even if you try to drag me through it.* She sounds petulant; more like Leto Murray, and less like the land.

"Can you hear her?" Martin whispers to Johnny.

The wizard nods. His expression is unreadable: a hustler playing poker on a Mississippi steamboat.

"Open the Gate, then," Martin says. "Please."

There's little change in the attitude of the silver wolf – but instantly the air directly behind Martin begins to shimmer. Turning about, he finds himself looking once again into that curiously multiplied reality through which he watched Johnny Horsefeathers tumble so long ago, at another Moment, another place. There, superimposed on the waving grass, is the interior of the fogou, its dark walls and dusty earth floor close enough to touch – but in the distance seems to hang one brilliant circle of yellow light, like the moon. After a few seconds of confusion, during which he wonders whether it really is a moon, and whether Leto's accidentally opened the Gateway to yet another world – or at least another time – in which the chamber has been opened to the sky, he realises it's the beam from the Bakelite torch, which he must have dropped. *The batteries are still full,* he thinks, in surprise. How much time have they spent in the Otherworld?

"You're still my friend," he says, suddenly. "Just like the crows. I won't forget."

Neither will I, comes the little girl's voice.

"Go on, bird boy," says Johnny, gruffly, staring down the slope. "Quickly. There's no time. Go!"

Martin looks behind him. *Pavor Potentia* has swallowed half the sky. Aeroplanes buzz across it like bullets. The faceless men are close. Horsefeathers is right: there is no time. He takes a deep breath, and steps forward. Once, in another world, he remembers, he boarded a train, not knowing where it was going or what he was supposed to do when he got there, only wanting to live, to escape the terror that had engulfed his world, the evil that had come between him and his place in it. He left Berlin with a name, a history, an identity; but somewhere on the journey from there to here, he lost all those things, and found only one. Now Elijah Rosenstein, grandson, orphan, pupil, is only Martin Stone, the boy who talks to birds. And Martin Stone is fleeing again, leaving a friend behind again. His heart feels numb. *At least I'll have Miss Fox,* he thinks. *And Leto will have Huma.*

He knows neither is really enough.

The portal swirls around him. He steps through it.

Leto watches Martin leave, and a small whine escapes her. She will miss him. Then she turns her eyes expectantly upon Johnny, who is also her friend, and her tail gives a faint wag, as if by itself. She's rather ridiculously pleased to see him; pleased that Halek-dhwer hasn't hurt him; pleased he's escaped the river woman, whose cold embrace Leto can smell on his clothing. But he has to go, and once he's through the Gateway it will be the sacred duty of the silver wolf to ensure he never, ever again comes through it.

"Leto," the wizard says seriously, crouching down in front of her. "You can't stay here. You're not part of this world, you're part of mine. You're not a wolf. You're my sister. My little sister. My father's your father, Gerald Murray. We had an argument, many years ago. A bad – a terrible argument. But I'd love to get to know you properly, as a sister. Wouldn't you love to have an older brother? Won't you come home?"

Leto shakes her head; not in denial, as a human might, because *of course* Johnny is her brother: doesn't he smell like Father? Doesn't the timbre of his voice carry an echo of Father's querulousness, Father's own, very masculine fear, which hides itself behind a veneer of confidence? If her conscious mind is surprised by the news, her sensual one is not. It explains so much: why Johnny showed her so much affection, so much kindness, when no-one else would; why she took to him so readily, trusted him so freely, when he was by all accounts little more than a stranger. His smell, his voice, his body were all familiar. And he's right; she'd have loved to have had a brother – *an older brother, anyway,* she thinks, with some residual feeling of resentment. But it's a pity he should choose this moment to come out with the truth: now, when it's too late.

Johnny – no, let's call him by his real name, now he's told the truth to Leto – Phillip Murray puts his hand out, ruffing the soft fur of her back. Leto likes the sensation; she leans her weight against his body, telling him, in the bodily way wolves speak, that she understands, that she'd like to have loved him, if she'd been given the chance. He's her brother, after all, the missing piece: that unspeakable ghost who haunted Father's eyes and drove her mother into jealous agonies. He's the one who smuggled her cucumber sandwiches and jam tarts, and told her her mother's cruel words are applesauce. She licks his hand. It tastes of salt and flame.

Phillip strokes her head, and begins to rub her underneath the chin, as if she were his favourite hound at the fireside. He slowly puts his arms around her, reaching over her back, under her belly. Then suddenly, before she's quite aware of it, he's picked her up, bodily, in his arms, and is heaving her into the shimmering light, through the Gateway she herself has created, into the world beyond.

Leto fights him, snapping and snarling, twisting her neck and struggling to bite in an effort to free herself from the hands that are gripping her so tightly, brother or no. The portal turns to glass, and shatters, like a shell shot mirror.

"Quickly!" Phillip shouts to Martin, bending low and running across the chamber toward the narrow tunnel, Leto in his arms. "Run!"

Martin picks up the Bakelite torch and shines it along the passageway. *Something is wrong*, he thinks, but he doesn't know what. He can feel it in the electric buzzing of the night, in every small vibration of the air.

Phillip scrambles to the entrance of the tunnel, and there he stops, unable to climb through with the limp body of the child encumbering his arms. He swears in frustration, and turns again to Martin. "Here," he says. "Sit with her. Look after her. And don't leave this spot. I'll come back with help."

"That belongs to Miss Fox," Martin says, as Phillip makes a sudden grab for the Bakelite torch.

Phillip looks as if he is about to argue – but then an idea seems to strike him. "Yes," he says, returning the torch to Martin. "Keep it. Wave it about in the entrance, so I can keep track of you." With that, he departs.

Martin sits still in the darkness, with Leto. The little girl is unconscious, her breathing shallow and faint, her skin cold and clammy. In the torchlight, he sees again, with shock, the blood running down the side of her face, thick clotted channels of red staining the collar of her dress; and the thought strikes him he couldn't see any sign of her injury in the Otherworld.

How can this be happening? Only moments ago she was walking about, running, scrambling through the stone thicket in front of him. She was talking to him, in her usual determined, troublesome, argumentative way – she even called the Gatekeeper, led both of them through the Gateway. Surely she can't have gone so quickly from such vibrancy, such life, to this. It can't be possible. It can't be right.

"Help!" Martin shouts through the opening, against the wind. "Help us! Help!"

Miss Fox has told the police everything she knows, which is really very little, and that mostly conjecture. Mrs Murray took her daughter for an evening picnic, and presumably feeling cold in the wind on top of Rough Tor, attempted to light a fire using petrol as an accelerant. The fire exploded, and Mrs Murray suffered serious burns. The police don't ask why Miss Fox saw fit to follow Mrs Murray, or question why anyone would be so foolish as to behave in all respects as Mrs Murray has done. She's a foreigner, after all; and therefore it's to be expected that she must possess a certain degree of idiocy. When Miss Fox explains that Leto is still missing, however, and describes how she found Johnny holding Mrs Murray in his arms, their interest in the situation seems to sharpen. The sergeant quickly directs two of his constables to scour the hillside in search of a little girl and a man whom Miss Fox hears him describe as "a suspicious character," even though she hasn't referred to Johnny in those terms. But perhaps Johnny's behaviour, and his repeated assumptions of blame, which she hasn't kept from her account, have led the policeman to draw his own conclusions. Besides, if Johnny witnessed Mrs Murray's accident, it's perfectly reasonable the police will want to question him.

She doesn't accompany Mrs Murray to the hospital, though she makes the offer to do so. The sergeant is clear she can be of no use to the comatose woman, and suggests she'll be far better off looking after the little girl, if they find her. Miss Fox flinches at the sound of that word: "if". If they find her. If she is all right. There are too many ifs, too many uncertainties. And Martin is still missing, too – though, she tells herself, she's not afraid for him. *The boy will look after himself,* she thinks. *He knows the paths.* Martin won't fall into a gully, or lose himself upon the open moor. In the few months since his arrival in Bransquite he has become, like she has, part of this bleak, unforgiving place: his passage over it, though never assured, will at least be eased. He won't freeze in this chilling, exhausting wind.

But though she tells herself all this, she can't quite make herself believe it. What if she is wrong? The thought of losing Martin Stone – the boy who came to her so unexpectedly, from a culture and a country so unlike her own, his arrival the result of an offer made without conscious reflection in a moment of thoughtless, impetuous generosity – that thought is suddenly too much to contemplate. *Whatever happens to the little girl,* she thinks, in a sudden burst of selfish, terrified, overwhelming love, *please, God, let nothing untoward happen to Martin! Because he is mine.*

Miss Fox sits down in a sheltered spot below the eastern side of Rough Tor, and waits for something to happen.

Phillip has left Martin holding Leto in the same position that he, himself, previously cradled her mother. The parallel, cruel as it is, doesn't escape him, but he doesn't allow himself to dwell on it. He's not entirely sure what happened during those last few seconds of their passage from the Otherworld. He remembers leaping through the Gateway, and bringing Leto with him; but somehow, somewhere, in the moment of translation between worlds, he remembers losing her, too: feeling her warm fur slipping from his grasp, her thrashing weight gone from him. He could almost swear that in that instant she escaped him and threw herself toward the ground, bounding away from him across the open steppe; and yet when he re-entered this world it was with an injured, human child in his arms. Has he lost Leto, or saved her? Who, *what,* exactly, did he bring back through the gate?

He casts his gaze towards the top of Rough Tor. The dark hillside is pricking with torch lights. *The police,* he thinks. His heart sinks, even as his hopes lift. Yes, the police will take Leto to safety – if the girl he's brought out of the Otherworld *is* Leto, and not a simulacrum somehow created out of the energy of the exploding gate – but they'll ask him questions, and make inferences and deductions, which perhaps will not go well for him. Can he lie to the police? Does he even want to?

He remembers being a boy, reading Euripides with his father. The ancient Greeks knew how to resolve a narrative crisis. When every other avenue has been exhausted, call on the God in the Machine: the underlying, deterministic power that dictates the direction in which matters must progress, even when that very progression makes it seem otherwise. Who is the God in *this* machine? Where is the higher power to which he might appeal, and which might spontaneously spring to life, reinstating control over those areas where he has discovered that he, a mere mortal wizard, has none; reordering his intimate actions, and those of everyone around him, in the service of the greater good to bring about the satisfactory conclusion of the play, reassure the audience of their continued enjoyment of civilisation. Does such a power exist? *Perhaps it does,* Phillip finds himself hoping. At least in a symbolic sense, like the Priest of the Grove was and is only ever a symbol, and the tragedy of Hippolytus that symbol rendered comprehensible via written words within a book, actions upon a stage. If it's not some kind of God, perhaps it's the accepted authority of the King, or of the law. Perhaps, Phillip decides, it's time for this flawed hero to surrender himself to the divine structure of tragedy, and call upon it. Perhaps, let me tell you, he is right.

"Ho!" he shouts. He begins to clamber towards the lights, waving his arms. The night air stings his raw skin, and he suddenly remembers the burns on his hands: strange how they didn't bother him in the Otherworld. "We're here! Here!"

The Cornish police quickly locate Phillip – or Johnny, as they still know him, on the south side of the Tor, and on his direction follow the faint light of Martin's torch to the fogou. They find the two children within: cold, damp and frightened – but the boy, at least, is uninjured and coherent, so they release him quickly into the tearful custody of his foster Aunt, and tell him to expect a visit tomorrow morning. Leto Murray, on the other hand, they drive directly to the Plymouth hospital to be reunited with her mother.

The Cornish sergeant inspects Phillip's

injuries, pronounces them superficial, and tells him, like Martin, to return to the village and wait until morning, when a constable will call on him to take his statement. It's plain to Phillip that the man regrets the lack of any credible excuse upon which he could have him arrested then and there. He has no doubt the sergeant will spend the remainder of the night gathering whatever evidence he can, from wherever he can, in order to find one. Dislike is etched upon his face like words upon a headstone. The notion of fleeing abroad and not returning to England until the dust has settled flashes through his mind. But, he tells himself, he's an innocent man; for all that he's cruelly deceived and used Evelyn Murray, he's not responsible for the fire, or – at least in any criminal sense – for Leto's injury. He's stolen nothing, harmed nobody – in body, at least. And what business is it of the law that he chose to bed his more than willing stepmother in order to take revenge upon his father? None, whatsoever – unless the Greek metaphor he used has a greater depth than he imagined, and British Law, like the Classical Gods, takes a meddlesome interest in family dynamics. He thrusts the memory of the guilty outburst that escaped him in the crags to one side. He hasn't done anything to contribute to Evelyn's accident, or Leto's. His poor, innocent little sister fell in the darkness and hit her head on one of the stones. It's the sort of mundane calamity that might befall anyone unfamiliar with Rough Tor who dares to climb it in the dark. *Blame Evelyn*, he reminds himself, darkly. *Blame the evil inside.*

And yet somehow, despite his determination to exonerate himself, the part of him which wept in the rain over Evelyn Murray's body refuses to be convinced. He wonders again: how much of the responsibility for what has happened is his? Is he really innocent? Or is Miss Fox right? Did he, through his arrogance, his stubborn refusal to see the people whom he sought to manipulate and deceive as human beings in their own right, with minds and feelings that were beyond his power to control, dig the hole that has swallowed his little sister? Perhaps there is no spell that can truly allow a wizard power over a woman's heart, especially one as complex and fanatical as Evelyn Murray's.

And he wonders again: was it really Leto he watched being stretchered away from the fogou and put into the ambulance? Was it really Leto; or is his sister now bound, as the prehistoric child was bound, into many thousand years of service as the Guardian to the Otherworld? Why did she struggle to free herself from his arms? Why was she so willing to give up her human life to become a bonded creature of the Earth? He remembers the portrait his uncle Ignatius Hart once made of him – how old Fireborn painted his face and body intertwined with leaves, as if he should have been the one promised to that fate: Green Man; Forest Priest; Sacrifice; Hippolytus; Phillip. Did Leto assume the duty because he failed even to recognise it? Because he, instead of doing his duty and carrying on his uncle's work, yoked his occult knowledge to the service of his own desires, and tried to use it for mundane, personal gain? Perhaps, he thinks, there's more to Mr Frazer's thesis than imagined history; perhaps, for all his faults as a scholar, the old man has, somehow, *accidentally,* fallen on a truth deeper and darker than imagination: that of an ancient soul connection between Man and

Earth; a mortal impulse to bleed, to give sacrifice in return for life: a bloody, breathy, bony Covenant of water and fire and stone, trust and thought and memory. Perhaps Evelyn, despite her craziness, was right.

And Phillip has broken it, has thrown away what should have been his birthright, in pursuit of petty, selfish revenge. What was it the Gatekeeper said, when it had him pinned to the ground? That the land accepted him, the faceless men looked to him as a prophet. He knows there was more, but he can't remember it.

It should have been me, Phillip Murray thinks. The more he thinks about it, the more it seems to him this has to be true.

And what his selfishness has wrought is not revenge, not shaming of the wicked, not punishment of the evildoer. He has brought down a landslide, an avalanche of catastrophe, when all he meant to do was throw a stone and crack a window pane. It has swept up both the innocent and the guilty, and buried them both beneath a pile of ice and stone.

You are unworthy to call yourself wizard, he thinks.

He returns to his uncle's house.

Chiswick, London,
3rd September, 1927.

Phillip,

I cannot imagine what the devil has got into you that you think it acceptable to address me in such manner. However, since you are determined to continue this defiant and destructive course, I am only too happy to break off our relationship.

I am sending all your letters, with this one, to your uncle Ignatius, from whom you may some day choose to collect them. Whether you do or not is of no interest to me. I expect never to see you again and if at any point in the future you decide that you need money or anything else from me you will receive no welcome in my house. You will inherit nothing of my estate and I will never speak of you again to anybody. You are not my son. You are dead. You were never born.

Gerald Murray.

Jack Wolf

Chapter Twenty Seven:
Deus ex Machina

Miss Fox wraps Martin in her arms, and takes him home, where she puts him to bed with an eggnog and the enormous ginger Fluffy curled up purring on top of the blankets. She doesn't press him for the details of what happened out on the dark moor with Johnny, or in the fogou with Leto; such matters can be gone through later, when Martin is rested and less distressed. She leaves him in bed until the arrival of the constable at ten o' clock the following morning with his notebook and pencil means that the story can be avoided no longer, and then goes to rouse him. To her surprise, the boy is already awake; she finds him sitting up in bed, looking out of the window at the stunted trees whipping in the Atlantic squall that's blown in overnight on the west wind.

"The policeman's here, Martin," she says gently. "Are you able to talk to him, do you think?"

"Yes, Miss Fox."

"I'll send him away, if you need more time," Miss Fox says.

"No," Martin answers. "It's all right, Miss Fox. After all, it's not as if talking's going to change anything, is it?"

Miss Fox wishes that it could.

"Where do you want to speak to him?" she asks. "I can ask him to step in here if you want to stay in bed awhile longer."

"No, I'll get up," Martin says. "I want to see my crows."

By eleven o' clock, the constable has taken down nearly all the particulars of Martin's story, and is about to close his notebook. Martin's statement has been thorough – although he's made no mention of the Otherworld, or Gateways, or silver wolves, because of course the man would think him mad. But he's given a clear description of Mrs Murray's peculiar behaviour in the village, and Johnny's actions on the way to Rough Tor – and his unexpectedly heroic, if panicked, response to the sudden eruption of the fireball. Then he describes his encounter with Leto, and the blood that was running down her head; and, though he's reluctant to do so, how she told him she thought her mother wanted her dead. The constable raises his eyebrows at that, but writes the words down without comment; it seems it is unnecessary, at this point, to ascertain whether Leto's fear had any basis, only to record that she expressed it. Then Martin explains how he led Leto to the fogou, and how she collapsed just after Johnny's arrival.

"He's Leto's brother," Martin says. "Did he tell you that?"

"Her brother?" exclaims Miss Fox, who has been listening in on the interview, dropping her knitting in her lap.

"Yes," Martin says. "It was all in the letters he left in the den. I know I oughtn't to have read them, but I wanted to know if he was a – well, a danger to Leto." He does not want to say 'a wizard'. It sounds too childish, and at the same time, too much the truth. "His real name's Phillip Murray. He's Professor Murray's son, from his first marriage."

"Oh, good heavens!" exclaims Miss Fox, in horror. "Her own stepson?"

"I don't think Mrs Murray knows," Martin says.

"What do you mean by that?" the constable asks.

"They were – I saw them through the French windows once, when I went over to visit Leto. They were kissing."

"Oho!" the constable exclaims. "Did you know about this affair, Miss Fox?"

"Yes, I did. Martin told me. It's the main reason I told him to keep away from the family. But he didn't tell me Johnny was Professor Murray's son! I thought he was just Mrs Murray's gardener. Though I did wonder about that, to be completely honest, for he was very well spoken. Oh, goodness, if I'd known the whole truth, I'd have tried everything I could to put a stop to it, even though it was none of my business."

"I wasn't completely sure, not until yesterday," Martin says. "He let it slip, when he was worried about Leto. I know it is a very wicked thing, Miss Fox. I didn't want to accuse them of it if it was not true. It's wrong to gossip."

"Of course it is," Miss Fox says, briskly. "Oh, but, Martin! It's not wrong to seek advice." Her voice

Mammoth & Crow

trails off.

"I think," the constable says, putting his pencil and notebook away in the top pocket of his greatcoat, "we'd better be taking a look at them there letters Mr Murray's got stashed in that den of his. I don't know if we'll need to take another statement from you, young man, but it's possible we might. You've been very helpful."

Miss Fox puts away her knitting, and shows the constable to the door. "Is there any news about Mrs Murray?" she asks, quietly, so that Martin can not hear. "Has she been taken to Plymouth?"

The constable begins slowly re-buttoning his coat, the top buttons of which he has unfastened in the warm kitchen. "Well," he says. "Her husband wants her transferred to a fancy hospital in London, but I doubt she'd survive the trip, to be honest with you."

"Oh, Lord!" Miss Fox says, touching her fingers to her lips. "And Leto? Is Leto showing any sign of recovery?"

The constable looks over her shoulder toward the kitchen, and wordlessly shakes his head. "Don't let the boy know, yet," he says. "He's been through enough upset, for a while." He turns up his stiff collar against the driving rain, and lets himself out.

Miss Fox watches the policeman cycle away down the lane, his bike wobbling perilously in the gale, and then returns to where Martin's sitting at the kitchen table, the ginger cat curled on his lap, staring blankly at the fireplace.

"I'll put the kettle on for elevensies," she says. "Don't worry, my dear. I'm sure everything is going to be all right."

Could it be possible, she wonders, for a

mother to deliberately hurt her child? Could there have been anything to Leto's accusation that Evelyn had wanted her dead? *Surely not. Surely, surely not.* Leto Murray was always an attention seeking child, much given to histrionics. Without doubt, it's much more likely she was exaggerating for dramatic effect. *And yet,* she thinks, *the poor little girl's now lying in a coma with a fractured skull.* Her mother might not have had any intention of harming her – but that's exactly what she's done, through her wilful ignorance, her reckless neglect of her daughter's safety. Not that she'll know that, now, of course. Perhaps, if the constable is right, she never will.

But did she know about Johnny? *Phillip.* That, Miss Fox thinks, is in some ways almost as dark a question as the other, even though it entails no lethal consequence, because both yes and no lead to terrible conclusions. If Mrs Murray didn't know the truth, then her seduction involved an exceptionally nasty fraud, of which she was the victim. If she did, then not only is she an adulteress, but a willingly incestuous one.

Human beings are wicked creatures, thinks Miss Fox. *We don't mean to be, but we are.* Wickedness seems to nestle in the human heart, haunting the shadows, waiting for the moment to reveal itself. All it takes is a little loneliness, a minor resentment, a wounding, and out it creeps, like pixie light upon the moor. We are all, sometimes, misled by it. But misled into incest? Into wanting her own child dead?

Perhaps it wasn't really Leto, thinks Miss Fox, *whom Mrs Murray wanted to do away with.*

"Martin, dear," she says, carefully, putting the

kettle on to boil. "What was in those letters you found? When did you find them?"

"A few weeks ago," Martin says. "On the day when I went to the fogou to find out if Johnny really was the tramp. The day before I saw them together in the car."

"That was why you were so worried that Mrs Murray was being tricked, isn't it?"

Martin nods. "I wasn't sure," he says. "I don't know England, Miss Fox, I don't know English names. Every second person in the village could have been called Murray. It could have been a coincidence, and then I would have been accusing them unfairly."

"Oh, Martin, I wish you'd confided in me," Miss Fox says.

Martin strokes the ginger cat, and doesn't answer.

"I assumed he was just someone she had met in London," Miss Fox says, helplessly.

"I don't think so," Martin says. "I don't think they'd ever met." Then he tells Miss Fox – in a rather awkward, disjointed fashion involving much stopping and starting, explaining and discussion – everything he found in Phillip Murray's private correspondence: how the son had fallen out with the father over his father's choice of wife, and how roundly he disapproved of the Professor's newly minted Fascist affiliations. "So Phillip is not a bad man, not altogether," he finishes.

"Well," says Miss Fox, pouring the tea. "People are rarely altogether anything. Even the wickedest despot can show kindness to his cat."

"Whatever he did to Mrs Murray, I think she deserved it," Martin says, consideringly. "She is completely in thrall to an evil ideology. Anyway, he tried to save her life when she was on fire."

"Yes," concedes Miss Fox. "He did. But don't begin to think revenging oneself on another is the way to eliminate evil, Martin, because it only breeds it. Even Euripides knew that."

"Do you think their affair was for revenge?" Martin asks.

"It's not as if we can know," says Miss Fox. "We can't ever be sure. But I think it must have been, at least on Phillip's part, and perhaps a little on Mrs Murray's, too."

"Human beings are so confusing," Martin says.

"Yes," says Miss Fox, sadly. "Yes, my dear, we are."

During the next few weeks, Miss Fox finds herself unexpectedly inundated with visitors. First to arrive is the vicar, who has had his car returned to him by the Camelford police, and is now quietly keen to pump Miss Fox for as much information as possible. Is it true, he asks her, that the lovely Mrs Murray is now fighting for her life in the Plymouth hospital? Dreadful, terrible, and so tragically avoidable. What could she have been thinking?

"Such a sorely troubled young lady," he says, thoughtfully. "I suggested that she might find some comfort in Church, you know, but, naturally, she was reluctant to commit. Young people these days see Church going as such a stuffy, dull, outdated thing – they would prefer religion to have more fizz, you know, more excitement, like the ancient Greeks and Romans: all sacred couplings and comic productions and tragic choruses, with the occasional blood sacrifice thrown in for good measure. Though I must say, she didn't strike me as the sort to approve too much of that sort of behaviour either. Spoke a lot about morality, and making sure her daughter was only exposed to proper influences." He sighs.

"I think Mrs Murray may have been thinking more of Mussolini than the Bible," Miss Fox says.

"Well, you know, I had no idea about that," says the vicar at once. "Didn't even realise – until I read about her accident in the paper – that her husband was associated with the Blackshirts. If I'd known, I would never have mentioned your refugee boy, of course."

"I am going to adopt him," says Miss Fox.

The second visitor, much to Miss Fox's astonishment, is Phillip Murray.

Phillip arrives in an official looking black car, of that make and style often commissioned by men from one or other Governmental Ministry. The car draws up outside the cottage gate shortly before teatime on the evening of the twenty fifth of August, and Phillip, alone, gets out of it and knocks upon the door. Miss Fox, who's heard the sound of the approaching engine, opens it before his hand has had time to drop to his side, and stands tall and stiff spined in the empty door frame, looking him over. For the first time, she notes consciously that she is several inches taller than he is.

"Good evening, Miss Fox," Phillip says. He's wearing a dark blue formal suit and a black Homburg hat, and his feet are encased in a pair of smart black brogues. In his right hand, he's carrying a battered leather suitcase. It looks curiously out of place. "Might I please come in?"

Miss Fox peers towards the car. The driver has turned the engine off, reclined his seat, and placed his chauffeur's cap upon the dashboard. As Miss Fox watches, he takes out a newspaper from the glove compartment, unfolds it, and begins to read.

"Well, Mr Murray," says Miss Fox, stiffly and deliberately. "I am surprised you dare to show your face."

"I understand your distaste for me." Phillip shuffles his feet, uncomfortably. "I suppose it wouldn't help if I told you I never intended things should turn out as they did."

"Not really," says Miss Fox. "How is Mrs Murray?" She doesn't dare ask him about Leto.

"It's too soon to be certain. But the doctors in Plymouth are confident that she is, at least, strong enough to survive being moved to London. She was lucky, in a way. The burns covered slightly less than thirty per cent of her body, which they say is the limit."

Miss Fox's gaze flashes to the young man's hands, which are hidden inside a pair of pale calfskin gloves, the sort a gentleman might wear to a society wedding. "And your own injuries?"

"Trivial, thank you, and healing. The Gods were on my side, it seems."

"So it does." Miss Fox looks again toward the car, her expression an unspoken question.

"I was given a choice," Phillip says.

"What sort of choice?"

Phillip raises his eyebrows slightly and nods his head, almost imperceptibly, toward the chauffeur.

Mammoth & Crow

"I see," Miss Fox says. Whatever choice Phillip has made, it seems the Ministry driver knows nothing of it, and Phillip is expected to keep things that way. "Very well," she tells him, coldly. "You may come in. Wipe your feet."

Phillip steps over the threshold, and Miss Fox shuts the door firmly behind him. "So," she says, turning to him with her lips pursed, as if he were an ill mannered schoolboy and she his Headmistress. "What have you to say for yourself, young man?"

It would have been easy for Johnny Horsefeathers to have attempted an outright lie, but, to his credit, Phillip Murray does nothing of the kind.

"I made a terrible mistake," he says. "I thought Evelyn was much stronger than she is: that she had knowingly seduced my father into a romantic and political association that would do neither him nor me much good, but bring dreadful harm to both of us. I thought she'd introduced him to evil, and was the cause of his estrangement from me. I didn't believe she loved him, and I was certain she'd betray him, given the opportunity."

"So, you decided to test her loyalty, at a time when her marriage and nerves were both under immense strain, and she was at her most vulnerable. How noble of you," Miss Fox says.

"I meant to prove her character," Phillip says. "And I succeeded – though, ye Gods! Not with the outcome I desired."

"Men!" exclaims Miss Fox, with unexpected vitriol. "Always thinking only of yourselves, and never taking the impact on the poor woman into account at all."

"You make it sound as if Evelyn was entirely

Jack Wolf

innocent. I assure you, Miss Fox, she is nothing of the kind."

"Sadly, I believe you," Miss Fox says. "But if she's no innocent, who corrupted her, Mr Murray? The whole Fascist project is designed by, and advanced by, men. All those ridiculous speeches by men like Moseley and Mussolini about building an empire of muscle and steel are speeches meant for men, about men. The world they propose is one that functions only in the interests of men. Where, *what* are women in their vision, Mr Murray? Wives and mothers of soldiers, at best. Barrack prostitutes, at worst. I suspect if Mrs Murray had found herself in a kinder, more supportive world – a world in which she might have learned her own worth as a woman and a human being instead of coming to think of her value as dependent on, and wholly set by, men, she might never have been drawn towards its ideology. Neither, perhaps, would she have felt any compulsion to have married your father. Nor even, feeling herself let down by him, to have surrendered up her tattered dignity to you."

"Were you a Suffragette?" Phillip says, surprised. "You sound like one. Did you chain yourself to railings, and exchange fisticuffs with the police?"

"No," answers Miss Jane Fox, drawing herself up to her full height. "I am a Quaker, and a Pacifist. While you, Mr Murray, are a cheat, a liar, and a cad."

"I suppose I deserved that," says Phillip, with a twisted smile. "But for what it's worth, this cheating, lying cad heartily agrees with you about the way the Fascists treat women. It's disgusting, and a cruel waste of feminine potential besides. You must not blame all men for Fascism, Miss Fox. I, for one, have always opposed it. I did not teach Evelyn to agree with it."

No, thinks Miss Fox, *doubtless that was some other cad, handsome and sophisticated and, yes, probably married too, with a swarm of little Mussolinis playing round his feet. But you did nothing to wean her away from it: nothing to make her question that evil ideology to which she is, most likely, still hopelessly in thrall.* She glares at Phillip. "Why did you come here?" she asks. "What is the meaning of the car?"

"Can we be friends?" asks Phillip.

"I don't think that's at all likely," Miss Fox says.

"A truce, then? Can we negotiate beneath a flag of peace?"

"There is," says Miss Fox, haughtily, "never any other flag worth flying. Yes, Mr Murray. I suppose we can. Come into the kitchen, and I'll make a pot of tea."

Phillip smiles. "What state would this world have to be in," he said, "if one could visit Miss Fox's cottage, and not be offered tea?"

Miss Fox casts him a very sharp look, but says nothing.

Phillip follows her into the kitchen, and sits down at the table, where the vicar did the same only a few days previously. The ginger tomcat, who's been curled up on the cushion, hisses, and slinks away towards the window, his hackles rising on the back of his neck, like spines. Phillip, sensibly, ignores him.

"I wondered whether I might speak with Martin," he says. "I have something for him. From my sister."

Miss Fox catches her breath. She hadn't been expecting Phillip to break the silence surrounding Leto, although of course she has known that, eventually, one of them must. "Martin's on the moor, with his crows," she says. "What is it?"

"A book. Her book. The Children's Encyclopedia."

Miss Fox sits down, suddenly, her legs trembling. "So, she – "

"No," Phillip says.

"Oh, Heavens!" exclaims Miss Fox. "How terrible! How stupid! I'm so awfully sorry, Phillip."

"I assumed you knew," Phillip says.

"No. I knew her injury was serious. But I haven't had word from the police since the day after the accident, and there's been nothing of her in the newspapers. Does the vicar know?"

"I've absolutely no idea. The funeral will be in London."

"Oh, Phillip!" cries Miss Fox, compassion for the young man's loss overwhelming the anger she feels over his many deceptions. "Your poor father! And you – to find your sister and lose her so quickly. It must be terrible for you."

"Please," Phillip says, holding up one pale gloved hand. "I'd appreciate it if you'd not offer me much sympathy. I don't deserve it."

"Well," says Miss Fox. "I can see why you might feel like that, right now. But when you do, finally, decide that you deserve it, Phillip, you may have as much as you need."

She stand up, and busies herself with the teapot and flowered china cups. She knows better than to offer platitudes. Poor little Leto Murray hasn't *gone to a better place,* and hasn't *been set free from all earthly suffering.* How could any child's world hold so little hope she could really be better off in the other one? Such words are consolation absent kindness. Phillip watches her.

"The police wanted to arrest me," he says, breaking the silence that's fallen between them. "The sergeant was convinced that I'd encouraged Evelyn to do what she did, and that I was somehow responsible – criminally, as well as morally, for the accident. At least they were still calling it an accident, and nothing worse. I was told to remain in Bransquite until further notice. It was obvious they were trying to work out charges they might be able to bring and make stick. I did, for a day or two, for I was still in shock, as you can imagine. Then, while I was packing my bags to leave – because however much I am at fault in this, I was not prepared to meekly sit around while some dull witted Camelford plod trumped up a charge against me – there was a knock on the door, and it was a man from the Home Office."

"Really?"

"I was as surprised as you are. It transpired that – I must glide over the details, Miss Fox, for believe me or not, I'm under oath – the Government wanted to offer me a sort of Plea Bargain, as they call them in the States. If I chose to serve my country, the investigation would be dropped. Of course, I agreed. As soon as I leave here today, the chauffeur's taking me to Whitehall. From there, who can say."

"It's war, isn't it?" says Miss Fox, leaning heavily on the counter-top. "They're readying for war."

"I'm not at liberty to say," Phillip answers.

"Oh, Lord!" exclaims Miss Fox, in horror. "How many more young men will have to sacrifice their lives before we human beings come to our senses, and stop this savagery?"

"How else would you suggest we tackle evil, Miss Fox?"

"At its root," Miss Fox says. "Before it has any chance to grow."

"But it *has* grown. It has swollen out of all control, like a giant boil. So what can we do now, other than lance it?"

Miss Fox thinks about Chamberlain, and how Hitler made a fool of him in Munich. Perhaps, she thinks, a shrewder politician, a stronger negotiator, might have had a chance against the German Chancellor. But what might have been the outcome of such a pact? Would Martin, and all those like him, have been left with no assistance whatsoever? Is peace worth its price, when that price is turning a blind eye toward horrors? A Fascist state is by definition an aggressive one, not easily swayed by reason or pity. It would have been impossible, she thinks, for even the cleverest rhetorician to have persuaded Hitler out of his imperial ambitions: the best result would have been a temporary neutrality, a castration of British power that would never have pleased the Whitehall hawks and bureaucratic paper shufflers, or the ladies on the Liverpool Street station platform.

"I will never agree that war is right," Miss Fox says.

"Not right," Phillip says. "But unavoidable. This must not only be a war against German expansion, Miss Fox, like the last one. It must be a war against an idea; and it won't be won solely by martial action. It needs to be fought in the minds and hearts of the English, too – men like my father, women like Evelyn – and banished so completely its possibility will never recur."

"I can't disagree with that," Miss Fox says. She arranges the china cups on the tea tray alongside the flowery pot, and carries it over to the table. The ginger cat makes a chirruping sound like a kitten, and begins to rub himself against her legs. "Why did the Government choose to approach you?" she asks.

"My father."

"He pulled strings?"

"No. God, no! We were not on speaking terms before this – there'd be no chance of a rapprochement now, even if I wanted one. The Home Office are aware of my father's connections. They're hopeful, I think, of my gaining access to some inside knowledge of the Nazis, or something of that ilk. The man seemed frightfully keen I should learn to speak German."

"I am surprised they've decided to trust you," says Miss Fox. "You've hardly cast yourself in a good light as far as that's concerned." She begins to pour the milk.

Phillip makes a non-committal sound. "The God in the Machine," he says.

Blackmail, thinks Miss Fox. *Or bribery.* She wonders which. She adds tea to Phillip's cup, and hands it to him.

"Thank you," he says.

"Don't mention it," replies Miss Jane Fox. A movement in the garden, beyond the windowsill auriculas, catches her eye: a fluttering of black wings in the branches of the apple tree. "Martin is home," she says.

Chapter Twenty Eight:
Mammoth and Crow

Martin Stone makes his way into the cottage, and takes off his raincoat and wellington boots. He's not been far; ever since the events of four weeks ago he's been reluctant to venture away from the security of his foster Aunt's home – and it appears his crows feel likewise, for not even the adventurous young ones have tried to tempt him to wander up over the high moor. But it feels cowardly, somehow, to abandon his visits to the open land without good reason. *What,* he asks himself, *is the worst thing that could happen?* Halek-dhwer is gone, finally freed from whatever geas kept her prowling the boundaries of the world; and now she's no longer Guardian of the Gate, it's unlikely his bear claw key could open a portal and lead him into an encounter with the faceless men. And even if, by some dark miracle, it does, he has no quarrel with them nor they with him: he passed on their message to Johnny Horsefeathers, as intended. It's not his fault the stupid wizard misinterpreted it.

But the memory of *Pavor Potentia*, and the actual moments that followed his escape through the portal, when he was sitting in the darkness with Leto in his arms, haunt him now as the faceless men do not. How could such a horror, manifesting in one world, influence the other? *It is war,* Johnny Horsefeathers said. But isn't Martin Stone already a casualty of war? It may not yet have been formally declared, but all the same it has begun, in acts of terror and repression, in the shattering of shop windows and the tearing down of orphanages. What is war, if it isn't this? He is one of the lucky ones. He was rescued – extracted from between the teeth of the machine just as they began to bite. But what of the remainder of his people? What of those who can't flee, who are too old, or too young, or too crippled to be given space upon the transport train? What of those who seek sanctuary abroad, only to be sent back to Germany? There have already been too many horrors, and these are just the beginning.

He hears voices in the kitchen, and his heart freezes. He thinks he knows who the visitor must be: someone from the local police, bringing the news about Leto he doesn't want to hear. He steels himself, and fights the impulse to run away to his bedroom and bury his head beneath the blankets.

"Auntie," he calls, buying himself an extra second of delay. "I'm back."

"Come into the kitchen," replies Miss Fox's voice. Then: "Phillip Murray is here," she says.

Phillip Murray? thinks Martin. Surprised, suspicious, he pushes open the door and steps across the flags.

Phillip is sitting at the table, drinking tea – just as he was doing on that dreadful day a few weeks ago, the day when he had come to tell Martin his hope of making him his apprentice, and Martin had run up the hill to tell Miss Fox his fear that Mrs Murray had kidnapped Leto. But he, the man whom he – and we – first met in the guise of a filthy tramp, is now dressed more smartly than Martin's ever seen him, in a blue suit, and a tie. He has been wearing a Homburg hat, but this one looks clean and new, and out of respect for Miss Fox, he has taken it off and laid it beside him on the table. A large leather satchel lies beneath the table, at his feet.

"Hello, Martin," Phillip says.

"No," Martin says, stopping dead in the doorway.

'Oh, Martin," says Miss Fox, as if she's guessed what's going through Martin's mind. "I'm so sorry."

So sorry for your loss. It is what Halek-dhwer said.

"I have something for you," Phillip says, standing up, scraping his chair across the floor.

"No," says Martin again. He can't go through with this. He turns around, and runs from the kitchen, up the stairs, and flings himself upon his bed. Tears sting the backs of his eyes.

A few seconds later, the shadow of the man falls over the doorway. "Martin," he says, softly. "I haven't come to tell you what you think. I don't believe Leto is dead."

Martin lifts his head from his pillow, and stares at the blue clad figure. Phillip Murray is trying to fill the space, he thinks, with as much assumed authority as if he himself were the Guardian, protecting the Gateway between realities from men just like himself: arrogant, vain, foolish men who imagine themselves powerful and wise, but are really nothing more than tinkerers.

"What do you mean?" Martin asks, even though he knows this is exactly what Phillip wants him to say.

The wizard comes quietly into the room, and sits down on the wicker chair that occupies the corner underneath the window sill. "Do you still remember?" he says. "Do you remember the Gateway, and how we ran from the *Pavor Potentia?*"

Martin stares at him. He hasn't been entirely sure that Phillip would remember. The Otherworld has a way of denying its own existence once one is no longer within it, as if eye and bone and blood – and some basic laws of reality – don't readily permit one to retain its memory. He nods.

Phillip sighs. "Good," he says. "Good. Then you'll remember that Leto had become the Gatekeeper – that she wasn't herself, not any more. You went through the Gate before me, so you didn't see me pick her up and jump – but she wasn't human then, and it's my belief she isn't now. I dropped her, Martin. She leapt out of my arms, and I dropped her. The body I emerged with was nothing but a fetch."

"A – fetch?" Martin's never heard the word used in that way before.

Phillip thinks for a moment. "A drop of water given human form. A reflection given flesh."

"So you think she's alive," Martin says. "In the Otherworld, at least – just like Halek-dhwer was."

"Yes," Phillip says. "I'm sure she is. But that can't be the end of it. I won't – we can't – let my sister languish there forever. We must set her free, Martin. We must get her back."

"I think," Martin begins, tentatively – for

Phillip, while he's been speaking, has been staring at him so intently he feels, for the first time in a long time, almost afraid of him – "I think Leto would say that she's free now, as she is."

"A bond-slave of the land? Impossible."

Martin does not reply.

"So," Phillip says, "To the matter in hand, bird boy. You remain my chosen successor, whether you want to be or not. I am off to war – the Home Office has plans for me that may well see me sacrificed in service of this country. So I'm giving you my books – my uncle's books, for the most part. You're free to read or ignore them, as you choose. Perhaps you'd do better to ignore them, but they're yours, regardless. And with them, I've brought something of Leto's that may open the Gateway, as the Lizard-bear's claws did."

"You're right, I don't want your uncle's books," Martin says, with a glare. "They're nothing but horsefeathers and applesauce."

"Think what you like," Phillip says. "But whatever you do with them, do not leave them for prying eyes to misread, and confused minds to misunderstand. I left a book that *I* considered applesauce in my uncle's old library, and Evelyn found it, and – well, let's say, I strongly suspect I'd have done far better by everybody concerned if I'd just taken the damned thing away with me and burned it. Leto's Encyclopedia, Martin, is a key now. I'm sure of it. And I know she'd be happy for you to have it. Even now, she may be waiting for you to open its pages and read it – or to stare into its pictures – or something else that you won't think of until you arrive in the right moment – your Moment, Martin –

so you can open a Gateway, and walk the paths again."

"Wouldn't that be stealing my way in?" says Martin.

"You know I can no longer go there," Phillip says. "I'd rescue my sister myself in a heartbeat, if I had the chance."

"All right," Martin says, slowly. Despite everything that he's been through in company with Phillip, he's beginning to wonder whether the man is, as he and Leto once feared, mad – though perhaps some degree of madness is an essential quality in a wizard. They never once, he thinks, considered *that* – and yet, the more he ponders it, the more likely it seems.

"It was supposed to have been me," Phillip says. "I should have been the one take on the Gatekeeper's duty, not Leto. But I failed. That was the choice I was supposed to make, bird boy, and I flunked it."

"You're wrong," Martin says. "The land wanted Leto. Have you never wondered why we saw the Otherworld the way we did? It's because that was how she was imagining it. She was making it, or it was making itself around her. It seemed jolly hostile toward you, I'd say. The Gatekeeper kept trying to kill you – and so did the river."

"I don't think Leto imagined *Pavor Potentia,* Martin."

"Perhaps not," Martin admits. "But she had some idea of what evil is."

Nevertheless, he realises, even while he's speaking, that it can't be true the Otherworld responds only to Leto's dreams and fears. The relationship between the worlds is much more subtle. Neither, really, is created by human desires; but those desires shape their skins, like breath rippling the still surface of water. And *Pavor Potentia* is older than Leto: older than Johnny Horsefeathers, too. Older, if the faceless man was telling Martin the truth, than human civilisation itself. Then he notices he's slipped into speaking of Leto in the past tense, as if she were really dead, or irrecoverably lost, and he turns his face away from Phillip and stares resolutely into his pillow.

Phillip Murray stands silently for a while, waiting, perhaps, for Martin to say something more. When the boy does not move, he places the leather suitcase at the foot of his bed, and leaves, closing the door quietly behind him.

When he's certain that the man is never coming back, Martin takes the suitcase and hides it away, unopened, on the very top of his wardrobe. It's going to be a long, long time before he takes it down and looks at it again.

Professor Gerald Murray first heard the gossip that was beginning to circulate around his wife – courtesy, though he doesn't know it, of Miss Fox's Hackney editor – only a few hours before he received the telegram that told him squarely that she'd been involved in an accident. He hadn't given a great deal of credit to the first piece of news, which was hearsay, after all – and if there was a part of him that was secretly pleased by the possibility of a legitimate excuse to get rid of Evelyn, he didn't show it. But he couldn't ignore the second – so he packed quickly, and sent a message to the owner of the green fendered motor car asking to borrow it and its driver again, in order to leave immediately for Cornwall. When he reached Bransquite, it was to find his cousin's house occupied by his estranged son, and his wife and daughter both in hospital in Plymouth.

A furious row followed, which concluded in Phillip, to his father's complete astonishment, shouting that if his stepmother had lost her bloody marbles and made a damn fool of herself with another man, it was Gerald's own fault for neglecting her, and in Gerald coldly stating that if he was in any way at fault, it was in not listening to Phillip when the boy warned him he was marrying a trollop. At this point, Phillip, notwithstanding his burned knuckles, punched him.

Neither man, when he thinks about it afterwards, has the slightest notion as to why.

"I fucked her," said Phillip, standing over his father. "It was me. I fucked her, over and over."

Gerald did not fight back. He picked himself up and left, bleeding into his handkerchief, to book into a guest-house near the hospital. They have not met since.

The Professor does not grieve, at least openly, for either his daughter or his marriage. Returning quietly to London, he keeps himself to himself, and ignores, as best he can, the increasingly tangled scandal that is springing up around himself and his family. Leto's funeral is a small affair, attended only – her mother being in intensive care – by himself and a few other people whose opinions he values. It doesn't occur to him to formally notify Nanny Gould of his daughter's death, even though the poor old woman raised the child from infancy: there's no place for an ex-servant at such a sacrament. He keeps his feelings buttoned up inside his chest, and only in private does he allow himself reflection on the fact that he has now lost both his children, and there's no hope of any more. He's never been, as I once remarked, a particularly affectionate father, and the desire for children has really always been Evelyn's, not his; but his heart hurts more than he ever thought possible at the loss of the little girl in the red coat and t-bar shoes whose endless chatter he always found so irritating, and whose existence he always largely ignored. He can't blame the child for her own death, as he blames Phillip for his exile, and naturally he sees no reason to blame himself; so instead he finds himself blaming Evelyn, in a way he's never done for any of her miscarriages. It was Evelyn's stubbornness, Evelyn's instability, Evelyn's ultimate faithlessness, which brought about Leto's fatal injury. Evelyn is as guilty of killing his daughter as if she'd intended her murder – and if he could have forgiven her for her affair, he can never forgive her this. He waits until Doctor Gaskell has confirmed that she's no longer considered likely to die, and then quietly packs her things inside a steel-bound trunk, and hides it in the farthest corner of the attic.

The Professor is so caught up in his own family tragedy that he's one of the few people in the country who is genuinely surprised when the BBC Radio Service announces the Prime Minister's declaration of war with Germany. The news doesn't come, of course, as a surprise to Miss Fox, or to Martin Stone, as they sit beside the wireless at the appropriate hour, listening to Chamberlain's dry voiced acceptance of the inevitable.

"Well," Miss Fox says, when the Prime Minister has finished speaking. "That's that, then. I wonder what will happen now."

"I'll warn my crows," says Martin. He pulls on his boots, and disappears into the garden.

Miss Fox turns off the wireless, and winds up the gramophone. *Summertime, and the living is easy.* She wishes she could agree with Ella; because living isn't easy, summer or winter. It's painful, and difficult, and often without any reward – except, if one is lucky, more life.

She thinks of her own father, and the falling out, and the man who came between them. *Was he worth it?* she wonders. *No.* No love affair, especially such an ill-fated, short-lived one, can be worth twenty years of bitter silence. What will her brother do, now another war has been declared? Will he face another call up, spend another lengthy stretch of time in prison? Or will he now, pray God, be considered too old to fight? How time has disappeared, slipping away like water through the proverbial sieve. She wonders what became of the man. Did he return after the Somme to his home city and his wife, and never give a second thought to the naive young Quakeress with whose poor heart he'd trifled? *It's quite likely,* she thinks. She wonders whether he is still alive. He was many years older than she was, and already, at the time of his call up, carrying an injury from Ladysmith. Perhaps – in fact, most probably – he is not.

And she thinks about Phillip, and Gerald, and the breach between them that is past any resolution;

and about Evelyn, who's lost her only child; and Martin Stone – Elijah Rosenstein – who at his young age has lost more than any of them, if loss is something that should have any quantity put on it.

But it is all so ridiculous, she thinks. Ridiculous, in the face of so much inescapable grief, to voluntarily create more. Ridiculous to perpetuate an estrangement that had no justifiable beginning, and even less cause for continuation. It is an act of violence: ridiculous violence, needless and pointless and born only out of pride; as foolish, in its own small way, as any war, and no less offensive to a forgiving, loving, pacifist God.

She looks out of the window. Martin, in the garden, is taking comfort from his birds, one on each shoulder, stroking their glossy black backs and petting their savage beaks, as if the wild things were fireside tabbies. Corpse eaters, harbingers of death.

That's wrong, too, thinks Miss Fox. Martin's crows are many things, but they're no more wicked or ghastly than the ravens who attended on the Biblical Elijah. They are thoughts, not terrors. Warnings, not omens, of human fallibility.

She goes to her bureau, and takes out her Parker pen and a sheet of writing paper. Then she sits down at the kitchen table. Her brother's home address in Fowey is as fresh in her memory as if she had been given it only yesterday.

But what of Evelyn Murray? What of Medea, Clytemnestra, Phaedra? She has fulfilled, after all, the role of villainess in this faery tale – and so, pace Euripides, pace Grimm, she should really be stoned to death, locked in her own oven, or allowed to die of a vanity induced apoplexy while obsessing over her reflection in a magic mirror. For consistency, I should have let her burn herself to death on top of Rough Tor. Now I should make her the story's scapegoat, pile all its sins upon her head and bury her memory deep beneath the stones of history. *A suitable end!* The Brothers would agree – and Martin's Crows with them. But neither protection nor purgation can result from the creation of such an abject, neither for the witch nor any one of us. So no. This is what will happen to Evelyn Murray.

Once she has recovered from her physical injuries, which in itself will take a considerable time, Evelyn will be transferred to a different kind of hospital situated in a village near the south coast. She won't want to go, but her caregivers, who have written their own story of what happened on top of Rough Tor, will permit no argument. Here she'll finally receive something of the comfort that the poor deluded woman has desperately needed ever since we met her back in London. It won't be enough, of course. It will be nowhere near enough. But the recognition that she is in need will constitute, at least, a start.

As for her politics, for her potential to achieve the moral redemption never offered by the Classical playwrights or the German brothers: well, who can say? Perhaps she'll repudiate Davenport and Mussolini, forget her tragic misunderstanding of poor old Frazer, and instead join the struggle against those dark potentialities that lurk so threateningly beneath the surface of this bright and oh-so-shiny machine age. Perhaps she won't. She will never, after all, want to conceive of herself as the victim of her own narrative. And it may well be that, at least in the matter of her radical political beliefs, Evelyn Murray's sense of self is still bound up so tightly in them that she simply can't accept that she is wrong. But if I can expect you to accept that Phillip Murray, despite everything we've come to know of him, is not wholly a wicked man, why shouldn't I ask you to extend a little pity towards Evelyn – even though she, poor damaged Red Queen, knows and shows so little of it?

What story would you have me tell of her?
What ending do you think that she deserves?

This is no common faery tale, pace Grimm's, pace Carroll or Lewis. It's a grit-stone, thigh-bone tale, with a Mammoth at its heart and a thrown spear singing in its blood. But since it *is* a tale, and I am still its teller, I'll offer you this partial resolution, frustrating though you'll find it. What happens to Evelyn Murray from then on is up to you. If you'd have her learn nothing from her experience, or die from overwhelming grief and guilt, then she will. If, on the other hand, you would redeem her, have her become instead a version of that *other* Evelyn, that un-manifest female potential who haunts the shadow fringes of reality like a ghost, who could have been so much, who could have *truly been*, you can. It's up to you. But I have to warn you of one thing: if in some other time, some other place, you hear from me or some other Storyteller that Evelyn's future didn't turn out quite the way you planned, don't come crying to me about it. That's the risk you run when you make up stories: sometimes you lose control of them. But if and when that happens, just remember this: though not all faery tales are true, some of them do contain a different kind of truth, which makes sense to the human heart on cold nights, when the dark is drawing in.

The Golden Bough quivers, and the Earth cries out: not with the birth pangs of a brave new era, but at the passing of the old; and in the Otherworld *Pavor Potentia* ceases, for a time, to swell, like drought starved fruit. But it does not shrink, or fall.

Leto is the white wolf. She is running. And now Huma is with her, or she is with Huma; and which of them is thinker and which thought doesn't matter. Perhaps there is, in actual fact, no difference. Huma is the Mother: the *Matriarch*. Her small eyes are sharp and bright in her gigantic head, seeing everything, forgetting nothing; her great feet cover miles in every step. Her tusks shine in the prehistoric light like long, white scimitars; yet she does no violence with them, and she never will. She is the spirit of the living land, and she lets Wolf run along beside her, loping long legged with her red tongue hanging out and her silvery tail waving in the breeze.

So, she says, in her rumbling voice. *You have come back. It is good.*

And Wolf presses her body against Huma's rough skinned knee, and weaves in and out between her ankles, playing beneath the massive creature as she plods forwards, like a toddler giddy with the joy of exploration. Wolf's reactions are fast and her muscles are strong, and her paws are swift. She is free. The mammoth loves her: she has no doubt of that. They're finally together, as she knows they should have been from the very beginning of this saga: Matriarch and child, each one a vital element of the world which they, together, are creating. Huma tells Wolf of the past, and of the future. She tells her of the world she has sustained since the coming of the ice: the spiders' web of life that depends on the waving steppe-land flowers that grow in her footprints, the cold, open skies that bring infrequent rain. She tells her of the warming Earth and the killing spears of men; and of the extinction soon-to-come of mammoth-kind, which will bring about the slow, gradual death of the steppe-land itself.

Run, little Wolf. Run, run. The waters rise: the air is turning into glass. The world's more full of weeping than you'll ever understand.

Huma caresses Wolf with the soft tips of her trunk, and holds her close against her; and Wolf looks up, and sees close at hand the ivory tusks, the massive head, alive and bright with personality. The mammoth's warm, sour breath ruffles her fur. And Wolf remembers, as if from a different life, the peat-tinged skull of a young bull she once saw in a British museum: an object, roped away, untouchable, empty, dead, not Huma's skull at all, not Huma's, never Huma's; and she can no longer comprehend how such a thing can be possible. The Mammoth Tribe aren't dead. Not here, not now. Huma is not dead. She's never been dead. She is still as vivid and fresh as the living soil from which that sometime-to-be ancient skull will, some day, be lifted – thousands of years away, in some future, in some other world. That Moment is not now, not here: it's not a thing Wolf needs, yet, in this place, to remember.

And Wolf remembers Leto's mother, and her father, and Nanny Gould, and they're the people of a dream: formless, faceless, unreal: shadowed images of things seen long ago in daylight, improperly understood. Of her previous family, only Johnny – who revealed himself to be her brother, who tumbled after her through the Gate and then inexplicably tried to steal her away – stands out in her mind with any clarity; and his shape is growing cloudy, her memories of him increasingly uncertain. But the memory of Martin Stone, the boy who speaks to birds, remains as clear and crisp as white hoar frost on winter leaves.

He will come back, too, in time. Everything returns, O Mammoth, Mama, Memory.

Black butterflies are flickering overhead. The wolf runs on, a silver river through the grass, through the valley of the shadow of the Mammoth and the Crow.

Come away, O human child!
To the waters and the wild,
With a faery, hand in hand,
For the world's more full of weeping
than you can understand.

WB Yeats: "The Stolen Child"